JAMEY

JAMEY

Novel of a Period (1967-1968)

BY EDWIN GILBERT

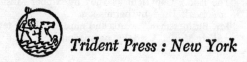 Trident Press : New York

Published simultaneously in the
United States and Canada by Trident Press,
a division of Simon & Schuster, Inc.,
630 Fifth Avenue, New York, N.Y. 10020

Printed in the United States of America

For my enduring friends

BETTY AND ABE : BRYNA AND LOUIS

NOTE

Though this is a work of contemporary fiction,
certain historical events have been transposed in time
or place. Of course the characters of the narrative
itself are all products of the author's imagination,
and are not intended in any way to resemble
or denigrate any persons dead or living.

E.G.

CONTENTS

PART I : *The Death of Flowers*

PART II : *The Gates of Academe*

PART III : *The Paths of the Rock Garden*

The destiny of any nation, at any
given time, depends on the opinions
of its young men under five-and-twenty.

GOETHE

PART I

The Death of Flowers

1 : THE CITY

REMEMBER THIS was back in 1967 and 1968, the man in blue will tell you when he talks about Jamey.

A time of the young: of wilting and death in the flower gardens of Tompkins or Haight, of the passing of june/moon, of the nudging of the status quo; when the medium of the message was a-twang with the guitars of folk/rock—a time reddened by blood and resonant with violence.

Not that the man will dwell on this. He will mainly tell you how many things have changed since those days. In the U.S.A., he says, changes happen fast. You take this neighborhood: remember all that furor? Gone now. Yet alive because of what happened to many of the people who were around here. This neighborhood: remember all those signs? The buttons? The way the kids used to dress? The microskirts? The runaway girls? The antiwar demonstrators? Of course the kids are older now. Many have changed, many are different. And now there are new kids and new griefs.

Jamey is older now. And he's changed too.

Used to see him around here. Nineteen, maybe twenty, he'd come down here with his guitar and do those songs or poems of his. Blue almost green eyes always looked like they were pressing back more than they showed; Jamey, a lanky kid in those white jeans, black windbreaker, sunglasses with the big white rims, hair straight and smoky yellow slanting across his forehead.

Yes, Sergeant Sims of the Ninth Precinct will reminisce, looking back, telling you: But one thing about Jamey—what happened to him I don't think I expected to happen; what I mean is, I never expected him to do what he's done. Maybe that's because though I knew him, I never got to really know or understand him. After all, kids aren't going to go out of their way to open up with you—not if you're on the force.

It is near summertime. Troubletime: the policeman's jaw is tight with it. He moves into the New York evening, which is still ashimmer with a dusk, amber and mauve. The dust of day is settling for the night on the leaves of yard trees and park trees, on the sooty cornices of derelict tenements, on the geranium boxes of renovated brownstones, on the fringed, faded awnings of old fruit stores with no names or numbers on their doors, on the shop windows of new boutiques with their new names: ELEPHANTS ARE COURAGEOUS reads the sign on the storefront near St. Mark's in-the-Bouwerie.

Across from the church where now the blue-clad figure of Sergeant Sims passes is the cinema of underground films, the current showing *In Quest of Erotica*. Sims moves along: he has seen, during the course of his rounds in the Ninth Precinct, bits and pieces of these films. May his mother rest in peace. Before him now he sees the youth driving the stripped-down Ford with the gaudy bumper sticker: NO EASTER THIS YEAR—THEY'VE FOUND THE BODY.

It is growing steamy, soggy.

All the familiar old-new sights looming: Corner of Avenue A and Ninth Street, a pale thin girl with Negro boyfriend. What makes her smile that way? She is holding in her hand a long white flower, now and then pausing to lift it to her lips to suck the stem.

It is all copasetic with Sims: he has been around a long time. His beat, his precinct thirty years on and off. And all these kids in the neighborhood, they're OK; he even likes some of them. (Something he wouldn't admit around the station house.) Sure, the kids are all right—as long as they don't make trouble, give him a bad time.

After all, he's a parent, isn't he? So how can you really hate kids? Yet Sims often intones a silent prayer of gratitude when he thinks of his son and how he is just a nice average boy holding down a nice job with Con Ed.

But one thing is for sure: whatever it is these new kids want or do, they are young in a way Sims has never seen the young.

William Sims is a bulk in blue—bulk of biceps, bulge of calf, a stalwart head that juts forward perpetually and which shows the creases of time and the city's corrosive air grooved into the flesh of face and neck. The alert eyes brown and warm, even at times kind, though this is not necessarily something to be flaunted when you're a member of the department. It might be said that Sims has developed his squinting, narrowing glance, the slightly belligerent thrust of his head as if to negate the possible hint of softness. But fear not: there have been times when Sims has had to be as nightstick hard as anyone on the force. . . .

Twing twingtwing
Bnng a-bnnng
Twinnng
Twinngtwinngtwinng
Rhhhppp—

The beat, electrically boosted, is rocketing out from Tompkins Square Park. The concert is in full blast. It reaches out. . . .

Rhhhpp
Bnnng a-bnng
Twinngtwinngtwinng
Bleeepphh
Rhhppp rheeepp

15

He reaches the park, closer now to the great decibel assault. Immediately, for he is swift to the scent of trouble, he sniffs how it is: a mob here, minimum of five or six hundred kids, barefooted or sandaled, wearing the too familiar vestments: jeans and jumpers, leather jerkins, vests of cat or rabbit furs, old army, navy uniforms and tattered frockcoats, people pendulous with Indian jewelry and beads and tinkle bells. Temporarily a part of this neighborhood now as the recent Puerto Ricans are, and shirt-sleeved, suspendered old-timers, the Jews, Poles, Italians, except that here in the park it is not always easy to tell the male from the female. That, to Sims, is what he cannot understand. Some people comprehend this. Sims doesn't.

But trouble already, for gawsakes? Too bad Cap Fink has to be away tonight of all times. Too gawdan bad. For the kids are beginning to spread out, some of them moving farther back, from the band shell, off the concrete, beyond the benches, and onto the grassy area.

Nix on that: their permit definitely states they are not to set foot on the grassy area. That's definite. Like the hours. They have to be out of the park by 11 P.M. Just about an hour from now.

But tonight they won't. Sims sniffs trouble as sure as if it has been borne in on a secret wind. This year it is the hippies. Year after it can be something else. Come and go. Tonight they are the majority. They don't get hot in the head as easy as the others. But those gawdan flowers. Makes it hard to cope with. If the park gets out of hand that'll bring in the Tactical Patrol Force. For sure.

Rheeep rheeeppp
Twainnng twainnng
Bnng a-bnnngbnnng
Brmm booom trappp bwaw zook zammmm—!

It's the local rock group: The Great Society Gross-Outs. They are playing, they are sprawled or standing or walking or dancing all over the mighty expanse of the band shell and some are singing, all the guitars slamming, and there is a big box with two flashing lights going on and off, red and green like traffic signals, and there is projected on the walls of the band shell overlapping

16

images, filmy and fluid in shifting trembling rainbows of colors.

All around the park little groups are dancing, girls and young men and women and teenyboppers and even little children, dancing mostly by themselves like animated projections of the music that is shattering in a fission of sound the East Village air.

These kids. Sims sees how they look at each other sometimes. Some, a very few, have some kind of mysterious calm. Do they mean it?

Rhmmmmm
Swnnngswnnngswnng
Rhooop rhooop eee
Rhappprhappprhappppppp
Dreeek dreeek trumtrummmmm

The lights spasm out and change and all the time many of the kids keep dancing in their jiggling beads and bangles and bells.

But what about the rules, the city rules, hmm? Breaking out now onto the grassy area.

As Sims starts over, he pauses: a murmur is rising from this mob like a benediction, and he sees the young man in the rumpled white jeans, black windbreaker, the dark glasses with the white rims—Jamey.

Jamey: the sound many of the kids are making. As if Jamey were a superstar.

Jamey is nobody. But Sergeant Sims knows who he is. Sims isn't that square, is he? Jamey is someone most people never heard of except down here. Jamey only gets down here on weekend nights and nobody knows where he is the rest of the week.

Jamey. Never around long. But when he is— He is stepping out onto the center of the band shell, his guitar strapped on. He draws the microphone closer, though he doesn't look like he's going to play or sing.

Jamey waves his arms, light strikes the shiny black sleeves, he lowers his head and the yellow hair shifts, curtaining his eyes. He brushes it back.

"Please, everyone—" Jamey calls out. He takes off the dark glasses. His eyes are faintly agitated. This dark greenish blue, crystal vivid as stained glass. "Please, everyone—open your eyes wide! A child is lost. She is two years old. Her name is Fara. She is wearing blue shorts and T-shirt. Light-brown hair. Fara. Please look for her. She has to be somewhere here in the park."

Jamey waits. Standing there. Not singing. Or talking. His songs are not always regular songs. He does them sometimes just saying them like poems.

Jamey waits. He stands by the microphone, long-legged in the white jeans, his thick straight fair hair in a rough slant across his forehead. He frowns now. Then abruptly he turns and walks off the band shell, motioning, as he leaves, to the band. A new set of rock begins, a rockburst.

Now the park is astir as people begin to look all around while, in contrapuntal wildness, The Great Society Gross-Outs get turned on, three bearded guitar players leap forward and the sound bursts and twangs from the banks of electric amplifiers, and one of the musicians, in a fur vest, snatches up the strobe light and flashes it around, and in the big box the red and green eyes begin to blink on and off again and the psychedelic images squirm and shiver on the walls.

Sergeant Sims is almost relieved: the search for the child will at least defer his running into grief with the kids spilling over onto the grassy area. He will stay put, around this gate, let the other men of his precinct fan into the park now.

He sees Jamey leaving the band shell. There is someone, a girl in tight washed-out jeans and sweater and long light hair, who catches up with him and now they are walking, looking around as they talk, and talking as they walk. This girl is slender and she is not barefooted and, by the standards of this crowd, not dirty. She could be from uptown.

Everyone is looking, turning, pawing around alert for the lost or missing child. Yep. The diversion is on, and Sergeant Sims allows himself a bit of hope that somehow all will go well. But then his weary eyes narrow in habitual apprehension as he sees more and more people edging onto the prohibited turf, and seeing that too many of them are holding or wearing those flowers or bells, so peaceful—and that is when it can be toughest to handle and can smell like grief.

Jamey, as he was known down here, hurried out of the side exit of the brick band shell to join the search. The young mother was waiting in the office beneath the stage with the manager of The Gross-Outs. She was in no state to make it into this mob, coming down after a near freak-out.

As Jamey moved amid the maze of people, most of whom were his age or near it, he noticed again how it was down here sometimes, how unlike other places or at home in the town he called Nittygritty City in Long Island, or even at school: sometimes like now you had this feeling of union with so many of the people you passed, the way they looked, digging you, smiling and easy.

Even granting he felt uneasy too. Sometimes. Not sure or believing.

Yet now, with people wheeling in all directions all over the park trying to locate the missing child, even now—or maybe because of it—there was this subtle current or union between him and the others. . . .

Oh, this could be of the best.

Could be. But wasn't.

Not with all of them.

Jamey never said it, not even to Laura, but he was beginning to think it, wondering if a lot of mediocre or phony kids weren't taking refuge in the scene, in the styles and manners, using the scene as a kind of cop-out. . . .

Still, once in a while, like now, he got this flash, this current around him, almost pantheistic, comforting, a harmony that couldn't turn him on elsewhere or with his family, at least not with his father.

Oh well. Let it all hang out.

Yes, Dylan, the times they are—aren't they?

Even now, as everyone searched, many of them continued to move in dance, stir, jut, bob to the beat of the rock, almost everyone responding to the sound from the band shell.

Plugged in.

Feeling that inner surge: and feeling no doubt whatever that the missing child would be found. . . .

"Jamey—" The voice came from behind him: Laura Barnes.

"Hey," he said. "What happened to you?"

"I just got here." Laura, long-haired, in clean jeans and

sweater, moving beside him among the clots of people along the curving concrete walk. "A policeman told me some child is lost."

"Yes." Jamey felt the glide of her hand on his, swift, warm, gone then. They kept walking, looking around on all sides.

Laura was saying, "How many little kids there are around here. This time of night."

Ahead of him, holding a baby, was a barefooted young woman; she was walking with a couple who had tagging along with them their five-year-old son, his head and shoulders, his entire small-boned body responding in an almost flawless rhythm to the rock, born to it.

Jamey and Laura crossed over to the playground sector, but no luck there. The music ceased. Another number. He looked back to see the lead guitarist step to a microphone, singing, the group behind him in the old Donovan special: "Sunshine Superman."

It was after they'd circled the concrete crescent of the park and were starting back toward the band shell that something drew Jamey's attention. Immediately he left Laura and ran over to the generator truck with its cables snaking across the ground, a crew working the film and light projectors on the roof. He stooped down and then, flattening out, crawled under the truck.

To find what?

A mound of dog. A mottled mongrel hound. Asleep in the shattering night. But from a distance it had looked like a—

He scrabbled up and out from the truck, got to his feet, but too quickly or carelessly, for as he straightened up, there it was, that tic of pain at the small of his back: he had to stand there, wait, test it, slowly trying to reach a straight firm position. Still waiting. Stupid. Careless. He always forgot.

Fuckleberry Finn.

"What is it?" Laura reaching him now. "Your back?"

He nodded.

"Oh, Jamey. You couldn't! Not again."

After an interval: "I think it's all right."

"Sure?" Laura smiling then in wry reminiscence: the grim summer of three years ago. "Is it really all right?"

He took a few steps. Slow. Brittle. Like an old man. Then he was making it. "OK," he said. Thankful, relieved. Straight as a sunflower. Yet he moved gingerly until he really knew he was all right. Less than five minutes later he forgot about it. He forgot about it because as they neared the west gate he was sure he saw the missing child. As Donovan's gift winged across the park.

"Come on." He led the way. A chunky policeman was blocking the path of a girl who was holding the child: it was Fara, yes, blue shorts and T-shirt. The hassle was tight when Jamey got there. The policeman stood hard center between the brick posts, attempting now to take the child from the girl: this girl about nineteen, her dark hair in twin plaits; she was wearing a faded old minidress bordered by an embroidered pattern of Indian symbols.

"Now looka here, miss—" The sergeant was all frowns, like a prune.

"Please let me go." The girl's gentle tone.

"Go where? That's what I'm stopping you for. Go where?"

"I'm getting this child back to—" The girl's voice was clear and open. Western.

Laura kept holding Jamey's elbow, as if to caution him. More neighborhood moved in, pressed against the brick posts.

"You were trying to run out of the park is what you were doing, and resisting the—" The policeman's jaw was outthrust.

"Will you please let me go!"

"Just give me the kid, miss, and you can leave. I'll handle this."

"Oh no—no, I refuse. Will you please forget it? Here—" With her free hand she drew a limp vinyl daisy from her hair and handed it to the law. Jamey still watching her, for there was something that hinted she was not necessarily the person her clothes suggested: the vinyl daisy was a tarnished one like a hand-me-down bauble from the past.

"Now looka here." His face knotted with impatience. "None of that. I have to make sure this child is delivered to her mother. How do I know where you're going when you go tearing out of this park? Now come on—" The thick hands were again reaching out, and the girl stepped back sharply as if she'd been scalded.

Jamey saw how pointless it would be to move in: it was this girl's groove, she'd resent him, just as she resented the law. She was obviously that kind of girl: yet it was a flash, this kid in juxtaposition to the burly bluecoat with his dutiful bluster; this brown-eyed girl who was trying to get under him with her politeness, her smile or her dime-store floral offering, this girl who could not have stood more than five feet one high, her dress a-swell with all she had, and her homeland's sun still gold on her legs: so much gender packed into such a diminutive package.

"Now looka here—" War between them flaring again. "Looka here, I'm taking this child back, it's my responsibility." But as he reached out his muscled arms, the little child bellowed in fright. The girl twisted away from him and dropped the armful of news-papers—the local underground paper—she'd been selling.

"Listen, you—" Her gentleness seemed to have run thin. "Listen, I don't think you have any right to touch her or stop me or anything, and no fuzz is going to lay a finger on her or me!"

Jamey stooped down and picked up the papers. "Can I help here?"

"Nothing to do with you, fella," said the policeman, but looking at him as if in recognition.

"I have to get this child to her mother and if it wasn't for this stupid—" The girl worked to mute her temper.

"Officer," Jamey said, "I spoke with the mother when it happened. So let's get the child back in a hurry, it doesn't matter who or how—"

"It matters very much," the girl broke in belligerently, again seeming to forget or ignore one of the tenets of her philosophy. "I refuse to give this little creature to anyone except—"

"Here, give her to me," offered Laura.

"Are you on his side?" The girl's eyes were bronze fires of indignation.

"No, of course I'm not, but—"

"All right." The girl, summoning a last effort, turned back to the sergeant. "All right, I'll take the child back straight through the park. You can follow me. OK?" Silence. "I mean, like let's forget it. Peace. OK?"

Officer Sims shook his head and lifted his visored cap to wipe the perspiration from his perplexed brow. "Sure. OK. Why not?" He harnessed his bulk, preparing to accompany her. It was at this juncture that one of his superior officers appeared and ordered him to join the other men of the force, who were converging on the restricted grassy area.

The hassle was over. The girl's face took on an angel's calm. She stroked the child, hitched her up close to her shoulder and started back toward the band shell with Jamey and Laura.

The girl turned to him. "You're not leaving now, are you?"

"What?" Then: "Oh, no." Then: "What's your name?"

"Poppy," answered the girl.

He introduced her to Laura, adding, "I'm—"

"I know who you are," said the girl who was Poppy. "I heard you last month one night, the first night I was in town."

"Where are you from? California?" Jamey said.

"How'd you know?" The girl smiled. "I think this kid is wetting its pants."

Jamey accompanied her to the office beneath the band shell and returned outside to Laura. He glanced at his watch. Fifteen minutes left.

Laura glanced toward the office door. "That's a cute kid."

"Yes."

"I didn't mean the child," said Laura.

"Oh," he said. Then: "Yes, she is. But like most of them, she's somewhere else. The wrong place."

"It's where she wants to be," Laura said.

He shook his head. "The wrong place." He put his arm around Laura's shoulder. "Where will I find you?"

"Out there adoring you in public."

"Save it." Jamey pressed his hand against the back of her head, that good feel of her hair. Hanging long. A tone like butterscotch.

He returned to the band shell, got his guitar and waited until The Gross-Outs finished their set. He sucked in the air. Then he stepped out onto the stage and readjusted the microphone. He did not use amplification. Just the mike. Voice and steel-stringed guitar.

He snugged the guitar against him. He looked out into the park. He lowered his eyes. He was ready. He'd written "The Lyndon Tree" less than a week ago. Ready . . .

"Well—" He talked it against the thrum of guitar.

There was this tree
A very fine tree
In his prime

A young tree
But his time was wrong, his time was the wrong time.
Yeah, there was this tree
A very fine tree
Hip, they said
Full of juice, sappy
A sapling in the green and groovy wood
With other trees.
But one day
A man, tan, wearing a banded hat
And a badge
Came along
And do you know what he did?
He tagged all these trees
That's right.
They were in.
Yeah, this tree that was so green
And happy in his prime time
His youth, the sap and slap of it
Tagged E.C.
By the tan toothy unyoung man
In the banded hat.

What is E.C., asked this tree.
It is E for Early and C for Cutting.
Well, what does that make me, asked the tree.
Why, said the man, it makes you a Lyndon tree.
But I don't want to be a Lyndon tree
I don't want to get myself cut down
I like it here
It's shady
Smells sweet in the morning mists
A leafy life is
For me.
Hey now, what kind of talk is that?
Said this tan unyouthful
Toothful of bad news,
What kind of talk is that?
Don't want to be one of the Lyndon trees?
What are you—some kind of Redwood?

No sir, I'm no Redwood,
I'm only an ordinary tree,

Juicy, sappy, leafy,
That's the kind of tree I am
And I like the green life
And the shade I bring to kids
Climbing at my knee
And the birdsong
And I don't want to be a Lyndon tree.

This tree, the man in tan decided,
Has got to go.
For this man was turned on:
His current was straight—D.C.
Well, you know what happened,
They tapped this young tree
For some far far place
Where there lived another race
Like jungle trees and trees with fronds
Alongside all the Lyndon trees
In this far far place.

Stillness only now and then
Just wasn't the kind of place
This kind of tree digs—
All that noise
Like roars and blasts and screams
All this din around this Lyndon tree.
But they told him again
How this far far place
Couldn't go on without the Lyndon trees.
Except that one day
The tree was being sawed
And quartered
Lengthwise—
Which at least was not as bad
As what happened to some of the other trees
Like the ones with the dark bark
First to go
Chopped into chips
Processed into pulp
And become newsprint for newspeak
So that many gurus
Around the Potomac

Could tell people how fine the show was going
In that far far place a thousand root years from home.
Anyway, this Lyndon tree
Sawed into four parts
Became a lookout
In the jungle
For cats to liberate everything in sight
In fields of fear
And paddies of blood
To flood the land with their might.
That's right.
Well, this now uprooted and quartered tree
Was no longer the same happy
Juicy tree in the green and groovy wood.
And then one day something else happened—
The lookout of the four-pyloned tree
Was blown to pieces
Which doesn't happen where the peace is
Does it?

And now the tree is gone
And some cat waved a flag.
Still the tree is gone.
A drag, just wasn't his bag
Was it?

Well, that's what happened
To the young tree
And many others, felled by the Lyndon blight.
That's victory, all right
For the fallen trees
In the far far night.

Ah: it was more than hearing people call out; it was more like their backing him or what he sang about. Jamey, for all his inexperience, could tell how the listening was and the way in which they'd been listening and the places where he had to stop, giving way to the way they dug him. Even though he did not agree with many of the people in the park, he knew he wanted what they wanted. It was only their way of getting there. Like this girl Poppy, lost, somewhere else.

The concert over. Jamey left the band shell. The Great Society Gross-Outs were packing up their instruments and amplifiers. He hurried out to meet Laura, though they did not leave immediately.

"What's going on?" Laura nodded toward the now crowded grassy area. Behind benches and iron fencing the population had swelled; the dozen policemen stood their stations, rigid, like blue statues along the periphery of the grass.

Jamey and Laura went over. The air was fragrant there, softly stabbed with incense.

The rhythmic thump of bongo drums.

And chanting. *Hare Krishna.* Young sounds touching the starless and nirvana-less night.

"Why are they just standing there?" Laura lit a cigarette, still watching the police, one hand hooked over the wide leather belt of her jeans.

"Waiting for the wagons." Jamey rested the guitar case against his leg.

"Isn't that—what's her name—Poppy?" Laura said.

He saw her almost at the same time, small, zealous, plugged in to the chanting. Despite the Eye of God, the diamond-shaped symbol embroidered in yarn on her dress, she still saved secret glances, hostile and defiant, for the policeman, the sergeant, hulk and bulk, standing splay-legged near her. Sitting everywhere now on the expanse of prohibited turf, there must have been at least two hundred people, the spillover from the concert, the same ragged long-haired middle-class harlequinade.

"Are we going to stay? I don't see why we shouldn't," said Laura.

Jamey said, "Not if it just means sitting here. I can't just sit here and turn off."

"It seems crazy, doesn't it, the cops not doing anything—"

"Not at all," he said. "They are known to be patient, benign, benevolent, tolerant, understanding, a real gas of sweetness. Let's go."

It wasn't until late the next morning, when they were reading the Sunday paper in bed in the downtown apartment borrowed from the brother of a college friend, that the absence of police action was accounted for.

"Look—" He held up the front page. "You want to know why the blue boys were so sweet last night? It's all here. All hell was breaking loose in Harlem. One blight at a time is all they can allow down in Lindsaytown. The price of peace downtown is trouble uptown."

Laura shook her head. "Are we coming down next weekend?" She buttoned the tops of her pajamas and began to brush her hair.

"I am. Aren't you?" he said.

"Try to keep me away." She tilted her head down and all that butterscotch hair fell forward across her face and down over her breasts. She kept brushing methodically.

"Why'd you ask?" he said. Silence. She shook her hair back, palmed it back and away from her face.

"M-o-t-h-e-r." She wrenched out the letters. "I mean, honestly, it's getting to be such a drag. She knows damn well I'm sleeping with you. Just as I know she's sleeping with Cliff. But no, we keep playing the same games. I mean, after all this time, what does she think?"

"It makes her feel good," Jamey said. "They're all hung up on games."

"Yes."

"At my house we play too," Jamey said.

"I-really-understand-you-son." Laura began the old college charade.

He took on the voice of his father, Frederick Mieland: "'Your mother and I get a kick out of your guitar. All that. Those things you write. OK. Swell. Part of growing up. OK now, while you're still in college.'"

"'But,'" Laura continued.

"'But,'" Jamey said, "'you're also building for the future, son, and one day when the business is yours—'" He stopped, gagged on this stereotype portrait of his father. He swung off the bed, picked up the ashtray and hurled it across the room into the kitchen sink. "The day I graduate from Mustang U. is a day I don't think I look forward to."

"Jamey—" Laura's conciliatory voice. Here or at school.

He turned. He thumped barefoot across the nylon carpet and sat down on the side of the bed. He felt her hand on his arm.

"You can't let it keep bugging you like this," Laura said.

"And now," Jamey said, "the newest thing is, why do I have to call myself just Jamey? How the hell am I going to answer that one? I can't say I'm trying to remove myself from the whole scene at home, the whole stupid lousy way you have to earn the bread."

"At least," Laura said, "we get away from it down here. For a while."

"We don't. We're talking about it again," Jamey said. "The thing is, it's getting tougher for me. After every weekend it's getting tougher to go back. It was bad enough while school was still on. But now. As soon as I hit Long Island and see all those plywood châteaus my father puts up—" He stopped. "To hell with it."

"Listen, Jamey, it could be worse," Laura said. "At least you're not stuck in the office."

"I cut that one up," he said. He rose, moved around the room again. He picked up his guitar and put it down. He went to the radio on the bed table, dialed in some rock.

"Look at it this way," Laura said. "How much better we've got it than a lot of people we know."

"Nobody has it very good," he said.

"The weekends are still something." Reasonable Laura. All that sober reasonableness: somehow it didn't seem to belong to her kind of face, a kind of Pre-Raphaelite face, the delicate tilt of nose, the pale-blue eyes with the sooty lashes.

"Yes." He glanced around the one-room apartment. The Sunday sunlight was blunted by the double drapes. The place was stamped by the owner's Junior Establishment taste: white walls decorated with two large abstract expressionist lithos and a few pop and art nouveau posters.

The music ceased and on came the DJ. The blabbing about which songs were top forty on the charts. He dialed it out and turned to another program. "Donovan's Colors," the arrangement by Van Dyke Parks, slashing and sliding and wallowing in and out of the sounds in magical distortion.

"Are you hungry?" he said.

"Not much."

"I am." Starting for the kitchen alcove. "You got me out of the blues. A little anyway." He picked up an ashtray in which they'd burned some incense last night, emptied it in the sink.

"I must have tried hard," Laura said. "But I'm glad."

A faint smile, glancing back at her. "That's the good thing about a girl with divorced parents. There's nothing like a tragic broken home to make you the daddy they haven't got anymore."

"Hee-hee-hee," she said. "I'm all choked up."

From the refrigerator he took out what was left of the bag of grapes. He brought them back to the bed, and he and Laura sat there eating the tiny water-green grapes.

Music still going. "Sometimes," he said, "I'm not sure what I really think about you."

"I hope that's good," she said. "Is it?"

"I don't know," he said. "I wish I had my record player here."

"Umm."

"You'd think after three years—" he began.

"You want to know something?" Laura said.

"No. What?"

"When I had the flu—spring vacation, remember?—well, I stayed holed up in my room at home and one day just for fun I started figuring out how much I'd seen you. And you want to know something? Those three years in actual time, that is—you know—actual periods seeing each other: it all added up to about a year. I mean, when you add it all up—"

"Maybe being a statistician—maybe that's your groove," he said.

"Oh sure."

"Was that all you had to do?"

"Well, it was better than listening to Mother and Cliff. Oh God—" She put down the hairbrush. "What time is it?"

"Ten of one. When are you supposed to be back?"

"Two." She sighed.

Jamey said, "That doesn't leave us much—"

"No."

"Why don't you call your mother, see if you can push it up," he said.

"I suppose I could." Laura pursed her lips. "The only thing is, I hate like hell to get involved in another of those filthy arguments with her. If I say I'll be late, she'll say where are you and what are you doing—"

Jamey immediately pulled her over on top of him. "Tell her."

She freed herself. "Thanks." Then she said, "I know those arguments with her, and I know one day I'm going to lose what cool I still have and just let her know I know she's sleeping with Cliff and why does she have to be such a hypocritical drag about it? But I just can't let myself do it, Jamey." A pause. "I'd just as soon not call her now."

"Try it anyway," he said.

"No." Laura looking more grim. "If I say I won't be able to make it, she'll jump at it right away and accuse me of lying to her and where was I last night. And she'll ask me if I'm with you."

"Tell her the truth," Jamey said, "how you found me flying on pot or speed, in the gutter, waving a Red Chinese flag and exposing myself to passing nuns."

Though Laura laughed, a frown began to form again. "Jamey— what did you mean before?"

"About what?"

"About not knowing what you really thought about me."

"What I meant? I don't know," he said. "Well, no— What I meant was if you'd really changed much since Mesa, Alabama. I guess maybe you're into a new—"

"I am certainly not."

"All right." He pulled her down to him again.

"All right nothing." She drew back. Not speaking now. Resting on one elbow. "I haven't changed," she said then. "If there's been any change, it's you. You're changing. The only difference in me is maybe I might like you a little more. What do you mean, I'm into something new?"

"Well—" He sat up. "You're sort of going back—rapping like a liberal. You used to be less safe and sound."

She swung away from him. "Well, you know what *you* can do!"

"I'd like to. But with you," he called after her retreating figure. She slammed the bathroom door behind her. He got up and followed her in. "Come on back, Laur—"

"Forget it." She turned on the shower.

"Look, all I want is to go back to bed."

"Well, go." The hissing of the shower now.

"It's not much fun alone," he said.

"I don't give a goddam." Laura piled up her hair and put on the white shower cap. But a smile began to sun up her features. "I'll be through in a minute. I have to shower."

"Do it later."

"I can't."

He reached out for her. "Since when?"

"Jamey, can I please take my shower!"

"Why do you have to be so clean!" He kissed her, unbuttoned her pajamas. "Come on. It's a silver Sunday, baby."

She slowly took off the shower cap and the long tawny hair fell, and she went back to the bed with him.

Radio a-blast: enveloping them, five guitars, twanging in electronic eddies, constricting, dilating as if in counterpoint to afternoon love.

But at first Laura was nowhere. Jamey kept trying to hold her very hard, still she wasn't totally there. He reached across her breasts to the crumpled bag of seedless grapes. He decided to put one in her navel. But this quixotic impulse was a mistake: the grape burst and mashed into her flesh, and at once she sat up and said he was being an absolute nut today and she didn't know what the hell she was doing with him.

As soon as she said this, everything seemed all right again and they had it the way they always had.

2 : THE CITY

ON FIFTH AVENUE near Thirtieth Street is the wholesale firm of Bemlen's Banners and Buttons, Novelties, Inc., known in the trade as B B & B Novelties (flags, bunting, buttons and allied items, catering to Masonic orders, conventions, campaigns, schools, sports, souvenir outlets). The company is expanding its premises, partitions are being changed, office space and stockrooms are being enlarged. Times are good. The firm is adding to its orthodox line a varied inventory of unorthodox novelties to catch up with the proliferating business of items for American youth. The president of the firm, L. K. Bemlen, Jr., is, like his father, an alert entrepreneur, a responsible citizen and active in the Lutheran church. The salesmen of the company are regarded as responsible family men.

Like Harry Folsom. Age forty-four.

He too will tell you about how he has seen Jamey.

Now Harry is closing his case, the novelties of the youth line, and he departs. Today is the day for downtown. He subways to Sixth Avenue and Eighth Street. The action has been here, the big tourist business. Later he will work his way across to the East Village.

He pauses in the subway tunnel before the mirror of a weighing machine. Harry is not exactly ashamed of his appearance. His fox-brown hair is short, bristly. Crew-cut. He is clean-shaven, clean-cut. He dresses sharp, not crazy or kooky. You might say more along the line of Ivy League, but not dull. Take his suit: it's a Durapress, Nowelt, Nylonethelene single-breasted with smoky buttons and pants half an inch narrower than some of the other fellas up at B B & B. His wife, Marta, admires the way he dresses, though his fifteen-year-old daughter, Linda, is not always as enthusiastic. But he'll say this for Linda: at least she sticks it out in Yonkers and doesn't hang around downtown in the Village with all those teenyboppers, who, say what you want, aren't so young they aren't peddling it around or taking pot or even LSD. One thing about Harry, whenever he returns from these junkets, he always makes it a point to see Linda doesn't get the idea there is anything interesting or stimulating about the way these kids dress or act. Harry knows a good father is a vigilant father.

Now in the smog of the mild late June day Harry makes his way from store to store until by half-past five he reaches Saint Mark's Place. Now his rhythm, his sharpness, his metabolism are changed, geared higher; a day's business always affects him like that.

He strides into another store, called The City of Psychedelphia, a "head" shop, featuring paper Tiffany lamps, buttons, mod ties, psychedelic posters, lights, perfumed cigarette papers, water pipes, beads, bells, etc. The co-owners are waiting on some kids; these owners are some old folks—Tom is twenty-five, his friend, Christina, twenty-one—and she is wearing a disgusting dress up to her ass, a disgrace, a fine example for any decent kids who come in here!

Harry has to wait until the customers are gone. His gaze is inevitably attracted to the bulletin board; all kinds of personal notices put up by the people of the neighborhood. Harry edges closer to the notices. Casually, as if bored, he studies them.

Lovely Chick & Friend (M)
Wishes Meet Attractive Non-Straight Young Couple
For Mutual Satisfactions.
Send Foto.

Poor, honest, loving Male anxious make San Francisco scene,
wants car ride (loves to fly) to West Coast with Att. (slim)
Girl with enough bread for two. Name of Peace.

Male: Driver Indefatigable. Gift for Cunnilingus. Seeks
desperate, clean, pretty women 19–39.

Former Bryn Mawr student who has Seen the Light is hung up
with Rent of 1 RM. APT. Desires roommate, male, with similar
pursuit of intellectual or/and erotic happiness.

Muses Harry, and his tongue moistens his lips, no wonder
these kids down here are giving their families such a bad time,
going wild, no responsibility, living on nothing but orgies, calling
themselves rebels or hippies or whatever. Nothing but an excuse
for goldbricking and orgies.

"Hey now—" Harry greets the owners as soon as they are free,
speaking, smiling, letting drop a few choice little words to show
he's hip, yes sir. "Hey, I've been waiting here all this time and if
you'll allow me, I want to show you guys some groovy items—"

The co-owners exchange quick wincing grimaces, though
Harry is spared, he is too busy opening his case to notice. He
must sell.

Most shops like this get their merchandise from makers here
in the Village—arts-and-crafts lofts or sweat shops—but B B & B is
moving in with better prices and deals.

When he looks up he sees this girl Christina leaning down to
examine the items. Her hair naturally is long, naturally there is
hanging a string of beads, but she's not even wearing a bra. The
informal type.

He says, "How're you kids fixed for—boutonnieres?"

"You mean buttons?" the girl says: she doesn't even get his
French touch. "We've got a lot. Too many. I don't know how
long we're going to stay in business. Even the drugstores uptown
are beginning to sell our kind of stuff."

Yes. Harry knows this. But he must sell.

"How about"—Harry holds up the cardboard of sample buttons with their printed slogans—"how about 'Moby Dick Is not a Venereal Disease'? Ha-ha."

While the girl wearily examines the buttons, he turns to the young man. "I'm anxious for you to see our ruby belly-button plugs and our new Buddha Beebee Beads. We're also ahead of the scene, man, with this item; no one in New York has it yet"—Harry reaches into the case—"the Mick Jagger handcuffs, the exact same, a replica, like the same ones he wore when those English bobbies tossed him in the clink. Lift 'em—don't they heft like the real McCoy? Going to be the hottest item we've had in ten years or—"

But Harry doesn't walk away with an order. Gets under his skin; got to compensate next place, unload more of this crazy merchandise and get out of this neighborhood of pot heads and perverts.

Why even come down here anymore? Business like this is now uptown.

What Harry needs is a stiff drink under his belt. He finds a bar, a decent one, and he orders a rye and ginger ale. He looks out the window. Across the way: underground films. Well, he hasn't stooped to that yet. After the second rye he decides this place is Dullsville. You take yesterday uptown, when he had a few high-balls in that new topless place, where at least you saw decent-looking people at the bar, not to mention the young waitresses, those big pink boobs staring you in the eye. . . .

Maybe he'll just take a peek at those movies across the street, just to see if they're—well, just to check. Call the family first.

Where's the phone booth? In back. Grubby there. Smells. Not clean. Nothing down here is clean. He calls his home in Yonkers.

"Hon? Harry. Look, hon, I'm still tied up downtown. You better go ahead without me. Those stores down here never close. All I can say is I'm glad Linda isn't mixed up with this gang of goldbricks around here, give you the creeps. What time? Oh, lemme see, say about ten, ten-thirty, have to grab a bite first. How's my little girl? Lemme talk to her, tell her her ever lovin' daddy wants to talk to her—"

Shortly after eight o'clock Harry enters the theater for the program of underground films. The place is only half full. People are dozing. He sets his case down between his legs. This kind of place you have to watch it. Well, looks like he's right in the middle of one of the pictures. The lighting is crazy, there is this naked girl moving around except you can't see her clearly because of that lighting, makes it hard to see what she's like. A disgrace, and all he can say is he'll never allow Marta or Linda to be exposed to this kind of stuff.

Now the light changes enough to see where you are, and it's some kind of church, all those candles on the altar. She is dancing around again and now she starts stroking one of the candles, the highest one, and now she's running her tongue along it. Talk about sacrilegious. You wonder they don't throw the manager in the clink.

Now she's working herself up into something, writhing, grinding, touching this candle again, kissing it gently and then for Christ sakes she falls in a faint and a figure like Jesus floats above her, holding a lighted candle. Why?

Harry stirs in his seat. Impatiently he waits for this disgusting film—not even a plot—to be over so that the next one can come on, and he hopes there won't be any of that tricky lighting that prevents you from seeing exactly what's going on. Here it comes, good, finally, the next one, a boy and girl, no clothes on, naturally, running along a beach, then into some sort of high green grass, really disgusting now the way the light moves, disgusting, you can tell the boy is putting the blocks to her but it's all seen through these high grasses, the way they move.

When it's all over Harry sees it is past ten o'clock and he steps outside into the wide avenue: for that welcome fresh air, a relief after all that filth. Two hours of it.

Hey, looka that. Corner of Second and Saint Mark's Place something is going on: all the traffic is gone. Hundreds of kids swarming all over. Music. Loud? Break your eardrum, all electric. A band of bearded wildos are playing rock 'n' roll on the roof of a Volkswagen Microbus.

Well, say. What's cooking here? Harry moves into the throng. The street is a mess, balloons flying everywhere, flowers scattered around everywhere on the stoops and fire escapes. Harry is pleased to see that some of the residents at least aren't buying all this; they're tossing vegetables and old junk down onto the kids from open windows. A few decent people left in the world.

"Say, what's going on?" he asks one of the kids, a girl of about nineteen, who is vacuum-packed into jeans and wears some kind of sarape and brass bells. B B & B still does a solid business in bells. "What's going on?" he asks her again.

This girl gives him a very sweet smile. Nice. A nice kid, despite the dirty feet. Packed into those jeans. She tells him what's going on tonight is that a free concert is under way and they have stopped traffic in order to get the city interested in turning the street into a mall, with trees instead of automobiles.

Mall. Trees. He looks around. Trees instead of cars? Some hophead must have dreamed that one up.

He moves forward. All these girls. Running around loose. The band atop the VW bus stops. A tall guy in white jeans, black glasses and with thick blond hair is climbing up to the top of the bus, past all those wires or cables that are run into that disco The Electric Circus. It is Jamey. He starts playing his guitar and singing or talking: Jamey.

Harry steps closer, inching forward slowly in the mob, inching forward and having to press right against this girl's little butt. He'll stay here and watch. The blond boy tilts his head closer to the microphone (a year later, Harry, who is something of a mimic, will try to imitate how Jamey did this):

Madrastown Madrastown
Oh we're all so lonesome, hometown lonesome
For Madrastown.
How the memories accrue, yeah
The way the haircuts are crew, yeah
On all the lads in Madrastown
A real mom and dad town.
A country club is there
Where the kids can dress sloppily
And folks play bridge and Monopoly
At the club where we all paid our dues
To keep out the niggers, the wops, the Catholics
and the yeah
Yeah life isn't so bad in Madras
Madrastown—

38

Harry wrinkles his nose, stirs. The girl in front of him has edged ahead. Oh well. This is Dullsville, that crap from the guitar up there. Harry ought to start thinking of getting home, out of here, all these dirty-footed kids pretending to enjoy that guy up there, but probably just hanging around until they can get socked in the hay.

And look at them wearing all that crazy junk, all those items, many of which came from B B & B Novelties. Harry calculates the amount of commission on sales he'll pull down this week.

Clearing out now. Halfway up the street, Harry, an innocent victim, suddenly turns, twitches, turns again to peer up with a bruised look at a tenement window: a carton of curdled yogurt has come hurtling down to strike him, his shoulder, the gray suit now splattered white, the milky rivulets creasing down his sleeve. At once in his rage he reaches for his breast-pocket handkerchief. It's not there. It's in the movie theater. On the floor, under his seat where he'd disposed of it.

Jamey put his guitar in its case. Session over. He was very warm. He was happy. He leaped down from the roof of the VW bus to the street. Saint Mark's Place was not easy to navigate, a thick gelatinous mass of people, the young of the East and the West Village, long-haired, shoeless, unkempt, along with some young professors from the grooves of Academe, and the groomed from uptown.

Like that poor cat over there with the yogurt slapped all over his shoulder.

Balloons were everywhere tonight, suspended like plump white polka dots in the night. Jamey moved slowly through the crowd: more kids nodded to him, some stopped to say something to him about his songs. It was very personal, the way it seemed to happen. He felt less of a stranger than when he'd first come downtown the beginning of May. Less than two months ago. Making it all this spring, leaving campus late Fridays after his last class, returning late Sundays. But now with summer vacation and living with his parents it was different. . . .

He made his way to where Laura would be, where the tree, an oak sapling, was set into mounds of earth that had been hauled, along with the tree, from Staten Island.

Laura was there, Laura, even longer-legged in the white stockings and band of skirt, the long amber hair straight down. She saw him. The faintest smile, the frosted lipstick on her mouth the hue of bing cherries.

"What do you feel like?" he said.

"What do you feel like?" she said.

They started toward Avenue A. "I appreciate that pad now that we haven't got it," Jamey said, and she nodded. At the corner he paused. He noticed the sign on the marquee of the theater a block down: an English raga rock group was there. He glanced at his watch. Too late to make it. "Some beer?"

"Sure."

Down Avenue A toward The New Annex. He said, "How'd you think it went tonight?"

"Just great. Really," she said. "Especially 'Lyndon Tree.'"

"What about 'Madras'?"

"Oh, it's really shaping up—"

"Needs work," he said. "But I—" He stopped. The girl who was selling the underground newspaper approached them.

"Hi, Jamey," she said.

"Hi." He recognized her then. Poppy. The diminutive girl who wore the same minidress he remembered from a few weekends ago, with its border of Indian symbols. Her dark hair in a ponytail, at her shoulder a black-and-orange button: PRAY FOR SEX.

"Which way are you all heading?" Poppy said.

"The New Annex," he said. "Can you make it?"

"I can't," Poppy said. "But I'll walk a ways with you." They moved south along the avenue, and then Poppy said, "Look, why don't you come back to the place with me?"

"Where?" Jamey said.

"Alan Bernstein's. I'm living there. Temporarily," Poppy said. "Why don't you come?"

He looked over at Laura, who said, "Sure."

Bernstein's apartment, he knew, was a crash pad. "Maybe I can pick up some beer—"

"Alan is a fan of yours. He's great. You know?" Poppy said. "He'd give away the teeth in his head. Have you ever made any records?"

"Hell no."

They turned east into Sixth Street. Poppy stopped once at a health-food store to buy a bag of organically grown wheat flour. "Well"—she was moving along now, barefooted and blithe— "there's probably going to be a mob at Alan's."

Jamey nodded. From the radio of a parked car "Baby You're a Rich Man," The Beatles in spiritual ode.

Poppy said, "I never see you around much down here."

"Oh—" Jamey hesitated. "I'm around."

"Like I mean during the week," Poppy said.

"Well—" Jamey paused. "I—I'm just helping out my father. For the summer."

Poppy said nothing. But Laura said he ought to come clean.

"Building. Housing developments," he said. "The trade that turns you off."

"Do you have to do it?" Poppy said.

"More or less," Jamey said.

Poppy considered this. "You must be strung out."

They were at the corner. In front of a store. He asked Laura to hold his guitar case, and he went in and bought two six-packs.

Alan Bernstein's apartment was a fifth-floor walkup near Avenue B. The stairwell, as they ascended, was fumed with garlic, fried fat, urine, wine, incense.

The door opened only a slit at first, then swung wide, and they met Bernstein, who stood in the kitchen entry—a doe-eyed, cadaverous young man with a tangle of walnut hair; he was bare chested, barefooted. He wore Marine Corps fatigue pants.

"Welcome," Bernstein said.

Jamey started to put the beer packs on the kitchen counter, but there was no place: a debris of dirty dishes, pots, pans. There was no refrigerator. He put the beer on an orange crate beside the two-burner gas stove.

"What happened about the dishes?" Poppy asked Bernstein. "Was it my turn or—"

"No. It was Mike's. But he had to clear out."

"Police?" Poppy said immediately. "Was it a—"

"I couldn't tell," Bernstein said. "They were polite this time."

"Where's MIKE?" Poppy frowning.

"Mike is all right. He got upstairs in time."

"I'll get him," Poppy said.

"Could be they'll come back," Bernstein said.

"You think so, Alan?"

Bernstein shrugged.

Poppy turned to Jamey and Laura. "It's a question of being scarce. Mike got inducted but he's not having any." She opened the door, this petite former zealot of Haight-Ashbury. "Oh, the stinking fuzz!" Muttering to herself as she went out into the hallway.

Alan Bernstein led the way out of the kitchen. In the next room, a large room with leprous walls, there were about a dozen people. At one end, by an iron lamp stand, circa 1922, some of the people were talking softly or reading; at the shadowed end on floor mattresses were the blurred silhouettes of three couples —one pair asleep, the others oblivious, making out, their bodies amorphous in the dimness, a slow dance, a wraparound, uninhibited, even innocent.

"Less crowded in here." Bernstein showed them into the next room: smoke, incense. From a record player the warm and beautiful sounds of the Far East trembled in the unfresh air: the multistringed sitar of Ravi Shankar.

People nodded and smiled. It was hot. A ceiling bulb and one candle for illumination. Jamey and Laura found a place on the floor by the window, which could not be opened.

Nearby on the floor was Kathy, a coarse-haired blond girl, tapping softly on a tambourine in accompaniment to the record's classical Indian strains; her Negro boyfriend, Carlos Jones, lay with his head in her lap.

On a lumpy heliotrope sofa sat two young men, one known as Hap, the other as Florida. They were passing a joint between them. They handed it down to Kathy, who shared it with Carlos Jones and then extended it to Jamey beside her.

Alan Bernstein put on Bob Dylan's "Blowin' in the Wind."

Jamey took two drags and then held the joint out for Laura, who would refuse. She did. He returned it to Kathy. He leaned back against the windowsill. Listening to Dylan. Ah yes. He loosened the collar of his shirt, tugged up his jeans. He tipped his dark glasses up onto his hair. Now and then he glanced at Laura.

Her hand moved over his. The room was very quiet. Vines of smoke rose, swirled, became as curled as Dylan's mane.

The joint, now a roach held by a bobby pin of Kathy's, came his way again for another drag; followed soon in the silence by a new joint and more drags. No place near a high, but soothing, yes, soothing. That was the truth forsooth.

He peered around at the others. All contentment? Half-smiles in their half-lowered eyes.

Being where they want to be?

Going where?

When?

But you could see no one cared all that much.

Total turnoff.

People like Poppy. He watched her. A waste?

Was he?

"'Xcuse me—" The voice of another girl as she emerged from the bathroom shower, naked, hair wet and shining; she held a bath towel (Hotel Winslow) as she stepped damply and briskly across the floor into the adjacent room. She almost collided with Poppy, who, along with a young man, brought in the beer and passed it around.

"Jamey, this is Mike. Laura—Mike," said Poppy. The fugitive from the Army was a big and rosy-cheeked youth, his blue eyes wary behind wire-rimmed glasses, his long hair rust red. He sat down near Jamey. "Hear you might play some," he said.

"He's going to." Poppy eased herself against Mike.

Alan Bernstein moved over to the side wall, which was decorated with graffiti and cutouts of hands and feet. An impudent upright finger was peeling off and he thumbtacked it back into place. When he turned back, he said, "Laura, I keep thinking I've seen you somewhere—"

"Oh?" Laura said.

"Yeah," he was saying. "But you don't work around here, do you?"

She laughed. "I didn't think it showed all that much. No, I'm with a foundation uptown. It's just a summer job."

Bernstein squatted on the floor. He looked, with his bare chest, his almost skeletal frame, the long thin arms, as if he might be capable of only the most delicate tasks; he certainly did not suggest the energy and strength it took to run this diggers' pad on what must have been an almost around-the-clock regime. "Well," he was saying, "I keep thinking I've seen you or"—a pause, the bony fingers in ruminative play—"I don't suppose—naw, couldn't be that—"

"What?"

"I was going to say it couldn't be you were ever down South, a place called—"

"I was in Mesa, Alabama. But that was three summers ago," Laura said. She had more of her beer. "That's where I met Jamey."

"Mesa! Hey, that's it, that's it!" Bernstein was exuberant. "That's right. I was there."

"You were?" Laura said. "You weren't in voter registration—"

"No," he said. "I was at the other end of town." Then: "Maybe where I saw you was around Liptrapp's Drugstore—"

"Oh, Liptrapp's. God yes, it must have been there." Laura laughed, swung her head to one side and pushed back the long fall of hair. "I went there whenever I could; it was the only damn thing you could do."

"The only place," Jamey broke in, "in that godless hole that had enough electric fans to give you relief."

"You were both in Mesa?" Poppy said. "I wanted to go down there in the worst way but that was the summer I had to stick at Berkeley. My parents were dying for me to go down."

"Your parents?" Florida seemed stunned. He stubbed out the butt in the ashtray, an empty can of cat food.

"Yes," Poppy said. "My parents."

Florida shrugged. Mike laughed, rose and went out to the kitchen, taking with him some of the beer empties. The boy with Kathy said to her, "You still getting bad vibes?" She nodded. "OK," he said. "We'll hang around." He raised his head, watched Florida rolling another joint. When it came his way he sucked in deeply, a sibilance of satisfaction, gave it to Kathy. Her mouth was dry now and not serene.

The music stopped, and Hap changed the record. Joan Baez. He stretched. A long yawn. "Got to go. Baby-sitting."

His job: guarding the small boy of a widow who worked a midnight shift at Kennedy Airport.

44

"Listen," Bernstein said to him, "if you're beat, I'll take it for you."

"You've taken enough for me, baby," Hap said. He slipped his black-soled feet into sandals. From under the sofa he pulled out his rucksack, unbuckling it, and took out a paperback.

The spindly, sluggish Florida cozied himself in the corner of the sofa. "If anyone's interested"—he addressed Bernstein—"I think I've got a line on that part-time job for the post office."

Poppy said that back in the Haight some of the kids had hauled garbage.

"Sure, if you have to," Florida said. "Hell, anything's better than having to ask your fucking father for the bread." He looked over at Jamey. "Right?"

"Umm." Jamey tilted the beer can to his mouth even though he knew it was empty.

"Me," Hap confided, "I really prefer panhandling."

Jamey said, "Is that a nice worthy ambition for an all-American boy?"

"Naw—" The boy grinned. "I'd really prefer a fine education at one of the finer colleges and walk into a fine executive job with one of the finer corporations and have a Country Squire station wagon, a caddie car for the golf course and an accountant who can cut corners."

"The scene I want to make," Florida drawled, after Hap had gone, "is the Saturday-night blast back home like with everyone getting stoned and your finger up your neighbor's wife and dragging to church the next morning with your mouth all sweet with chlorophyll."

Someone laughed. From the adjacent room, the girl with the bath towel around her middle thrust in her pale face. "Hey, Alan —somebody here looking for Richard. Have you seen him?"

"No, I haven't," Bernstein said.

Silence.

"Wanna split now?" Carlos Jones asked Kathy.

"Not yet. Why can't you wait?" Kathy looked uptight. The jitters that sometimes score the pre-acid takeoff.

"All right," Carlos said. "But this won't even get us off the ground."

Joan Baez' gentle question: . . . *just a little rain—/ What have they done to the rain?*

Florida said, "Jamey—you still in school?"

"Yes," Jamey said. "Still." One more year.

Laura? The same.

Florida said, "I've had it, man. My folks flipped when I quit. But who needs 'em? And when you *do* need them, do they dig?"

"Baez digs," said Jamey. *And rain keeps falling like helpless tears—/ And what have they done to the rain?*

Later, when Alan Bernstein turned off the music, he stood looking down at Jamey and Laura. "How about that!" He shook his head. "You two in Mesa."

"Three years ago," Laura said.

"I don't know why it seems a lot longer," Jamey said.

"Yes," Bernstein said.

"We never made it, did we?" Jamey said.

"Well, no, we never did, I guess. But—"

"I mean," Jamey said, "we got a few things going. But in the final analysis it turned out to be just a very small drop in a big leaking bucket."

"We got rid of some guilt," Laura said.

Jamey nodded. "It was really a fantasy, when you think about it."

"That slipped disk of yours wasn't," Laura said.

"A fantasy, I mean," Jamey said, "thinking we could buy off all that hatred with a little work and a little marching."

"The trouble is," Poppy said, "every time you get a good thing going, something happens. I don't know, it just begins to fall apart."

Again the door opened. A young man asked, "Anybody seen Eddie Morrison?"

No one had.

"I mean," Poppy was saying, "like everything that was happening at the Haight, the whole scene was beginning to embarrass me. People playing hippie, hyping it for TV and all the straight magazines. As for acid—well, the syndicates—" She shook her head. "I know one kid, a connection, who was killed right on the corner of Cole and Carl, shot by mobsters. I mean, the meth scene got so bad some of them carried guns. And robbing people all over the place." She paused. "We really had something going, but now—"

"It couldn't be," Jamey said. "Maybe the kids themselves—"

"What do you mean?" Poppy said. Kathy passed the joint to her but she said no, she'd wait until later, for Mike. Back to Jamey again: "What do you mean?"

"I mean," Jamey said, "a lot of the people using the scene just as a kind of cop out."

"I wasn't using it as a cop out," Poppy said at once. "You're not serious, are you?"

"I was only asking," Jamey said. Then: "Why'd you come East?"

"Why? Well, for one thing Mike and I had to—I mean, like Mike couldn't very well lay down for the draft board," Poppy said.

Jamey said, "You going back?"

"I don't know," Poppy said. "You mean to the Haight?"

"Yes," Jamey said.

"No. Never," Poppy said.

"What are you going to do?"

"How would I know?" Poppy said. "Who knows what anyone is going to do? Stay around here, I guess. Unless this scene falls apart too."

"Come on, baby." Carlos Jones turned to Kathy: "If we're going to drop that cap."

"You haven't got it on you?" asked Alan Bernstein.

"Sure, Alan, we got it on us, just waiting for the po-leese to come lick it off," Carlos answered, and laughed.

"Well, you know what I mean," Alan Bernstein warned.

Another youth pushed open the door. "Ace been around to-night?"

"Not since yesterday," Florida said. "He's sitting out bail."

"Were you serious, Jamey? Before?" Poppy was looking at him. "Serious?"

"About people using the scene just to cop out?"

"I wanted you to enlighten me," Jamey said.

Her pale cheeks stained with color. "I thought you were on our side."

"I am."

"Shit, man, who cares?" For the first time, the Negro, Carlos Jones, cracked the shell of his seeming, dreaming indifference. "Who cares if people cop out of the scene or even if we cop out of Vietnam? Who needs it?"

"I know, I know." Jamey knew, he knew. But he could never really get much beyond today. Tomorrow wasn't here yet.

"The only thing is—" Laura began, not finishing now: a harsh confusion at the door.

"Mike—Mike!" Poppy cried out.

The russet-haired Mike was running across the room; he almost threw himself into the bathroom, pushing the door shut after him and slugging in the bolt. Somewhere a cup and saucer rattled.

At once Poppy changed her position: she moved over to sit down cross-legged on the floor in front of the bathroom door.

As simultaneously Alan Bernstein hurried into the adjacent room and on through to the kitchen entry.

"What is it?" Jamey said.

Poppy's shoulders were rigid. She shook her head. Florida lit a stick of incense. Kathy and the Negro were on their feet now. Poppy motioned for Jamey to play the guitar.

He opened the case and removed the instrument. He'd just begun to pick out chords when Alan Bernstein returned. "It's all right, Poppy. They were just looking for Mrs. Shanlon's daughter."

Poppy's face softened in relief.

The police, Bernstein said to Jamey, were looking for another runaway kid.

Rising now, Poppy knocked very loudly on the bathroom door. "Mike," she called. "It's OK, Mike!" Then: "Mike. OK, Mike!"

The sound of a window being lowered or raised. The door bolt clanked back and the big, unclumsy Mike emerged from the bathroom. He looked around, then dropped to the floor, and then Poppy sat down beside him.

"Christ," Mike murmured. His palms were moist, his long hair ruffled, ruddy as autumn leaves.

Florida settled down again. He started rolling a new joint.

"I can use some," Mike said.

"I was waiting for you," Poppy said to him.

"Arc we going, baby?" Carlos Jones said to Kathy.

"What's the rush?" Kathy's voice was still raw; she peered up at the scabrous ceiling. Her long gold hair looked dry, unwashed, and hung down the back of her T-shirt, reaching the big blue printed numeral: 69.

Carlos shrugged. "OK. It's your trip."

Florida lit up, dragged, passed the joint up to Kathy.

"Jamey—" Poppy's voice. "Aren't you going to play?"

"What?" He reached for his guitar again, but without warning let it thud back into its case. "Come on, Laura."

He stood up.

"Jamey—" Laura said.

He said something about having to leave.

"Oh—" Poppy's bright, sad voice followed him. "Oh, you're—you're pissed off, aren't you?"

Jamey gained the door without needing to answer.

3 : HOMETOWN

LATE AFTERNOON. The secretary, Miss Louise Yates, age thirty, sits at her desk in the office of Mieland Homes, in the reception room with its interiorscape all Kountrylodge Knottypine.

Here in this Long Island town that Jamey likes to call Nitty-gritty City.

She turns on the glitter-faced desk radio (like the color TV set in Mr. Fred Mieland's inside office, it is a gift from the local distributor, who appreciates a kind word a builder like Fred Mieland might pass along to home buyers).

Almost five o'clock. That music now, she likes it. Herb Alpert's Tijuana Brass? Nice to dance to. If she ever went dancing much . . . Jamey coming in the door now; Jamey wouldn't think much of this music.

Jamey in a real tizz. Natch. His face all suntanned from his outdoor work with the crew, his blond hair all roughed from the wind, and sawdust still in his hair and his hands unwashed.

"Oh, Jamey," she says, "your father said he couldn't wait. He had to go, but—"

"Couldn't wait?" Jamey's blue-green eyes show sudden rage. Par for the course. Has his father's temper. Natch.

"He said for you to wait," Louise tells him. "He'll be back. Does this radio bother you?"

"What? Oh. No."

"It's Herb Alpert and his—"

"I know, Louise."

"Why don't you sit down, Jamey." She tries to placate him. Maybe she doesn't get to meet any men like Jamey, but even if she was his age would she want him? Well, all right. Who is kidding who? Louise Yates at this point will take just about anyone. And maybe you think Jamey's father doesn't know it. Not much he doesn't. But Fred has his good points and he can be fun when you get him away from here. Only it's too sneaky to suit Louise. But it has to be that way.

The only thing so far as Jamey is concerned is he always makes her feel ninety-five. And there's not all that much difference between them, not actually, about ten years is all; they even went to the same high school; of course she was there earlier. But this boy was unlike the ones she knew, he was even different from most of the kids his age. When she started working for his father, Jamey was on the wild side, used to play with a small rock group and getting very bad grades. Until his last year, suddenly then he was making the honor roll. High on it. As if he'd never been anywhere else. Then he nearly ruined it, he was almost kicked out of school that last year for that song he wrote and sang about the English teacher Otis Oaker. He'd sung it in the gym during the senior dance. People still sang it around school even though Mr. Oaker was gone, promoted to head of some junior college in Southern California:

Oh, Mr. Oaker, our hero
We hold him in fear, oh
Yes, he's severe, is Mr. Oaker
Disciplines the girls, after school
For breaking the rules
But, mothers, your fragile flowers
They are a-bloomin', after hours

In Mr. Oaker's English class
Oh, Mr. Oaker, he digs Shakespeare
And yeah, he digs Blake, our hero
Turns us on to tears
Hear him recite that free verse
And remember his free hand
For in Mr. Oaker's English class
If you let it roam, he'll let you pass.

When it happened, all this furor about Jamey's song, Fred Mieland hit the ceiling and had to go around town apologizing to everyone, including Mr. Oaker. Mrs. Mieland never mentioned it, but she is strange sometimes. According to Fred.

Louise says, "You know what I was just thinking about, Jamey? Old Mr. Oaker."

This makes Jamey smile, not much, but some. That smile when it is full on could be, well, awfully nice. And let's say he did ask her out sometime, maybe she wouldn't say no, at least if his father wasn't around. Not that she would, not actually.

"Listen, Louise, how soon do you think he'll get back? I mean, I rushed over here from the job when I heard he—"

"Oh, it ought to be practically any minute, Jamey. Honestly. Why don't you sit down?" she says.

Jamey still stands.

Tijuana Brass is over. Radio news on: "—the report on the war in Vietnam. But first a message of importance.

"Does dirt or grime stick on your kitchen floor? Is your sink clogged? Is the toilet sluggish? Well, here is a secret. A new cleaning compound has been discovered. . . ."

Then the war report: "The Defense Department is encouraged by today's Kill Ratio—one hundred nine Americans killed to nine hundred twenty-two of the enemy!"

Jamey draws in his lips. He goes to Louise's desk, mumbles excuse me and turns off the radio. He moves away from it as if it were contagious, a vile disease.

"Kill Ratio! Jesus Christ!" he mutters, his back to her as he stands looking out the office door.

Well, there's going to be a real donnybrook around here when the old man gets back. Louise just knows it.

Jamey left the reception room and went into his father's office. He sat down. That didn't help. He hoisted himself out of the Kountrykraft chair in the Kountrylodge Knottypine office.

Beyond the door Louise Yates had turned on the radio again. *"Does dirt or grime stick . . ."* and more gabblegabble about cigarettes and deodorants and hand cream. *"Look at your hands."*

Christ, almost five-thirty. He didn't know why his father had sent for him. Almost five-thirty. He had to get home. Shower. Get this sawdust, all this muck out of his pores. The day's work. Look at his hands. *Look at your hands.* Calluses. On his hands. On his feet too. Summer work. Everywhere except. No callus on the phallus?

He looked at his watch again. The minutes were killing his night. Tonight again he would go into town to Tompkins Square; it was going to be a good night, a flash for him, far from the two-by-four, Easy-Down-Payment world of Mieland Homes.

And *Kill Ratio!*

But no splitting here yet. When his father sent for him, got him off the job to come to the office, there had to be a reason. A reason he didn't want to think about. Too much going tonight.

Maybe he'd better call Laura. But just as he started to the desk, his father appeared.

Fred Mieland, who, unlike many of his fellow builders, did not come on strong, all hustle and bustle, hearty and farty, not Fred Mieland, not Jamey's father with his solicitous gaze for the community, his almost perpetual smile (that Fred Mieland, people in the town were always saying, he has the nicest smile. And talk about nice, he gave us two rolls of insulation left over from another job. Free. Talk about nice). Fred Mieland in the office now, tall, vigorous, thin except in the melon-like middle, neat in tan pants and tan shirt. From the breast pocket there rose like a minute pipe organ the multicolored ball-point pens, pencils and markers. No father like some of the fathers of his friends at school, no glib or glossy psychiatrically oriented, quasi-hip, demi-square "intelligent parent." No, not Fred Mieland, with his plain cunning and his fondness for cheap bourbon and his hobby at the piano, those surprisingly adroit fingerings of Bing Crosby or Perry Como or Andrews Sisters songs, his voice in nostalgic tribute to the soothing pulp of yesteryear's lyrics, his eyes sweetly lowered, so that even Jamey's mother, once a music teacher, would stop whatever she was doing and listen to her husband and think of what it had been like before his soft smile had strayed from her to favor the community.

His father.

But gone was the smile. "Where were you? I waited for you before; what the hell happened to you, Jamey?"

"I was only five minutes late," Jamey began. "The truck—"

"You know how I get jammed up here Saturdays, Sundays, in and out—" He went at once to his desk. (*Member Long Island Developers and Builders Association,* a baroque certificate announced on the wall above his chair.) He lit a cigarette, this week's new brand, longer, and lower in nicotine and tars. "Have to talk to you." The crimson flush of his flesh was bleached by weather and whiskey. His brown hair was straight and thin, only sparsely threaded with gray, though his ginger moustache was soft and youthful. The skin around his eyes and mouth was marked by all the darts and creases he'd engraved there with his goodwill smile. He was appraising Jamey, frowning with concern, irritable, loving concern. "Look at you. Jesus, Jamey, I hate to see you looking like that. Filthy!"

"I—"

"Filthy," his father said. Then: "Hate to see you looking like that. I'll never know long as I live why you choose to work out there when you—"

"Dad, you've told me that one thousand times."

"Choose to be out there when you could be in the office here with me. Selling."

"Is this what you wanted to see me about, to tell me this again?" Jamey said. "Just to tell me all this for the one thousandth time—"

"Now wait a minute. Take it easy." Fred Mieland abruptly summoning his smile, that warm and familiar beguilement: When-I-show-you-this-little-house-Mrs.-Smith-you're-gonna-walk-away-with-the-key-in-your-little-pocket. "Tell you, son, what I wanted to discuss, why I called you. It's Jim Fowler. Happened today."

"What happened?"

"Very sick. Came down with a hundred-and-three tempera-

54

ture. Some virus. And I can't afford to lose help, this time of year."

"In other words," Jamey said, "you're shorthanded in the office."

"More than shorthanded. Hamstrung," his father declared. "He's been my right arm. A real ace. His selling record—"

"Look, Dad, I—"

"Now I'm here alone. I don't have to tell you what Saturdays and Sundays are. Lookers all day long and half the night," his father said. "That's why I have to have you here tomorrow."

"Tomorrow? I can't," Jamey had to say. "I just can't make it, Dad."

"Can't make it?" His father swung around in the chair, opened the desk drawer that concealed the bar, drew out the bourbon and a shot glass. "Can't make it? I see."

"I just can't. I've got an appointment."

"Laura?"

"No—she's in Washington on her job," Jamey said. "But I have to be downtown in the Village."

"I see." Came the same flat tone. "Guitar and—"

"I'm never here weekends," Jamey said. "You know that."

"That's true. I know that," came the flat response. Then: "Listen, Jamey, when I first wanted you here with me, you said nothing doing. You wanted to work outside with the crews. That was last summer. It was the same this summer. I was a fool. I let you do it. For what? Now that I'm caught shorthanded, now that I need you, you have more important things to do!"

"I don't know why you have to flip like that," Jamey said. "It was decided I could work outdoors."

"Well, I decided wrong." Fred Mieland downed the bourbon; he kept looking at Jamey, the brown eyes squinting in bewilderment. "Will you tell me, tell me how you're ever going to learn the goddam business if you're out there with the goddam crew all the time?"

"Look, let's not get hung up on that again," Jamey said.

"Is that all you know—hung up?" Fred Mieland floundered between paternal affection and paternal exasperation. He turned and pointed out the window. "Look at that. Sixteen houses in that tract alone. That didn't happen by itself. Somebody did a little selling around here to make it happen. And who is it all for? Who's going to get it all? And you talk about hung up!"

"Listen, Dad"—Jamey couldn't let it pass—"don't try to snow me with that. Don't make this business something you did for anyone but yourself. It's your own ego. You would have done the same thing whether you had a son or a two-headed monster or no one at all. That kind of noble sacrifice really burns me down!"

"Is that what you think, Jamey?"

"Yes." But regretting the outburst already, suffering his father's bleak and desolate gaze.

"I see." Fred Mieland was uptight: there would be another blast. But there wasn't. He reached for the bourbon, another shot of the harsh amber. He looked over at Jamey. Abruptly he laughed. "Your mother—she said yesterday, last night, 'Fred, you just don't know how to handle Jamey.' Well, maybe she's right. I don't know." Calm and compromise? "I don't know. But I'll tell you one thing I know. You're a smart kid and that's all I care about. That's why I need you in here. If you were some chump I wouldn't want you." He drank. The smile began to spawn. "So let's forget tomorrow. OK? I'll manage it all right. May push me, but I doubt if we'll go into bankruptcy." Then: "Snifter?"

"No thanks." Jamey eased back into the chair again.

"OK, we'll forget about tomorrow then," his father said. "OK, son?"

Jamey nodded. He lost his frown. He saw his father as he'd seen him now and then when he'd been a child.

"Swell," Fred Mieland said. "And you can start in the office next Saturday."

"What?"

"Need you here beginning next Saturday. We're forgetting this weekend."

"Next weekend? But I can't—" Jamey burst out. "I'm going up to that college—"

"What college?"

"I told you about it the other day," Jamey said. "But you didn't listen, you never listen! You've forgotten. I'm going upstate with The Gross-Outs for that free concert. It's part of a Negro—"

"Oh—" his father began. "Oh yes, that's right. I remember. I was listening. Heard every word." The put-down had slowed

56

him. "Well, OK. Go ahead, son. Swell. All for it. Glad we haven't got that headache around here yet."

Jamey waited.

"All right, Jamey. You go to that thing." Then: "Sure I can't give you some of this bourbon?"

"No thanks," Jamey said. "And I don't think you ought to have it either, Dad. It's your third."

"You worried about me?"

"I was thinking of your ulcer."

"How else can I relax?" his father said. "Guess you think marijuana would be better, huh?"

"I didn't say that," Jamey said.

"Well—at least you're worried about your old man. Guess that shows something." The bourbon glass still in his hand. Then he placed it down on the desk. "You're right, son. I'll listen to you." The tribute was warm. "OK, son. We've got an understanding. You begin in here a week from next Saturday. Can't say I don't try to go along with you. Next Saturday a week. After all, won't have you around too long; middle of September you'll be back in school. Gone again. So let's specify it, huh? You'll finish out the summer here in the office."

"Dad, I—"

"Hmm?"

"I—I don't really—I mean—" Jamey tried again.

"What's that?"

"Nothing," Jamey said.

"Nothing? You going to tell me again you don't like showing our houses, selling 'em? That's the line you always give me. I've always taken it. Tried to understand. I always tried to go along with you. Your mother—I'd never hear the end of it if I didn't. But goddammit, you're not a kid anymore. You're twenty years old. No more line, no excuses. I'm not going to take it anymore!" His father showed that edge of harshness the community never saw. It was reserved only for the people he loved. "So this time, son, I expect you to go along with *me*. For a change. And understand *me*. For a change. You're moving inside where you belong." He rose and came around to Jamey. He grasped his shoulder. "Can I count on that?"

Jamey felt the warm nearness and the pressure of the hand.

"Maybe you don't know it—or believe it"—his father's grip clenched harder on Jamey's shoulder—"but having you in here is going to mean a hell of a lot to me." An interval. "OK. That's specified now. We're set. OK, son?"

Jamey could not shut out his father's beseeching presence.

"We set, son?" The eyes burned with the need for the word.

"Well—" Jamey said.

Fred Mieland waited no more. Half a word was good enough. He moved away. To the wall. To the great calendar he went. Jubilance in tan. From his shirt pocket he snatched one of the colored pencils: SATURDAY. JULY 15. He enclosed the date in a mighty red circle.

July 15.

The whole summer.

Death in the sun.

"This we got to celebrate, son!" The bourbon bottle in hand again.

Jamey accepted the glass and found himself drinking to his own defeat in Nittygritty City, U.S.A.

To New York on the third weekend night of July, on the old super-beefed-up Harley-Davidson, Jamey rolled, wheeled: helmeted and goggled, in white jeans, black windbreaker, his guitar strapped onto the saddle seat behind him, bent into the hot wind, rubber searing the parkway, spurting straight, curving leaning, streaking like a white comet: but late, late, late. Ten-thirty P.M. When he was due at nine. But instead being held up with lookers, buyers, showing them the model homes: the horseshit trail, telling them of all the joys of Mieland-built love nests, oh yes, and all the easy miracles of credit that they (and his father) could depend on from the nearest bank.

A rain of starlight fell from the summer sky. Past eleven o'clock when he parked the motorcycle on West Sixty-seventh Street, and with his guitar he ran, long-legged, overanxious as a boy, the mass of dark-blond hair roughed in flight, running into Central Park, to the Sheep Meadow: dark shapes huddled, dense as thickets, everywhere in front of the illuminated Parks Department platform and band shell. THE ARTS AGAINST WAR read the giant blue-and-white banner above the stage, the arts being mostly poets and folk or rock singers. Promised for the peace rally were Pete Seeger, Joan Baez, Phil Ochs, Tim Buckley. And groups like The Doors, The Mothers, Country Joe and the Fish, and The Great Society Gross-Outs.

As soon as he reached the side of the shell, he met Terry Bruner, the wild-maned lead guitarist of The Gross-Outs. "Where've you been, man? You know what time it is?"

Yes, and how Jamey knew!

"I mean, we finished our last set almost two hours ago," Terry said.

Two hours.

"Lot of record people around tonight," the guitarist said.

Two hours. Fuckleberry Finn!

It was then that the lean and bearded young director of the concert joined them. Recognizing Jamey. He had heard him last month in Tompkins Square. "Sorry you didn't make it," he said, fingers in staccato play against the clipboard in his hand.

"I couldn't. I got hung up out at—" Jamey coughed, cleared the clot of anger and dismay from his throat. "But I mean"—he swallowed again, facing the director—"would it be possible—I suppose it's too late for me to go on—"

"You've got to be joshing," the man answered. "Unless you think you can follow Baez." A mourning glance, and murmuring sorry and hurrying away.

Alone then: looking up, seeing nothing, while from the shell Country Joe and the Fish stormed off with electric organ, guitars, voice: *So put down your books and pick up your guns . . .*

Jamey started moving, not stopping, not wanting to, not looking back. Two hours: that's all that had kept him from being here, from being part of something that meant something to him, the only thing that could flash him on.

Two hours: how how how? For what?

For Fred Mieland, who was using him, working him harder and longer, as if to make up for the past two weekends, when Jamey had been downtown and at the college in upstate New York.

His father hand-picking tonight with that explosion of houselookers in Nittygritty City. Yes.

Tonight. And Laura still in Washington. Three letters a week,

Laura, loving and right and reasonable, and yes, wouldn't you know it, still trying to sell him the reasonable philosophy of the "Thoughtful Middle."

Diddle the Thoughtful Middle.

But being with her. Not just making out.

Oh Jesus, what a black night. He was out of the park, beyond meadow and music. On the street, staring at that miserable motorcycle, he could have kicked it flat. As if it had been responsible for his being too late.

Where now?

Where? Downtown.

Rolling now.

Get some grass somewhere.

Rolling and the music lost, and to hell with it. Half an ounce of grass. Where?

Not Alan Bernstein's place. No. Which is where he went. East Sixth Street.

Asking for Poppy then. Or Mike.

"She's not here anymore." The quiet, cadaverous Bernstein stood in the kitchen entry of the diggers' haven.

"Not here?" Like a sudden bring-down.

"No."

"I—I was looking for them."

"Why?" Bernstein asked.

"What?" Jamey heard himself croak the word, a moron: lost, sunk, submerged, almost without voice—back three years, that same aching, locked, bruised sensation in his chest, the way it used to cut him up during that first college year, no ready voice to say things that should have been easy to express, hung up, avoiding people, never hacking around the Student Union, closing himself in with his work or with records, listening to records, or tapes—messages from the gods—Jelly Roll, Muddy Waters, Woody Guthrie, Seeger, Dylan . . . always the records or tapes, sometimes playing or humming along with his guitar until by accident when his sound system broke down, one night alone in his room, when he was just picking at the strings, he started talking, grieving to himself, grooving out his dissatisfactions with himself and half the world, but saying what was underneath his tongue, getting it out then, making it work with the music, that's how it began, finding a second voice. . . . "You—do you know where she—where they are, Alan?"

"Poppy got a small pad on Ninth Street. Six-fifty-three East. It's the rear door, on the third floor," Bernstein said. "Anything wrong?"

"Wrong? No," Jamey said. "Say, Alan, I could use a little pot— can you put me on to a—"

Alan told him the nearest and safest connection was a friend of Florida's who lived down the street, the apartment directly above Leahy's Health Store, Macrobiotic Foods.

The connection—a young man with cloudy eyes and blond hair much lighter than Jamey's—was in. He knew Jamey was not a real head but he also knew he wasn't a narko. He let him have half an ounce of Panama for ten dollars. It was the most Jamey had ever paid. At college when you wanted half an ounce you connected for five or six dollars, though it was never Panama or Acapulco prime leaf.

Jamey zipped the plastic bag into the pocket of his windbreaker. A few minutes later he parked the Harley near Tompkins Square. He started eastward for Poppy's.

"Hello, how're y'all tonight?" A bearded youth, flanked by two gaunt girls, addressed the couple just ahead of Jamey, two tourists from a straight part of town. They paused to look down at the sidewalk: spread on the pavement was the torso of a plastic dummy attached to a pair of black pants on which lay scattered a number of coins. "How's about it?" the beard said to the uptown pair. "Like to drop some pennies on the magic good-luck suit?"

"Well—" The man consulted his lady companion. "Why not?" He carefully brought forth several pennies, which he dropped onto the pants.

"Mighty kind," murmured the youth, but as the couple moved off he called out amiably, "And I hope y'all have a nice orgasm this evening."

The couple halted, or rather froze, not certain if they had heard correctly. But then the man retrieved his poise and in the elegant accent of starchiest old guard New York answered, "Thank you. I hope so too."

The panhandling put-on eased Jamey's tightness. For a moment. He hurried on. He found the tenement building near Avenue C, its mulberry facade trellised with fire escapes. Into the hallway, a whiff of bad news, and up to the third floor, but climbing the stairs without spirit, his young legs slowed by an ancient inertia, still unable to drop the weight of the night's disappointment.

There was no name on the door. He knocked and no answer. He knocked again. He waited. He tilted his head against the door. There seemed to be no sounds. It was difficult to hear. A radio somewhere above going with the wild power of The Fugs.

"Poppy—" he called then. "Poppy—"

Life within. "Yes."

"Jamey."

Soon a twice-turned lock and a bolt pushed out of its slot and there she stood, shadowed, the half-light behind her. "How'd you get here?"

"Alan."

"Oh." The wide eyes still trying to dig him.

"Where's Mike?" he said. "He's OK, isn't he?" Jamey looked beyond her into the room.

"Yes." She admitted him and locked the door. "I don't know why I never expected to see you again."

"Why not?"

"Oh, I don't know—you were, like that night at Alan's—"

"Hell, I—"

"Look, we'll be done in a minute." Poppy, he saw now, was barefooted, wearing nothing but a man's shirt held together by a single button. Her hands were wet, dripping. "I'm just finishing Mike's hair."

Jamey stood the guitar against the room's only chair. He stood beside it. The bathroom door was ajar and he could hear the splash and slish of water and the great submarine groans of Mike. He shouldn't have come here. Mistake. He didn't know just what he needed or wanted, except to push out his blues. It was better to be here than— He glanced around the squalid one-room apartment which Poppy had daubed yellow with paper flowers, and lighted with a candle to augment the lamp by the yellow coverlet of the floor mattress. There was a pile of books beside it: Lao-Tzu's *The Way of Life*, *I Ching*, Tolstoy's *Essays*,

Bertrand Russell's *War Crimes in Vietnam,* Lorca's *Poems,* Treblig's *Rock: Sounds of American Youth.* Except for the last one, Jamey had read them all.

"Hi!" Mike called out from the bathroom. "Jesus! Easy!" he cried. Poppy pushed his big head back down into the sink.

Jamey noticed the USO picket signs against the back wall, residue, he supposed, of a recent all-girl protest: IT'S NOT HIP TO GET THE CLAP, read a placard. Another: 1 OUT OF 4 GI'S BRING HOME THE CLAP FROM SAIGON BROTHELS.

In the bathroom Poppy was rinsing out the shampoo: it rose from Mike's head like a foam of black blood. When he emerged, massaging his scalp with a ragged towel, he said, "The roots keep getting dark. I never appreciated the way I used to neglect my hair. Man, it's a testy thing, a drag, keeping me this fire-engine red," said the former history major from San Francisco Southern College.

"How long have you been doing it?" Jamey said.

"Poppy's been doing it. Since we left the Coast."

The image of these two nailed Jamey down: he saw them breaking out of the West Coast on their cross-country escape from police and FBI, the real and imagined shadows in their push East. But the two of them together in their special thing, now in his luckless night . . . "Maybe," he tried, "maybe you can let it grow back, Mike. Maybe by now that draft board has forgotten you, lost in the files—"

"I doubt it." Mike kept toweling his hair. "It was the way I laid it out for them."

"What it was, was spitting in the eye of authority. They couldn't take it." Poppy lit a cigarette.

Jamey touched the pocket of his windbreaker: to turn on now. Yes. One small joint. He decided to forget it.

"Actually," Mike was saying, "I did it twice, you know. I sent the draft board a letter originally, telling them I wouldn't go. I said I wasn't even a legal Conscientious Objector because the law about it was immoral and there's no way to be moral within an immoral law. That didn't work. They classified me one-A."

"A Lyndon tree," Poppy said.

"Yes," Mike said. "It was a lousy week. We'd lost hundreds of Marines and they needed more flesh. So I went back for another physical. This time they were waiting for me good. But I wasn't having any. I was up on acid. Didn't work, not even that. The docs just shoved me down the line, not even a look or a listen. Stuff me in the uniform. That was the order. I wore it one day. That was all." Mike threw the towel onto the mattress. He got into jeans and a T-shirt. "I got hold of Poppy and we decided to get out. I figured it's more important to function, I mean, work against the war, than get myself stupidly deballed in some mine field. So we split for the East. Her parents gave us the bread."

"Your parents," Jamey said, "must be among the great." He turned to her, conscious only then of what he was looking at, the dark hair unpleated now, the crests of her breasts like peaks in the limp surface of the man's shirt, her finely tapered thighs, the slender ankles, small narrow feet and all that sparking power in her eyes—the life-seeker (or retreater from life?).

"My parents," she was saying, "are maybe too great."

Mike reached under the chair pillow and brought forth a large manila envelope. He slipped it carefully into the pages of a copy of *The Saturday Evening Post*. "How'd you beat it, Jamey? The draft."

"My back," he said. "I'm one-Y."

"At least you don't have to shake the Feds."

"Not yet," Jamey said.

"You know, you look"—Poppy was studying again—"I mean, you really look wiped out tonight."

"I was supposed to make it to that rally in Central Park," Jamey said. "But I got there too late."

"Christ, I'm late too." Mike put on his dark glasses.

Poppy went to the gas burner. "The water's ready if you—"

"No time now, baby." An excitement seemed to have turned Mike on. He brushed his hair in a final hurried effort.

"Would you like some anise tea?" Poppy asked Jamey.

Jamey declined. To Mike he said, "You have to leave right now?"

"Have to." Mike had a midnight meeting uptown near Columbia University. He worked with antiwar groups, setting up workshops in organization, leaflet-writing, distribution. He was helping plan the next march on New York's induction center, and coordinate draft resistance on college campuses.

"Listen," Jamey said, "I've got my bike, I can ride you wherever you—"

"I'm meeting three other guys. But thanks." He turned. "See you, baby."

"Mike," she said, "please be careful."

"Right." To Jamey: "See you. Peace, man."

Poppy locked the door. She made the cup of anise tea and then sat down on the rugless floor, the shirttail draping her thighs.

"Does Mike always take off like that?" Jamey finally seated himself in the chair. The room was so quiet, all sound plugged out.

"Oh, not always," Poppy said. She put down the cup. "You never know. Sometimes he's gone in a second, sometimes he's up here like for two or three days. The problem I have is trying to keep him from—I mean, he just can't afford to take any chances. Like next month. That march on the induction center. He's supposed to keep himself scarce. Last time he went right down to Whitehall Street and he was almost grabbed by the cops. What happened to you tonight? You looked so uptight when you got here I hardly recognized you."

"Oh, I—I had one of those lousy black nights," he said. "We—my father—I had to show those plywood châteaus until the last looker was ready to fall into his hundred-foot Chevrolet Impala."

"Can't you—well—I mean, like just quit?" Poppy said.

"You're thinking of your father, Poppy. Not mine."

"Oh, my father is no paragon. But compared to most—" She smiled up at him. "I mean, you know, the kind of marriage they have is like not real. It's enough to piss you off forever, it's that good."

"You're hard to please."

She didn't answer. Then she said, "I don't suppose you feel like some guitar, do you?"

"I really don't, Poppy."

She glanced at the bolted door. "Look, let's go somewhere—"

"All right. Where?"

"I don't know," she said. "Just somewhere—"

"I picked up some pot before," Jamey said.

"Oh?"

"I got it from a friend of Florida's." He broke out the plastic bag.

"Oh, you mean the guy he's working for now," Poppy said. "You know Florida's pushing for him."

"Isn't that pretty stupid?" Jamey said.

"I suppose it's a way of getting it cheaper," she said.

"I forgot the paper," Jamey said. "Nothing wrong with me tonight."

Poppy rose and went to the kitchen cabinet; she brought back a packet of Zig-Zags.

"Thanks." He emptied the grass carefully onto the floor, then began rolling the joints, twisting the ends. He looked up once. "I'm used to more sanitary conditions. At school I do this on record covers."

She laughed.

For an instant, watching her, small in the voluminous shirt, sitting beside him on the floor, thighs slender, the small feet tucked beneath her, he grew conscious of his own silence, finally speaking then. "Where do you feel like going, Poppy?"

"Oh—just let's go."

He lit a joint and placed the others back into the plastic bag and put it into his windbreaker pocket. He took a long drag, sucking the air in through his teeth, passing on the joint to Poppy. She drew on it and then got up and put on a record. "I'm glad you came by, you don't know how glad," she said.

Not as glad as he was to hear it, yet almost killing it: "Laura's in Washington," he said. From the record the verve of Simon and Garfunkel: *This feelin' of fakin' it/ I still haven't shaken it, shaken it . . .*

But when he looked over at her, she was still standing by the machine, not seeming to be at all with it, plugged out. Then she came over to where he was sitting on the floor, her hand extended, and he passed up the joint to her. She stood there and they finished the joint, and then she went into the bathroom.

When she returned she was wearing an old miniskirt, a khaki bush jacket, open and beltless, and sandals. Around her neck she had a plain thong of leather with a small brass bell. "I don't know"—she was tying her dark hair into a ponytail—"sometimes, like now, I—you know—I don't even feel the grass. Other times, a few drags and I'm into it."

"Yes."

"You didn't get that pot just for here, did you?" she said.

"No."

"I mean," she said, "since you don't use it much."

"Not a hell of a lot." But Jamey felt obliged to add, "I—well, I like it for when I'm tight or down, but I don't particularly need it for anything else. I mean, if I'm doing something I really like—" His glance shifted to the guitar case. "I like to be in total control. I won't go near acid." He got to his feet. "Anyway, if I like what I'm doing, I get turned on without it. That's a nice record player."

"My folks sent it to me," Poppy said.

"They did?"

"The old one I had at Berkeley I gave away," she said.

She switched off the machine. They left the apartment. Poppy locked the door and put on her shoulder bag.

"Wait a minute." Jamey turned back. "Give me your key, I forgot my guitar."

"Oh, pick it up later." Poppy started ahead of him, down through the stairwell's evil, true odors.

Outside they walked up Ninth Street to Avenue B: starlight still bathing the city in false beauty; above Tompkins Square a faint silver halo like a distant carnival.

He and Poppy walking slowly. "It must be hot in Washington," she said.

"What?"

"I hear it's a hell hole in summer."

"Yes." Passing tenements and storefronts.

"Too bad she has to get hung up there," Poppy said.

"It's the job. She's been there over a month." *Dear J, it's not only godawful hot here but I'm parched for love—any way you want to spell it. And I think you (or your father) a bastard for ruining last weekend.* Laura's last letter still in his room at home. *Instead of you, I'm concentrating on people from the foundation, all of whom are very enlightened. "Liberals" in the best sense— I can hear you groan, and I know my dear mother would really be pissed if she could hear them, but I don't see any other answer between the extremes of the other sides. . . .*

"We were talking about it—going to Washington—Mike and I. On that march on the Pentagon."

"Yes. I want to make it too," Jamey said. "But I don't know how I can tear myself away from all that fascinating work I do at Mustang U., those fascinating professors I get to hear."

She laughed.

"Hi." Poppy greeted a passing Negro and his pale-haired, blue-jeaned, barefooted girl.

"Hey, babes," the boy said.

Presently another voice.

"Hi, Gee-Gee." Poppy neared a ragged, shabby young Negro in a knitted skullcap. He was leaning against the black iron fence of the park. Gee-Gee's smile was slow. He murmured, "Loveya."

They stayed on Avenue B along the eastern perimeter of the Square. "Let's get a Coke," Poppy said. "It's funny how he—Gee-Gee—how he's like just slid down the hill. He used to be all over the place this spring. He was in jail behind acid and ever since he can't make anything, not even much sense. I don't know—sometimes around here lately I get the worst vibrations. You know? I mean, like something's not going down at all. Maybe it's me. Look, why don't we go in here? Have you been here?"

"No," Jamey said. It was a storefront place, candlelit, and called The Is. A wilted cardboard sign in the door announced:

INTER-LOVE
IS
INTER-BODY
Soft Drinks. Come in.

The Is was packed. There's no biz like Is biz. . . . Little light, pullman deep, the walls had Day-Glo posters illuminated by black lights, the ceiling glowed with Tie-Dye bunting.

Groping their way through, couches, chairs, mostly floor cushions, losing balance, incense and cigarette smoke in milky lavender tendrils, but in all this Jamey was getting what he wanted or needed tonight, this smoky womb, a good place to be when you wanted to lose a feeling or find one.

Toward the rear, Poppy found a place: a free edge on a black, sagging, imitation-leather couch, occupied by a bespectacled, bearded youth and a stockingless, sandal-less girl: they were sprawled back, relaxed, beatific, her legs across his lap.

"Hi." The girl shifted her legs to make room for Jamey.

"Hi," Jamey said.

Cokes, the ice clacking cool against the warm, dim sound of music, a melancholy raga. And Poppy, on the ledge of couch, beside him. Poppy did not take much room.

"Before more environment gets going," a young man addressed the darkened figures in the spectral room, "a friend of ours, Steve Saint Stephens. He just came in from the Square and we'd like him to read a poem of his."

Steve Saint Stephens, age nineteen, in faded jeans and Free-store cutaway frock coat, a great daisy in his buttonhole, stepped up onto the piano bench and gravely read from a black copy book:

What is it, child,
people do not fuck up to you, child?
out among the outraged?
is there nothing but the soft-on for you?
among the outraged and the unloving?
and the eggsuckers?

Is it true, child,
this wanting their applause?

Why do you want their unlove?
Yet, who can say no to you
if their applause feeds
your still unweaned soul?
But how, child,
to comfort the outraged?
Can I tell you how?
There is no way
unless, my child,
you go out
and dress in blood uniforms:
Neat neat neat.
With armbands, remember that:

White white white.
And march, child,
Make a phalanx:
Step step step.
And cry the patriot's song. Hear?
Clear clear clear.
Yes, this is what they pray,
all the unloved, punch-card, soft-on men
And your worms will be
their prayers.

Some people clapped, there were cries of "Peace," some people laughed. Poppy seemed dejected. Jamey felt he could not go back home.

A young man in sunglasses and yellow jockey's shirt—he was a co-owner of The Is—appeared holding a big spool of movie film. Quietly he moved among the dim and supine figures, draping the strip of film over heads or shoulders or around bosoms or between legs. "We're all more together now," he said contentedly as he looped the film across Jamey and around Poppy's bosom.

"Umbilical," Jamey said to her.

She rested her head against him. "This is the first night I've been able to get out—you know?"

"You ought to sound better then." Jamey fingered the strip of film. "Does this happen here all the time?"

"I guess, yes, I suppose so; they just start with anything at hand and let it go at that," Poppy said. "But like every night this week almost, I've been in that pad. Mike doesn't insist, he begs me to get out, get some air, but I can't do that, I mean, somebody has to be in in case some cop or some nosy Fed decides to drop in on us."

"That's lousy," Jamey said.

"Well, no one's making me do it. I don't know, I never used to get down like this," she said.

The couple beside Jamey stirred and then they changed their position: the girl moved her bare legs and the boy shifted so that her legs were scissored with his, the film intertwined between them.

"Is everyone—is everyone in a state of inter-awareness?" the jockey-shirted co-owner called out, and immediately the quiet darkened room erupted with a blast of sound. Jamey guessed it was a blank video tape projected onto a wall accompanied by electronic sounds of wildest and varying pitch.

He felt Poppy tighter beside him. The long hair of the girl next to him grazed his cheek: a bond was sure as hell coming into being, a celluloid bond that in some crazy way was working; artificial or contrived as it had seemed at first, it was having a certain effect: you could almost feel or sense the communion among everyone, the pound and rack of sound on you had a way of making you lose yourself in it, making it easier to merge with those around you and to see beyond what the mind's eye held, and if some people had come in here afloat on acid or grass, you couldn't tell and it didn't matter.

All you could tell was that everyone seemed to be removed from the outside.

Which, for Jamey, could only be fine. Down the line.

For Poppy too.

Whatever the awareness added up to, it was good and it was moving down from his mind, groinward.

Sound, *sound:* inter-blast of dissonant clashes, and now images in palest shades began to shimmer on the walls, the colors like scarves of wind. . . .

Someone near Jamey, a young man, got up from the floor. He started for the blue light bulb, the men's room. The strip of film trailed behind him so that another man rose and, not to break the celluloid link, followed him, and that in turn caused his girl to join, and the girl beside her was on her feet too. The sound track ceased and someone began to work a twirling, blinking light box so that it darted all over, on everyone, as now the film, still unbroken, was being carried along by person after person, and now Jamey and Poppy were on their way and the recumbent couple on their couch was in action, following them, and slowly, in the darting light and laughter, each of them made his way following the first Pied Piper into and out of the men's room and back to where he had come from.

Poppy seemed easier now, the brooding beneath her brown eyes layered now with that sparkle of mischief or liveliness that he had not forgotten. When they settled back on their end of the sagging couch, their hands met and held and he slid his arm behind her. It was a good time, full, suddenly.

The light show faded out, but now the long line of film had been broken at several places and lay in coiled fragments like black confetti on the floor or still spiraled around people.

Music on, this time The Beatles and their Sergeant Pepper, far from the Asian shore but already on the way, part of the Beatle vision, and the young man nearby who had led the celluloid daisy chain in and out of the toilet, a happening created by his bladder, this guy and his girl were sitting erectly facing each other on their floor cushions, leaning forward in a marathon of kissing.

"They sort of look like two tilted Buddhas," Jamey said.

Poppy smiled. "Buddha was a dropout from his family."

"They weren't like yours," Jamey said.

No reply from Poppy.

He said, "Are you very much in the Eastern thing?"

"I have been," she said. "In yoga on the Coast. I used to go twice a week to the Swami Sathanda's, twice a week out to his ashram near Oakland. You know, he looked like Allen Ginsberg, except his beard is longer and pure white."

Poppy lit a cigarette as if to break off further questions. But he said, "How long were you into it?"

"Well, not all that long, but I put a lot there," she said. "We did asanas in class and we chanted Om. You know. All of it. It can make you very peaceful. I loved him, I mean, you know, I really did. Now—well, I'm more or less out of it, except that it stays with you. The Swami was very anti-acid. He never—you know—put you down for it, like he was very patient, but he always said the psychedelics get in your way."

"Do they?" Jamey said.

"Get in the way?" Poppy said. "I think that depends on a lot of things. I mean, I never dropped a single cap after that. But for everybody it's different. People like you, maybe you just refuse to—"

"No, what I mean," Jamey said, "is the way people take it up here—they get into yoga and try to make it in a week or a month. Total nirvana piping hot while you wait."

"It was never like that for me," she said.

"I didn't say it was, Poppy. All I said was—" Cutting across his words, across The Beatles' chant, came the siren piercing, outside, near, close, closer. Until sudden silence inside and outside, and Poppy, like many other people, stirred in sharp apprehension.

The dark cavern of The Is was emptied in fire-alarm time. He and Poppy got out to the sidewalk: the nightstreet was a glare of lights and revolving beacons and everywhere the police, the patrol cars, emergency trucks, the paddy wagon.

More tourists now. Almost 2 A.M. The elderly citizens of the neighborhood aroused, shuffling in bathrobes, at the windows and fire escapes, and more and more kids from the Square.

"What is it?" Poppy asked Steve Saint Stephens.

He shrugged. "It's not good."

A girl behind them said, "I heard somebody was killed."

It was two people. Policemen were coming out of the tenement now, carrying sheathed bodies in the long canvas slings.

While other officers and plainclothesmen were already hauling in "suspects" or going around asking questions. And Poppy said she wanted to leave.

"What happened?" Jamey asked a bald man in slippers, baggy pants and suspenders over his pajama tops.

"What happened?" The old resident's voice was harsh. "I'll tell you what happened—two kids are dead is what happened in this goddam cockamamie neighborhood!"

Poppy had already turned and left. He saw her moving quickly north up Avenue B, her dark ponytail undulating behind her, the brass bell tinkling against her chest.

"Poppy—" He caught up with her.

She swung around. "I don't know why you had to stay there. It's—"

"I wanted to know what it was."

"Why? Couldn't you tell?"

"Sure. I mean, I knew it was nothing but bad news. But for me—" He hesitated. "Well, I just tried to find out. It's important to me."

"OK." But her walk accelerated: Poppy in miniskirt and light cotton bush jacket, her small body, the narrow feet in compulsive, graceful escape.

73

The sight of the covered corpses moved with him and with her, and he saw how the agitation was still flaming her eyes.

As soon as they were back in the pad, he went across the room for his guitar. Roll home. Time to leave. Back to Nittygritty City.

"Don't go," Poppy said. "I mean, do you have to go?"

He looked at her. "I don't have to, but—"

"Oh, I know I'm down. I'm sorry, Jamey, I don't know, I can get the worst vibes sometimes."

"I guess tonight we've got enough between us to go around," he said.

Poppy remained where she was, by the record player. Jamey was still holding his guitar. After a moment she said, "What happened to that grass?"

He broke it out and got the papers. Poppy put on The Beatles, and brought the album cover and dropped it onto the floor mattress. He sat there and rerolled the joints he'd fixed earlier. The elegiac sounds of "Eleanor Rigby."

"I don't know—" Poppy was beside him now on the side of the mattress. She looked down at her bare knees. "I mean, all week it's been like this. It's getting bad as the Haight. Maybe it's going the same way. Like Tuesday, right downstairs here, a person I know, a wonderful girl, got mugged—she only had a dollar on her—and all her clothes ripped off. I don't know who jumped her. They say some speed freak did it."

He lit a joint and gave it to her.

"Thanks. What happened last week was even worse—not actually, but in a way, to me, it was." Poppy sucked in the smoke. "Mike and I had no money, my check from home was late and we were hungry, so we took our plates and went to the Square for some free stew." She shook her head. "We had to wait a long time, it was a long line. But we never made it. People were pushing and shoving and then some Puerto Ricans and hippies got into a real hassle, trying to keep their places in line. They were like animals. It was disgusting. I lost my appetite. What we did, we went to the EVO and borrowed some bread from a friend. I mean, it's just getting that way, so terribly fucked up. It wasn't anything like that just three months ago." She passed the joint back to him. "And then tonight. I don't even want to think what happened there."

Neither did he.

And listening to "Eleanor Rigby."

And for a while there was nothing between them except the grass. Knowing a little more about her would have been good but he said nothing. Now and then she would look up at him, and then her eyes grew easier, and then he found it easier to be with her and to let fall the hangups out at Mieland Happy Homes.

Poppy's smile could be very soft. Like now.

Another joint and then the roach too hot and he dropped it into the ashtray on the floor.

"Amorous is what pot makes me sometimes," she said. "Sometimes."

"Not me," he said. "It never hits me like that." But kissing her mouth then and not stopping, not stopping for a long time, and Poppy's palms, her fingers against the sides of his neck.

"Ahhh—" All of her life juice soft in that single sound, still kissing him, her mouth changing under his, his under hers.

Changing now, there grew that haze, that good buoyant haze, light and sweet in his head and heavy and sweet where his jeans pulled tight, a good haze, a maze within, around him, and her, Poppy now easing off her skirt and he slowly, slowly as she, easing away his clothes, heavy, floating and trembling, her body clear, blurred, and feeling that suffocating flash all through him, slowly, still slowly her breasts to be tasted, devoured, not stopping, even drawing away, looking, globes in this gold haze, her eyes closed, yet seeing him, ah Poppy, she had so much, so much, this way of offering, of giving in a pure giving way, meeting him, wanting it the way he did, her lovely small belly upward now and he found her, touched it, tendering it, pleasuring it, the core of her need, tendering it and her hand sliding down to him until he pressed his need into hers, and hearing it again: "Ahhh—" breathless this time.

What he felt afterward was not that zero limpness that usually happened, or even that sense of not having known all of it that he sometimes had with Laura. What he felt was all of Poppy's giving; it was almost drenched in its own pureness. "Poppy—"

"Hmm?" Beside him. Her eyelids lowered though not in sleep.

"Nothing." How could he say it?

Then she said, "I'm glad you loved me like that."

"I'm glad you loved me like that," he said.

"Let's again," she said.

"Yes." Saying then, not wanting to, "I— Is Mike—"

"Coming back? Probably. I never know," Poppy said.

"I meant—" But what he wanted to ask would sound wrong, somehow wrong or out of place.

"Some coffee?" Poppy said.

He said yes: her nakedness moving before him now. After she put on the water to boil, she went into the bathroom. When she returned she was wearing the voluminous unbuttoned man's shirt.

Into his jeans. But now the airless room was too warm. He left his shirt and windbreaker on the floor: delay it, not leave, not even wanting to think about leaving. . . .

His mouth pot-dry. And the bitter taste of what he hadn't been able to talk about. Yet, if she didn't mention Mike, was it totally up to him? (Had he, for that matter, said anything about Laura?)

Was there more to learn? Cool is the rule. But how? Poppy moving around in that open shirt, small and loving and digging him: or could it be that the great way it had been between them was not just because it was Poppy or the pot? But him.

Could he have been that different? Better?

He wasn't all that super great. Not usually. He didn't have all that much experience under him; enough, yes, but tonight—what happened tonight happened more out of inspiration, leading him into it, a new trip. . . .

"I've got some hard-boiled eggs here. I'm starving." Poppy's voice.

Maybe it had been like that for her too. Poppy. All that softness now. The loving message all over her. Though earlier it looked as if she'd never make it out of her corner, as if she had some kind of fear of discovering something unwanted in her life, Poppy holding up that bright belief of hers, that search that sometimes, like when they were out earlier, seemed to be getting past her, beyond her, putting her down, yet Poppy not believing she could lose her beliefs. . . .

Was he that much different from her? Maybe. Nothing—he

was that sure of it—nothing could shake him from what he believed in.

"No handles left." Poppy put the coffee cups on the floor by the mattress. "You have to wait for it to cool off."

"The same can be said for me," he answered when he saw that she did not come back beside him, but settled herself nearby on the floor. He said, "Poppy—"

"What?"

"I—I—well, it can wait," Jamey said.

"Let's put on a record," she said.

"No. Don't bother," he began again. "I was just going to say—I'd like to see you—maybe sometime during the week or next weekend, unless—"

"Oh sure, Jamey." She blew on the coffee. "Let's."

"I mean, you have no phone here," he said. "Maybe we ought to make a definite—"

"I'll be here most of the time." Tasting her coffee.

The message reached him. "All right. I'll come down when I can get away."

Halfway through her coffee, Poppy said, "I'll put on some music." She got up from the floor, she paused, impulsively she leaned down and kissed him on the mouth, and started across the room.

She stopped, turned: a knocking in rapid rhythm on the door, and the key in the lock. "Oh, it's Mike." She moved back to the entry.

Jamey tightened his belt, looked down to the floor where lay his shirt, windbreaker, shoes.

"People still straight up around here?" Mike stood there in jeans and T-shirt. He took off his sunglasses. He smiled over at Jamey. "What goes?" Then to Poppy: "Everything OK?"

"Yes," Poppy said. "How was it uptown, Mike?"

"OK."

Poppy put on a record: "Rock the Boat."

"Smells mighty good in here." Mike stretched out on the mattress next to Jamey. "Whew!" He sighed. "Is there by any chance any left over for Daddy?"

"Sure." Jamey was thankful for the opportunity to move: but he had to reach to the floor for his clothes, gingerly fingering

77

the pocket of his windbreaker as if it were a live wire, finding the joint, the last one. He lit it for Mike. He glanced toward the door, he looked at his watch.

"It went OK actually?" Poppy was saying.

"So far." Mike sucked in the smoke.

"I'm late as hell," was all Jamey could summon.

"If you want to stay, Jamey—" Poppy said.

"Sure, stay here," Mike said.

"I couldn't," Jamey said. No choice then, having to stand up, put on the rest of his clothes, doing it, or trying to, with slowness, naturalness. The duel of the cool. "You must be beat, Mike."

"No. After we finished the meeting all of us went up to this professor's pad." Mike's cavalier stance. A pose?

"Oh?" Poppy said.

"Nobody much turned on," Mike said, "but it was a good scene. Maybe you should have been there, baby. To protect me."

"Why?" Poppy sat down on the edge of the mattress.

"In case you think you missed something." Mike's tone was genial. "There might have been some chicks there."

"Why not?" Poppy said. "It was your trip. I was all right."

"Were you? Was she, Jamey?" Mike said. "Well, I hope so. We don't like to kid anyone around here. Do we, Poppy?"

"Look," Poppy said, "if everybody made out, what's the hassle, Mike?"

"Here—" Mike handed her the joint. "We never hassle."

"That's right." Poppy said it like the partner of a pact. Then: "I want to hear about the meeting."

Jamey went across the room for his guitar.

"Hey—you're not going," Mike said.

"I—"

"You don't have to," Poppy said. "I mean, like why go all the way out there? Why don't you stay?"

Jamey zipped up the windbreaker, reached for the guitar. "I really can't make it."

"Hell, lots more room in here than it looks," Mike said.

"Thanks, Mike. I've got to ramble." From what? being cutsey-coy, inhibited by their invitation, resenting Poppy for it. And Mike.

Beyond that, what burned him down was Mike himself.

For if Jamey had admired him or made him special, Mike seemed to go out of his way to kill it, Mike going about his work almost frivolously, for kicks, a gas. All his covert antiwar work performed at risk to his liberty or life—all this seemed to be like some kind of desperate put-on. . . .

But who was the put-on for? Jamey? Poppy?

Or a world whose absurdity Mike kept seeing in spite of all he was doing?

What was wrong was that Jamey didn't want to see Mike except in one way, a one-track, one-tone, dedicated unhuman being: it was like trying to paint the portrait of someone who refused to sit still or who kept grimacing or grinning and changing his features. . . .

"What's the matter, man?" Mike said.

"Nothing, Mike." He turned; his smile went to Poppy, but it was unsure or false, the wrong string plucked, music marred.

4 : HOMETOWN

AT HOMETOWN NATIONAL—Your Friendly Bank: Get Your Loan over the Telephone—one of the officers, Frank Beldon, Jr., sees Jamey Mieland coming in on this September afternoon.

Frank Beldon, Jr., sits at a desk near the marble-veined Ionic columns of the entry, for in addition to being a vice-president of H.N., he is its chief public relations man, a greeter of recognized talent, a plump man with putty complexion, a man Frederick Mieland has admiringly called "a great bullshit artist."

"Hello there, Jamey," Frank greets Mieland's son.

The boy with the thick straight blond hair slanting across his forehead nods, says hello. Wearing an old windbreaker and faded corduroy pants and ankle-high shoes with side-buckled straps.

"Anything I can do for you, Jamey?" Frank Beldon, Jr., buttons his brown tweed jacket. The emblem of Rotary is on the lapel. (It is one of his specialties, giving talks at Rotary or Chamber of

Commerce and several other local organizations, one of which he never discusses with anyone.) "What can we do for you today, young man? Not planning to break the bank, I trust."

Jamey Mieland takes off the big sunglasses. He says he wants to transfer his savings to the bank in his college town.

"Certainly. I think we can arrange that little thing." Frank Beldon, Jr., pushes out some papers. "Just sign these, Jamey. And we'll walk it through. How's your dad today? After all, haven't seen him since day before yesterday."

"He's fine."

"Fred Mieland, he's one of a kind," says Frank Beldon, Jr. "Well, what's this make it, Jamey, your junior year?" Frank likes to regard himself as sophisticated and up to date, not one of your old fuddy-duddies, and he likes to show the kids he keeps up with them.

"Senior," Jamey corrects him.

"How about that now! The way time goes, huh?" Frank Beldon, Jr., says. "Well, guess you won't have much time anymore for your guitar and—" He pauses, netted by a memory. "Say, bet you you forgot a certain day—when you were only thirteen years old. Forget that day?"

"Which day?" Jamey asks. Doesn't even recollect! Or doesn't he want to?

"Why, that day a certain little boy—" But Frank Beldon, Jr., decides, when he notices the way Jamey is looking at him, that he will not air this reminder of the past, smarter not to mention that time when Jamey got caught stealing records, or was it sheet music? At Gharman's Music Store, the day Frank happened to stop in at the store right in the midst of all the fuss, as Mr. Gharman was on the telephone telling Fred Mieland about it. Fred naturally was crushed. Making it worse, what does this boy do? He runs away, stays away for twenty-four hours, nearly drives his mother frantic. He is in New York all that time, until the police locate him and Fred Mieland has to go in and get him. The kid's been in Greenwich Village. In his pockets they find some brochures and price lists from a place called The Jazz & Folk Center. . . . Now that Frank thinks about it, looks like Jamey still finds time to hang around New York. "Well—all I started to say," he improvises, "is that a certain little boy is pretty big now and getting famous in the hometown already. Or didn't you know about it, Jamey? But we keep track." Then: "Got a nephew of mine, and he heard you a few places, don't know where—New York, I think." But Frank Beldon, Jr., knows exactly where. "Yes, my nephew told me about you." A laugh, friendly, from Hometown National—Your Friendly Bank. "Told me about seeing you and" —another friendly laugh— "you had me worried there for a while; thought you'd turned into one of those peaceniks. But your dad says you've been sticking on the job out here most of the summer."

Jamey gives him the papers. The dark look in the boy's eyes cues Frank Beldon, Jr., back to the safer topic. "Going to get the old sheepskin this year, eh, Jamey?"

"Yes."

"A.B. degree?"

"Yes."

"Understand you've given up the idea of being a teacher." Frank Beldon, Jr., believes Hometown National ought to show genuine interest in kids.

"Yes."

"You know—" Frank cannot resist saying it; these days it's his blind spot, claims his wife. "You know, there's a place I'd like to tell you about—"

"Where?"

"It's where I sent my nephew Phil a few years ago. Mackinac Island, up in Michigan. Moral Rearmament is there, and I tell you, Jamey, in my book there's no better place for a young—"

"I doubt if that's for me, Mr. Beldon."

"How do you know it's not?"

"Well, I—"

"Come on, don't be bashful. What were you going to say?"

"Just that—well, I don't like some of their affiliations, for one thing." Jamey's answer somehow surprises him. It shouldn't. Obviously the kid has been brainwashed by Village or college Lefties.

"Now, Jamey, I don't know who you've been talking to, but we all ought to be very proud of what Moral Rearmament stands for."

"Yes," Jamey says. "I think I've got to get going."

"Right," Frank Beldon, Jr., says briskly to conceal his irritation. "Glad we could be of service." Then: "I know your dad is going to be pleased to have you in the business. You plan to start in next year?"

No answer. These kids could use better manners.

And Frank Beldon, Jr., is tempted to say a few things that are on his mind. He'd like to ask this boy, for example, how come he writes these kind of songs, rock, folk or whatever you would call them. Because his young nephew Phil, who despite Mackinac Island is unfortunately going downhill fast—a disgrace considering they've always given him everything he wants, car, TV, radio, everything, yet look at him—Phil saying how wonderful Jamey—calling himself Jamey—did those antiwar songs and those songs about how terrible life is in the USA!

How come Fred Mieland allows his son all this? If he's working for the old man you'd think Mieland would have more control over him. If Jamey was *his* son, you can be sure he'd know where Frank Beldon, Jr., stood all right! It's kids like Jamey who can fall into the wrong hands.

But of course Frank Beldon, Jr., being a sophisticate, knows how it is with kids. And how it is with the bank. He must always try to remember this. An account is an account. Today's school-kid is tomorrow's saver and borrower and interest payer. He knows, like it or not, what these kids mean to a bank, to the local economy.

Take your local merchants: take Gharman's Music Store. In the last four years, since this whole craze for The Beatles and all the other noisy crazy bands and rock 'n' roll singers, Gharman's Music Store has tripled its volume in record sales, in musical instruments like guitars, harmonicas, drums. Tripled. And you take Frolik's Sport Shop. Sure old man Frolik, like most decent people in this town, thinks the way these kids dress is a disgrace, yet who knows better than Hometown National how Frolik's inventory in jeans, bell-bottom denims, flower shirts, Western boots, work shirts, bush jackets has more than doubled in the past year alone; his accounts at Hometown National, long on the skimpy side, are now very respectable indeed. And you even take Poole's Book and Stationery Store, dying for years; now even Poole says business is up, that the kids are buying books the way they never did before. Of course it depends on what kind of books. You take all those new dirty ones. Frank Beldon, Jr., speaking privately as a sophisticated man, reads these books too. He must; it's his job to keep his fingers on the pulse, isn't it? You have to be up to the minute today.

"When're you leaving, Jamey?"

"Tomorrow."

"Well. I want to wish you all the luck, young man. We'll be keeping an eye on you. Say hello to your dad and your mother."

Into the chaos of his packing his mother returned. The late last sunlight before dusk spattered in his room. "Jamey, won't you want these? I found them in the basement."

He was on the floor sorting out his record albums.

"Jamey—"

"Hmm?"

"Jamey, I asked you a question."

He looked up from the color-streaked patterns of album covers.

"These posters." Mrs. Mieland held up the thick rolled sheaf. "Aren't you taking them back to school?"

"No, I don't think so, Mom." Glancing at his watch: no call from Poppy. Past seven o'clock.

Poppy's voice. That sound.

"Why not? You had them in college all last year," his mother said.

"No more posters," Jamey said. "I've had it."

Perplexed, his mother said, "What should I do with them?"

"Give them to some kid in the neighborhood," Jamey said.

"All right." But she kept holding the roll.

"Maybe Laura would like some of them."

"She's seen them a thousand times at school, Mom. And she has her own."

"I never did see what anyone saw in them." Mrs. Mieland placed the posters on the foot of the bed. Tentatively she began to unroll the large sheets. "People on motorcycles. Or that Uncle Sam with the black beard."

"Allen Ginsberg."

"Who?" his mother asked.

"Never mind, Mom."

"Well, you used to spend all your money on them and I just can't understand why you're suddenly turning up your nose." Mrs. Mieland touched her cloud of gray-blond hair.

"It's just—they were all right when I started getting them," he said. "I mean, it's just that they meant something a few years ago, but now everyone—I mean, now it's strictly Diners Club."

Past seven o'clock. He got up and opened his door.

"Well, all right." Mrs. Mieland began to roll up the posters again. But then he saw the trouble she was having. "Here, Mom— give that to me."

His mother worked her fingers. "Maybe it's the weather."

Jamey said, "Look, Mom, I think—I've always thought it—but I think if you just forgot about weather, diet, doctors, and started to play the piano a little, just a little every day—"

"How can I? I tried, you don't know how many times, but—" Mrs. Mieland sat down on Jamey's Kountrykraft maple bed. She turned on the lamp.

"It was a mistake, a hell of a mistake, Mom. If you hadn't given up teaching—I mean, with all the pupils you—"

"Your father never wanted it. You know that."

"Yes, I know it." Jamey stacked the roll of posters by the door and went back to the mounds of albums on the floor. "But you should have fought him on it."

"Fight your father? Nobody can." She held her blue gaze upon Jamey. "Can they?" Her way of reminding him that he too had been cornered this summer. Just as, many years ago, Fred Mieland cornered his wife into giving up her piano pupils and becoming a neurotic, arthritic lady of unwanted leisure.

"Well"—his mother looked away—"that's water under the dam now. I'm sure if I'd wanted to teach badly enough, I would have found a way to do it. Fred is usually right about most things."

"For godsakes, Mom, stop always taking his—" Jamey let it go; he'd been there too often. He resumed sorting out his albums.

His mother said, "You know, I like your hair that way now, Jamey. I didn't for a long time. But I kind of like it now."

"Tell my father."

She stirred then, studying his suitcase. "You're not going to

85

leave with a suitcase like that; it's the worst mess I ever saw. I'll—"

"Don't bother; it's all right, really, Mom. I'll pack it over."

But already his mother was emptying the contents of the bag, a cornucopia of socks, shirts, shorts, tapes, sheet music, books. "What's this? Oh yes." She held up the program from the Newport Folk Festival. "I don't know why you're keeping it, Jamey. They don't even have your name on it."

"I was too late. I didn't know about it in time."

"You never told me," his mother said.

"It was a foul-up all around," he said. "Except that I at least did get a chance at it."

"Why didn't you tell me?" Mrs. Mieland said. "Was it on TV?"

"I don't know." Then he said, "I didn't want to mention it at the time. I had a big row with Dad. He took the message for me and forgot to let me know. Deliberately. That's why I went anyway, and when we got to Newport—"

"We? Who's we?" his mother said at once.

He hesitated. "This friend of mine."

"A girl?"

"Yes."

"Who? You never tell me anything. Who was it? This new party—what's her name? Poppy—Poppy what?"

"Edwards." And where was she? No call. Zero.

His mother began the repacking.

"Look, Mom—I wish you wouldn't bother with all that." And please, no more questions.

"Somebody has to do it, and it's not you," she said. Holding up a snapshot: "You still want this old picture, Jamey—you and Roy Billings?"

"I guess."

"He's nice-looking. For a colored boy. Is he still at college, still living on your floor?"

"No. Roy moved." And Jamey still cut up about it.

"I know you don't believe it, but I'm old enough to take care of myself." His mother still sometimes waited up for him at night.

"You don't know how to pack, and don't tell me what you can or can't do! I know!"

He watched her for a moment, his mother, whose once slim

and energetic body had become sugar-fatted, sluggish, living her no-life in Nittygritty City.

"Hey—hey, son!" From downstairs his father's voice. "For you. Telephone."

Jamey scrambled up, leaped out of the room, knocking over the big rolled sheaf of posters and a stack of record albums.

"Hello?" He gripped the phone: it could be somebody else.

"Jamey—"

"Poppy, what happened to you?" But his fingers softened around the instrument, he leaned against the wall, the wallpaper this cornpone of Colonial American life, replete with bewigged gentlemen and demure, bellow-skirted ladies, horses and carriages and pillared manor houses (all the wallpaper in the house was a gift to Fred Mieland from the wholesale distributor in Long Island). He lowered his voice now; he saw his father in the living room. "What happened?"

"I'm trying to get away. But I lost your directions."

"Christ, Poppy. It's almost eight o'clock and—"

"Everything went wrong here," she said. "That mimeograph machine Mike borrowed broke down and he had to stay here while I went out to try to find someone who could fix it, and we just finished now," Poppy said.

"Listen," Jamey said, "are you sure it's all right?"

"What's all right?"

"Coming out here?"

"Why?" she said.

"Well, you know—"

Poppy's laughter seemed unnatural. "I love you best when you don't dig. Look, can you give me the directions again?"

He told her which subways to take and the stops to watch for. He would meet her at the Rego Park exit.

Poppy said, "If you weren't leaving for school tomorrow, I'd never do it. No, forget it. Yes I would."

"Laura?" his mother said when he returned to his room upstairs.

"What?"

"Was that Laura?" his mother said.

"No."

"Oh." Mrs. Mieland had finished the repacking. "Must be that

87

other person, not that anyone around here ever gets so much as
a look at her."

"Aw, come *on*, Mom," Jamey protested.

"Well, after all—" She paused to listen. From downstairs came
the sound of the piano and Fred Mieland's voice: the piano
which originally brought them together and ultimately separated them. For now it was only his father who touched the keys,
Fred in his nightly pleasure making the sounds of another
time: . . . *wrap your troubles in dreams and dream your troubles
away . . .*

"What time are you calling for Laura tomorrow?" his mother
was saying.

"Around noon." Jamey was borrowing the station wagon, driving into New York, picking up Laura and her gear, and then
going on to school. He'd return the car next weekend for his
motorcycle.

"I think you're finally getting to be a ladies' man," his mother
said.

"That's me."

"What happened to all your handkerchiefs? I thought you had
at least half a dozen—"

"Mom, you know I can't stand handkerchiefs. Every year we
go through this."

"But if you get a bad cold—"

"I never get a cold."

"No, that's why I nursed you with pneumonia for three weeks,"
his mother said.

"That was a century ago."

"A century? Three years. Two days after you came back from
that march in Alabama," his mother said.

Less than an hour and he would see her. Assuming she got
away in time or didn't get lost on the way out.

"Well, I think this is better now." Mrs. Mieland tried closing
the suitcase.

"Yes. That's fine." He went to her then and kissed her, a warm
kiss on her tepid, neglected cheek. "Thanks a lot, Mom."

"You're sure you don't want anything else to eat before you go
out tonight?"

"No. I'm fine."

His mother was smiling at him then, a resignation of creasing flesh, and Jamey, not wanting to show the sudden pinch of his love or pity, winked at her: an overhearty wink, almost comic-book. Yet . . .

After she left he looked at his watch again. He picked up his guitar. For a while he settled down, chorded his way through something—a folk/rock idea—"Everything to Live for"—he'd been working on. But it didn't groove. He put on a tape he'd made to test something else he was into: *Time's Runnin' Out.* While from below, at the piano in the living room, Fred Mieland still sang away, that Crosbycroon from way back.

And Jamey now almost smiling at the moment's overplay, the mix:

JAMEY'S TAPE:	FRED MIELAND'S VOICE:
Listen Papa, Father, Daddyman	. . . wrap your troubles in
Hold that American dream hard	dreams
as you can	And dream your troubles
For time's runnin' out, time's run-	away . . .
nin' out.	. . . aren't going your way
When I try to hip you to how it is	And skies are cloudy and gray
You say keep on the ball, get	Just wrap up your troubles in
down to biz	dreams
But don't you see: time's runnin'	And dream your troubles away.
out?	
Gotta get your credit card, swim-	
min' pool for the yard	
Sign for whatever you pine for	
Buy, fly, ball a call girl	
Do it all but you won't dare look	
around	
For the dream's runnin' out . . .	

Soon he got ready to meet her: he'd go earlier, pick up the beer on the way. He'd take along his portable Zenith FM. The blanket was already strapped on the back of the bike.

He went into the bathroom. He brushed his teeth.

"Jamey—" His mother's voice from the downstairs hall. "Jamey, it's the telephone. For you again."

"For me?" In dread. "Who is it?" Almost hesitantly he started down the stairway.

"I don't know, dear. But it's not a female for a change."

"Oh." Relief quickened his steps then. "Hello?"

"Hi, man."

"Who is this?"

"Mike." A pause. "Mike Stone is the *nom de paix.*"

"Oh, Mike. What's wrong?"

"Nothing." Yet the voice was not the same. "I just wanted to get the names and addresses of those guys you told me about— you know, at school."

Jamey gave him the information on the campus draft-resistance group: Lyle Stinnett, the law student, and Roy Billings, the Negro student who had lived across the hall from Jamey. Lyle and Roy: two cats who were of the best.

"I'll send all the stuff out tomorrow," Mike said.

"Fine, Mike."

"One thing, Jamey—could I maybe get you to do some of your songs for that war protest we were talking about?"

"Yes—sure, Mike."

"Wait a minute—Poppy wants to talk to you."

Poppy? He turned so that he had his back to the living room. The phone was warm and moist against his fingers.

"Jamey—"

"You mean you haven't even left yet—" he began.

"Well, no—I— Mike is all involved here and—" Poppy said.

"What was that before, about the mimeographing? I thought that was supposed to be the hangup?"

"It was. But—" An extended silence. "Listen, Jamey, I meant to ask you, did you get that letter today?"

"What letter?"

"The— It was from that record company. Avant Records."

"No. I didn't get any mail at all today. How was—"

"I mean, I forwarded it to you," Poppy said. "It came care of The Gross-Outs but nobody knew your address and they asked me."

"Oh." Avant Records. "When did you send it, Poppy?"

"Yesterday—no, night before. Maybe you ought to check with the post office, I mean, in case it got lost."

"Yes." He glanced down to the telephone table, where mail was kept; he opened the drawer. Nothing.

"Jamey? Listen, Jamey, he's gone back upstairs, Mike's gone now. I couldn't talk before."

"For Christ sakes, Poppy, I was just getting ready to go out and pick you up," he said through his dismay. "What do you mean, you couldn't talk? Talk about what? That letter?"

"No. About Mike."

"What about him?"

"I'm not sure, but it's depressing. I mean, I never expected anything like this." Poppy's voice had become breathy, more rapid. "We had a good thing, but now it's—"

"I still don't—"

"Look, it's impossible to discuss here," Poppy said. "Maybe I can see you next week or week after—"

"Week *after?* Jesus, Poppy, will you at least tell me what—"

"I told you. I mean, he's always been decent about everything, we've always had a good relationship. As you know. Now he's trying to bust it," Poppy said.

"He's leaving you?"

"No, not that."

"Oh."

"I mean," Poppy said, "now he's gone—I don't know—straight. Or something. He's like jealous. Like he suddenly owns me. The funny part is that he likes you—I mean, he thinks a lot of you. Maybe that's the trouble. The fact that it's someone like you." She waited. "He's never—not once has he ever got in my way and I've always told him he's just as free as I am, but now all of a sudden the whole relationship is different. I mean, he's suddenly, well, extremely sensitive. How about that? And I know he's been balling that girl from Barnard. But all this week I notice he wasn't the same, including one night he started shooting meth. When he came down he was worse than before. That's when I found out. Two nights ago. And tonight he just refused to let me go out to see you. I mean, like the whole scene between us is almost unrecognizable. I told him it was your last night before school, but that only made it worse, and on top of that I don't want him going on speed again, it's not for him— Look, he's calling me. I'll write or call you, Jamey—"

"Hang up. I'll call you right back."

"No—please don't," Poppy said.

"What?"

"Please don't. Not now," Poppy said.

"Listen—"

"I've got to go—"

"Poppy—"

"I'll call or write."

"Listen, Poppy—I'm coming back next weekend to bring back my folks' car, and I'll— Hello? Poppy?"

But she had already gone.

It was raining, a salty glisten in a pepper-dark sky. Raining when he loaded all his gear into his father's station wagon that morning; raining when he'd gone to the post office to hassle about the lost letter from Avant Records; it was raining now on the parkway to New York and the windshield wipers thudded in steady rhythm like twin metronomes, like the metronomes his mother used to have on her piano for her lessons, for the lessons she had given Jamey.

To Laura's now. Past two in the afternoon when he finally sweated out a parking place on East Ninety-fourth—yet another affluent alley clotted by all the poison-spewing cars of the fatcat life.

Christ, was he going to be uptight like this all day? It started last night and was still with him. That hassle about the Vietnam war with his father at breakfast. The missing letter. And Poppy. And Mike. Bad-news day, a great way to kick off the beginning of his senior year. If that mattered.

And now on the ninth floor of the apartment building, Laura's mother, Marion Barnes, greeting him in the foyer, where all the luggage and cartons were stacked, leading him into the living room, this safe-and-sound, ivory-walled morass of reproduction French furniture and French art, and those magazines on the coffee table, caricatures of middlecat miniculture.

"Jamey—come in. Sit down. For a minute." Marion Barnes was great to look at. If you unplugged the sound. She had one of those athletic bodies (golf, ride, swim, torso slim, limbs trim) with light hair in short boyish cut as if to show even more contrast to the rich long fall of Laura's hair. Mrs. Barnes today was all autumn season—brown dress, stockings, shoes. "Aren't you awfully late, Jamey?" Marion Barnes metered out the words in crisp cadence.

"Took me most of the day to park," Jamey said.

"Hello there, fella." The patronizing voice of Cliff Robison, an easy lounger in the rigid French chair, midday Scotch in hand. Cliff, about forty-five, dark-haired and ruby-cheeked, easy and correct—not a Dartmouth dropout, but dropped by Dartmouth, Laura liked to say about him. Cliff Robison, you could see, made a good shackup for Marion Barnes, though maybe you wouldn't see it right away since he and Marion were always playing the game.

Mrs. Barnes went to the hall door. "Laura," she called. As she resumed her place on the beige sofa, she said, "It's awfully nice of you to help Laura with all this junk."

"I'll start loading up." Jamey was not tempted to linger in this territory.

"What's your rush?" Cliff Robison was being very cordial today. "Marion, if this were my place I'd fix Jamey a drink."

"No thanks," Jamey said.

"Come on. Join me. First of the day," Cliff said.

"When Cliff visits us"—Marion Barnes was into the game—"when he visits us he always expects to be waited on."

"Hand and foot." Cliff said it with the elaborate mockery that was meant to tell you it was all just a friendly put-on.

"Yes—well—" Marion Barnes paused, turned. "Jamey, do sit down. It has been a long time, hasn't it?" Palm fluffing up the sparse hair. "Tell me, how's the—uh—the folk singer these days?"

"Oh, Mother, for godsakes!" Laura had come in. "Jamey, I'm just about ready."

"OK." He looked up at her: the August sun of Washington was still on her September face.

"Oh—let me see, when does my plane leave, Cliff?" To Laura: "Did I tell you the funniest? Well, Cliff has to go to Charlottesville on business, so he's switched his flight to mine. Isn't that the nicest? Laura darling, you're not wearing *that*, are you?"

"Yes, I am." Laura was in tight corduroy pants and a turtleneck sweater of amber like her hair.

"What I meant, Laura, is that you're going back to school, not to the East Village." A sniff and wrinkle of her perfect tilted nose: looking at Jamey now. "I must say, I couldn't be more relieved Laura isn't going down there anymore. If nothing else, at least that job kept her in Washington for the rest of the summer. I can't tell you how many nights I used to sit up when Laura went down there to stay with her friend Pam." Mrs. Barnes said it as blithely as if she believed it. "And I take it, Jamey, you won't be going down there for a while either. My God, when I think of what's happened—that lovely girl from Greenwich murdered. People like that—"

"That Greenwich girl isn't the only person who's been murdered there," Jamey said.

"To Mother she is," Laura said.

"Well—" Jamey stirred on the sofa. "Maybe we ought to get started."

"Tell me, Jamey—" Marion Barnes said. "You know we never do get a chance to talk much—tell me, are you planning to go on with your music, your folk songs, or are you going to have to 'put up with' your father's business?"

Jamey frowned: it was coming again. "I'm not sure, Mrs. Barnes."

"Oh, come on, Jamey, after all this time you can call me Marion. I couldn't be that old, could I? But as I was saying, about your father's business. Cliff and I were discussing it just last night —Cliff invited himself over to keep me company while Laura was at that lecture." Mrs. Barnes hesitated. "But as I was saying— where was I, Cliff?"

Laura interposed, "You were giving Jamey the works, Mother."

"How can you say that?" Mrs. Barnes said. "All I meant was that we were talking about him and Cliff was saying what an opportunity, a marvelous opportunity Jamey had if he—"

"What I was saying"—Cliff Robison rose and lit Mrs. Barnes's cigarette for her—"I was saying a fella like you, if he wanted to, could move right in and upgrade the whole business, bring a whole new dimension to that ball game."

"Yes." Mrs. Barnes crossed her slimtrim legs. "It might just be the cleverest." Peering at Jamey through the veil of smoke. "Or am I talking out of turn? For all we know you may have something altogether different in mind. I remember you started out wanting to be a teacher."

"I don't know what I'm going to do," Jamey said. "I mean, my father likes to run things his own way." He decided not to say more. Mrs. Barnes and Cliff were once again trying in their unsubtle way to influence him. Mrs. Barnes, having made a total disaster of her marriage with Dr. Barnes, though now living high off the alimony hog, did not want Laura to get burned on some unstylish future with Jamey, just in the event a future was involved.

"Look—" Laura's embarrassment was as much for him as for herself. "Before everybody here starts reorganizing Jamey's life, I think we'd better get going."

"Darling, no one is trying to reorganize anyone's life," Marion Barnes said. "We know better." But she must have felt that it wasn't often that she could corner Jamey, for she proceeded to say, "Of course I don't want to make sounds like a mother but, Jamey, I'd appreciate one thing, knowing what happened last year on the campus. I'd appreciate it if you don't try to force Laura into any of those— Well, you know what I mean. After all those demonstrations and protests last year, I don't think it's fair to ask Laura to—"

"Mother! For the—" Laura began.

"I think"—Cliff put his highball aside—"I think all your mother was trying to say was simply that she expects you not to use college for a place to tell the government what to do about the Vietnam war or how to handle the race riots. The Democratic party, I'm overjoyed to say, is very much up the creek, but let's remember this is still our country and we have our commitments to honor; let's just not forget there's still such a thing as honor." A thin laugh. "Well, after that, I think I'll pour myself a double." He was being very cutey-cute, tilting his crew-cut head sidewise, punching his cheek in mock chastisement as he moved to the liquor cabinet, striding across the room in suit of cavalry-twill.

Jamey was on his feet. Laura was already in the hall.

"Now just a minute." Mrs. Barnes rose from the sofa. "You may think Cliff was joking, but I don't, and— Jamey, I really mean what I say, I won't have Laura getting—"

"Goddammit, Mother, stop it—!" But Laura's rage thickened

her tongue, and Jamey, feeling the blood hot in his neck, bent down and lifted her suitcases.

This day would not be of the best.

But it had stopped raining by now. The station wagon groaned like a Gypsy caravan with all their gear, all his music equipment.

"I could have died," Laura said as soon as they were under way. "God, she drives me up a wall!"

"Forget it, Laura." But he'd been up there himself, even before he'd walked into all that bad news on the ninth floor.

"I mean, of all the absolutely lousy taste. My father would have died!" Laura was saying. "And then that whole thing about Cliff just happening to fly the same day—"

"Yes," Jamey said.

"Oh, am I glad to get away!" Then Laura said, "You know, when I was a kid, and even later at prep school, sometimes when I got badly hung up on something I used to practically beg her to tell me what to do. But no. She was always afraid to take a stand. So it was always: 'Well, what do *you* think, Laura?' And now when I'm old enough to know what I'm doing she's suddenly giving me advice all over the place. God, what a joke!"

He turned the car into the East River Drive, going northward. He opened his duffel coat.

They didn't speak for a while, as if each of them needed time to get down from that wall. Laura kept sitting hunched down into her turtleneck sweater. He knew it was more than her mother and Cliff getting under her; she'd been like this last time he'd seen her, last week.

He knew or felt that today she would get around to it: this ride to school was too long not to go unused.

He would not or could not blame her. Out of his anxiety, he heard himself mumble, "What is rock, said the hen to the cock."

Laura turned. "What did you say?"

"I woke up with that stupid line going," he said.

"Oh. Did you finish it?"

"What's the point?" he said. "What is Zen, said the cock to the hen." He switched on the radio. He switched it off. He should have known the reception would be all scratch on this expressway. "Today I couldn't put anything together."

"After what happened at my place I can understand it," she said.

"It was before that," Jamey admitted.

"Like what?" Laura sat more erect now.

"Well, somebody from Avant Records sent me a letter—"

"Really?"

"I never got it."

"How come? Avant Records. What happened, have you any idea?"

"No."

"I mean, how do you know they sent it?"

"A friend of mine—well, actually it was Poppy—"

"Oh." Laura's tone falling a sudden octave.

"It was sent care of The Gross-Outs and they thought she might know my address. I guess she didn't have it right."

"Did you leave your forwarding address?" she said.

"Mustang University." He hoped his old joke would win a smile.

"Yes." But no smile. "How is she?"

"Poppy? Oh, she's all right."

"Couldn't be as dull as you're making it," Laura said.

"What I meant"—Jamey pushed back the hair from his eyes—"all I meant was, she's all right considering all her hangups."

"So is everybody," Laura said.

"You're never all that hung up, Laura."

"You want to know something? You're wrong," she said.

"Then you keep a lot to yourself," he said.

"So do you," she said. "Now."

"I wasn't talking about myself." And he hoped he wouldn't have to.

"Well," Laura said, "since I got back I really haven't seen enough of you to know what you think."

"Christ, Laura, put it away, will you." Before she could reply he tried the radio again. The newscast voice came through the scratch; he didn't want to hear the news and he didn't want to hear the scratch. But he bent forward to listen: "Today's Kill Ratio is . . . Another race riot in Milwaukee . . . The government is ordering an extra two thousand troops to be on hand for the Pentagon Peace March in October. Another march is planned on the induction center of New York. Have you heard about Dex Deodorant? Are you getting bypassed, ignored? Then try Dex, the Super Deodorant with *super sex power!*"

"Jamey, for godsakes—!"

He turned it off. "I prefer commercials to the news."

He remembered last September when he'd driven Laura to school, how great it was all the way in the yellow and vermilion autumn day.

But they weren't strung out like this last year.

It was when the city was behind them and they had stopped for gas and coffee at the Valentine Palace, glowing orange and babysweet blue along the parkway, that Laura put down her cup on the table and said, "I can tell you one thing, I certainly wouldn't want to have her hangups."

"What—who do you mean?" Though he knew.

"I mean Poppy." She rose to leave.

"Oh." He moved ahead to pay the check. The action might break up the way it was going between them.

But in the car, as she fussed with the buckle of her shoulder bag, she said, "I mean, when you consider living like that."

"Like what?" He nosed the car into the traffic stream, now curving eastward. It would be a bad hassle, and Mustang U. was still a time away.

"Like the way they live," Laura said. "People like Poppy and Mike—those people have a whole thing about it, don't they? I mean, it's perfectly OK sleeping together but you go your way and I'll go mine. Right?"

He eyed the radio again. But if he turned it on it would look like he was trying to cop out. Which he was. And if it had been anyone but Laura . . . "Yes," he said, "I guess that's more or less how it is."

How it is: and yes, here was Laura cutting him up, getting right into it. How, after what had happened at her place today, how could she still move in on him in cool reason, even granting there was something under it.

Sometimes some rules get broken:

Laura, despite her mother, was pure reason born out of chaos.

And Poppy, with her hip, simpatico parents, was pure chaos born out of reason.

98

"I suppose," Laura was saying, "it's OK if you really want it that way. Some people can be like that. But God help you if something like love gets in the way. What happens then?" Her look was on him now.

"How would I know, Laura?"

"I mean, you take Poppy and Mike. I don't see how that can be any kind of serious relationship. Do you?"

"It's serious now," Jamey said.

"You sound grim," she said.

"What?"

"Nothing." Laura shook her head. "Nothing."

To the radio then. Getting the last track on The Byrds. Coming in now on the overspin, The Beatles, "A Day in the Life."

Spanning ahead, clean, lethal, the parkway. And the trees and fields no longer there, crushed away, though even now the road was almost obsolete for all the fatcat cars, and already the computers programming new routes to build and other trees and fields to crush. The Beatles' tale.

"What time does registration start tomorrow?" Jamey said.

"Nine, I guess." Laura looking straight ahead. "And something else. People who go in for those involvements—what about venereal disease and God knows what other cruds you can pick up. You'd think people like that would at least think of things like that. I mean, if being selective or sensitive means nothing to them— Oh, I'm being a drag, I'm sorry. Just pretend you don't know me."

"Can't you please put it down, Laura!" But Christ, why did it have to be her? If he didn't feel the way he did about her, if it was anyone except Laura . . . "Look," he tried, "why don't we just—"

"Pretend I'm not here. OK?" Laura looked away, out to the no-scene bleakness.

"No, it's not OK." Jamey glanced over at her again.

But Laura wasn't there. Then without warning she moved, turned, her arm going around his shoulder and a hand on his leg, and leaning closer, her kiss light, gentle, like snow.

Now in this age of confusion—Joan Baez softly, purely singing —*I have need of your company* . . .

Her long light hair stirring, ruffling, silky on his cheek. For a long time she stayed close like this, not talking, not wanting to start cutting him up again, or maybe just waiting for him to say something. He wasn't sure what he could say; he kept his attention on the parkway traffic. Until a red light shone ahead at a junction of new road construction and he had to stop and wait and Laura drew away and opened her shoulder bag and took out her lipstick.

Jamey said, "Laura—about what you were talking about—"

"Hmm?" She looked at him. "I—I was just talking."

"About Poppy, I mean," he said.

"All I meant"—Laura hesitated—"was, well, not Poppy as such but people who—"

"I know what you meant," Jamey said.

The red light going green then and the car gaining speed, spurting off from the pile-up of cars behind him. "Look, Laura" —his vision hard on the road now—"I—about Poppy. I saw a lot of her and Mike—"

"Oh?"

"I mean, I saw a lot of her," he said, "without Mike."

For a while, a long while, it seemed as if she hadn't heard him. Then she said, "Well, why not? I saw people in Washington."

"What I'm trying to"—his voice getting raveled—"I mean, Laura, what I'm trying to say—"

"You don't have to say it."

"I—"

"Jamey, don't bother," she said very quietly. "What makes you think I didn't know?"

"Then why didn't you say so, instead of—" he began.

"I told you it was all right," Laura said. "If you want to make out with people that's up to you." Still cool, incisive, rational.

Which made it worse.

"Christ, Laura—"

She interrupted him. "I had this stupid idea you took such a dim view of all those people—"

"I did—I do. But—"

"But what?" Laura said. "Oh, why bother, Jamey, why bother— to hell with it. And you don't have to look that way, all lost and put upon. I mean, in case you don't think I'll live through the day, I have news for you: I'll make it." Then: "I'm used to people giving me the—"

He shouted across her words: "Are you through?" His hands rising in guilt and rage from the wheel.

"Watch where—"

Fiercely he grasped the wheel again: he swung left, veering away from the shoulder of the road, the high whine of tires piercing, breaking through the *whoosh* of cars passing on the parkway.

Nearing the University. Another semester, another year, and how it always looked a little better than it was, always giving you that hope, that surge that this year will be the one when you discover something. Or uncover some new light on yourself.

Always that hope.

Except today he was too down. Plugged into blues. He and Laura coasting in now, hardly talking, or talking almost like two archetypal squares around the punch bowl of a faculty party, or maybe it was like they were straight out of "Dangling Conversation."

Their mouths moving. Lip service.

Maybe it was a mistake, his telling her. Maybe there's a right and a wrong time for the truth. And this had been the wrong time: when you saw what it did to her.

COLLEGE AVENUE SOUTH. TO THE CAMPUS.

Lip service: "You're taking that lit of Crookshank's, aren't you?" he said.

"Which one?" Laura said.

"Currents in American lit from eighteen fifty—I think—to the present. It's two terms."

"Yes. Unless I switch to Sutter's seminar," Laura said.

A mile more. Then: "You know," Jamey said, "except for that one postcard, I never heard a word from Roy Billings all summer. I wrote twice but no answer."

"Ummm."

"I mean, when you think how much I used to see him."

"Yes," Laura said.

Soon then, he said, "Well, we made it. Again."

She nodded.

Again. Here it was. The University sprawled on slopes and levels from the river to the hill. Alma Mater Mustang.

"Looks the same in spite of all the new stuff they keep building," he said. Change without change. Like bucking the war. All the antiwar work and Vietnam still on fire. Like the Negroes. All that rioting and their lives still ghettoed. Messages that never get there.

Laura still silent.

He said, "Look at this traffic. Almost like New York."

"Yes," she said.

From everywhere students were wheeling in on the campus, many in their own cars, and it always seemed to Jamey that all the cars were red Mustangs. Though there were all the others—the scaly, beat-up beasts of pre-fatcat vintage, and the TR's and MG's and the phallic XKE's, and all the bikes—Hondas, Harley-Davidsons, BSA's and BMW's. ("I had to take two busses to get to high school," his father liked to tell him regularly ten times per annum.)

This was the University. With the mobile student population wheeling or parking around the architectural crazy quilt of the campus.

Nearest the river, where Jamey was driving now, was the College of Liberal Arts, his territory, a huge quad of beech and locust trees and one Colonial (1780) manor now housing the Dean and his staff and assistants. Flanking this were blocks of serene classic-columned halls (1830–1859) and mansard-roofed redbrick Victorian structures with towers and captains' walks (1875) and sudden lines of horizontal granite-faced, slabbed cubes (1959). In the center the dining hall (1926), of native stone, collegiate Gothic like a mighty chapel out of early Princeton via Oxford.

Upriver the Medical School and hospital, another fungus growth. Inland now past the Engineering College, the School of Fine Arts, College of Business Administration, School of Journalism, School of Music, School of Nursing, and College Hall, that white marble Parthenon shielding the office of Mr. Alvin Adams Ross, the Chancellor, Prime Minister and Führer of the University—these buildings all solid, stolid, plain and polychrome, low and high, narrow and wide, square and round and even rhomboid.

"To cook up an architectural goulash of the American University," Jamey wrote last year in *The Review*, "start with a basic stock of redbrick Victorian Gothic, add a pinch of genteel Georgian, a sprinkling of blandblond 1929 Moderne and a lavish chunking of neo-Saarinen Contemporary. Mix and stir, bring to a boil of alumni taste, then vomit."

Uphill again, along The Best Part of Town—Fraternity Row: terraced turf rising, sloping up from the wide pavement, and crowned with the splendid residences in styles of Virginia Plantation, New York Tudor, Massachusetts Rustic, Connecticut Revolutionary, Rhode Island Federal and Nowhere Modern. Gilt Greek letters, like coats of arms, were encrusted over doorways or in pediments. (The DKE's had in their hallway a Confederate flag autographed by the Governor of Alabama.)

Jamey turned right, drove up to the plateau, treeless and bleak, this high plain where stood the newest complex of deluxe women's dormitories for juniors and seniors: six bronze-bricked buildings known as "The Husband Trap."

To the curb in front of Building B to deliver Laura's cartons of new curtains, bed cover, pictures, posters, wastebasket, lamps, record player, records, books, clothes. Here only seniors could enjoy the privilege of living in a room alone and the casual curfew rule: just leave a number or address where you can be reached. More free than a sorority, a life Laura had decided against, causing terrible times of trauma for her mother. Whom did Mrs. Barnes blame for this catastrophe? That's right. Jamey, Jamey, I call your name.

In the September dusk now they unloaded her gear. It took four trips up and down the stone steps. This came as a kind of relief to both of them, though now that it was over and his hands were empty and Laura stood there holding her ski jacket and skis, even the lip service came with effort. The ceiling and wall lights of the foyer were very bright, the foyer was bland and substantial like the waiting room of a newly prosperous dentist. TRASH BAGS MUST GO TO CURB MON WED FRI, read a notice by the elevators.

"Well—thanks a lot, Jamey."

A junior in minikilt on her way out said to a friend who had just entered the dorm, "Hey, Smith—what's for dinner tonight?"

"Roast beef."

"Wow!" said the kiltie.

"Yeah, but don't try cutting it. Have to pick it up in your hands and chew it to pieces."

"Ohhh!" came kiltie's groan.

"Look—" Jamey said in the foyer's deadness, "maybe later we could get some coffee at Niko's. I'll call you, huh?"

"I've really got to get this place fixed up," Laura said.

"Well—well, listen, Laura, we'll get together tomorrow anyway."

She nodded.

"Hey, Barnes!" A girl in fun fur greeted Laura vociferously, though looking at him.

"Oh, hi—hi, Betsy," Laura answered.

Elevator doors sliding shut.

"Well, I better get upstairs." Laura turned and then turned back. "I hope you get that letter."

"Oh. Right."

"Well. Thanks again, Jamey. For everything."

"I'll see you then," he said to her, her smile gray in the foyer's shine.

PART II

The Gates of Academe

5 : THE CAMPUS

THE TREES tell it: it is October. And on this smoky afternoon
Jamey Mieland is summoned to the office of the University's
Chancellor, Alvin Adams Ross. Behind the anterooms of his
secretary and work force, the Chancellor sits in his chamber, the
carpeting deep, hushed to the tread. The staffs of the American
flag and the University colors rise to flank his desk, making for
the man a vivid frame. Vivid too on the walnut walls are the cer-
tificates, diplomas, commendations and other high honors con-
ferred on Mr. Ross during his decades of distinguished service
to the academic community.

Ross looks youthful for his age. His brown hair is almost free
of gray. His nose is bold and dominates a face still quite tautly
fleshed. The eyes are clearest blue. Blue is his suit and a gold
chain spans the vest. Even seated in this high-backed leather
chair he shows a lofty bearing not unlike that of Charles de
Gaulle.

This is the Chancellor now confronting Jamey Mieland, Class of '68.

This is the Chancellor who, on Friday, will be confronting the First Lady.

Confronting campus trouble.

Lady Bird.

But today's business cannot be bucked to the Dean of Men. Too risky. Needs the seal of this office. This is in Ross's basket: Mrs. Lyndon Johnson is not only to speak (on Beautification) at the University, she is being the Chancellor's guest Friday. (Secret Service is already crawling all over the place to "prepare the premises for Mrs. Johnson's comfort.") And student protests and demonstrations are now in the making.

"Sit down, Mieland." The Chancellor, despite a well-grounded antipathy for this young man, moves his arm in a friendly sweep, though never losing the authority that has marked him as the University's outstanding trouble-quasher and fund-raiser. "I hope, Mieland, all goes well with you since the last time you were brought to my attention."

"Yes, sir." The boy, of course, does not fail to perceive the irony of the Chancellor's reference to the stormy past: this boy with the thick straight wheat hair, jeans, half-boots, black sweater. He is not the most reassuring or soothing part of the student landscape; not, at any rate, in the Chancellor's view. For he cannot quite forget or forgive Jamey Mieland for what happened a year ago when he instigated and led the movement against the no-drinking regulations of the school.

Infuriating too is the fact that Jamey Mieland himself drinks very little. But no, inflaming the students with his cries that the no-drinking law was a "howling hypocrisy" and also illegal, he defied Ross's repeated assertions that "as long as I am Chancellor of this University drinking will never be allowed." Yet Mieland pressed the issue into both the student and administrative law tribunals. He set this off one April evening, witnessed by the local and regional press, by climbing up on Scott Memorial Fountain in the quad of the College of Liberal Arts and proceeding to drink down a can of beer. Thus breaking the law. And thus forcing the case to be tested in legal channels, while at the same time firing up the entire student population. In the end the regulation had to be revised so that drinking was now permitted at any "University-registered function."

"What I wanted to talk to you about, Mieland, is this—" But he waits: he sees that the young man, still mystified, has lost some of his poise, the blue-green eyes glinting anxiety, the long fingers no longer motionless. "Since the responsibility of the First Lady's visit is directly upon me, I wanted to hear more of what you people have in mind about the nature of Friday's demonstration."

"Well, sir—" Jamey Mieland moves forward in the chair. "The committees met with the Dean and Chief Kavanaugh this morning. I think everything's been cleared."

"Yes, I know all that, Mieland. I was asking you about the *nature* of the demonstration."

"Our group is planning a silent protest. Though I'm not sure about the other groups. There will be a few speeches," the student says.

"And you'll be there with your guitar," the Chancellor says.

"Well, it depends, sir."

"I see. Is that all you can tell me?"

"I'm only on the steering committee of—" the young man begins.

"Mieland," the Chancellor interrupts, "I know you have more than a little influence."

"I—"

"Now this is not simply the case of some government official being on campus," the Chancellor says. "This is the First Lady. And regardless of how one feels about the conduct of the Vietnam war or anything else, she is a lady and she is the President's wife. It would be nothing less than a disaster if your demonstration changed its nature, if it turned out to be violent, vulgar or tasteless. Though I have every hope we can depend on our people to act with discretion, and like gentlemen." Then: "Tell me, how many students are you expecting?"

"About three or four hundred," Jamey Mieland answers.

"Chief Kavanaugh informs me it could easily exceed five hundred."

"We're trying for that," Jamey Mieland admits.

"As long as it's quiet and in good taste." The Chancellor's

theme reprised. "It was carried off fairly well when Mrs. Johnson was at Yale, though at Williams there was an unhappy incident when some students walked out during her speech." A pause. "What about your signs, the picket signs? If there is any obscenity, I warn you, it will not be tolerated." He waits. "I'll trust you to make it your business to pass along the word."

"Sir, the SDS—I mean, our group is only part of this, sir. There are other groups and we expect people from all over campus to be there and even town people," Jamey Mieland says.

"What about the Provos?" The Chancellor's nose twitches imperceptibly as he recalls how some members of this activist group chose to lower their pants in a previous antiwar demonstration.

"I don't see how I can speak for them, sir."

The Chancellor studies the lanky young man. Then he says, "You know, Mieland, I wouldn't like to think I've become too cynical, but I've been thinking about student demonstrations, not only this year but more or less historically. And as far as I can see nothing has ever been accomplished—except perhaps to bring on the suppression of human rights. In other words, I can't help but believe that all these mass protests will be futile and will change nothing."

"Well"—Jamey Mieland looks uncomfortable—"all I know, sir, is you just can't let it happen, I mean, you just can't sit around and let certain things go on without trying to do something—"

"But why not use the proper means to show your feelings, like the democratic election process?" the Chancellor asks.

"But there's no real choice, people don't have a real choice. I mean"—the student hesitates—"all we have is—more like an illusion of democracy. But show me a candidate running without the machine or some other big interest behind him, and I'll show you a loser. Voting just doesn't make it. Anyway, it's too late now—"

"You know, Mieland, for someone tilting at windmills, *you* seem to be the one who's being rather cynical, aren't you?" The Chancellor caps his meager triumph by quickly reverting to the immediate concern. "At any rate, we'll depend on you to see that this demonstration will in no way put the University in an embarrassing position with the White House."

"I beg your pardon, sir?" Jamey Mieland moves forward in the black leather chair.

"I said we will depend on you."

"You mean—actually?" The boy raises a hand to slant back the rough blond hair.

"Why not? I can't think of anyone better," the Chancellor says.

"There are—there are a lot of people," the student declares. "There are six or seven at least. And what about someone like Reverend Tillou?"

"Come now, Mieland." The Chancellor must smile as he visualizes the young Assistant Dean of the Divinity School. "You know as well as I do that the Reverend Tillou is much too exuberant: he'll be the first man with the pickets and the protesters, and the last man to leave. No, this office feels this is a student affair and we're confident you can find a way to keep this from getting out of hand."

As if for the first time Jamey Mieland recognizes the true purpose of this meeting. "But—what if it's impossible? I mean, no one can tell what can happen, how can one person control it?" He leans forward. "I just don't see how I can promise anything like that!"

"Someone must. The Board of Trustees expect a guarantee from me. Just as I expect this responsibility from you," the Chancellor states. "When I am with Mrs. Johnson on Friday I want to be able to reassure her. After what happened when Dean Rusk was here, we— Well, advance planning must now be much more thorough. We don't want to depend on force of any kind. But I believe you're the person who can keep this thing within decent and tasteful bounds." A nodding of the head now, a clearing of the throat. The interview is over.

Jamey Mieland stands up; the color seeps into his face.

As now the Chancellor looks off toward one of the noble windows, turns back again. "That will be all for now, Mieland. Thank you."

The boy has gone. Alvin Adams Ross shakes his head: you would think he had nothing on his mind except the stratagems of student protests.

Of course, if he wanted to be crassly honest, he might admit that since the advent of this large minority of vociferous American youth in troublesome, tempestuous upheaval, he, Alvin Adams Ross, has benefited considerably by more public exposure—press interviews ("In your opinion, Mr. Ross, what percentage of the student body is involved in political protests and do they belong to the New Left?"); feature articles ("A College Chancellor Looks at Today's Youth and the Widening Generation Gap"); TV ("Tonight's panel includes Alvin Adams Ross, who will discuss Changing Sex Mores on the American Campus").

Yes, his image has indeed bloomed and many handsome offers have come his way.

The Chancellor peers toward the door which Jamey Mieland has just closed upon leaving. Alone now. And peace for an instant before, alas, the harassments resume: next week's meeting on the proposed budget, $73,000,000. And Friday, Lady Bird.

Jamey, carrying his rage and his books, left the office of Ross-boss. He was badly burned down. And he couldn't move fast enough down the marble steps of the neo-Parthenon administration building, as if by fleeing the scene he might lose or drop the responsibility the Chancellor had thrown at him.

He tripped on the bottom step, he almost fell as he reached out trying to catch the manila folder of anthro notes and the three books that had slipped from his grasp and which now lay on the pavement. He bent down and scooped up the books and the folder.

Fuckleberry Finn's day.

He hurried. The motorcycle was in the parking area in the rear. He packed the books into the saddlebag, jammed down too fiercely on the kick starter and roared off, driving the Harley like a hard-core scramble nut.

At the third intersection he lost the light and had to wait, and almost right away he saw Laura. She was with another girl. He waved to her and started to angle the bike in toward the curb, edging forward in front of the trembling-for-takeoff fatcat cars.

He was running short on time but he had to see her, even though a minute now probably wouldn't be much different from any of the other minutes they'd talked on campus or in lit class. It was the kind of bind he couldn't handle: he still couldn't pursue her and he still couldn't turn off when he thought of her or saw her. Yet now, after Rossboss, how he would have liked to see her, tell her what happened, discuss it with her.

Laura wasn't waiting. For an instant she seemed to hesitate, she touched the striped knitted scarf looped around her neck and hanging down behind long as her hair, but she only nodded, waved and turned in the other direction, so that when he drew up to the curb, she and the other girl were already on their way.

He watched her. And then started up once more. Late. And too much to get done. Tonight's schedule was too much. Typing up all the anthro notes and starting that piece for lit, and getting on the phone to call SDS people and some other groups. It would be a new role for him, the cautious moderate: he'd never been into that slot and he wouldn't want to tell anyone why he was in it now.

And in less than two hours Mike and Poppy. Arriving at the Greyhound Bus Station.

Poppy making it.

He wheeled uphill past the Liberal Arts College and up to Beech Street, where he lived, a street of old trees and red-brick Victorian houses, part of the off-campus complex of University-registered living centers for upper-class students. He parked in front of his place, number 17. It was on the corner and like the others it had been converted and was studded with gleaming trim and appliances to become yet another style, Mod-Vic Collegiate: four floors of red brick and aluminum storm sash and that wild mansard tiara.

Up the stoop into the square hallway: smudged buff walls and a pay telephone and a bulletin board and two synthetic-leather benches and a sack of somebody's laundry. He picked up his mail: a letter from Nittygritty City. His father.

Up the oakwood stairway, almost colliding with Keith Owens McNulty, a senior known as K.O., his arms stacked with library books.

"Hey, Jamey." K.O. stopped midway down.

"Hey."

"Roy Billings was here a while ago."

"He was?"

"Yeah, about an hour ago," K.O. said. "Has that guy changed since last year! Well, seeya."

"Listen, K.O. You going to be at the demonstration Friday?"

"Don't you know it!" said the always energetic campus hotshot eager-beaver overachiever, whose father was a Chicago manufacturer of caskets and other mortuary supplies. "My dad," K.O. liked to say, "is a big man in the underground movement." K.O. was a member of the Young Republicans; he was also a wheel in many other organizations and attended all events regardless of political or intellectual level. He also speculated in the stock market and had a finger in several commercial enterprises both on and off campus. When the literary magazine, *The Review*, ran into financial disaster, K.O. was the man who took over the management and though he didn't much dig or approve the periodical's contents, he sold enough advertising space to pull it through. So that Jamey always felt an unabashed affection for him.

When he reached the second floor front, Jamey saw the note that was inserted in a slit above the lock in his door. It was from Roy Billings. He read it as soon as he was inside and free of his books. He was not prepared for what Roy had written: "If Friday's protest is going to be all silence, count me out. But if anyone wants my draft card they can have it. I'm all for handing it to Lady Bird to take back to Washington and give it to that mother—"

Jamey read it again. He went back and closed his door. Directly down the hall was where Roy Billings had lived, but this fall he had taken up residence in a building that was occupied exclusively by other Negroes. When Jamey had gone over to see him to find out what happened, Roy had said quietly, "It's nothing, man. I just decided I want to live with my friends."

"I thought I was your friend," Jamey had said.

"I mean my people," was all Roy had said, and never talked about it after that, and though they saw each other on campus, Roy seemed preoccupied and sometimes even hostile.

Jamey went immediately into the bed alcove and dialed Roy's telephone number. No answer at first. Jamey waited, he sank down on the bed: the session with Ross still had him ungrooved.

He looked around. The place needed straightening up, but

he'd been gone all day, rushing out this morning for his nine-o'clock. He had to clean up before Mike and Poppy came. It was what he called a one-and-three-quarter-room apartment, the three-quarters being the box of bathroom and the alcove that held a double bed, telephone and clothes closet. From here in the alcove you looked through the arch to the main room, of good size and high ceiling. There was a deep bay window and when you stood there you could see the street and the trees below. There was a table, and hanging above it, a bright Japanese lantern light. And there were four lacquered black Italian chairs. In the middle of the white room was a secondhand studio couch and two worn armchairs.

Low across the entire left wall ranged the bookshelves, on which was his audio equipment: stereo record player and speakers, tape recorder, FM radio components, racks of records and tapes and piles of magazines and newspapers—*The Oracle, The Los Angeles Free Press, Ramparts, Avatar, The Village Voice, EVO, Crawdaddy* and old issues of mimeo newsletters from Israel Young's Folklore Center.

The only focus of decoration was in the center of the wall, a brilliant blue dove he'd cut out from a poster. Lower down and off to one side near the bay window was a framed photograph of Woody Guthrie, which the now dead folk singer had not been able to sign when Jamey, a stranger, had managed to visit him in his sickroom in the State Hospital in New Jersey. Hanging nearby was another memento: a program of Bob Dylan's first concert at Carnegie Chapter Hall in 1961, when Jamey was thirteen years old. (How slavishly he would imitate him, how long it went on before he began to find his own track.)

"Hello?" Roy Billings' voice suddenly in his ear. He shifted the phone to his other hand.

"Roy? This is Jamey. Sorry I missed you. I got your note."

"Yes," Roy said.

"I mean"—Jamey groped for a way to start—"I was kind of bugged by what you said. We're counting on you for Friday and all the people you can line up—" As he paused he was sure he heard a faint sound on the line.

"Hello, you there?" Roy was saying.

"Yes." But Jamey listened hard.

"Jamey—what's going on?" Roy said.

"I don't know. I thought maybe at first it was somebody trying to get me, but I can still hear it," Jamey said. "Maybe something's wrong with the line."

"Couldn't be you're being tapped, could it?" Roy said.

"Naw," Jamey said.

"Why not?" Roy Billings said. "The FBI isn't particular."

"I don't know, but—"

"Look what happened last May. Remember after that sit-in on the Dow Chemical recruiter—don't you remember Ed Ryder's telephone was tapped?"

"Yes," Jamey answered. "But—"

"Well."

"It's just that I—" Jamey stopped. "I can hear it all right." Then he said, "But you'd think if anyone wanted to tap my phone they'd do it so that I wouldn't know it."

"Not necessarily, not necessarily," Roy Billings said, with that very precise diction of his. "Sometimes those mothers want you to know you're being tapped."

"I doubt it," Jamey said.

"Sure, it's a form of harassment. Like a threat," Roy said. "Listen, I know. It was happening in Cleveland this summer after the riots. I know." Then: "Anyway, about Friday, doesn't sound very appetizing to me—and if any of those intellectual giants of the FBI are listening in, let's make it worth their while. Listen, Jamey, I'm against the idea of silence—it's too refined. But what about getting as many people as possible to turn in their draft cards? Put them in a box and present them to Lady Bird to take back with her."

"Roy, cool it." But Jamey wasn't sure what to say now. He couldn't tell Roy or anyone else about Ross: it would look like he was asking everyone to help keep the Chancellor off his back; it would also kill the spirit of the protest. He said, "Look, Roy, you don't want to talk about turning in your draft card Friday. I mean, is that any way for you to show your appreciation for the life, liberty, equality and opportunity your country has given you?"

"Oh, you're making me feel real bad," Roy answered, and even laughed.

Jamey tried it straight: "What I think, Roy, I think we ought to hold off this Friday, save it for when it means more. I mean, Mrs. Johnson is only here to talk on Beautification, and I don't think it calls for a big stink. What we want mainly is to get a turnout, a really impressive turnout. Some good speeches and a deliberate fifteen-minute silence."

"You must be out of your head!" Roy's rebuke came sharply. "We're not eating that custard anymore! Fifteen-minute silence? What's that going to gain us? What's the matter with you, Jamey? You're still giving me the same Boy-Scout liberal cop out all you people have been trying too long!"

"'All you people'?" Jamey was stunned. "What is that supposed to mean, Roy? I thought you knew how I feel. Since when am I 'you people'?"

"That's how it comes across," Roy said.

"It is? Then you ought to know me better," Jamey said. "I mean, all the time we used to— Don't you know how I stand?"

"Sure."

"Well then—"

"Forget it. The time is too short. Too short." Roy chopped it off.

Jamey hung up. For the second time this fall he was flattened by the difference in Billings. Of course he knew why Negroes were changing, turning to their own, no longer relying on the white Establishment. Even so, for Jamey this was bad news: he didn't believe in separatism for blacks or anyone else. The only choice you had today was between coexistence or no existence. . . .

He stared down at the bed table. The alarm clock showed ten minutes to five. Time leaping up at him. Mike and Poppy due in on that six-o'clock bus.

He rose. Slowly, almost absently, he pulled off his black sweater. He was drenched with sweat. The Rossboss sauna. And this salty way of Roy's—another unanswered question about Friday.

Again the Chancellor's voice boomed its bass warning. And Jamey hurried his undressing and went into the shower. He came out clean but still uncool.

He sat down on the bed again, the towel around his neck. He

picked up the envelope, opened the letter from his father (dictated to Louise Yates).

DEAR SON:
Answering yours of the 4th.

Too bad about the man from the record company. Know you must be disappointed. Know how you stewed until you finally got that letter. But to look at the bright side, it isn't your fault when a company changes its personnel. Maybe you'll realize now that though the building business is tough, the record game is probably a rat race. Doubt if you'd want to get mixed up in it seriously. Not for the long run. You know my opinion on this subject. The office is certainly quiet. Not like it was the last part of the summer when you were helping to hold down the fort. House is likewise, according to your mother. Since you left, weather's been against us, but sales of units 129 and 130 are being closed next week, finances set with Hometown National.

A sharp sigh: Jamey impatiently scanned the rest of the letter.

. . . you're on the homestretch now. Won't be long before we wake up and it's June. Brings me to the fact that we're starting work on the addition for your office. It's one way to justify the payroll for crew during slack winter weeks. Have to have a place for you to hang your diploma in. Need I say more?

No! Jamey shouted to the empty room.

Meanwhile your Mother and I send our love. Good luck and keep your nose clean.

Your loving Dad.

He put the letter down. He had to start calling some of the people about Friday.

But he couldn't make it yet. He couldn't fade that feeling. Most of it probably came from Roy Billings, and it wasn't only the way he'd changed. And Laura. On that street corner. And now this hot communiqué from Nittygritty City!

Even the prospect of Poppy arriving, even that marred. Mike with her.

A long low-down day with no rise, no surge.

Let it all hang out!

He reached for the telephone to begin his calls: Bob Lothar, an editor of the campus newspaper who was active in SDS (Students for a Democratic Society); Gary Einsberg, a premed, who was leader of the popular middle-of-the-road NCSN (New Committee for the Study of Nonviolence); Jim Wade, a divinity student; Susan Sayres, a senior and prominent in WOW (Women Opposed to the War). And he would also talk to K.O. McNulty. K.O. would help round up support among the jocks and maybe even some right wingers. The last call—and the toughest going—was to Lyle Stinnett, a law student and chairman of CCA (Council for Campus Action). But he would also be seeing him later tonight after Poppy and Mike got in; Jamey had arranged for them to stay at Stinnett's apartment off campus.

Before he could begin, his phone rang. He was surprised. It was Laura. It was the first time during their uncomfortable truce that she'd taken the initiative.

"Jamey, I'm calling because of this thing on Friday—"

"Since when do you need an excuse for calling me?" he said. "What the hell happened to you this afternoon? I wanted to see you but you took off before I even—"

"Well, look," Laura broke in. "A lot of people I know are going Friday, but the poop is that it's going to turn into some kind of brawl and I assume you know what's going on, what the plan is—if any."

"I know all right." Jamey felt the first relief, being able to voice his anxiety. "I wish I didn't."

"What do you mean?" she asked. "Why so cryptic?"

"I wasn't being cryptic. It's just that—actually it just happened, and, Christ, I'm glad you called," Jamey said. "You know when I saw you before? Well, I was just on my way back from Ross-boss."

"You were? What happened?"

"That's what I wanted to tell you," Jamey said. "What happened was that I had the luck to be the guy singled out for this deal. I'm supposed to be the monitor who keeps the kiddies quiet."

"The demonstration?"

"Yes," Jamey said. "Ross really threw it at me."

"God, Jamey. Isn't he kind of laying it on?"

"I guess. But after last year—"

"Yes, of course," Laura said. "Oh, he must love you." Her tone soft, soothing. Then she said, "In other words, if anything goes wrong Friday, it's on your back. Right?"

"Right," Jamey answered dismally. "What it is, is that I have to make sure Ross won't be embarrassed with his house guest."

"Then it's definitely going to be a nonviolent demonstration?" Laura said.

"Fifteen minutes of silence. Or something like that."

"Oh, that's good. That's what worried me," Laura said.

"Christ, I'm glad you called," Jamey said again. "There's nobody else I can tell this to." He listened now: the sound was not on the line—at least he couldn't detect it this time.

"Well, look, Jamey," Laura said then, "maybe it's all for the best. I mean, after all, it's only Mrs. Johnson, and though I'm not holding any brief for her, it just seems to me—I don't know—unfair if this thing got violent or anything. Don't you agree? Don't you?"

"Well, naturally I agree. Silence is the only kind of protest that makes sense in this case," Jamey said. Yet: "I mean, emotionally it's the way I feel about it. But in my head something tells me it's too easy, simple. I mean, in my head I'm against it. I don't like to think we're being had—that good manners, womanhood, Beautification are going to sell us all on a polite little whiteglove antiwar show that ends up as nothing—" But his rage rose now even as he tried conscientiously to quell it.

"But, Jamey, you know what could happen if people get steamed up and—"

"Yes, certainly I know," Jamey said. "You should have heard what my old buddy Billings had to say a few minutes ago. Anyway, don't worry, I'll do everything I can."

"You sound like you're still kind of frazzled," Laura said.

"Well, this isn't my groove, Laura."

"Look—" A long hesitation. "Look, maybe, if you'd like, I might come by later. I haven't even cracked a book yet, but later I could come by and hold your hot little head."

"That would be great, Laura, I'd love it—except the only thing is—"

"Except what?"

"I have to go to the bus station. At six. Mike is due in."

"Mike?"

"Yes," Jamey said. "With Poppy."

"Oh," Laura said.

"But as soon as I know their—"

"Oh, it doesn't matter. Never mind, Jamey." Laura's voice had lost its new buoyancy. "It doesn't matter. See you tomorrow." She ended the call.

He thrust the phone down into its cradle; the lamp on the bed table shuddered from the impact.

He was ready for the shower. Again.

For a few minutes Jamey, naked except for the towel around his neck, moved around his room: what the hell was he doing here? Why was he into all this?

The ache of old questions arched through him. And the new answers: to be beyond this, needing nothing, relying on nothing except maybe a guitar to help rid himself of the ache and the answers.

Yet year after year he returned here. He'd bought it. Like everyone else: he had an education. Did he have knowledge?

He had everything and he had nothing.

He could feel all this. He could unplug the sound of Laura's voice.

He went to the far wall to the bookshelves. He put a record on the stereo, Tim Buckley's "Hello and Goodbye."

He lay down on the floor, stretched out on the acrylic carpet. He closed his eyes and he listened. But the Buckley saga only stirred him up again. He rose and turned it off. To regain time lost, he dressed with the careless speed of his freshman days, when after physical ed he was the first to clear out of the locker room, his hair still shower-damp.

Now, back in the bed alcove with no appetite for the job ahead, he began his telephone calls to the people about Friday. A meeting was arranged. It would be at the apartment of Lyle Stinnett, at 7:30 P.M.

His anthro notes would go untyped. That piece for lit, "The Influence of Dylan Thomas on Contemporary American Poets," would never get under way. My, my. Also, before Friday morning, for Medieval Music 4, he had to cover all the variations of plain chant, troubadour-trouvère and development of organ through motet. Et cetera. Never get it done. If that mattered. They wanted you to get the right answers, not the concepts; the facts, baby, not the meaning. . . .

Cram it and ram it: The Influence of Dylan or Rylan or Bayler or Mailer. In first year high school had he needed any of it? Taking for his own Salinger or Hesse or Tolkien or— And giving them back.

The influence of Dylan the T——, as if that was of any consequence to anyone except the prof who would show his department chairman the neat papers of the neat minds of Mustang U. . . .

What counted? The work of the man, that counted. D.T., his work, just that. Was anything else needed? Not for Jamey. Reading him, mouthing, even singing the Welshman's lyrics could be like the greatest of highs . . .

The bus station was less than a ten-minutes walk. He got there late but luckily the bus was not on time. It drew up in front of the station restaurant at quarter-past six, its bright silver flanks yellowed by the grit of travel. See America First.

At once, as soon as he saw her, fatigue drained from his bones, an incipient headache cleared, a stupid Welcome Club optimism overtook his darkest forebodings: Poppy.

Poppy in microskirt of faded corduroy, fishnet stockings, thin turtleneck and Navy pea jacket, her bronze-dark hair tied back with an orange scarf: not a sign of even a button or a bead or a bell.

Poppy, the brilliant ocher of her eyes in the pale oval of face, emerging now like a diminutive saint from the cavern of the bus, a backwash of ordinary mortals watching her, passersby pausing to look up as she stepped down from the bus. Diamond in the dust.

Poppy, a-smile, her small hand outstretched, grasping his, drawing it close to her, the oval face raised and kissing him then.

Where was Mike?

"Take it easy, man." Mike's voice close by. And Jamey uncertain, disappointed, yet somehow pleased, a boost seeing him, the big familiar Mike, the dyed hair ever wild and red, Mike with the sun shades, but no sandals or jeans, wearing shirt, black tie, old chinos and a tweed jacket of olden times (circa 1964).

Mike was carrying two blue and battered flight bags and some manila envelopes.

"It's great, Mike, it's great to see you." Jamey's pleasure, though certainly dimmed, was nevertheless genuine: his admiration for this draft counselor, this bold fugitive from the California arm of the Selective Service system, returned with all its former power.

Even though it had lapsed the last time he'd seen him—the weekend after school had begun when he had returned the station wagon to his family. That weekend had been not of the best: Mike flying on speed, lifting him beyond his jealous torments, the methedrine jazzing him up until he was ready to take on the entire New York police, or anyone else or anything else; but coming down, sagging down, his weighted eyes heavy on Poppy, this passionate pacifist again threatening war on her.

(Or Jamey?)

But now he seemed more like the early days of this past summer. Different too. As was Poppy. Or was it that all of them were coming on too strong?

"Man, we've got lots to catch up on, huh?" Mike's arm around him now. "Where's this pad of Stinnett's?"

"I talked with him a little while ago," Jamey said. "We're meeting everybody there at seven-thirty. It's not far from here. I thought maybe we'd get something to eat." He turned to Poppy. "There's a fairly good joint around the corner notable for pizzas, minute steaks and French fries, enough grease to turn on the entire American Medical Association. No unbleached flour, Poppy, and no organically grown anything, no anise tea."

"Ooooh, it all sounds so good. I'm so hungry I could even eat Diggers' stew." Poppy between them now as he led them across University Avenue, passing the Co-op, and down Kent Street, past the bookstore and Able's Music Store and Prell's, Gentlemen's Haberdashers, to the next block, where many restaurants flourished and where, wedged between a cafeteria and a white-tablecloth club, was Niko's. Nobody knew who Niko was.

Niko's at this hour was full: it meant waiting by the cage of the pizza chef.

"Hey, Jamey—" the chef called. He was a drama major with

whom Jamey had a long and superficial friendship, and who had made campus history two years ago when, with deadly aim, he threw down a bowling ball from the fifth floor of his dorm, deliberately just missing the Assistant Dean of Men, who was mincing prissily down the street.

"Hi, Bill. Listen, these people came miles for one of those poisonous pancakes of yours," Jamey said.

"A few ahead of you. But OK." He smiled down at Poppy. Then into his performance he went. For a performance is what it was: he reached for a ball-like lump of dough, he then hurled it high into the air, catching it on the descent, not quite catching it but rather letting it lightly ride, stretching and twirling on his upthrust knuckled fists; his fists like blunt pivots as he kept tossing and spinning the doughy disk, until he achieved a big flat wheel of dough ready to receive its garden of spices, herbs, cheese, tomatoes and anchovies before being spaded into the oven.

When the sideshow was over, something of the gaiety of the group seemed to have ended too. Jamey felt uneasy. Poppy and Mike had stopped talking.

A young man on a stool at the counter nearby leaned over to his friend in cool conspiracy for weekend plans.

"Hey, man, we've got a line on a house on the Cape. Six couples. OK?"

"Oh, yeah. Very definitely."

As now four students on their way out, stopping to talk to the Cape Cod swingers.

"Hey, Smitty."

"How the hell areya? How'd you make out in that French quiz?"

"Not too bad. I hope."

"Great."

"You ought to see the chick sits next to me. Built?"

"No shit? Rough, huh?"

"Uh-huh. Kinda piece you dream about."

"Yeah? Well, don't kill yourself."

Jamey led the way down the long aisle between the counter and the booths to the free booth in back. A student waiter cleared the Formica and took their order.

"The smell of coffee, catsup and French fries. Nothing takes me back to school like that," Poppy said. "You know?"

Jamey sat opposite her and Mike. "Fill me in some more, Mike," he said. "I mean, how long is it going to take you here?"

"I'm not sure." Mike removed his sunglasses. "I have to get to Dartmouth, Syracuse, Cornell and U. Conn. and Yale before next Wednesday. What we want to do is have as many Eastern campuses as possible organized so that when the buses get to Washington everyone will know what to do and where to do it before we start marching on that five-sided outhouse. Anyway, I thought we'd split here by tomorrow, but I'm going to try to squeeze my schedule so I can stick around and see how you people make out with Lady Bird."

"You look kind of beat, Jamey." Poppy spoke for the first time. She slid out of her pea jacket.

"Well, I'm carrying this heavy study load," Jamey said. "Which is stupid."

"No time for balling any of the campus talents?" Mike led off. With what hope?

Jamey said no.

"Why not?" Poppy asked serenely, but the eyes in mischievous play.

Jamey tried to cool it with a grin but it died on his lips. To Mike then: "Are you going to go to Washington yourself, or is this just—"

"Hell no, I wouldn't put my face near any of that fuzz," Mike said. He would be mainly concentrating on the campus people, leaders or monitors who would be organizing the bus trips to the capital, outlining data for the trip and tips on self-defense in the event of hassles with police, marshals or militia. "What time are your buses leaving from here?"

"Practically at dawn," Jamey said. "Lyle Stinnett is in charge. But there's been a hangup. The company that we planned to rent the buses from has just announced they ain't taking our tainted money. They said pressure was on them not to carry the 'Commie peaceniks.'"

"Yeah," Mike said. "What're you going to do?"

"Stinnett is lining up an outfit from out of town," Jamey said. He had been watching Mike more carefully. No evidence of the recent run on speed. His eyes sparkled blue and clear; his cheeks were ruddy; his mind a-bristle as of yore. If there was any change at all it was in the way every now and then he would side-glance at Poppy, a hasty, almost furtive, feverish shot of a look.

"Oooh, look at that lovely poisonous stuff!" Poppy declared as the waiter placed the three succulent bubble-hot pizzas before them. "It could like almost replace sex, couldn't it?"

He and Mike ordered beer, Poppy tea.

For a while they did not speak, making the most of the Niko specialty.

"Here, Mike—" Poppy put in his mouth a small wedge of the pizza. "You like anchovies."

A student waiter changed the music on the record player behind the counter: Judy Collins in Leonard Cohen's "Suzanne." They listened to this, and when it was over, Poppy said, "That's nice. I've never heard it until now." Then: "Have you ever heard from that guy who wrote you? You know—Avant Records?"

"No."

Then Poppy said, "The Gross-Outs are going to make their first record. Did I tell you?"

"No. When did it happen? Who is it for?" Jamey said.

"I don't know when it happened, but when I ran into Terry Bruner he was all full of it." And Poppy told him how Bruner, the lead guitarist of The Gross-Outs, had said the group had a contract with a new label, a small company.

Now in the musicless room the sounds of the other people around them became more audible. Poppy nodded toward the booth behind Jamey and said in a half-whisper, "Some things just never change, do they?"

Jamey listened. He heard the familiar fragments. A freshman getting the fraternity treatment, or part of it, coming with unethical zeal in advance of the regular rush season.

The Greek god now saying, "Well, tellya, Mitch, I'm not going to disparage the Tri-Gams, but let's face it, I mean, let's look at the logistics. The Tri-Gams have a lot to offer. Right? But let's look our way, the Delta Phi's. Like we have eighty-one brothers and—count 'em—a hundred and sixty-two little sisters. How d'ya like that kind of arithmetic, Mitch?"

Mitch says, "Well, uh, would you tell me a little more about the brothers?"

"Y'betcha, Mitch. Well, we've got a pretty well diversified gang: one Delta Phi, for example, is from New Canaan, Connecticut, his father is a wheel with NBC; another Delta Phi is from Chicago, his old man is president of Elways Steel; another Delta Phi is from Los Angeles, his dad is a judge in Superior Court—but listen, Mitch, I don't want to bore you with a *Who's Who* of the brothers or how many guys at the house are in varsity sports. Let me just say, before I forget it—and I guess this'll be of some interest to you, Mitch, and I don't care how many other houses you go to. I mean, what we have—and even the Greeks don't have a word for it—we have a house mother who is real hip, I mean hip, you know: when a girl's in your room, this HM is suddenly blind and deaf and keeps blasting with The Beatles and The Doors on her record player. In other words, Mitch, I don't have to tell you what a gas our parties can be—"

A new selection from the restaurant's stereo killed off the Greek.

"How would you say it stacks up here?" Mike was asking.

"What?"

"The student body, how is it here? How many people here really get off their ass to do something?"

Jamey nodded toward the booth behind him. "You heard it, Mike. That's the scene. For the most part. Except for the usual small gang."

"Yeah," Mike said. "That seems to be it at most campuses. But it's a hell of a potent small gang."

"I don't know," Jamey said. "I mean, what's actually happening? What gets through? Not much."

"You're wrong, man." Mike played his fingertips against the flame of his hair. "The message is getting through. And something else too, baby. Who in the Administration likes the idea of going out of town to speak or attend meetings? I'll tell you: no one. We've got them boxed in. When the Secretary of State has to sneak into a place like a thief, and needs two thousand cops to protect him, we've got 'em boxed in!" Mike finished his beer. "Look, we have to start moving."

"Mike, will you wait? Don't start taking off." Poppy was still munching on the last wedge of pizza. To Jamey: "Like he's got a firecracker inside him. I mean, as soon as he decides he has to leave, that's it, the whole world has to stop so he can leave."

"Baby, finish up. We have to leave. I've got lots to go over with Stinnett." Mike crumpled his paper napkin into a ball and crushed it flat on the tabletop. "She always eats like a kid, trying to make the dessert last forever."

"Everybody wants the dessert to last forever," Jamey said.

"OK. I'm outvoted. Let's split." But Mike's rosy countenance darkened, a sudden rawness had come into his voice. Jamey was astounded. The flareup, almost paranoid, was that intense.

"Mike, I want more tea. We were on that bus for hours and I—" Poppy began.

"All right," Mike said. "How do I get to Stinnett's?"

"I'll take you there, Mike. Why don't we wait a couple more minutes—"

"How do I get there?" Mike said.

Jamey gave him the directions. But then Poppy put down her cup and reached for her pea jacket.

"No, you finish, you have some more tea, baby." Mike pushed her back down onto the seat. "You keep my friend company."

"We really ought to get over there." Jamey recognized now how easily this scene could break apart.

At the cashier's near the door, they paid the checks, and Jamey called to the pizza chef: "Bill, it was a masterpiece."

"Thanks."

Jamey said, "You're going to be on hand for Friday, right?"

"Oh sure," Bill said.

"You better make it," Jamey said, as Mike and Poppy left the restaurant.

The pizza chef leaned over the barricade of his kitchen. "Hey, Jamey, who's your little friend?"

"A friend of my friend," Jamey said.

"Tasty, hnn?"

"You be there Friday, Bill."

"Right." The pizza chef peered out the window at Mike and Poppy. He said wistfully, "The family who lays together stays together, huh? Who said that?"

"Shakespeare." Jamey started out to the street.

In the languishing twilight, the three moved off toward the south end of the town, to the off-campus apartment of Lyle Stinnett.

Jamey now said, "Incidentally, Mike, in case you want to call me—don't. It's possible my phone is tapped. Don't ask me why anybody would want to go to the trouble of doing it, but—"

"You sure?" Mike seemed calm and easy once more.

"I think so." Jamey told him of the call to Roy Billings.

"They must be hungry," Mike observed.

"Yes," Jamey said. "But I doubt if they'll do anything about it. I mean, what the hell can they do?"

"Nothing," Mike said. "Just reclassify you one-A. The Uncle can use your services."

"If Uncle Sam needs me, I'm going to go." Jamey saluted.

"How far is this pad?" Mike said.

"We're almost there." The apartment building was of recent construction: faceless, with the personality of a computer punch card. Lyle Stinnett's apartment was on the third floor, and his extra bedroom would save Mike and Poppy the price of a motel. Jamey preferred not to think of it.

He introduced them to Stinnett, and Lyle immediately took the flight bags into the other room. As soon as he returned to the small foyer, he gave them his official and effusive welcome. Lyle Stinnett, a liberated spirit from Virginia, had determinedly shaken every vestige of his Southern background except his accent, which was redolent of hot buttered biscuits and smoked country ham; he still had a certain courtly manner and a brand of teasing humor.

"You don't have to say a word," he announced, "your rights are guaranteed by the Constitution. You don't have to open your mouth. I may happen to like what you say but I don't approve your right to say it. Now let's get down to business here." He nodded toward the living room, where the other people were sitting. "I'll just fetch this lovely little gal a small drink 'cause I wouldn't want to see her lose that look. I'll say this, Jamey, you always have the nicest-looking ladies in tow. Is it your guitar?"

"It's all my money and high connections." Jamey followed them into the living room. He saw, with disappointment, that Roy Billings hadn't come. The others had: Bob Lothar, of the campus paper, Gary Einsberg, the premed, K.O. McNulty, Jim Wade, Reverend Tillou, Susan Sayres and another girl. Normally Laura would have attended. He was surprised to see Lincoln Karr there; Link was an economics major and very much nonactivist in campus affairs.

Everyone was drinking beer or coffee. Lyle came back from the kitchen with cans for Poppy, Jamey and Mike. Most of the people were sitting on the floor.

"Jamey," Lyle Stinnett said, "we've been talking for a while, and though we aren't getting anywhere, at least it's been dull." He addressed the others: "I'd like to hear what Mike here has to say—that is, I think we might benefit by it. He's a pro in this business."

Mike said, "Maybe later, Lyle. Thanks."

"All right," Stinnett said. "Then let's hear it from your side, Jamey, as per our phone talk earlier."

Jamey shifted on the floor, hunched up his knees, glanced around at the other student leaders. "I guess I know how most of us stand," he began. "Some of us—that includes me—are getting around to what Sartre says: 'There is no reality except action.' But this Friday, we're hung up on a special situation because Mrs. Johnson is not an official part of the scene." Jamey went on trying to explain his stand for a silent demonstration. "I know this kind of has the aroma of compromise. But the trustees of Mustang U. and the jolly green Chancellor happen to be very sensitive at the moment. Lady Bird is staying at Ross's house. In other words, it's become a personal thing too."

"He's bucking for some federal funds," one of the group commented.

"What the hell do we care what he's bucking for?" said another.

"Hey, Jamey, what is this?"

Jamey said, "Look, we have three things coming up: the march on the Pentagon, the New York Induction Center and the CIA recruiters who're coming here. It just seems to me that we should pile up some credits for when we need them. Why waste it on Lady Bird? I'm against it. I think we'll pull a lot more students if we keep the demonstration a quiet one, no violence. No stuff. If anyone is looking for that, don't count on me." He paused, adding, " 'It ain't me you're lookin' for, babe.' "

"I buy that," said K.O. McNulty.

Jamey got up and went into the bathroom, leaving behind him now a dissonance of disagreement among the group. But in the end, with the beer gone and not enough coffee to go around, he pulled a majority opinion to his side. Lyle Stinnett and Gary Einsberg were the holdouts.

"Jamey—" Lyle was calling from the kitchen now. "I swear there's not a grain of coffee left. Looked everywhere. Would you do me a favor? See if the Doughertys have any. Or try Andy and Paula—"

The Doughertys, a young married couple, language majors, were at home, but as it turned out, with just enough coffee to get breakfast.

When Jamey came in, the living room held that heavy-sweet fragrance: Dwight Dougherty was smoking. He offered Jamey the joint. Jamey said not tonight. When Dwight's wife, Claire, returned from the kitchen, her husband handed her the joint as she sat down on the studio couch beside him. Last year this couple used to have friends in, dropping acid about once a week. But there'd been some bummers. Since then they'd become conservative, sticking only to pot.

Jamey then tried the students farther down the hall. Though the card on the door read Andrew Ryan, Paula Heston lived there with him. Technically, on University records, she was registered in residence at a women's dorm. She was in fine arts, he in architecture. They had often helped get out signs and banners for demonstrations.

Yes, Paula Heston said, and turned off Jefferson Airplane ("Hymn to an Older Generation") on her way into the kitchen. "Tell Lyle he might as well keep this. We owe him I don't know what all." She gave Jamey the can of Medaglia D'Oro. Paula was a somber-eyed, handsome girl of long legs and long hair the color of teakwood. Andy Ryan swung around on the high stool by his tilted drafting board and lit a cigarette. He was gaunt and fair and bespectacled. Corduroy pants and open button-down shirt. "Sit down, Jamey."

"Thanks," Jamey said. "But we're still in there rapping about Friday. You're passing the word around, aren't you?"

"Sure thing," Andrew Ryan said.

"We've got about twenty-five signs done. They're in Straton Hall. Everybody pitched in," Paula Heston said. "One of the people brought one by earlier." She went into their bedroom and returned with the sign, a small one with small carefully wrought lettering. "This girl in Design Five did it." She held up the little placard:

LADY BIRD BEAUTIFIES
WHILE LYNDON BOMBS

"Oh, that's of the best," Jamey said. He laughed. "A whole song, a whole kind of fuguelike thing could be built all around it—"

"You ought to do it," suggested Paula Heston.

"I can't even find time to finish the ones I'm working on," Jamey said. "Thanks for the coffee."

"How's Laura Barnes?" Paula Heston said.

"Oh—she's fine," Jamey said.

"We'll see you Friday," Andrew Ryan said.

Later, in Stinnett's apartment, after the coffee was brewed, the final plans for the demonstration were refined. It was around midnight when the group broke up. Mike was still in conclave with Stinnett when Poppy followed Jamey out into the hall. She had been uncommonly quiet during the evening. She said, "I wish there was someplace we could talk."

"Yes," Jamey said.

"I mean, like it's just been too much for me, Jamey," she confided. "Is there anyplace I could see you?"

"The trouble is, Poppy, you picked one of the worst times of the year. The next couple days. Saturday's the game; that would have been better for me, I'll be out from under."

"We'll be gone by then."

He nodded.

He looked at her, his gaze private and painful.

"Well, listen," she said. "Can't we—"

"The only possibility would be, say, around five or half-past tomorrow. Could you—"

"I will. Where?"

"There's a place, The White Cat. It's close to my last class. It's the only time I can get away. Unless you could make it much later, like near midnight." All his unfinished studies rose before him, a tower of guilt. He gave her the address.

She said she would be there.

"You sure Mike won't get—"

"I don't know, but—well, I'll make it. I have to," Poppy said. "If I could let Mike go to Dartmouth and Syracuse ahead of me— but I couldn't do that. Look, I better get back—"

Her eyes reaching out to him in that way. Being with her now in this stupid, furtive corner only made his need more unbearable.

Oh, this was not of the best.

Poppy, go back.

Go West.

Poppy is come out of the West. . . .

So faithful (?) in love (?)

By the next day, working through half that night, he had cut down half of his work. (For what?) At five o'clock, after his philosophy lecture (young one-eyed Professor Scudder on the concepts of anxiety and absurdity in the work of Sartre and Camus), he hurried to The White Cat, Poppy already there waiting outside on the sidewalk, in the same corduroy microskirt and sweater and carrying her Navy pea jacket, her hair today hanging straight, ribbonless, scarfless—he saw her half a block away and his chest felt as if he'd been running.

"God, am I glad to get here," he said. "I wasn't sure this morning if I was going to make it. I had to squeeze in time to get to the campus security office to file the plan for Friday. Of all the goddam things. Christ, these people burn me down. You'd think we were planning to slip a bomb in Lady Bird's pocket. You OK, Poppy?"

"I guess." Then: "I just couldn't wait until now. What is this place?" She looked at the small windowless whitewashed facade with the black door. A sign: COME IN AND GOOF.

He opened the door for her. "It's just a place." Which was true, for it was part store, part coffeehouse and hangout, part pay telephone where you could get messages. Music going all the time.

"Hey, Jamey."

"Hi." Greetings to the pair behind the counter: the girl was working for her doctorate in history, the man was an assistant instructor in computer systems engineering. This little enterprise was a casual and often part-time project, for The White Cat closed during midterm exams or if the two decided to go skiing. The instructor had transferred from Yale and out of undergraduate nostalgia had modeled this place somewhat after The White Rabbit in New Haven. Stereo sounds suffusing the black-lighted room: *Outside the gates of Cerdes sits the two-pronged unicorn . . .* Brooker's voice breaking over The Procol Harum.

Through the dim incense-fumed room to the L-shaped black-lighted space in the rear, just an army cot, people sitting there with coffee. Jamey and Poppy sat on kegs in the corner and someone brought in the mugs of coffee. In the charcoal haze you could make out the gaudy gaiety of the posters by Cryk.

"I guess you can't smoke in here," Poppy said.

"No, at least not as far as I know." He sipped the coffee, then put the mug on the floor.

"I think I only have one joint left," Poppy said.

"I have some. I picked it up today. I thought if there was time enough, I mean, if you could get away, we'd go someplace—" He had stopped earlier to see a friend of his, from whom he bought grass once in a while, a senior active in experimental cinema, a member of the University Film Society. Jamey had seen him in the basement of the Audio and Film Center adjacent to the Fine Arts Building, found his friend there bent over the Movieola, and they'd gone into the john and Jamey bought a nickel bag. It was good pot, his friend assured him, and this was usually true; it wasn't all prime leaf, of course; it had stems grated up in it and maybe a few seeds, but it was never bad. This friend bought it from a city dealer and he used the profits to purchase his own film equipment as well as lights, projectors and other materials for his mixed-media studies.

Poppy stirred on the uncomfortable keg. "It's nice here. I like it. I don't even want to think of leaving." Her hand over his, for an instant, then she lit her cigarette.

"When are you supposed to get back?" He watched her face: the smoke rising, a pale and diaphanous veil in the black room.

"I'm meeting them at seven. Listen, Jamey, what am I going to do? I don't know how or when it's going to stop, I just can't take it anymore, the way Mike is, I don't know how to cope—" She looked up at Jamey and then looked away. The two couples nearest them sitting on the army cot, leaning back on the zebra-striped air-filled plastic pillows, had stopped talking. Now the music from the other room, The Fish in "Eastern Jam."

When the two couples got up and left, Jamey and Poppy took over the cot, sitting back against the air cushions, and Poppy said, "I mean, I don't know; maybe if I could get away with him, maybe if he got behind some acid it might break this thing."

"I wouldn't try it, Poppy."

"Oh, I won't, don't worry. I'm too scared after what happened back home. I'm having enough trouble keeping him off speed. Though he's been fine for a week, like he's been busy and I've hardly ever left the place except to buy whatever we need. But how long can I go like that?" Poppy did not even pause; she kept talking, her voice low, breathy, rapid. "Would you believe this, Jamey—when I said why didn't he make this campus tour alone, he almost flipped, not right away, but—you know—he came back about two hours later, flying on meth, and scared the hell out of me, I mean, like the way he was, all that drive and threatening me, he grabbed me once and lifted me up as if I was—was a pillow and said he'd throw me out the window, I mean, this just bewilders me, bugs me all the time. Oh, he's fine here, in front of you and the others. It's the minute we're alone that he can start. You know in the hall last night when we were talking? Well, what were we talking about? He kept asking me later, and did I telephone you today and why did I have to go with Stinnett this noon to the Co-op? I mean, this is how it gets, and when you think what we used to have going, what a decent relationship we had. It's not only that though, all this wild possessiveness; he's turning paranoid on me. I look at him sometimes now and I don't know how I could have ever loved him, and even if I didn't, our relationship was wonderful. You remember. We were free and we looked after each other. Now look at it. Just when everything he's been working for is coming up—"

Jamey said, "This all started to happen when I—"

"Yes. But he likes you. He digs you."

"I feel the same way about him."

"I know," Poppy said.

"He's a special guy," Jamey said. "I mean, what he's doing, the risk he—"

"He doesn't think of it that way," Poppy said. "You know how he feels. He says no matter what happens to him here—like even if he gets caught—it won't be as bad as being part of the war. But, God, if only he wasn't so kooked up about me and—then, well, there was this other thing—"

"What?"

"Not now. Jamey, listen, is there anyplace we can go? Oh, Jamey, I wish you could be with me. All the time."

His arm under the small of her back, around the small waist, being with her. All the time. How? Strawberry Fields. Forever.

"Oh God—I'm so fed!"

"Poppy—"

"I don't know. I'm so fed. I mean, it isn't only Mike. It's everything. I get this feeling, Jamey, sometimes, like I'm choking. The whole scene now, it's just getting—I've never been worried before."

"Worried about what?" Being with her. All the time.

"About me," she said. "I mean, I'm fed with what I've got, with what's around me, and I don't know what I want. Maybe it's coming here, maybe that's it. I mean, when I left California I never wanted to see another campus. Now it looks different. Like what am I doing hung up in that place in New York? It's nowhere, isn't it? I mean, it used to be fine, but it's nothing—"

"You're not talking about maybe going back to school?"

"I don't know," Poppy said.

"All I've been thinking"—Jamey voiced it for the first time, though it sounded unsure, probing, as if he was listening for the truth beneath the tone—"all I've been thinking is am I wasting my time here and should I get out? I mean, I don't know if I can groove on this anymore. If I had a reason—it wouldn't even have to be a good reason—"

"If you got out what about the draft?" Poppy said.

"I don't know. They can reclassify me. I'll fight it any way I can," Jamey said. "I mean, if they decide my back is all right now. But if I get out of here, where do I go, where, how? My father keeps boxing me in, he counts on me now. He's waiting until I walk in with my great big gold seal from Mustang U. He talks about it much more than he used to, it's in every letter." Then he said, "Maybe, Poppy, what'll happen is that you'll start in again and I'll get out. Christ, what a lousy black idea that is." Kissing her. Unaware or uncaring about the three people who just came in and were sitting nearby on the kegs, as a track from "Magical Mystery Tour" began. "Listen, I've got a lot of work, but if you could—I mean, if you can stay out awhile, is there any way you could stay away for a while?"

"Why?"

"I thought I'll get the bike and we can scramble out of here, out of town, I mean, not far. To Platt's Landing. It's dead there. On the river. We could go there, if you—"

"Oh yes, let's. Let's."

"What about Mike?"

"I don't know. He's with Stinnett. But I can't call him, I can't tell him anything; no matter what I tell him he'll— Oh, let's go, let's, Jamey."

Jamey was back at The White Cat in less than fifteen minutes. His blanket and the FM packed on the Harley. Poppy was waiting at the curb. She was wearing her pea jacket. She got on the bike, settling herself in back, and as they started off she edged up against him, the crescents of her arms clamped around his middle.

Uphill, upriver, the Harley snorting, gaining speed, and soon the dim lonely lights in view, Platt's Landing. He parked the bike. The riverfront street of this no longer popular resort was an invalid now, crutched up by one neon-red bar, a sad diner, a boarded-up marine-repair shop. He got the blanket and the FM and led Poppy down the cracked concrete stairs to the shore and to the old gray pier sagging there. But beneath it, on the marsh grass, it was cool and private.

Jamey put down the blanket, and they sat down and he turned on the FM, tuning in on Cream, the middle of Clapton's guitar. They sat there and listened in the dimness above the riverbank, no life anywhere except the swoop or peep of a marsh bird or the drifting lights of a river tanker: soon the river would begin its winter freeze and the shore trees would be gaunt.

There was a scudding of clouds across the moon that gave this October evening a dappled, elegiac blur.

Now The Doors. "Light My Fire." Poppy clasping her knees,

more brightly saying now, "I don't know why, this reminds me of some places like between Monterey and Carmel, I mean, the kind of misty lonely look. You know? It's not the same, but there's that feeling."

"Yes." He toned down the music. They sat side by side not talking anymore, Poppy so quiet, as if to erase somehow all she'd said at The White Cat.

Then she opened her pea jacket, turning to him then. An offering.

When he drew her to him, she sighed and arched her hope and her despair against him. Jamey could sense it, just as he felt his own unsureness and his rampant discontent.

"Oh, Jamey—" She breathed his name in that good way. "Oh, Jamey."

"Poppy. Baby."

A long flat barge plowed sluggishly through the waters, blunting its way upriver.

Jamey brought out the small envelope of pot and the papers, and he sat cross-legged and rolled two joints. He lit one and handed it to Poppy. She sucked in and returned it to him; after he had inhaled he kissed her and they parted their lips, letting the smoke rise, fan out between them. From the radio, The Byrds in "Space Odyssey."

Oh, this was of the best.

Yes.

And when they finished the first, they had a second, and that was all.

It was getting cooler, a chill mist edging in from the shore, though by now they were immune or indifferent to it, Poppy slipping out of the microskirt and sweater, and when they were nude he pulled the blanket up from one side, then let it fall, for Poppy in the magenta evening was something he couldn't deprive his eyes of, yes, the young breasts modest yet full, a joyful palmful, ah yes, so much gender in this diminutive package, the subtle swell of her belly and the slim eager thighs and the small narrow ankles, Poppy like an offering, not only to him but maybe to love itself, for this is how it was or could be with Poppy, now his nakedness shielding hers from the cooling outer world, though that was not enough or not the true loving, not for Poppy, who

138

had to give you all there was to give, as if her giving was the last love rite in the world, so that his giving was the same, that surge inside him taking him over the crest of all past loving, her slipping down and caressing him, her mouth, the joy of her tongue warm over him until he could not bear it, moving then, sitting up swiftly, swiftly as if not to lose that surge or essence, Poppy dainty yet weighted, as he held her there impaled until she shattered the night and collapsed on him and they fell sidewise, falling in helpless dizzying descent from some height as if the bed of matted marsh grass had been a mountain cliff.

Soon the hunger and thirst that often hit you after pot. He said for her to stay here and he'd get coffee and hamburgers at the diner. He dressed. And suddenly he laughed.

"What is it?" Poppy naked beneath the Navy pea jacket.

"'Jeez, I can't find my knees.' Remember that?"

Poppy laughed. But when he returned from the diner, with the cartons of coffee and the hamburgers sheathed in soggy paper napkins, her head was tilted downward, she was sitting there hunched into the pea jacket.

He put down the coffee and the sandwiches on the blanket. She looked up, smiling, then she got to her feet, the blue coat open, and she stood on her toes standing tight against him, drawing away then. "Do we have to go back? This place is so nice."

"I'm living here now, haven't you heard?" Jamey said.

"Yes," she said. "Oh, wouldn't I love to live here, right here."

"Me too," he said. "Thoreau with hamburgers."

They sat down and had the now tepid coffee and the gristle-meat in its blood of catsup and it tasted so wonderful and he could have eaten three more.

Poppy said, "Have you ever been to Walden Pond?"

"Once." Jamey told her of that one time he'd gone there on the Harley, all hyped by this lecture series on Emerson, Hawthorne and Channing. "Just to see what there was about it. But it was better in his book."

Poppy sipped the coffee, holding the carton with both her hands. She looked up and in a compulsive way said again how this place reminded her of that stretch of coast between Carmel and Monterey, which was more rugged and rocky but which had this nice blurred lonely feeling.

"There was this boy." Poppy addressing the rim of the coffee carton, Poppy talking up a groove tonight, so unlike Poppy. "It was during my sophomore year. I guess I was pretty stoked for him. One Sunday when his parents were away—they were in Hawaii on their twenty-fifth wedding anniversary—we went to his house out in Carmel Highlands. Right on this rocky beach. Like here except very foggy. Spooky, I mean, like we were wrapped in it. We'd dropped two caps before going down to the beach. It was his idea. Well, we went down there, and nothing much happened at first and then the fog started getting very blue and then paler blue and then wavering into orange, like all the molecules were changing. The sea started coming in like faraway music, louder and then fainter, louder and then closer. That's when he said he wondered what it would be like, I mean, doing it then." Poppy waited. "I'd heard a lot about how it can be. Anyway, the way we ended up, it was—"

"How was it, Poppy?" Jamey heard himself ask; he had vowed he wouldn't.

"What? Oh. Well, that part of it was nice," she said. "I mean, it was like fantastic, slow, floaty—that's how it seemed, though it wasn't. Anyway, the way it ended up was the worst. A real bummer. I think it must have been three or four hours when everything, the colors and the music, just went away and then there were these really gross images—the sea or the waves began to look like the house I used to live in when I was a kid and there were these two rocks turning into my parents and they were looking at me, that was obviously because I must have felt all this guilt, even though I don't think I really did; what was so horrible was the different things coming back, like when I got my finger stuck in an iron garden chair when I was eleven and it began to turn purple, then black, and I started to scream and faint and then my mother worked it loose, or tried to, and my father running around trying to get help. When I came down I was so depressed it stayed with me for days, I know I never made any of my classes on Monday. His trip was bad too, maybe worse. He kept telling me about it afterward but I was too shook up, I scarcely heard. A week later he was killed. Crashed his car into a tree on the Big Sur. I don't know how it happened. I don't know if he was high. Anyway, it was awful. That's when I went into yoga. My parents had been into it and they were all for it." Poppy paused. "They're always into everything. Even before I am."

But he wanted to come back to the trip, he wanted to know more of how she really felt, but Poppy had delivered herself of that, at least she believed she had. So he never got there. All he said was, "Poppy, you never let loose like this before."

She didn't answer. "I think I'm cold." She took off the Navy pea jacket and put on her sweater and then put on the pea jacket again. She looked at him in the dimness. "I don't know. It was being out here, I guess. That's part of it. I started to tell you something else before, but I didn't; I mean, I thought it would like ruin the whole night—"

"Tell me what?" The music had given way to a talk show; he turned it off. He pushed himself back against one of the pilings.

"And also," Poppy was saying, "I couldn't talk about it in front of Mike. But what happened was, day before we left for here, I got this letter from my father. He—" She stopped; an old man, holding a flashlight, a can and a fishing pole, was passing by. She watched him. Then she said, "He was in his office in school and someone knocked on the door and came in. An FBI man. He wanted to know if I was his daughter. My father nearly died, he was sure something had happened to me. It turned out that the FBI wanted to talk to me because they were looking for Mike and they learned we used to see each other a lot around Berkeley. Anyway, that's it."

"Does your father know Mike's been living with you?"

"Oh sure," Poppy said. "That's why he's so nervous about this. He told them I'd gone East and that I was just—you know—traveling around visiting friends. He said he knew nothing at all about Mike. God, when I got that letter I changed overnight. I mean, I was very down on this whole campus tour—except for coming here. But after that letter, I couldn't split soon enough, and I'm in no rush to get back."

Jamey said, "I wish you could stay with me."

"Oh, so do I. I could, but—"

"I know you can't."

"But I can't go back to that apartment either. I mean, if I go back with Mike and they come up looking for him, which they

141

could do any time now, I mean, that would be the end of Mike."
Then: "The terrible part, Jamey, is that I should leave him, I
should. But how can I? I mean, I couldn't do that now."

Jamey said, "What about maybe you and Mike moving here?"

"How do you mean, Jamey?"

"I was just thinking. You could live in town here. Why not?"

"Oh, that would be— No, he'll never go for anything like that.
Never."

"Why not?" Jamey said.

"For one thing, he really has to work out of New York. But
there's the—the other thing." She stirred and edged over closer to
him.

"You mean me," Jamey said.

She nodded. "Of course. He'll translate it that I want to be near
you," Poppy said. "And I do."

"Look, Poppy, I could at least suggest it," Jamey said. "Anyway, you've got to tell him about what happened with your
father."

"I'm not even sure he'll believe it."

"Show him the letter or call your father. You can do it from my
place," Jamey offered.

"Yes," Poppy said. "But I know how it'll work out. He'll say
why don't we move, find another pad somewhere, and that'll be
something I can't say no to." Then: "Oh, Jamey, if at least we
could only work it out—living here, I mean. Though I know it'll
never work. I mean, I know he'll be back on meth— Oh, Jamey,
what—I don't want to know what time it's getting to be, I don't
know what to do—" She pressed against him and then she said
couldn't they have one more joint before going back.

They smoked in the murky cooling night. He turned on the
radio and they listened, not saying anything, for a long time.
Donovan's delicate Scottish lilt.

And Poppy's hand, cool and slender, under his sweater.

But suddenly there was this feeling, Jamey felt it coming down
on him and around him: he felt enclosed.

Enclosed.

Not that he minded, it was just that it was new or unexpected.
He knew what it was to be encroached upon—his father, some-

times Laura or his guilt, the Chancellor. But that was not the same.

This sensation was different, this being enclosed.

Maybe he even wanted it. Still, it didn't go down, at least not yet. And yet, he wanted all of it to be of the best, just as coming here had been of the best, Poppy's closeness, her essence, her femaleness, how he wanted it. Then why this unwanted sensation? Like a warning or a fear or a kind of cop-out?

When they returned to the campus it was almost ten o'clock. He let her off near The White Cat. She said it would be bad for them to show up at Stinnett's and risk the hassle with Mike. She was right, and so it was left, simply, that she'd gone to a movie. Which was all she could say except the truth. And neither she nor Jamey could blow the truth at him, not at Mike, not now.

Back to 17 Beech Street. He tried to get into the rhythm of ordinary nights, the shower, pajama pants, the music, the settling down at the table in the recess of the bay window to finish the studying.

But unlike the ordinary nights, he couldn't focus on the books at all: his mind kept drifting back to the riverbank and Poppy there and all she'd said and how it was with Mike, that great indefatigable Mike doing all he had to do, untiring, his neck far out for the ways of peace, yet hung up in his own private war. . . . Jamey's thoughts kept wavering, fluttering and always drifting into that shore (like Monterey fog?).

But when he was able to turn off, what took its place was tomorrow. The demonstration.

Finally he ended the music. He got out his guitar and stood, disconsolate, leaning against the window of the bay, and he quietly played random songs of others and then he tried his own "Everything to Live For," but he wasn't there, not now.

What he did then was surprising, though it wasn't: he'd felt it working on him ever since they'd been at The White Cat this afternoon, and the way Poppy had been, and he worked on this because it was like an escape or a different track for him, because it could be light of heart and stranded with fancy and private. He called it "The White Cat." He got a start on the melodic line, bending it now to the beginning of a lyric:

143

The White Cat
Is a nowhere place
Where the smoke curls up like ebony lace
But the colors of my mind entwine your face. . . .

Early afternoon on Friday, a gray and uneasy day, Mrs. Lyndon Johnson and her secretary in the mighty Continental reached the house of Rossboss. It was just a few minutes before Jamey got there, having time between classes. He went across the street. He watched the meager show of student pickets walking up and down beneath the sunless russets and saffrons of the autumn trees. The Chancellor's two-story white clapboard Colonial manor house, with its Palladian window elegant above the paneled front door, looked dim and empty; though of course Secret Service people were already bushy-tailed occupants.

That's when he saw the rather fragile blond girl with the delicately painted sign: LADY BIRD BEAUTIFIES/ WHILE LYNDON BOMBS.

Mrs. Johnson stepped out of the car, indifferent to the display of pickets. She looked, from where Jamey stood, much more attractive and certainly younger than he had expected. The pickets paused and waited until the First Lady had passed and entered the house.

Two men not far from him were watching Jamey. They made no attempt to disguise their interest. He thought of his telephone line. It was all stupid. Like a cartoon about The Police State.

He moved off.

To higher learning.

On Friday afternoon at four-thirty, with guitar, he arrived at the quad of the College of Liberal Arts. Lady Bird was scheduled to make her speech in Ames Auditorium at five o'clock.

Students were milling around; it looked like a turnout. He was surprised to see so many people who on campus had always seemed very straight and traditional; uninvolved in events like this. Advance announcements in the campus paper of the "silent demonstration" had drawn them here, as Laura had said it would, as K.O. McNulty had promised. "Promise me a silent show and I'll deliver," K.O., the always eager-beaver overachiever, had said yesterday. The Chicago world of wholesale mortician suppliers would never be the same after K.O. entered the field.

There seemed to be a K.O. McNulty or a Lincoln Karr at every school, the guy everyone admired or envied. Like The Kinks singing "David Watts."

Jamey made his way to the center of the quad, to the Scott Memorial Fountain (Cornelius Elijah Scott, Class of 1889). He leaned his guitar against the marble lip of the giant basin: unsacred ground where a year ago he had stood and downed the can of lager and broken the Chancellor's hope of a dry campus.

Soon Lyle Stinnett, tall and ambling, appeared with Mike and Poppy; and then more student leaders joined them. Other people were setting up microphones and running lines into the mock seventeenth-century-Gothic dining hall which rose anachronistically midway between the fountain and the concrete umbrella that was the auditorium.

He saw Dwight and Claire Dougherty.

Gary Einsberg and Bob Lothar arrived. They were carrying bullhorns. They gave them to two of the monitors.

Jamey kept seeking one face: Roy Billings. But Roy was not around. Not yet. At this moment, even more than earlier, Jamey felt the loss of his friend and ally. A year ago he would have been at his side. Six months ago Roy would have been here. Calendar time was getting to mean very little anymore.

Another look around the quad. His anxiety lodging itself. He turned back to consult with the others of the ad hoc committee. He saw Laura coming then. She was with Lincoln Karr, and Susan Sayres, the earnest chestnut-haired history major, and Sue Burke.

Joining them now was Reverend Tillou, the young Assistant Dean of the Divinity School—Tillou, reedy and tweedy, hazel-eyed, hair still crew-cut as of olden times, his fine aquiline nose already a-quiver with the challenge of this protest.

"Listen, fellas," Reverend Tillou said at once and with unashamed exuberance, "I don't mean to butt in but I have a spectacular idea as a follow-up to reinforce our show of silence. Why don't we ask everybody to fast tomorrow? Omit dinner. When Mrs. Johnson returns to Washington the news will catch up with her. It would be spectacularly impressive. For some reason it means something when Americans sacrifice dinner. What do you think, Jamey? Lyle?"

Jamey said yes. Susan Sayres agreed. Laura felt it was too much. The others might have been too hungry to give an objective answer. Someone said, "No—not on a football weekend."

Lyle Stinnett was doubtful: "It's action after the fact."

Reverend Tillou was undaunted. A smile cracked his craggy young face. He left them, striding off, long, strong, tough as a gong, to stand with the divinity students and the chaplain gathering now to the left of the fountain.

A phalanx of local police had formed to safeguard the First Lady's arrival at the auditorium. She would be escorted by the Chancellor.

Inside the auditorium Mrs. Johnson's secretary, who'd come to the University two weeks previously to see about the arrangements, was standing in the foyer talking with the press and passing out mimeographed copies of Lady Bird's speech to people from campus publications. Television crews were a-bustle in a labyrinth of cables and cameras and audio equipment.

"No one is working harder at peace than the man who's our President," Mrs. Johnson's secretary told one of the group.

Jamey waited. He was warm in the chill afternoon; he opened his denim work jacket; beneath it was a black turtleneck sweater. His forehead was warm. He kept pushing back the thick blond hair. His nerves were getting tight: he could tell, he could see, that certain people, like Bob Lothar and Lyle Stinnett, now that the time was here, were growing restive, impatient. You could see they were probably already regretting their decision on the protest.

He looked back and he saw Mike. And Poppy.

He saw Lincoln Karr frowning in contemplation.

Sue Burke was nudging him. "Where did those people come from, those pickets passing Straton Hall?"

"I don't know." Jamey was not overjoyed: half a dozen students on their way to the auditorium were carrying signs, all grossly obscene, with intimate suggestions for the President's personal life.

As they moved past Straton Hall and other dorms, another group, a clot of high school and town people, were also arrowing in on the auditorium. They were carrying signs urging SUPPORT FOR OUR BOYS IN VIETNAM and JAIL THE DRAFT CARD BURNERS.

146

Jamey and Gary Einsberg took off. They ran through the now thick crowd of milling students, they reached the picketers, a line of zealous freshmen, just ahead of two campus policemen. It was not difficult to turn them back. Jamey assured them they could flaunt their messages *after* the First Lady had gone.

In less than half a minute, as Jamey and Einsberg returned to the fountain, the Continental limousine arrived and Mrs. Johnson was quietly guided into the foyer of the auditorium.

A reporter from *The New York Times* had sauntered over. He spoke with Susan Sayres, Lincoln Karr and Laura. Why, he wanted to know, had it been decided to hold a silent demonstration?

"Because"—it was Laura who answered—"demonstrators are usually featured as irresponsible or misfits. I mean, here on campus most of the people are very responsible. It's like saying everyone here smokes pot or takes LSD. A lot do maybe, but the great majority don't and the great majority are responsible and reasonable." She glanced over at Jamey and then walked away to rejoin Link.

"Jamey—" Roy Billings was standing in front of him. Roy, in corduroy suit with a vest that didn't match, and wearing his glasses, held a cardboard carton. On the side, printed in large black letters: DROP YOUR DRAFT CARD IN HERE. SEND YOUR COMPLIMENTS TO WASHINGTON.

"Hello, Roy," Jamey said. "I was looking all over for you. I—"

"Yeah." Roy seemed cordial. "Before this little prayer meeting gets going, Jamey, we're just passing this around."

Jamey looked at the box. Lightly he said, "And you want a little help from your friends."

"I—" Roy began.

As now Chief Kavanaugh of the campus security office, accompanied by a gray-suited man, reached the fountain. "Mr. Billings, I don't think anything like this is called for. Nope. Not here. It is not on the plan filed in our office."

Roy Billings turned. His round brown face held the hint of an impudent smile. "It was a last-minute idea," he said to the Chief. Chief Kavanaugh paused, fingered the blue coat of his mock uniform. He was a robust figure, with heavy-lidded blue eyes and filaments of white hair sprouting from his large ears. "The First

Lady," he said very slowly, "the First Lady is going to take"—consulting his watch—"is going to take the rostrum in there in seven minutes. We can't have any disturbances. Better to make sure of this now instead of too late." He looked at Jamey. "Mr. Mieland, according to the plan you filed with our office—"

"We plan to follow the plan"—but Jamey knew his cool was going.

Chief Kavanaugh arched his silver brows as he studied the carton in Roy Billings' hand. He consulted his gray-suited companion. The man identified himself—FBI—a quiet, bland man who was firmly muscled beneath the anonymous gray suit. He spoke to Roy Billings: "The federal law requires you to carry Selective Service registration cards at all times. Failure to do this can result in a delinquency ruling, a one-A classification and an immediate induction. And"—a portentous pause— "today, with the First Lady at the University—"

Roy Billings interrupted: "Can I say something, sir?"

"Of course."

"You see, sir, I don't care," Roy Billings said quietly to both men. "You see, where I come from Beautification isn't going to help much, and so today we—"

"You have every right to say what you wish, as long as it is not with the intent to incite—"

"Some of us"—Roy Billings resumed even more quietly, and looked down at the carton in his hand—"some of us don't see much percentage in getting killed for 'freedom,' or any of the other wonderful benefits some people don't seem to get at home."

"The First Lady," Chief Kavanaugh said, "is going to take the rostrum in five minutes." A pause. "We don't want to see any kind of disturbance. If this is to be a silent demonstration—"

"It will be," Jamey said, but out of impulse and conviction, and also out of some inchoate need to regain the rapport of his friend Billings, he pulled out his draft card from his wallet and dropped it into the carton. "This is silent," Jamey said.

"That's right. It surely is." Lyle Stinnett stepped up with his card and let it fall into the box.

Chief Kavanaugh looked away from his watch long enough to witness this. But before he could intervene or even speak, Roy Billings lifted out the two draft cards.

148

"Now listen, Roy—" Jamey said.

"Just a black silence, you see." Billings handed back the draft cards. "Here's the thing, Jamey—if you liberal people joined in, they're apt not to take us seriously enough. A lot of people don't, you know."

Billings, the carton under his arm now, moved off, erect, calm, making his way to the cluster of Negro students standing near the Gothic dining hall.

By this time the long quad was dense with people, close to a thousand students.

Chief Kavanaugh said the First Lady would be taking the rostrum in exactly three minutes, and then he and the man in gray separated. The Chief moved with impressive strides to the auditorium, leaving a nimbus of anxiety around the fountain.

Gary Einsberg said, "Hey, Jamey, I thought you were going to sing some of—"

"Too late now," Jamey said. He then hoisted the microphone up to the marble rim of the fountain. A minute later he leaned forward and said, "Your attention, everyone. Your attention, please!" He had to say it several times. Then he said, "Would everyone now please remain quiet. We're going to remain silent for the next fifteen minutes. Thank you."

Thus it began. He leaped down to the ground. Slowly the students began to turn around to face Ames Auditorium. Slowly the tide of voices receded, and then this mass of demonstrators stood still and did not utter a sound.

While inside, the wife of the Commander in Chief would be speaking on beauty.

Jamey, at first, was surprised, relieved by the perfect show of silence. His tenseness began to ease off. Once he looked over to see Laura, seeing her in profile, the delicate tilt of her nose, the long amber hair, the dark lashes, Laura in open suede coat, holding notebooks, standing beside Lincoln Karr and Susan Sayres and Sue Burke, Laura looking straight ahead, ah, how cool. Three years ago in Alabama she had had all that daring and zoom, Laura bending over him that night when he lay on the street, nose bleeding, temple bruised, welted, his back injured, left there after the "slight fuss" with two citizens. That Laura had certainly altered, hadn't she? Not stopping loving him, but slowly inhibiting, chilling that first magnolia passion, taking second looks, drawing back, veering off to the middle road. Just as he had done. Until this year, this year of the Rubicon . . .

Beyond her, Jamey saw Lyle Stinnett with Mike and Poppy. She turned almost at the same instant to net his glance, but looked away again as Mike motioned to her for a cigarette.

Ticking of time: andante. The clock on the auditorium facade showing only four minutes had passed.

A thousand people and all this stillness unbroken.

So far unbroken. The mass of students standing, bareheaded, facing the auditorium. Facing in silence toward the unseen target.

In a way, as the time beat on, in a way it became impressive, this protest. Dignity. Responsibility. Like Laura told it.

Yet something was absent: that slow rage or resentment that gave tension to the ritual, that infused it with the blood of involvement—the feeling Roy Billings had all the time.

Silence.

Looked from here as though he would make it. He and the jolly green Chancellor. If anything went wrong, what then? Probation? Or worse?

Did it matter truly?

During this silence, like a Mass without music, he could ask himself what if he didn't make it? What if he ended up on the wrong side of the college gate? If that happened, it was his mother and father more than himself who governed how he would feel.

Your education, son.

Someone—Lyle Stinnett—nudged him back to the outer silence, which suddenly was no more: scores of people looking up, rightward toward the flare of sound.

Yes. It had been too good to believe or to last. From the right on the second floor of Noyes Residence, a dorm for lower classmen, from the now open casements came—

Oh no! Yes! The music, the raw electronic rock was unmistakable—someone's stereo blasting with the anticulture invocation of The Fugs. Hundreds of people around the fountain and the hundreds near the dining hall now turned, stirred, kept looking up to the second story of the dorm.

Already a guard of campus security was sprinting into the dormitory.

Jamey waiting an agonizing half-minute now. Some people laughed. Some grinned. Some began to snap their fingers or bob their heads. Jamey stood there watching, biting his lower lip in a spasm of new anxiety. Then people started getting restive, they seemed now to be bored and then they turned back to observe the silence again.

Seven minutes left now. Or seven years.

The Fugs had become muzzled. The quad all dignity and responsibility: Oh, Laura, Laura, I call your name.

He looked at the clock once more, the black hand not moving, but time moving, measured, tortured.

Still biting his lip, still standing so rigidly. Lyle Stinnett whispered, "Five minutes to go. You happy, daddy?"

Jamey didn't answer. Now instead of this tight waiting he began to feel a kind of boredom or impatience. He saw far in the front that someone had raised a large sign: HELL NO WE WON'T GO!

Someone tried to pull the sign down. Like a flag in a storm it shivered and twisted and tilted as its holder tried to keep his grip, and then it fell.

Three minutes to go. He whispered to Stinnett, "If this works—"

"What?"

Jamey shook his head.

The clock at last showed what he had been waiting for. Immediately he was back up on the fountain. Into the mike he said that the demonstration was now over. "Thank you very much," he said.

Some applause. It grew. The volume became rhythmic, strident: maybe it would even penetrate Chief Kavanaugh's rostrum in the auditorium. Then as quickly as it had begun it subsided, petered out into foolish, almost embarrassing quiet. Leaving suddenly behind a suction of anticlimax. Or disappointment? Or unfulfillment?

But it was over. Monitors using their bullhorns were urging people to leave the quad in orderly fashion.

All according to plan.

Where was Roy Billings now?

The FBI so polite. Taking off.

It was over. Pledge kept. Home free.

Free. Clean. Clear. He turned to look for Poppy. As he turned he heard the voices, high decibels of anger, not in one place but in several. But you couldn't quite tell what was really happening: small fights, brawls or recriminations harsh in the October dusk. It was as if some of the people, after the enforced or unnatural span of silence, needed to let loose.

It was there, yet it wasn't a deadly sort of trouble. Jamey wasn't sure what to do or if anything at all should be done.

The voices from the bullhorns came more urgently.

That seemed to inspire more chaos.

Poppy was motioning to him then, in pantomime playing the guitar. Then Lyle Stinnett picked up the guitar and handed it to him. Andy Ryan and Paula Heston pressed closer to him, and Andy said, "Come on, Jamey."

Gary Einsberg, in gray sweatshirt and tweed jacket, climbed up on the basin of the fountain and spoke into the microphone, calling for attention. It took a few minutes but it disrupted the cores of disunity in the crowd. Close call.

Jamey, strapping on his guitar, got up on the fountain. He readjusted the mike. As quickly as he could he tuned the strings. From a small knot of enthusiasts came cries of "Lyndon Tree." But of course he knew that he would be violating Rossboss' injunction; it would not be the kind of thing that was "tasteful" or "gentlemanly." Instead, because he had never done it before, he sang his newest, "Everything to Live For." He tilted his head down. The guitar, the color of meerschaum, was almost the same tone as his hair. He looked up:

Oh, you're lucky bein' twenty-one
Says the man
But why ain't your faces bright as the sun?
Says the man.
Can't understand
The youth of this land
Just can't understand:

You've got everythin' to live for
Haven't you?
Oh yes, you have.
Then why do you go 'round like soreheads?
Ain't we got rockets
Hey, and poverty pockets
Yeah, and those nuclear warheads?

   (What more do you want? What's got you down?
   In the land of honey and the Bunny Club.)

You've got everythin' to live for
Haven't you?
Oh yes, you have.
So why do you bug us and bait us?
We're facin' stilettos
Hey, and guns in the ghettos
Yeah, and gassin' the bastards who hate us.

   (What more do you want? What's got you down?
   Why, when I was your age, didn't have two nickels to rub.)

     But listen now, all you college men with honor keys,
     When you graduate and ship overseas
     You may get killed but you'll have your degrees.

You've got everythin' to live for
Haven't you?
Oh yes, you have.
This ain't no place to goof off in
Look at your flag a-flyin'
Hey, and the CIA a-spyin'
Yeah, and eyein' you from cradle to coffin.

   (What more do you want? What's got you down?
   Cameras print your fingers and photograph your flub.)

Yeah—if you can take what we give
You've got everythin' to live for.

Not everyone had heard him. The sound system had broken
down or been broken. Loudspeakers on the dining hall went

dead, so that he had been audible only in parts of the quad. Though now some cheers began and some clapping, and it grew, rising, becoming sharply fierce, like rain slanted by a sudden rush of wind.

It was unexpected. He hadn't been sure about it. It was unexpected. But the moment grew. This moment that was of the best.

As now, unseen by most, the First Lady and her party left Ames Auditorium and drove off.

Jamey saw it. Exit. Gone. The End.

Mrs. Lyndon Johnson could go home and say the student opposition had been real nice about it. Chief Kavanaugh, proud of the success of his surveillance, joined the escorting squad of Secret Service and town police.

A success: Jamey could almost say it. He'd held up his end, the promise of silence had been kept: attention, Rossboss; yes, yes, Laura.

Unfortunately, the song, while diverting the initial trouble and shielding the First Lady's departure, had acted to rouse other people to a new excess of enthusiasm. A group of SDS students, maybe nine or ten, pushed through to the fountain, climbed up onto the marble rim.

"What do we want?" one of them shouted out.

"Peace!" chanted the others.

"When do we want it?"

"Now!" More people joined in answer.

It was now Lyle Stinnett who, like the others, had to release his zeal: it was as if everyone wanted to project or continue the spirit of the song now that Jamey had stopped.

"Will we go?" Lyle's rich voice boomed.

"Hell no, we won't go!"

"Hell no, we won't go!"

It was happening, Jamie saw it coming, his first success had been too soon: like a Fourth of July celebration in which the Roman candles do not streak their rainbows in the sky until the holiday is over, the first of the demonstration didn't really get ignited until now.

The cries were carrying in widening circles, reaching out everywhere in the crowd, though only about half the students were actually responding. But without warning then, a new and ugly lava of sound erupted to the right of the Gothic dining hall: a vanguard of kids, some of them members of the high-school Anti-Communist League, were clustering together to intimidate the changing group.

"Hell no, we won't go," the students were still chanting.

"Fuck you, you will too!" the high school gang shouted back. "Fuck you, you will too!"

The cross-bombardment began. Two monitors, their bullhorns pointing toward the dining hall, began calling out, urging the people to please disperse. But the two warring groups heard none of it.

"Come on," Jamey said to Lyle Stinnett, "we better try to break it up."

"Let's go!" Stinnett's towering figure leaped ahead, along with Jamey, Bob Lothar, Gary Einsberg, Andy Ryan and the others.

A right angle, formed by the flagged walk in front of the dining hall and the pavement in front of the dorms, had become the focus of action. Jamey and the others ran straight for the two groups, who were facing each other shouting out recriminations, their voices often unclear, overlapping each other, a particular cacophony of anger not uncommon in many other places in America during this time. . . .

They parted; Jamey went to the left end, Stinnett to the right, others to the center, and they tried to calm the students, get them to ignore the threats, cool it and leave. But at this point they were in no mood to listen, the fever was high in them, in all of them. It was not a good scene and it became worse now when a number of town people, mostly factory workers (where had they come from?), joined the ranks of the high school group, so that now the day trembled with louder cries, hoarse, stammering, inarticulate curses and threats harsh in the academic air, and more and more college students moved in, but soon it became obvious that words left most people impotent, dissatisfied, so that some of them began striking out and fighting got under way, and then one of the townsmen, seeing Roy Billings and three other Negro students, called out, "Let's get these dirty peacenik bastards!"

"Draft card burners!"

Jamey saw it then: the stalwart, gray-haired man in the work shirt swinging his brawny arm in a fierce arc, knocking the cardboard carton of draft cards out of Roy Billings' hand.

And Roy lunging his fury out, grasping the man's thick wrist, trying to throw him. Another Negro student was picking up the carton from the ground when two high school boys jumped him, drawing at once a rush of college students into the melee.

Jamey saw that Roy's glasses had been knocked off, broken, and the man in the work shirt was shoving him back, both men talking, grunting, shouting, and Jamey moved in, elbowing his way between them, trying to elbow them apart, but all this did was bring in more campus people and more town people, but by then the older man's fist cracked against Jamey's face and he staggered back and fell.

Mike's voice above him. Mike plunging in to attack the man: "Why, you sonofabitch!"

Mike and the middle-aged worker bending, tilting back and forth in locked combat, but Mike freeing himself expertly and, his arm rigid, like a scythe, chopping the man down.

It was like another signal, a torch or flare bringing more town people and more students into the fray, and the fighting grew more vicious and wild. From somewhere the first units of police appeared.

Jamey was picking himself up when he saw the two policemen turn and stop Mike, who was trying to withdraw.

"You a student here?" One of the policemen detained him.

"Hmm?" Mike wiping his wet face, stroking down the savage red hair.

"You got your draft registration?" the second policeman said.

Mike clearly was delaying their interest, wiping his face, blinking his pale-blue eyes, patting his pockets looking for his sunglasses, finding them, seeing they were broken now.

"You got your draft card?" The policeman studied Mike.

Jamey looked around, looked back. But there wasn't enough time to work out any kind of intelligent plan to get the law away from Mike or Mike away from the law. All he knew was that this confrontation was pinning Mike in the one corner he couldn't risk being in. So that all Jamey could do was what he finally did: he moved into it, putting himself almost directly between the law and Mike: "Listen"—he addressed the law, blindly attempting to create any kind of confusion or diversion—"nobody here has any right to come on this campus to—"

That was when Ben Nettleton, a college official from the Chancellor's office, interceded. Ben Nettleton—hazel-haired and freckled, a plump figure who often did little necessary hatchet jobs for Rossboss—Nettleton addressed Mike: "Are you a student here?"

"I—"

"If you are not, please leave this campus," Big Freckles stated. Turning then to Jamey: "Let me see your campus pass." As if he had never seen him before.

Jamey stiffened. "Why should I?"

Silence: even the two policemen turned away from Mike to witness this mild insurrection.

Covertly then, Jamey tried to reach Mike with his eyes. Mike got the message, and Jamey turned to resume his defiance of the Chancellor's aide. "What if I refuse?"

Sounds now from the street in front of the auditorium: two green vans; more police.

"If you refuse, you can be suspended." Freckles made the warning loud enough to draw closer the ring of students who had formed.

"You can't suspend people for that," one of the students called out.

"What is this, a Fascist campus?" Another indignant voice.

Jamey grateful for all of it, seeing Mike carefully edging away, and Jamey going on: "What if I happen not to have my campus pass with me?"

"You mean what if you refuse to show it, isn't that what you're saying?" Nettleton seemed short of breath.

"Well—I mean, I didn't say that, you said it," Jamey retorted. Yes, Mike almost in the clear, moving ever closer to Scott Memorial Gate.

"You can be suspended for this," Frecklehead announced. Then: "And right now you can consider yourself under disciplinary probation. We've had enough, more than enough of this on this campus!" The gray eyeballs flinty with rage.

Mike making it, lost now, somewhere beyond the gate.

"Hey, Jamey, he can't do that!" someone called.

"What the hell is this?" Lyle Stinnett stepped in.

And with him, like a backwash, he brought the same gang of high school kids and some of the factory workers.

"Give it to 'em!" the town men urged the police.

"Yeah, give it to 'em, dirty peacenik bastards!"

"You can shut your ignorant face!" Stinnett answered, and then it started all over again, the cries now more hoarse and bellicose, the battling even wilder, though it didn't last, for the two green vans had regurgitated at least thirty policemen and more vans arrived, and the law came running across the quad, truncheons raised like lances, charging now in a blue phalanx, reaching into the moiling roil of the mob, and two of the policemen pushed Jamey off in the direction of the vans. When he hesitated they locked him in their grips. He resisted then, trying to free himself, not because it was possible but because it was still necessary to continue creating his own center of chaos. As he kept twisting in the blue tentacles he looked all around just to make sure, final sure, that Mike was not anywhere in sight. He wasn't.

In relief he slumped, let his weight drop, so that the policemen had to lift him and carry him to one of the green vans.

Inside on the two hard long benches of the van he saw Roy Billings and fifteen other students. One of them was a girl and her nose was bleeding. A Negro sophomore was holding his hand to a livid welt just under his right ear; the shirt sleeve of another student had been ripped away. Jamey looked down to notice for the first time that his kneecap was exposed and bloody in the gaping hole torn in his corduroy pants.

The engine started.

Poppy. Where was she, what had happened to her?

His guitar. Back by the fountain. What had happened to it?

Escorted—pushed—into the van now was Lyle Stinnett. Jamey edged over to make room for the law student. Immediately Lyle said to the other students, "I just want to tell everyone here about your rights. You don't have to talk when we get to the station. You'll be allowed one telephone call, I think. And just to make sure these bastards don't bug us, I'm going to call Professor Wyatt; he's on the law faculty and he'll come down." To Jamey: "How're you doing, daddy? How's your old back?"

"Great," Jamey lied. Then: "You think he made it, Lyle?"

"Mike, you mean?"

Jamey nodded. With a wad of Kleenex he dabbed his knee.

"Last I saw him," Stinnett said, "he was vanishing through Scott Gate like a thief. That man can move, can't he?" Then: "That was a nice little maneuver you made. You ever think of going out for football?"

"If he can make it, if he can get out of town—" Jamey said.

"What about that nice little gal? I surely do like her," Stinnett said.

"I don't know. If she went back to your place—"

"I'll be mighty pleased to look after her," Stinnett said.

One more student was assisted into the van and then a policeman got in and pulled the double doors shut, and the van jolted forward. Once Jamey got up to go across to the other bench to talk to Roy Billings, but the law directed him back to his seat.

Through the high grilled apertures of the moving vehicle, Jamey got swift glimpses of the free sky, streaked yellow.

Jamey wondered now if the others in the van felt as he did: this sensation of the bizarre, of disbelief, while at the same time feeling that it was somehow familiar and unstrange, and certainly believing it was happening.

What counted, however, was that it was he, not Mike, who was hung up here. If Mike made it out of town then at least the whole ugly scene would have been worth it.

And Poppy?

(*The White Cat/ Is a nowhere place/ Where the smoke curls up like ebony lace/ But the colors of my mind entwine your face. . . .*)

The precinct station nearest the campus was less than twenty minutes via van. It was of neglected brown brick. When they were unloaded Jamey was surprised to see a crowd of students outside, shouting encouragement to them and impolite injunctions to the fuzz.

Now the campus cargo going inside, about forty people filing into the muster room, all pale aquamarine walls and the clicktick of teletypes. All of them lined up like acolytes before the high oak altar of the desk officer: questions and answers and getting

159

the white arrest card, going upstairs then for fingerprinting, and filling out the card, though not all of it.

Not the kind you sent home to the folks: *Dear Mom* . . .

Prisoner's name . . . Sex . . . Color . . . Crime Code . . . Drug Code . . . Time and Date of Arrest . . . Pct. of Violation . . . Charge . . . Specific Offense (if drug involved, specify type) . . . Name of Arresting Officer . . . Shield No. . . . Complainant's Name . . .

Back downstairs in the glare of the white fluorescence. You are allowed to make that one telephone call: *Hello, is that you, Dad?*

Lyle Stinnett telephoned Professor Wyatt.

They were all escorted then into the green and grilled limousines of the police department and hustled to the night court. By this time the game was over, of course. Jamey was losing that arrogant and watchful spirit that had held him before. At least Mike had made it beyond the law. Five years in prison and/or . . .

Waiting in the court, huddled together, all of them in a room of evil smells, like hoods waiting to be processed.

Professor Wyatt of the law faculty arrived prepared to ask the college to appeal for withdrawal of charges—disorderly conduct, resisting arrest—but discovered that nimble Frecklehead Nettleton had already signed the complaint. The arraignment proceeded and the judge paroled everyone and set the hearings for November 12 and 13. Chief Kavanaugh had finally made the scene and watched it, nodding gravely from time to time. Reverend Tillou and several young professors had also come.

It was past 10 P.M. when the group of criminals was let loose into the innocent American night. Jamey and Lyle Stinnett were starting back, getting back to Lyle's pad; it was the only base Mike and Poppy had and if Mike was still around he would be there. They had just reached the bottom of the courthouse steps when he heard Laura calling him and he turned.

"I thought you might want this." Laura was holding his guitar. She was with Lincoln Karr and Susan Sayres.

"Oh Christ, Laura, I was worried about it—" He took the instrument. He thanked her. Her long amber hair was very bright in the lights of the night street.

Link Karr said did they want a lift; he had his GTO around the corner. Jamey said yes, and Link led the way, a senior with light-brown hair, quite a jock, an ace in tennis and lacrosse, but his grades always above average. Jamey had seen more of him this year because he'd seen him more with Laura, seen them at showings at the Film Society, at lectures and rock concerts; last week they'd sat in front of him in Ames Auditorium for the Simon and Garfunkel appearance. Though Karr politically was a very moderate cat, he had good instincts and Laura was probably making them better. It left Jamey uncomfortable but how else could he feel?

And also what could he expect? A girl like Laura was too attractive, she had too much to offer to sit around waiting for him, waiting for a few good words and some in-between love to groove on; she was bound to get someone else turned on, and if it wasn't Link it would be some other man. Right? Right.

They got into the car, Jamey, Stinnett and Susan Sayres in back, Laura and Karr in the buckets, and shortly they were in front of the apartment building where Lyle lived, and they said good night and hurried up to the third floor.

The apartment was empty. Mike and Poppy had gone. There was a note from Mike on yellow legal paper on Lyle's worktable:

Lyle—When you see Jamey tell him thanks.   M.

That was all. Except that on the floor near the bedroom there was half a package of organically grown dates Poppy must have dropped in flight.

The empty room now suddenly full of her.

O Poppy . . .

(Farewell, Ruby Tuesday?)

6 : THE CAMPUS

THE TREES are nude, blackly noble against the silver of a November sky, a chill noontime on the Saturday of the Big Game. In Able's Music Store on Kent Street, the proprietor, Dave Able, balding and middle-aged, a devout nonreligious Jew, a cultured nonintellectual, a pragmatic idealist, tells people there must be almost as much excitement on campus today as there was last month when Lady Bird was here. At least it seems that way. Never has football drawn such an influx, the campus thick with parents, an army of old grads in town; many of them are in the shop now, browsing as they did when they were students and the store was run by Dave's father. (Paul Whiteman, Red Nichols, Bix Beiderbecke, Bing Crosby, Tommy Dorsey, Benny Goodman; Gershwin, Kern, Youmans, Rodgers and Hart, Cole Porter.) They are browsing now among the racks of Sinatras and Show Music and the newest albums of the University Glee Club. . . .

Dave Able, near the doorway, presides on a dais behind a high counter, flanked by cash register and turntable. From here he surveys the action and checks to see that his three young assistants (all relatives) are roaming around offering to be of help to the nonstudent lookers. Dave Able fingers his rimless shades; they keep slipping down and he tips them back onto the thin ridge of his nose.

With the dexterity of a DJ he drops another record on the turntable, selections for the delectation of the alumni: a track from Mantovani's *Golden Hits,* and after that a track from *Man of La Mancha* or *Music to Watch Girls By.* On these Big Game weekends you have to accommodate your ways to the tone and temper of the visitors. Just as at the barbershop a few doors away, they put on extra help to handle the rush of boys who have to get their long hair trimmed so that the old man won't blow his stack. Dave Able has no children, alas, no son; but on what his wife, Rona, spends on fur or jewelry, he could send a son through college. Not that he begrudges her. She wears them only to prove something to her family. No, money is not the prime thing these days, business is good, too good to complain. And if rock or folk/rock is still a bit harsh to his sensitive middle ear—personally, he is a chamber music buff—well, that's the way it is, or, as those disk jockeys on AM radio keep saying every five minutes, "That's where it's at, baby."

Even so, Dave Able considers himself more than superficially aware of the taste and trends of the rock scene on campus. He can, and often does, discuss it with students. After all, he makes it his business to keep up, doesn't he? Wouldn't he be a *schmuck* not to? He reads the best, scans the authorities: Richard Goldstein or Paul Williams or Albert Goldmanor . . .

With a boy like Jamey, who has just come in, many a time he has had good talks. Personally, he thinks Jamey is *meschuga* for not going into rock professionally; he'll never understand this lanky blond kid. . . .

"Hello, Jamey. How goes the celeb?" For the kid's name has figured in newspaper accounts of the demonstration during Lady Bird's visit, and now a magazine has come out with a photograph of him standing on Scott Fountain with his guitar. He notices the boy is not putting on the kind of face he usually does when he comes in here; usually there is that half-hidden smile and the sea-colored eyes are less tense. He likes to wander around the store studying the albums, not just rock, though it's mostly the folk/rock he buys. Often, especially in the winter, Dave lets him listen to new records in the back, in the private office, but that's a privilege given to very few students, not that they ever ask for it. Unlike his father's time, when students wouldn't buy without listening first, the kids nowadays don't have to listen, they know in advance what they want and why they want it. But with Jamey it's different. He does more than just listen.

Today Jamey has on what looks like a new pair of olive corduroy pants. He wears a high black turtleneck sweater and an old suede jacket. "Anything special, Jamey?" Then: "You like that Otis Redding you got?"

Jamey's face softens. Yes, he liked it, and he talks about that one track, "I've Been Loving You Too Long." Then Jamey says, "Dave, are there any tickets left for the Donovan concert?"

"Right with you." Dave Able turns to attend to one of the grads, who is buying *Glee Club '67*. Another man, also wearing hat, topcoat, button-down shirt by J. Prell and striped tie, purchases a Herb Alpert and the recording of Chancellor Alvin Adams Ross's address to the National University Council. After the men have left, Dave consults his diagrammed book of the seating plan of Ames Auditorium. "For the Donovan? Let me see—naw, not much left, Jamey. They might have more tickets at The White Cat."

Jamey says he has been there.

"Well," Dave says, "I've got a few left in the very first row, but you know you can get a stiff neck looking up, and there's some left in the second balcony—"

"The first row then," Jamey says.

"Two?"

"Just one, Dave." Jamey hands him the money.

Maybe now, since the kid is here, he'll put on that record by Leonard Cohen, a Canadian poet who sings his own songs.

Dave Able turns back to Jamey. "You know what I got in back? It's not out yet. The new Bob Dylan. I just got it in, and if you want to go back and listen to—"

"Not right now, Dave. Thanks."

"No?" Dave frowns. "I remember when you couldn't wait,

when you practically tore a new Dylan out of the shipping box in the stockroom. Remember that?"

"I sure do."

"What's the matter today?" Dave ventures.

"Oh, nothing. I want the Dylan, but I guess I want to wait for a while." Jamey speaks slowly, reluctantly. "I mean, there's so much bullshit going down about it, I just want to wait and hear it later."

"Certainly. I understand." Dave recognizes that this is obviously not one of Jamey's prime days: ever since the demonstration when Lady Bird was here (even before that), something has been wrong. Maybe now it's his being on probation or maybe it's something that happened in Washington when he was on that march on the Pentagon. Who knows? Dave Able will keep his mouth shut. Instead he wants to get to another matter. He leans forward across the high counter. "Tell me, you going to make a tape of that thing you did when Lady Bird was here? Reason I ask is, a lot of kids have been in and asked if it was on tape or a record— No, I'm not kidding, I've had a lot of inquiries. Even before the newspapers. You're not going to do anything about it?"

"Well—right now, no." Jamey listens to the Leonard Cohen.

"Why not?" Dave Able says. "Look, I hate to repeat myself, Jamey, but when are you going to do something about this? Go to one of the record companies. It isn't too tough. Not nowadays. In my day you had to beg for an audition. Now it's a different story. I think, personally, you're crazy. Especially now after the newspapers. I heard one of them quoted your lyrics—"

"Part of it."

"I don't understand, Jamey. Personally, it's none of my business, but I think you're making a serious mistake. I can say that. I know you for a long time. Give it a try at least. After all, now you're a celeb, kid."

"One thing, Dave. I don't think I'd like it."

"Like what?"

"The music business."

"What do you care? That's not your concern," Dave Able says.

"Well, I mean—you know."

"All I'm talking about, Jamey, is you. Not other people. Remember, Dave Able is telling you this sincerely, this is not the old craperoo, kid."

As now two men, class of '40, hats, topcoats, striped ties, are at the counter with their purchases. Four albums: two Glee Clubs, a Richard Rodgers musical, an Erroll Garner.

Dave Able, in homage, puts on another recording of the University Glee Club, featuring all-time favorites of the alma mater—songs, chants and cheers.

Jamey steps away to leave, but Lincoln Karr has come in. This athlete is high scorer of the varsity lacrosse team. It's a game Dave Able, of all people, happens to enjoy. To him it is a rite of spring.

"Hey!" Lincoln Karr nods. He wears a mustard crew-neck sweater and brown tweed jacket.

"Hey, Link," Jamey says.

But there is a kind of woodenness between the two students, a certain stiffness or absence of ease.

"You look like you're still on DP," Link says.

Jamey nods.

"That hearing in court—I hear it's been put off."

"Yes," Jamey says. "It has. Until the end of the month."

"Sounds like somebody has connections, huh?" Link says.

"Oh, nothing corrupt like that," Jamey says. "Just that one of the girls, who got a slammed nose—you know, Sue Burke—it turns out her uncle is a wheel in the State Department and if a big stink starts in court it might embarrass him, so the word has come down to stall, delay it. At least that's what I heard from Stinnett."

"That's a break anyway," Link says.

"For everybody except maybe Roy Billings, who already received a letter from his draft board," Jamey says.

"No kidding. Rough," Link says. Then : "Going to the Donovan concert?"

Jamey says yes. He just bought his ticket.

"I got them last week—" Link Karr stops. Then: "Saw your picture. Terrific. The way that demonstration was written up, I wasn't sure I was there. Of course I was just more or less on the sidelines."

"They make the whole thing sound like it was a goddam football game," Jamey says.

"That's a fact. Well, got to take off. Going to the game?" Lincoln Karr asks and then the afterthought: "Oh, that's right, you're not very gung-ho in that department, are you?"

"I'll probably be around," Jamey says.

"You will?" Lincoln Karr is surprised.

"Well, just the part before the game," Jamey says. "There's that Sing-In at chapel—"

"Yeah. I know. I said maybe I'd show up for it," Link says. "I think it's going to be pretty corny."

"Probably," Jamey says. "But it's about the only kind of thing you can crank out now, I mean, for today if you want to get to the parents, the alumni. What the hell else is there? I mean, for me, as long as I'm on DP—"

"Oh, I don't know." Link loosens up, grinning. "You might as well beat up a few people, just to keep your hand in, Jamey. I mean, the campus can get pretty dull."

Jamey tries to match the other's smile.

More seriously then, Lincoln Karr says, "Of course, with the alumni all over the place, an antiwar Sing-In can aggravate a lot of people."

"Maybe that's the point," Jamey says.

"Sure, I know," Karr says. "But, you know—I mean, let's face it, why rub their noses in it."

"Why the hell not?" Jamey's tone seems suddenly hostile.

"Well, I think I might sit this one out today," the lacrosse captain from Baltimore says. "How's that knee, Jamey? Any better?"

"A lot. Thanks," Jamey says.

"Great." Karr's smile brings a fine luster to his face. "Well, see you."

More grads are lining up with their albums, waiting at the high counter as Dave Able puts on the flip side of *Glee Club '67*. He sees Jamey waving to him now, and he waves back. He turns to the men in the snap-brim hats, the topcoats and the regimental ties. He takes the money of their eager nostalgia while in counterpoint the Glee Club chants away to the merry bells of the cash register.

Across the late-autumn campus that midday Jamey made his dolorous way, looking at no one, moving out of habit to the dining hall in Scott Memorial quad, but when he'd almost reached the Gothic building he changed his mind and went all the way back to Kent Street: he was not up to seeing that many people at one time. Instead he stopped at Niko's for a pizza (was it a century since he'd brought Mike and Poppy here?). The pizza was good and it was even better because someone behind the counter decided to lay down "Like a Rolling Stone"—nice old way-back, rough-edge Dylan.

Afterward he went back to his apartment on Beech Street. There might be a letter from Poppy. In the entry-hall rack of boxes there was nothing. Four days since he'd heard, and then all she'd written was her new address. She'd moved from nowhere to nowhere, another pad, and maybe Mike would be safer now—ah yes, Poppy, more shadow than substance sometimes, a rare rainbow, seldom a sunset, a zephyr more than a storm, around him and under him and never there. Ruby Tuesday hello and good-bye . . .

Maybe even being away from her, maybe even that would be tolerable if everything else would get right, but nothing had and nothing was, everything that happened kept putting him uptight: the whole hassle with the police on campus and with the troops at the Pentagon, all of it left him shaken, the unreality of it, the sense of not being in America yet knowing this was what it had become, the way he had once felt in Mesa, Alabama. . . .

Coming back here with a heart not in it, his studies not getting to him. The professors—most of them—were unplugged, failed to turn him on anymore. . . .

If he left school—and the idea no longer startled him—what would he be getting into? The building bag. Mieland Homes, Inc. Nittygritty City . . .

Or another induction physical . . .

The gravelly voice of Dave Able still echoed, the only sound that got to him. For weeks now there was nothing much to hold on to. Oh, there were a few good moments like when he'd felt that flash after singing "Everything to Live For," discovering how he had been able to reach other people and inspire them to share his feelings; and the spurt of satisfaction seeing Mike lose the law; and then that moment of hope in the primrose Washington morning arriving in the capital with the busloads of students, meeting across from the Pan Am Building, walking down Seventeenth Street to the Lincoln Memorial, that first real flash, the sense of communion when he saw the thousands and thousands of people assembling on the grounds in front of that majestic, Doric-columned monument which loomed before him with such repose, serenity, peace.

Peace.

That's right. Lay the peace on me, man. Tell me a fairy story, Mommy.

Getting back to campus and reading the accounts for a week, certain papers and magazines doing that blackwash job, putting down the march with all those clichés of hippyshit instead of really digging how people felt, but lies and deceits was all that was going down and if you—

"Mr. Mieland—?"

He was confronting a man in the foyer of the apartment, and even before the man showed his credentials Jamey knew who he was.

"I hope you've got a few minutes." Mr. Arthur Olsen Regis spoke just as mildly and politely as his FBI colleagues that day of the demonstration in Scott quad. "I know you people don't have much time, but I figured maybe Saturday might be better. At least before the game. I assume you're going to the game—"

No.

"Oh? Well— Look, would you rather talk upstairs? It doesn't matter. We can stay here. Just a few minutes. And I must tell you, of course, that you have the absolute right of silence if you choose. Cigarette?"

"No thanks." Jamey wanted to tell him to shove it, yet, here again, he was drawn by that force that is sometimes hard to resist: being part of something that dazes you with its unreality in the real and commonplace world.

It would just take a few minutes, Mr. Regis assured him again, and since Jamey seemed reluctant to invite him upstairs to his rooms, they might just as well sit down over there on that bench beneath the windows.

"This is just a friendly inquiry." Mr. Arthur Olsen Regis sat down. He opened his brown topcoat, as if thereby to reassure Jamey that the interview would be brief. He was a compact figure, an unobtrusive forty-five, of oyster complexion, snub nose and short upper lip, very white teeth, stubby fingers, well-groomed nails. His hair was neat and black; it rippled back from his forehead in short neat waves like a washboard. He could have been a space scientist or an insurance executive or a hangman. "I want you to know how much we appreciate your giving your time now," he was saying. "I'm sure you can be of help to us."

"Help? In what way?" Jamey said.

"Let's put it this way," Regis said in that pleasant, sympathetic manner. "I've got a job to do and that is to see if I can get at some of the things that bother you people and the reasons why."

"You mean, like why did I turn in my draft card in Washington?" Jamey said.

"Well, since you mention it, it would be helpful to know if you did it out of, say, some emotional impulse or perhaps because others did it or if it was the policy of some group," Regis began.

"No, no one else was involved," Jamey said.

"In other words there was no organization, no group at all?" Regis gently pressed it.

"I can't say, sir." There was only one way for Jamey to repress his feelings. He said, "I got my orders and they are secret, they come on microfilm."

Blithely Regis proceeded: "Mr. Mieland, it would be very helpful if you could tell me what made you do it."

"Oh, I just did it for kicks," Jamey said. "Just a fun ball game."

Regis chuckled, yielding. "But seriously, of course I know you disapprove of the war in Vietnam—a lot of us wish it didn't exist —but you say you did this on your own. Correct?"

"No, sir. I was coerced into it," Jamey said.

"All right." Another laugh. Then: "I know you weren't forced into it, though sometimes people do a thing that has reasons that go back to other things or other people."

"How true." Jamey glanced at his watch. He wished he had his tape recorder here, hidden in his pocket or his fly, to immortalize this fine fucking fragment of American Life at Its Democratic Best.

"Let's put it another way, if you don't mind," Regis said ever so

170

kindly. "Do you think you would have done it if you didn't have a one-Y or a two-S deferment?" Adding, less gently, "In other words, weren't you pretty safe turning your card in?"

In rage Jamey started to answer but held back: these people were looking for everything except the truth. His sense of safety was what they wanted to establish, not the true reason why he did what he did. "I'm a lot safer than some of those poor guys who aren't in college or who have no physical disability, yes," Jamey said. "But in the long run I don't think anyone's safe from anything in this country. Not anymore."

Regis sat up. He was really plugged in now. "You really believe that, Mr. Mieland? Or is it something you hear around or read—I know how bull sessions are. Everyone has a gripe about the state of the world. Of course your friends must all feel the same as you do. Lyle Stinnett, Roy Billings, people like that."

"No comment, the Senator said," Jamey said.

Mr. Regis took out his 100's. "Smoke?" He extended the pack. "No thanks."

"I envy you. You're smart not to touch them," Mr. Regis said, and lit up.

"Not much point when there's pot, speed or acid. Right?" Jamey said.

"Mr. Mieland, all jokes aside—and I like a good joke as much as the next fellow—but to get back to our discussion. What we're interested in learning is how students formulate their intellectual beliefs. For instance, would you say it comes mostly from books that are part of your curriculum? Or is it sometimes some professor whose views stimulate you, or a visiting lecturer or perhaps some person who happens to be visiting the campus. I realize it's hard to put your finger on a thing like that, but—"

Maintain thy cool!

"No, I'd say, Mr. Regis—of course I'm just an average cat—but I'd say I picked up most of my simple ideas just from listening to decent everyday Americans like the President and some of his generals and the men who make riot-control equipment—you know, people who are really helping to make us the most beloved nation in the world."

Mr. Regis inhaled his cigarette.

Dashing through the foyer was K.O. McNulty. "Hi!" he called, and bounded up the stairway.

Mr. Regis shifted on the bench. "I meant to tell you that was quite an interesting song you wrote. I heard it. I thought it was very clever."

"Thank you."

"That's what college is for, a place where we can all speak our minds." Mr. Regis generously offered this pronunciamento. "I suppose that wasn't the first time you've ever done that song, was it? That is, have you played it for many of the students or people in your own circle?"

Jamey pursed his lips; he wondered when Regis would get onto a new track. He decided to call it. "Look, Mr. Regis, I thought you were trying to clear up certain questions about me. But all that seems to interest you is who is the sinister leader or leaders of the Communist Conspiracy on campus, who all the Kremlin agents are. And have I been redwashed and by whom—"

"Mr. Mieland, I've tried to level with you, but I think you're being unfair and unnecessarily facetious. As I said, I have a job to do and I appreciate the time you're kind enough to give me. But—well, let me ask you a hypothetical question. What would *you* do about Vietnam? How would you resolve it?"

Jamey said, "I'd say what Senator Aiken suggested: just announce we won the war and withdraw. It's simple."

"What about our military commitment?" Regis said.

"I don't think killing, bombing a people ever works," Jamey said.

"It worked in the Second World War."

"At least," Jamey said, "at least that war was *about* something."

Mr. Regis crushed out his cigarette in the ashtray. "You might have a point there, of course. I was in the Navy myself. In the Pacific."

Jamey looked at his watch again and said he really had to leave.

"Just one bit more, Mr. Mieland. Along the lines we were talking. That big demonstration when the First Lady was here—would you say that was set up, that is, organized on the spur of the moment or more planned by some particular group or by people off the campus."

Regis was right back grooving on that same track. "I really couldn't say, sir," Jamey said with heroic restraint. "It just sort of grew."

Then Regis casually said, "Do you happen to know a young man by the name of Michael Sturdevant?"

"Who?" Jamey said. He could ask it convincingly because Mike was someone you somehow never thought of as Michael Sturdevant.

Regis repeated it.

"No, I don't think I do," Jamey said. "Should I know him?"

"I don't know. Should you?" The FBI man, for the spark of a second, was charmless and naked.

"Mr. Regis, if that's all—"

"This Michael Sturdevant is not a student here, he's from California, but we thought he might be around," Regis said.

"I'm late, sir, and—"

"Oh—sorry." Regis rose. "I don't want to detain you."

"Have to be at that Sing-In at one-thirty," Jamey said.

"Oh yes. Well, enjoy yourself. And thank you very much for your time." Mr. Arthur Olsen Regis buttoned his brown topcoat and left the apartment foyer, moving with honorable strides into the free sheltered streets of academe.

The first thing Jamey did when he reached his rooms upstairs was pick up the object nearest him, a coffee cup, and hurl it across the room to the opposite wall. The mug lay shattered on the floor, shards from the temple of his temper.

Feeling better, though not much, he went to the bay window, to his worktable: books there for his attention, neglected last night, neglected totally and without conscience while he bent to pleasure, over his guitar, the pleasure of that kind of work, refining his melodic line, working out the rest of the lyrics for "The White Cat," finishing it. All it took was that letter, the second one from the man who had been with Avant Records and who was now a producer with a new label. It reached Jamey this time after the newspaper accounts, though what really reached him was the fact that this man had sought him out long before the Lady Bird incident.

Now he went to the bathroom and rid himself of the virus Regis. A few minutes afterward, as he was leaving to go to the

Sing-In at the chapel, his telephone rang. Into the alcove, to the bed table. What now? Who? The Chancellor's office? Roy Billings? Poppy . . .

"Son? Jamey, how are you? Not getting you at a bad time, am I?" Fred Mieland coming on too strong, all that rigor and vigor, pour me a jigger. . . . "You OK, son?"

"No. I just finished talking with the FBI." He disliked having to lay it on the old man that quick, but it would get to him one way or another and better he heard it now, from him.

"What's that?"

"I just finished talking with a man from the FBI."

"I heard you all right," his father said, "but I thought maybe I heard wrong. When did this happen? Today? Was it about that—uh—fracas when Mrs. Johnson was there or about what happened in Washington?"

"How'd you guess?" Jamey said.

"I didn't guess," his father answered. "And I still don't know why you had to do all this. I know how you feel but why did you have to tell the whole world? Well, never mind. The reason I called is—uh—it's more or less about the same thing. Your mother is having a fit. Before I put her on, let me tell you what happened—if you want to hear something crazy." Fred Mieland's voice became more subdued. "Last night, almost midnight, the phone rings. I'm dead to the world. I didn't get it right away. But listen to this, Jamey. Someone—he wouldn't give his name—someone called and said I better get hold of you and talk some sense to you, that people in town here did not like those anti-American songs or what you're doing, turning in your draft card and starting all this mess—"

Jamey said, "Could anyone have been—you know—kind of putting you on?"

"Oh sure, it's possible, always possible, all the jokers I know around here," Fred Mieland said. "But whoever it was called me, you could tell they meant it all right—they spoke without stopping and then hung up."

"Do you know anyone who would actually do a stupid thing like that—I mean, make an anonymous phone call?" Jamey said.

"Certainly not. Do you?"

"No. But then my opinion isn't worth much," Jamey said. "The way the FBI has taken over this campus is just as incredible as that call you got last night. I'm sorry about it. How's Mom?"

"I don't have to tell you, do I?"

"No, I guess not," Jamey said.

"She wants to talk to you," Fred Mieland said.

"Listen, Dad—that call—did they say anything else?"

"Oh, not much, just some malarkey about if I valued my business I'd better shut up my son."

"What did you—"

"I told you, I didn't get a chance to say anything," his father said.

"Christ," Jamey protested, "are they worried I'm going to blow up the White House?"

"Yeah. That's right," his father said. "All the same, Jamey, I don't know why in hell's name you have to go around raising all this stink. Why? Can't you just go to college without all this outside stuff all the time, getting us—getting you in trouble." Hastily his father corrected himself.

Jamey said, "Maybe my mistake is going to college."

Silence. Then: "What was that?"

"Nothing."

"All right," his father said after another interval. "Look, you stick to your schoolwork. I called to tell you what happened here, but I don't want you to worry about it. I know how much studying you have to do and I don't want you to stew about this. Just forget it. I'll call your mother now. I want you to tell her that the world's not coming to an end. OK, son?"

But after he'd finished talking with his mother, he still felt shaken by what he'd heard. His first rough encounter with the police after the silent demonstration, the action at the precinct station and the courthouse, the FBI being given open sesame on the campus was even worse, but the vision of back home, an anonymous telephone call terrifying his parents in the middle of the night—this is what really cut him up.

He snatched up his short coat and put it on over his sweater and left the apartment, starting now for the chapel in Stadium Park.

Some day this was.

A day in the life. Of Fuckleberry Finn.

And now that first view, the Georgian chapel, all rose brick and white wood trim in the park across from the football stadium, and all the cars, the station wagons parked for the pregame booze festival of the alumni. Nearing the chapel steps, Jamey was in no state to appreciate the scene or what it signified: all those students (but a small percentage of the campus) milling around finding a place to sit on the stone steps, all those bare heads, the fleece-lined suede coats, the mackinaws and leather jackets and duffels, all those well-intentioned students here for the Peace Sing-In—another naïve liberal act, another Boy Scout jamboree, another liberal error: trying to fight a fort with a feather.

He saw Gary Einsberg, the premed, with his sister, Verna, who was visiting; he saw Susan Sayres, and Sue Burke, whose pretty nose had been carelessly bruised by the local fuzz; he saw Paula Heston with Andy Ryan and the Doughertys, all those well-meaning liberal-spirited cats always rallying to all the good causes, naïve as himself, and here they were again all set to crank out the inspirational songs to edify the alumni, to get the message to them before the football game, another attempt that would go down the wrong way, for only a handful of alumni would tune in. . . .

When would they begin to dig?

But it was good to see another member of the faculty join the antiwar group now—A. Ajay, the dark-eyed and svelte professor of art.

There on the top row of the steps, standing up, was Laura in her suede coat, her hair long and bright in the pewter day, Laura talking with Link Karr. Ah yes, Link had obviously changed his mind, he wasn't going to sit this one out after all.

One thing at least: it was definite now. For the first time. Nothing said, but definite, no more half-tries, no more half-motions. He and Laura . . .

"Hey, Jamey—" It was Gary Einsberg, Gary waving him over, saving space on the steps. Jamey took the place, sitting down now between the premed student and his sister, Verna, who was one of those fair, blue-eyed girls who have to go through life insisting to people who must have their stereotypes that yes, she is really Jewish.

"You didn't bring your guitar. How come?" Gary Einsberg was saying.

"Can you blame him?" Dwight Dougherty said.

Jamey started to tell them about his interview with Mr. Arthur Olsen Regis. Reverend Tillou joined them now and said that he'd just telephoned the FBI office in town and told them that their presence on campus was disruptive. "I also told them," the exuberant clergyman said, "that no agent has the permission of the Dean to be on Divinity School property for the purpose of interrogation." That was the Rev, for whom Jamey and his friends were planning a surprise dinner by way of a long due tribute.

"Well," Jamey said, "they sure as hell didn't stay away from my place. I could have shut up, of course, but I don't know, I just had to go through with it to believe it."

"Yes," Verna Einsberg said. "I mean, I can see why you'd do it."

"It was a mistake," Jamey said. He was going to tell them about his father's call, but by now the sing was getting under way. A young instructor from the College of Music called for attention and suggested an order of songs and then it began, a ragged choral group with more enthusiasm than pitch or harmony.

Yet it did get going, beginning with the standards of all past peace marches and civil rights chants, and ending with Dylan's "Blowin' in the Wind." After the first round Paula Heston and Andy Ryan held up the large placards they'd brought along, for now several dozen members of the alumni had stopped to listen or watch. The two placards announced: PEOPLE ARE BEING MURDERED IN YOUR NAME. And YOUR UNIVERSITY DOCILELY PREPARES STUDENTS FOR DEATH.

Yes, and there were Frecklehead Nettleton and Chief Kavanaugh standing by to protect life and property.

As the alumni stood and looked. There were many couples, but most of the people were men in their coats and their felt hats, standing there, their paunches flubbed out, their faces flabbed into creases of bewilderment (What the hell do those kids want, they never had it so good!) or disapproval (Good God, you send them through college for what? For all this Commie crap!).

But the Sing-In was more or less ignored by most people. For it was party time along the long line of station wagons on the parking green between the chapel and the stadium. . . .

Jamey watched it as if for the first time, as if he were viewing some primitive African rite: yes, the tailgate cocktail party and picnic was gaining momentum, station wagons, row on row, with the rear gates open like tables and all the fatcat barbecue and cocktail appurtenances flashing and glittering, the long-stemmed glasses or decorated laminated paper cups; and the Scotch and bourbon, the gin and vermouth, and vodka, ah yes, and the matrons in knee socks and houndstooth-check coats or coats of horizontal striped mink, and beaver, as well as pre-preppies in long thrift-shop raccoons, while Dad the Grad, hair neatly, cleanly cut and in the J. Prell uniform tweed jacket, Dad the Grad blissfully tinkering with that hibachi grill, supervising the charcoal fire, as now the steaks and burgers began to sizzle and sear the air with their fine fatcat smells while the martini brigades clustered around the tailgates, those martinis going down ever faster while more and more health-giving outdoor-living cigarettes were being lit and the Scotch and bourbon and vodka and gin flowed, and transistor radios played soothing palp to dream by. . . .

Only now and then did some of the tailgaters pay much attention to the young voices from the steps of the chapel, glancing over between drinks, shaking their heads and smiling at each other, very indulgently now, booze smug: *Don't worry, those kids will get it all out of their systems and settle down one day just like the rest of us!*

As soon as the game started, Jamey left, returned to his rooms.

Now what?

An envelope under his door. Familiar stationery.

Yes.

A note. *It is requested that you report to the office of the Dean of Men at 2:30 P.M. next Wednesday.*

But somehow that didn't get under him this time, though he didn't know why, unless he was just getting inured or tough-hided or maybe just plain disgusted or indifferent. He dropped the note in the wastebasket beneath his worktable.

Alone and all the studying to do, and putting on some music.

All familiar, all normal. Except that suddenly Jamey had this sense of aloneness. It was different from solitude, which he usually welcomed and made the most of. But loneliness was something else, and today he wasn't sure how to cope with it.

There was the Donovan concert tonight, at least there would be that.

But a day, an afternoon, like this could bring him down, feeling like this, and he didn't know what to do.

And the apartments above and below his with that daytime silence that only happens on a football Saturday.

In the raw drab chill of late autumn maybe you could feel unnecessarily alone. What would it be like down by the river, by Platt's Landing?

Or right here. If Poppy were here.

Always this scratching of his nerves, knowing her, and knowing how she had that way of sparking all his senses. Poppy where today? Or tomorrow?

All afternoon Jamey hung in that limbo of nowhere, not really studying and not really listening to the records of folk and folk/rock, all those songs which were of the best, but somehow not grooving on any of it.

He was early for the concert that evening, waiting outside Ames Auditorium, hungry for friends, thankful as soon as Lyle Stinnett arrived with Sue Burke, and then the Doughertys and Paula Heston with Andy Ryan, and Gary Einsberg with his sister. He lost them all at eight o'clock, but yes, he would see them afterward at Andy Ryan's apartment and he'd bring some beer.

Alone now in the first row, a place for his legs, but a pit. The vast auditorium peopled from first row to last. Waiting, students waiting, almost no one in sight who could be a day over twenty-four. Impatient clapping and whistling until:

Upon the great span of stage (where Lady Bird had Talked and Beautified) there walked out a ruby-cheeked man of middle height in a light-gray business suit—someone said he was Donovan's father—who in his quiet businesslike way lit the sticks of incense in the pots on the table in the center; he poured water into a large paper cup; he placed cough drops on a paper plate; he checked the microphones. When all was in readiness, he stepped forward in his gray business suit and said with quiet authority and pride, "And now—I give you your evening star."

This was the first time Jamey had ever seen Donovan, Donovan crossing from the wings to the center of the stage, moving slowly, with grace, in long white robe and sandals and beads, a topaz or amber ring on his right index finger, Donovan now adjusting his guitar, tuning it, Donovan's choirboy face crowned by soft raven curls.

Everyone palpitating, expecting to hear that one song that had preceded the young Scotsman years before. Instead there came other songs, a varied repertoire of rock—folk, Indian, classic, baroque—but always delicate and with the poet's thrust, those Donovan landscapes; and those humanscapes; Donovan reminiscing on Greece . . .

Yet later, as the concert went on, as Donovan also sang with that exotic group backing him—flute, organ, bongos, drums— Jamey discovered something: he was listening to all of it, digging it, while becoming more and more conscious of another voice, the one he'd heard earlier and at other times, only now it came with more insistence and he found himself yielding to it, yielding to something that was much older than he knew.

He would look back on this night, the time when he decided. A bigger night than other nights. Epiphany at Mustang U.

As now, after all the ovations, Donovan reached over to the table where the flat basket of flowers was, and began scattering the carnations out to the students, gently tossing them in spray bursts of white and palest pink, and then serenely turning and walking away, cool and gentle in the now kinetic concert hall.

Yes, and Jamey deciding it.

High on the decision, as good as stoned on it, and not even half a joint needed; though by the time he got to the party he had some grass with him, and two six-packs. When he reached the apartment shared by Andy Ryan and Paula Heston, the pad was already a-blast with talk and music. Paula took the beer to the kitchen and came back with a chilled can for him.

He stood there, holding his beer, looking around, seeing everyone, seeing them suddenly out of some projected nostalgia, seeing them like figures in a tableau, a scene he had to imprint on his memory now in the event he would never see them again: the Doughertys on the studio couch with Gary Einsberg and Susan Sayres; on the floor on cushions were Gary's sister, Verna, and the date he had set up for her with another premed; standing near Andy Ryan's drafting table was Lyle Stinnett with Sue Burke, whose nose was still faintly discolored from the copbop; seeing Andy Ryan sipping beer, taking a rare nighttime reprieve from work at architectural school, Andy looking less harassed, his gaunt frame less rigid. And dimly hearing them talk about the Donovan concert—a concert to them, something else to him— and now Andy putting another stack of records on the stereo, The Rolling Stones dropping down first.

Jamey listening, yes, though not talking now, keeping his smile, like his decision, to himself, not wanting to part with it, this treasure he carried away from the Donovan concert: tonight, maybe tonight would be his last Saturday night on campus. . . .

And soaring on the strange, exciting prospect. Except thinking of those of his friends he'd miss—looking now, already with the eyes of memory, at Lyle Stinnett, seeing the tall Virginian, the teasing eyes, hearing that voice resonant with a honeyed melancholy.

And maybe tonight or tomorrow would be the last time he'd be seeing him. After almost four years . . .

While The Stones kept going and everyone getting more earnest, very very earnest, right? Hearing it all around him from the studio couch or the floor, conversing about guess what? All the nights, all the years he's been hearing (and saying) all of it:

"La Guerre."

"Washington—"

"—old Lyndon De Gaulstone."

Fine. Great. Of the best. But he'd had it. He was aching to run, reach beyond the campus gate, the creeping snooping Feds, get out, be part of what was happening away from here, a chance to keep his guitar out of its case, far from the Frecklehead Nettletons and the Chief Kavanaughs, away from the Dean of Men and Rossboss, and yes, Laura Barnes and Lincoln Karr, and those faculty voices that no longer turned him on. . . .

"Hey, Jamey"—Stinnett's eyes a-glint, his arm around Sue

Burke's waist—"how come you didn't bring our buddy Regis along tonight?"

"Hmm?" Jamey came back slowly. "Yes. I should have."

"Wouldn't be the first time," Stinnett reminded him.

"Incidentally," Jamey said then, "when he cornered you today, did he try to pin you down on Mike? I mean, did he ask if you knew him or—"

"He did just that," Stinnett said.

Jamey frowned. "I just hope they're not closing in on him." And Poppy. What about Poppy . . . maybe seeing her in a day or week . . .

"I hope not." Stinnett paused. "You know, sometimes it doesn't take much to get fed with this place the way things are going around here. If it wasn't for the draft I probably would have departed—"

"Even so," Andy Ryan said, "even if you can duck the draft, any place you go or any job you apply for, there's always that question: 'Have you ever been arrested?' And that's what we're going to have to face."

"Right." Gary Einsberg moved into it.

"All I know," Stinnett said, "is that I've only got another year to go. There's always Canada. Did you read that literature on Canada, the stuff Mike left here?"

"I'd rather try to stay right where I am," Gary Einsberg said.

Jamey said nothing. The Stones getting into "The Lantern."

"Come on, Gary, don't give us that," Andy Ryan said. "You'd quit tomorrow if you could. The same for me."

"You really mean that?" Jamey pressed it, as if overeager for someone else's reassurance. But why?

"Really would what?" Verna Einsberg joined them.

"They were just talking about being fed and quitting here." And then Jamey heard himself add, "I could leave tomorrow morning and it wouldn't be too soon."

"Really?" Verna said. Her blue eyes were pale and when she was unsmiling and serious she could be very pretty. "Well, I guess the idea is something everybody has. I had it once, and it certainly looked good to me."

But not as good, as hot, as it looked to him at this instant. "Did you do anything about it?" Jamey said.

"Oh sure, I certainly did. I had two years at Hunter and that was enough. At least I thought it was."

"Why—what made you decide to do it?" Jamey kept watching her now.

"Well, it was a question of getting away from home," she said. "I mean, I just didn't get along very well with my parents."

"That sounds familiar," Sue Burke said wryly.

"I mean," Verna said, "I didn't really tell myself that at the time. What I told myself was something else—" She turned and glanced toward the open door of the kitchen: her date was in there giving a helping hand to Professor Ajay, who was fixing *kibbeh* and other Syrian delights for later tonight. "I mean, well, everyone has his reasons for quitting, whether they're true or phony. What I thought I wanted to do was live alone and get a job on my own. And I did it. Receptionist and general nuisance in an art gallery. But this man who ran the gallery, he must have been very insecure. He let me go and replaced me with this Bennington girl who had one or two degrees. She did the same work I did but I guess she represented something to him. It didn't register on me at the time, but that's probably what it was." She paused. "Or maybe he just liked her better."

"That's sort of a special case," Jamey said: The Stones rolling great, spiced by some old Sergeant Pepperoni.

Someone was smoking, a new fragrance in the room.

"Could be," Verna Einsberg said. "But after that I got kind of hung up. You have this peculiar feeling after a while like you're missing something or that something's hanging over you that you didn't finish up. But it's still there. It was for me anyway. Then what happens is that though you get away from your parents— and it's a terrific feeling—you find it's suddenly not all that easy to make it—I mean, it's harder than you thought, it really is. Plus I think I did it too quickly. I think if I'd—you know—given it more thought, I never would have quit."

"But you're back now," Jamey said. The smell of grass more pervasive. He saw one of the couples go into the bathroom and lock the door.

"Oh sure."

He kept looking at her: but he was losing that high that had winged him to the party. Somehow this nice-looking girl rapping with all that conviction brought him down, way down.

He moved to the drafting-table stool after she had gone to the kitchen, and he brought out his plastic bag and papers and rolled some joints. He passed one to Sue Burke, another for Andy Ryan and Paula Heston. He drew in the smoke, sucking, hissing it in as if he could hurry that first cloud of euphoria.

And who the hell asked Verna Einsberg for her personal history? And who cared. That was her hangup. Not his.

"Say, Jamey"—Paula Heston so somber-eyed and noble-browed, and so voluptuous in that sweater and miniskirt—"about that thing we talked about—you know, in jail, for the Rev?"

"Yes."

"We were discussing it before with the Doughertys and we were thinking how about Sunday night December first? That would give us enough time to set it up." She waited. "Is that all right for you?"

He nodded. Had he already forgotten this dinner they'd decided to give for Reverend Tillou? About fifteen people. They were going to chip in to really lay down a banquet for this greatest of Divinity School cats. Yes, that would be a night he wouldn't want to miss, seeing the Rev's craggy face, the wide exuberant grin when he walked in and they'd all be waiting for him. . . .

Jamey would make it. Somehow he'd—well, he'd what? Why didn't he tell Paula now? If he was leaving they'd better not count on him or his guitar. Why didn't he tell her that now?

People like Verna Einsberg could really be a drag.

By the end of the second joint he began to feel easier. So did everyone else. Except for Verna and the Professor.

Piercing the smoke, the voice and the harmonica and harpsichord of Country Joe and the Fish in their TV idyll: *Into my life/ on waves of electrical sound/ and flashing she came—with the twist of a dial* . . .

And later, dry-tongued and hungry, all of them sitting around on the floor with paper plates eating Ajay's succulent *kibbeh* and the rice stuffed grape leaves. Yet Jamey, though among good friends, still feeling lonelier than he wanted to, and it wasn't only because he was the only person there who didn't have someone along with him.

184

Afterward Sue Burke and Lyle Stinnett went down the hall to Lyle's apartment, and Gary and his date vanished somewhere. Then Jamey left. It was 2 A.M. And he had not parted with the word.

No. He only said good night, not good-bye. Good night as if this were a Saturday night like any other.

Yet as soon as he was straddled on the Harley and wheeling off toward Beech Street, he turned back and made for Kent Street instead. He was not ready, nowhere near ready to go to sleep; he was wired into something that charged him with this anxiety, as if he'd let himself be sold, conned, as if someone like Verna Einsberg, straight as a gate, could have undermined all his resolution. . . .

Or was it something other than this nice well-meaning chick from the halls of Hunter?

Whatever it was getting under him, all he knew was suddenly not wanting to go back to his apartment, end up alone, not for a while. . . .

He went to Niko's: at this hour the long Pullmanesque restaurant was almost empty, a blinding white neon oasis, no music going now. Several students in one of the booths were leaving, the pizza oven was no longer afire. Jamey hesitated; maybe he ought to go someplace else, but then he saw sitting at the far end of the counter Roy Billings, Roy alone, reading a paperback, and he went down the long aisle and sat down on the vinyl stool beside him. Except that he felt constrained when Roy looked up, these years of friendship and feeling constrained like this.

"Hey, Roy"—Jamey said it too heartily—"where the hell have you been? I haven't seen you around at all; don't tell me I'm all that much poison—"

"No. Of course not." Roy speaking in that precise way of his. New, black-rimmed glasses had replaced the ones that had been crushed during the antiwar demonstration. Roy closed his paperback. Closed it reluctantly?

"Seems like the only time I get to see much of you these days is in a paddy wagon or in jail"—but Jamey failed to reach that easy familiar tone of yore.

"Looks like that, Jamey, doesn't it?" Roy answered, and contemplated his black face in the electric whiteness of the wall mirror.

Jamey spoke to the counterman: yes, coffee, no cream. Roy lit a cigarette and then Jamey saw him glance leftward: two men, on their way to or from a night shift at one of the factories in the area, had come in and seated themselves at the other end of the counter; one of them ordered coffee and opened his newspaper.

Jamey tried to keep the talk going but reaching Roy was an art he was suddenly clumsy in, and it wasn't until Roy began looking more often at the people at the end of the counter that any real communication between them happened. "Recognize him?"

"Who?" Jamey glanced leftward. "Which one?"

"The one with gray hair and the lumber jacket," Roy said.

Jamey looked again. "I'm not sure—oh, yes—must be that same guy." Jamey's voice must have carried, for both men turned to regard them: there was the stalwart, gray-haired, meat-muscled man, and his white-haired, rather frail companion, sickly and slight even in the mackinaw, but the other one, the big one, that was he, all right. . . . "That's the same guy, I think." Yes; the day of Lady Bird's visit—this same bellicose worker who during the antiwar hassle beat up Roy, or would have, if Mike and Jamey hadn't broken in.

"Yes." Roy very cool. "Yes, I believe he's one of the people we had some trouble with that day. I made the mistake of not breaking all his teeth. I think too many people got in my way."

"Like me, huh?"

No answer.

Roy sipped his coffee and again studied his image in the glass, raising his eyebrows into a deep frown. Last year how many times he and Roy had come to Niko's for midnight home fries with catsup, toast and coffee, all those good sessions really turning on with him, and going back to Beech Street with Roy living on the same floor, and Jamey feeling proud of this friendship.

Jamey used to like to tell himself that if anyone knew what it was like to be a Negro it was he, yes, Jamey really knew what it was like, Jamey really dug it, Jamey was one of the few white men who knew what it was like to be black.

But when any white man tells you that, beware; he may not know it, but he's riding the supershit special.

And Jamey riding it with the best of them.

"You go to the Donovan concert tonight, Roy?" Trying now to keep the mix very bland.

"Donovan?" Roy said it as if the Scottish singer were some mythical or planetary figure.

"Yes."

"No. Why should I?"

"I don't know, Roy. Since when wouldn't you go?" Jamey let his resentment surface. "You went to the Arlo Guthrie and when Country Joe and the Fish was here last week—"

"True." Roy left it at that.

Jamey drank his plastic mug of coffee. It was a stupid mistake sitting down here trying to cosy up to Roy. "Well"—he put down his money—"I've got to get back. See you, Roy."

"See you."

Jamey started toward the front of the restaurant.

"OK I say," the stalwart figure in the work shirt was saying to his elder friend. "OK I say; if these kids want to listen to all that music, go ahead and listen. But I say it's going too far when they don't stand for the National Anthem like it happened at that rock and roll show—The Country Fish? Did you see that editorial about it in the *Banner?*" The brawny hand slapping the newspaper. "I'll tellya, makes a man good and goddam mad!"

"That's a fact," the other said.

Jamey kept moving. Ever since that concert a week ago, the local papers had been having an orgy of indignation.

"What I'm saying is I don't give a damn they want to hear that rock and roll, that's their business, but there they are, somebody paying for the college education and paying for their cars while they try to take any yellow way out to stay out of the draft! And then they won't even stand up when the National Anthem is played! I'll tellya, if I had a kid like that I'd kill, see him dead first!"

When Jamey reached the now empty pizza chef's cage, he looked back, to see that Roy was getting off his stool and going over to the man.

"Were you talking about me?" Roy standing by the man who

was hulked on his stool, the *Evening Banner* still in his mighty hand. Roy looking deceptively slender.

"Huh? Talking about you?" the worker said.

"I was one of the people who didn't stand up that night." Roy Billings sounded cool but Jamey could detect the tightness. "I just wanted to tell you so you wouldn't have to keep raising your voice in case people couldn't hear you."

"What?"

"I just wanted you to know," Roy said.

"Sure." The man put down the paper. "Anything else on your mind?" Without angling his body, and only slightly turning his head, the gray-haired worker kept talking. "Seems to me fellas like you got something to stand up for."

"Like what?"

"Like what do you think? This country is what!"

Jamey started back. "Roy—"

You could see all light leaving Roy's dark eyes, only something cold and flat there, as without warning he jutted his hand out and spun the man around on the stool and then, letting go, striking him, the blow glancing off the side of the man's mouth, but the force bringing a thin spurt of blood. The elder man was on his feet and calling out to the kitchen. The swinging door creaked open and the counterman appeared, and then Roy calmly walked away.

He did not get more than a few steps when the factory worker lunged after him, a burly figure, heavy and broad of back, yet very agile. He reached out for the Negro and pulled him around and held him rigid in his cable arms. "All right, you little chicken bastard, get going"—he released Roy—"get out of here, I don't want to kill you!" Not finishing, and Roy's fist streaking out, but the man warding it off, reaching out again and in an almost helpless tantrum flinging Roy down against the countertop, and his thick blunt fingers around Roy's throat, Roy's head against the Formica.

As the man's friend kept twitching his bony hands together and muttering, and the counterman stood there unmoving and saying several times, "All right, break it up, break it up."

By then Jamey had already moved into it, coming into it from behind, having that one advantage, and being as careful as he

188

could about his back, he was able to pull the man's arms loose from Roy's throat, and as the worker wrenched around, Jamey swung as hard as he could and got him just below the right ear. The man reeled, swaying back, turning in wildest rage to see it was Jamey—a white man!—who was attacking him, so that he spewed out more of his fire and misery and joy: "You fucking dirty Commie bastard!" Leaping forward for Jamey, and Jamey, trying to duck and step away from him, slipped on the shiny floor and fell back, but catching himself, expertly breaking the fall, gripping the side of one of the booths.

Roy was back now, Roy after the man with a lion's murderous pounce, and then Jamey rushing in, the two of them on him, front and back, though by this time several students had hurried in and it took almost all of them to subdue Roy and the factory worker, breathless now, breathing in fierce harsh gasps, but still solid, stalwart, powerful, his lust unrequited.

When it was finished and the two men started out, the worker stated in the neon brightness that he would report this to the police and to the University authorities. "And this is just the beginning, we're not through with you!" His gray face the hue of fuchsia as he shouted the threat at Roy and Jamey.

"Fuck off," someone called.

And it was all over.

Quiet settled in the restaurant; the counterman said it was lucky the boss wasn't around. Jamey and Roy sat down at the counter and the counterman said maybe they'd like to have some more coffee and he sure hoped the boss wouldn't hear about this, for crysakes. But smiling then, saying to Jamey, "Jesus, a good thing you jumped in; that guy could have choked Roy to—"

"Where's that coffee?" Jamey said. He sat very straight. His back seemed none the worse.

Roy was putting his glasses on and rebuttoning his shirt collar.

"Coming up." The counterman poured the coffee from the Silex.

Jamey looked at Roy. "You all right?"

"As far as I know. Why?" Roy said.

"Oh—nothing. Just asking." Jamey lifted the plastic coffee mug, so light and heftless. He glanced toward the front of the restaurant. "Funny how bad news like that keeps turning up around here."

Roy tried his coffee.

"When that trial comes up, I can tell you now," Jamey said, "that's the kind of cat who will get there early to get the front row." Jamey knew it was unnecessary small talk but he felt obliged to fill the still bewildering void of silence. Then he decided to tell Roy of his decision to leave tomorrow. No. Not now. Yet, why not?

But he let it go after that and just sat there like Roy, looking into his coffee.

"Listen, Jamey—" It must have been five minutes before Roy spoke. "I'd appreciate it if you did me a favor. You and your friends. I know you're always working conscientiously on this liberal kick, but look, don't sweat it, huh? I know you're sincere, for what that's worth, I know you've always been sincere, but do me a favor, give up, forget it, let it rest. I wouldn't bother telling you this except I happen to like you, so let's not sweat it, OK?" He reached into his pocket and put some coins on the counter.

"Now wait a minute, Roy, what the hell kind of way is that to talk to me?" Jamey swung around to face him.

"Will you listen to me?" Roy Billings said very quietly now. "I want you to forget it, I don't want you to keep on kidding yourself. You see, this country is going to go down, it's got to. It's a racist country, it really is that, always has been. It lives and feeds on ignorance and lies, so it has got to go down. And if I have to, I'll go down with it, but not without first helping it go down. It has to die. What people like you are trying to do just doesn't cut the mustard anymore."

That was all.

Roy stood up: there was that flick of recognition as he saw Jamey's face; he hesitated, and then he reached out in some sort of impulse of benediction, and touched Jamey's head.

Roy turned away and walked out into the campus street.

Soon Jamey left too; and then he straddled the Harley again and again started for Beech Street.

Under him, though, was the sudden anger, resentment, a sudden flare of hatred for Roy which just as quickly he saw was

190

nothing but hatred of himself and resentment of being rejected, cut down by a person like Roy. . . .

But knowing this didn't help.

Down on the starter and gassing the Harley, scrambling across the campus in the still and starless and aching night:

Bombing uphill, yes, so that he could summon all his arrogance and tell himself all the things that would make his exit a triumph:

Racing now, racing toward what? That last gate—yes, tomorrow he would go, no copping out on this decision: he didn't function like some people, like Verna Einsberg, for example; he never turned back once he started. Racing away from Roy and toward what?

Toward the bloodrush of rage on his father's bourbon-blushed face, the dismay in his mother's watery eyes . . .

Toward Mike . . .

Toward Poppy . . . Ah, yes, Poppy, yes . . .

Toward the draft board (reporting in and bucking another physical) . . .

Toward the place where he would use his guitar, yes . . .

Across the campus universe now, gunning it ever uphill, the buildings bulking up, shadowless monsters, passing all the cars, all the couples making out in their Mustang mating machines: Gownies and townies, farewell! Greeks and freaks, veeps and creeps, so long! Rossboss and Regis and Big Brother, *ciao!* Laura Barnes, *adieu!*

Give up, forget it . . . What people like you are trying to do just doesn't cut the mustard anymore. . . .

Tomorrow at this time the campus would be a landmark place, a marker in the landscape of Jamey Mieland, yes, onward and upward, everything to live for. Right? Yes, if you could beat it.

Beat it for what? Success Fame Fortune?

Well, you see, it's like this, Dad. (How would he tell him?)

Fortune Success Fame in the Tradition American Great.

Why?

Who said?

Fuckleberry Finn Must Succeed!

You must: are you suffering from Horatio's allergy?

Never mind. Get into it, man. Cool it. Ignore the ache in heart or groin, sing it out. What kind of dream is the American dream?

Wet.

Yes. And what else?

Myopic. The campus a last refuge from the supershit society, except even that refuge works only if you believe in the dream or the myth. . . .

And still the killing and the Kill Ratio is the order of the day and what happened to the daydream?

And who had been helping to build the lie? And who was the man who liked being benefactor to his black friends? And who fumed at the realization that this good groovy, guilt-easing game might be over?

Right: none other than one Jamey (Mieland)!

Yet racing now to pass that last farewell gate of Academe, to make it, to get beyond the daze of dreams, to go where he could do the only thing he knew or hoped he knew, and even if he wasn't sure enough yet, he knew where he had to go to find out.

PART III

The Paths of the
Rock Garden

7 : THE CITY

PANDEMONIUM IT must be on this spring (April Fool's) night. As per. Calmly Carol Lachman, the veteran (age thirty-five) PR girl of Raven Records, turns to the boy with the shaggy blond hair. "Sorry about this," she says. "It'll be a while yet. I hope you're not nervous."

"Nervous?" Jamey pushes back his hair.

Carol lights a cigarette. This boy's audition will have to wait all right. While pandemonium reigns.

Three-ring circus. As per. Here they are, the Raven people, gathering, meeting, waiting. They are renting time in this recording studio on West Twenty-third Street from Vanguard Records, renting it beginning at ten tonight. But of course even now there's a population explosion going on in the control booth, the anteroom, the great recording studio and the small glass-walled recording chamber.

Step right up. See the lights, kiddies: here in the control booth, sitting high behind Carol at the great span of the sound board with its myriad dials and levers, recording on the eight-track system, is the master mixer and blender, the sound engineer, and beside him Maynard Solomon, who is producing the Joan Baez for Vanguard—not songs this time, but an LP of her poetry readings. . . .

In front of the sound board and tape equipment is the long row of folding metal chairs where Carol Lachman is seated beside Jamey, where the Raven brass will soon be. . . .

While at the right in the adjacent glass-walled anteroom is gathered one of Raven's newest rock groups, The Gingerbread Bicycle—all five members there with their girl friends or wives, all smoking, drinking beer or Cokes, the empty Coke bottles already showing a debris of cigarette butts, this young crew casually costumed in old jeans, boots, a blue admiral's coat, suede jacket, leather jerkin. Tonight they will be beginning to record their second LP (their first was a breakaway, high up on the charts and soon to reach Gold Record status). Two of the group are studying some music sheets, others are leafing through this week's *Billboard* or *Cash Box*. One of the girls, a college junior, is doing homework. . . .

And Joan Baez is working in the small recording booth to the left of the main recording room, finishing up Vanguard's session.

"Joanie—" Maynard Solomon at the console switches into the little booth where Baez sits, the poems on the table before her. "Joanie, could we just have that again? Once more to cover."

Baez nods. This time you hear her asking the leader of the studio musicians grouped in the lofty recording room, "How many times before I come in on this one?"

"On the third measure, Joanie," answers the leader, and readjusts his earphones.

"All right," Solomon says from the sound board. "Rolling on six." He enters the note in his log.

Carol Lachman, skin so pallid, eyes so darkly intense, sits there listening, observing, noticing now and then the lanky young man beside her, Jamey Mieland, the scuffed buckskin shoes and tan jeans and black turtleneck; he is leaning forward, elbows on his knees, head resting on his upturned palms; he scarcely moves, he seems almost rigid, as if caught midway between his interest

196

in Baez and his apprehension about himself and the trial still before him.

Carol, at the end of Baez' next poem, looks at her watch. What time will she make it home tonight? Soon Vanguard will finish up and then the Raven people will begin and only God knows when they will end and only God knows what time Carol will get back to her sixth-floor apartment just off Riverside Drive; her husband will be watching some late late TV or reading and on his sixth cup of coffee. He is a low-budget experimental film-maker and Carol's salary is necessary to his survival. She married him in 1958, three years after she was graduated from Barnard in 1955. Childless—not that she has any choice—she likes her work; she likes Raven Records because it is still an indie label, still fairly intimate and successful. It is run by two "associates"—Syd Held and Zak Silberman. They are not easy to work for; they are not known for their patience or their courtesy; they are, however, very exuberant and intuitive: they sign artists on instinct, but if the artists fail to make it early in the race, Raven drops them. In today's market there are that many rock groups and singers to pick from; they grow on trees and the season is all year long.

Now Syd and Zak have arrived: they are cool and prosperous and dressed in high-button (Brill Building Mod) suits. They are the oldsters of the firm, Zak being thirty-eight, Syd thirty-six, a team of two who have a way of interrelating without word, sign or signal; they will back each other up or veto each other, whichever offers maximum profit for the firm.

But when the wind is their way they are zealous and all joy all over the place. They are unlike certain other record-company executives. Unlike, for example, a man like Maynard Solomon, who in his quiet authoritative way is decidedly of the intellectual caste.

None of them, however, is like Raven's newest producer, Clement Vogel, who has just dashed in—Clem seldom walks or saunters. Clem is producing The Gingerbread Bicycle; he is the one who has brought in this boy Jamey to audition.

Clem Vogel is getting on. He is twenty-seven, five years out of Princeton. Slim, of middle height, nonathletic, an indoor specimen, he has long unruly brown hair, exotic sideburns and a bold nose. Clem Vogel, in his black Mao jacket, stops to shake hands

197

with Jamey. "Look, I think maybe we'll listen to you first tonight, no point in your hanging around half the night, which is what goes when I work with The Gingerbread. OK?" He sort of makes it sound like street talk, as if he were going out of his way to suggest he never saw the inside of a college education: his bag is folk/rock, and nothing else in his life, including his wife, is as dominant. "OK?"

Jamey says yes, the sooner the better; nerves tighten his smile.

Clem Vogel, for a minute only, sits down, leans over and gives Carol some instructions for tomorrow, and she shorthands them into her notebook. Clem looks over at Joan Baez, then he rises, greets Solomon and hurries into the anteroom to confer with The Gingerbread Bicycle. Only for a minute. He is back and pausing now for a hasty exchange with Syd Held and Zak Silberman. Then, like a butterfly, he comes back to the first flower. "Listen, Jamey, what are you going to do? I discussed it with Syd and Zak and I want them to hear 'Everything to Live For.' What else?"

Jamey frowns. "I was thinking maybe this new thing I've done."

"What kind of new thing?" Clem Vogel asks. But with zeal, consuming interest, as if the answer could be the secret of life.

"It's called 'The White Cat,'" Jamey says. "It's very different from all my others."

"Different? Well, why not? How is it different?" Clem Vogel says.

"It's a—well, it's just a love-mood kind of thing," Jamey says or confesses.

"You've got it." Clem Vogel reaches into the slit pocket of his Mao coat and brings out a small pad and a big black Magic Marker and scrawls several words down. Then he says, "That other one, 'The Lyndon Tree.' It's long but I think our people ought to hear this too."

"Are you sure?" Jamey says.

"I shit you not, Pedro," answers the former English major from Princeton. And up he stands now to dart back into the glass-walled anteroom for serious discussion with The Gingerbread Bicycle.

Carol turns to Jamey. "I have almost no information about you."

"What?" Jamey says.

She repeats it. "But there's no rush. I mean, naturally we'll want to see what happens here first."

Carol Lachman does not press it further. Too soon to get into it; first you had to see how the kid makes out in this audition. Clem would be sympathetic, but Syd and Zak would be strangers: if they voted no, the boy would be out in the alley; if they voted yes, he would get the Raven treatment, the associates would spare nothing to push him. In the beginning.

And Carol Lachman would start to feed the whole program into the PR machinery. She would have to spend a lot of time on him and with him: there were worse fates.

In these short ten years since she joined Raven Records, she has witnessed remarkable changes in this industry. These kids who are now making the folk/rock scene are doing more than just making music; some of them are helping to create all kinds of trends and changes; what they have to say in their songs or poems is a long distance from the june/moon past of pop music; these kids put out ideas and styles, social commentary or political satire that a lot of people under thirty pay a lot of attention to and buy a lot of records to prove. The associates at Raven, like many others in the industry, may not care one way or the other just so long as the records are sold. But even many of the occupants of 1619 or 1650 Broadway have to recognize that what is happening today grows out of something beyond mere music-making. And if some people, like Clem Vogel, raise the value of the super rock stars to the ridiculous level of high art, Carol Lachman would be the first to recognize that, valid as this viewpoint might be, let's not get carried away, huh? Let's not confuse these modern minstrels with Walt Whitman or Dylan Thomas or Robert Lowell. . . .

Yet, looking back, remembering how people used to blast these kids, all the moaning and groaning of the square world all during 1967 and until now—the way the kids protested the war in Vietnam, the way they worked, kept working and pressuring public opinion; a new life style.

And now peace possible.

For this these kids would have her vote.

And bless them.

It is now half-past ten and Joan Baez has finished for Vanguard

Records tonight, and now Clem Vogel leaves The Gingerbread Bicycle and returns to the control room. Now it is time for Raven Records.

To Jamey he says, "I guess you can start tuning up that gun."

Clem unbuttons the Mao jacket. Carol suspects that in the privacy of his own apartment or out at the house of his parents in Stamford, Connecticut, he is seen wearing more traditional clothes; but this suit, like his sideburns, is merely his way of transmitting on a more empathetic wavelength to the young rock artists he works with and hopes to inspire.

It is all part of the current bag. But Carol admittedly prefers this scene to what it was when she first became part of it way back in 1958.

Jamey is removing his guitar from its case. Clem Vogel goes around to the dais in back, to the sound board, and talks with the sound engineer. Joan Baez has now come in from the small recording booth while in the big one the musicians are beginning to pack up their instruments.

"All right, Jamey," says Clem Vogel, "any time you're ready."

Yes, he was ready: for a hole in the floor, a chute to zoom down in, a laser ray. To vanish.

Now that the time was at hand, now that the break had become real, now that he was here—where was he?

Now that he might get what he wanted—did he want it?

Truly want it?

Is that what he had fled from? Finally. Four months after the day that polite cat from the FBI had tried to nail him down, four months after that night of the Donovan concert and the potshot party at Andy's and Paula's and the restaurant hassle with Roy Billings, that unwanted farewell from Roy, four months since he hurtled away on the Harley across campus all plugged in to all that bravado . . .

Jamey never turns back.

But he had.

First it was the trial; then his mother. The law school lawyer advised him that his chances at the trial would be much better if he was a student than if he was listed by the University as a dropout. This turned out to be true. He and the others who'd been arrested during that battle with local police got off; the case was dismissed by the judge. It was easy.

Too easy? For last week Jamey, Roy Billings, Gary Einsberg and the others received notifications that their draft status would be changed from 2-S to 1-A—General Hershey's punitive little fist reaching out and slugging.

The trial behind him, except a lot of people in Nittygritty City still talking about it and telling his father about it, not letting it die.

And then once again when he decided to leave school, calling his father to prepare him for the blow, and a nurse answering. Jamey's mother down with pneumonia; she was being taken to the hospital. That weekend he came home but of course he couldn't wire them in on his plans, not at a time like that, putting it off, going back to Mustang U. Going through the motions for a few weeks and then getting himself involved in the McCarthy Presidential primaries in New Hampshire, bussing up with Lyle Stinnett, Gary Einsberg and a lot of other students. Including Laura Barnes. The Sleeping Bag Brigade. All of them spreading out to the towns assigned to them, making it from door to door trying to rap with the people about clean Gene. In Portsmouth, where Jamey was, he got response; the thing was that McCarthy got through. Jamey stayed on when the others returned; on two successive weekends in Concord, he did his songs for nighttime gatherings of students from different schools and once McCarthy was there listening, watching with that diffident smile. A week later in Keene, Jamey gave an informal concert, a last-minute improvisation, but the kids digging all of it, and that newest of his, "In New Hampshire," a frankly partisan rock ballad which he'd put together hurriedly on a melodic line in the spirit of Yankee folk tunes. It began:

Hear ye, hear ye
From Concord to Keene, Dover to Laconia
You'll hear the promises of all the runners
But you'll know only Gene will sincere ya
And you'll know the others only phony ya
For it doesn't have to be winter to get snowed
In New Hampshire
No, it doesn't have to be winter to get snowed
In New Hampshire.

It was in Portsmouth that he ran into Mike again, the first time since the day he'd scrambled out of that campus rumble last November. Jamey was right in the middle of North Bow Street when he saw Mike, who was on his way to Hanover on resistance work; he was staying out of New York as much as possible. Much too hot. He had to leave Poppy there, he could no longer risk involving her. As if Jamey didn't know about it.

Had Jamey seen her lately?

Well, not much. Jamey said the half-truth standing there in the street in that raw March wind, and seeing Mike's robust face tilted, pink dappling the whites of his eyes from fatigue or meth, then looking up searching Jamey's face, turning away then as his bus came, calling out something as he ran to make it, and Mike waving once from the bus door. . . .

Had Jamey seen Poppy lately?

Yes, Mike, I have. But not during the McCarthy campaign.

But when the New Hampshire experience was over, he waited no more. And as soon as he was able to set the audition, he split for New York. K. O. McNulty (now a Nixon man) said he'd bring in Jamey's gear next weekend in his new Olds (the Mustang had to be traded in; after all, as K.O. said, it already "had a lousy seventeen thousand miles on it"). And drop it off at Poppy's place.

And here now. New York. Now. And after this crucial session here, it would be down to Sixteenth Street. To Poppy.

But now. Here in this recording studio. And all those faces facing him: Clem Vogel, Carol Lachman, Syd Held, Zak Silberman, the studio musicians and The Gingerbread Bicycle. All bringing their attention his way: in a way more terrifying than the police or the FBI, or even the prospect of his father's face when he found out, or his mother's. . . .

Someone saying his name and introducing him to Joan Baez.

Meeting her now, and then Baez moving past him to Maynard Solomon, Baez all slimness and easy grace in the dark-blue pants suit, the tawny vinyl boots, the long hair all black sheen, the vivid young features that formed the sculpture of her profile.

He turned and went out to the big recording room, coming right back, going to Vogel and asking him if he couldn't wait until Baez and the Vanguard people left. But as it happened, almost immediately they did, and Jamey went back out to the recording room. Some of the musicians were still there, idly watching him.

He saw inside the control booth that Zak Silberman was consulting his watch, the gesture not one of patience. Syd Held wetting his lips, scratching his thick corkscrew hair. Clement Vogel stretching out, the Mao jacket hanging open, the thrust of his nose like a signpost directing all eyes to Jamey.

Jamey drew over a high stool. He tried as best he could to summon his cool, becoming very busy, his left hand moving along the neck of his guitar, fingers fussing over the frets, checking the pickup and bridge.

His head and eyes cast downward, yet seeing, feeling the attention of the musicians who still lingered in the big room, holding their instruments, waiting, watching him. Just as, in the control booth, The Gingerbread Bicycle, more restive, eyeing him.

Jamey's head already moist. The heat in here. The lights. A July noon in April.

And then into it: "The Lyndon Tree."

Somewhere about midway through, it came, the voice from the control booth: "All right. Thank you."

Jamey looked up, swallowed. Yes, he'd heard it correctly, Zak Silberman talking. "No offense," Zak Silberman saying then. "But since Lyndon's bowing out and the war's going to be over, why don't we get on to the next song."

Jamey nodded, still frowning, unnerved: *The war's going to be over.* . . . Did that mean everyone was supposed to act as if it never happened or as if it had nothing to do with a lot of other things bugging everyone?

He wanted to finish it anyway, but he knew this kind of song was already ruined by the break.

"All right." He bent over the guitar. Silence. Then into the second one. "Everything to Live For."

When he finished he did not look around. He heard footsteps. People leaving behind him—the studio musicians?

Then slowly, plucking the intro, slowly in a psychedelic curve, a cascade of minor chords, singing now:

The White Cat
Is a nowhere place
Where the smoke curls up like ebony lace
But the colors of my mind entwine your face.

The White Cat
Has walls dark as teak
The rock's so loud we can't even speak
But yes I address the pale rose of your cheek.

Oh yes, remember the White Cat
That hangout place with the strobe-lighted dome
Where it's much too dark to read a palm or poem
Though if love is bright does it need a sunny home?

The White Cat
Is a nowhere place
Where the smoke curls up like ebony lace
But the shine of your lips with mine I trace.

When Jamey looked up nothing had changed; the world had
not tilted. He glanced leftward at the studio musicians. They
were still there; some were smiling and one of them gave him an
emphatic nod.

Somehow that was what counted then, what they thought. So
that when he went back into the control booth where the Raven
people and the rock group were, he was less intimidated.

"Sit down, Jamey." The voice, that of Syd Held, was a hospi-
table one.

"I think," said Zak Silberman, "we can use your *shtick*."

"Jamey"—Clem Vogel was standing now—"we're all agreed. Tomorrow let's get together. OK? Meet me at the office at three.
We've got a lot to rap about." His arm around him in a swift
embrace. "Pedro, I see nothing but glory and art and bread."

"Sit down, Jamey," Syd Held said again. Jamey took the metal
chair beside the associates.

"Before you and Clem start tomorrow, some questions," Zak
Silberman said.

Jamey was still not there.

The Gingerbread Bicycle began moving out to the recording
room.

"I understand, according to Clem, that you have no other commitments. Is that right?" Syd Held asked.

"Yes." Slowly Jamey was coming back.

"What about school? When do you finish up? We can't put our heart and pocketbook into this if you're not free to move with us," Zak Silberman said.

"I've left school."

"Oh? Definitely?" Zak Silberman said.

"Yes," Jamey said.

"When?" Zak Silberman asked.

"This afternoon," Jamey said.

Syd Held leaned over, hair all oily and coily. "You mean you flunked out or what?"

"No, I quit."

"I see."

More paternal, a wider smile, Syd Held said, "Your parents—how do they feel about this, Jamey?"

He swallowed. "They—I haven't told them yet."

Syd Held gave him an affectionate jab. "Be a good idea if you dropped them a hint."

"I plan to," Jamey said.

The Gingerbread Bicycle were setting up in the high recording room preparing for their session. Clem Vogel was back at the sound board. "OK, Jamey, meet me at the office, three tomorrow."

Jamey nodded.

"Carol," Zak Silberman said, "you can lock into this, right? Start in on his bio."

That was it. No blast. No glasses raised.

Take off, man, they suggested in their rough and tender way, we've got work to do.

But, of course, it was all there, a submerged excitement, a-bubble just below the surface, everyone very cool. You could only really see it in Clem Vogel's eyes. And Jamey could still hear it in his chest.

As if this was where he was trying to get all his life and never really knowing it? Or was all this a phony euphoria, and even forgetting already the way one of the associates coldly resisted a protest song this soon, as if the war were something that happened long ago. . . .

Strapping his guitar and his small canvas duffel bag onto the Harley, unlocking the bike and then driving down to Sixteenth Street (instead of to Nittygritty City and to the parents who didn't even know he was here or what he'd done).

But he was still much too flashed on to go home: a radiance was in him and he wanted to share the shine with Poppy. She had two classes tonight at The New School, but she certainly would be back by ten-thirty. It was past eleven now. Gunning the Harley and already passing the bulking facade of the old Port Authority Building, then east into Sixteenth Street, gray and anonymous to this latest of Poppy's addresses. He left the Harley angled between a pickup truck and a Volvo sedan. Into the shabby narrow apartment of brick the color of cordovan, into the cube of tiled foyer and pressing the bell. There was no door buzzer; you had to wait until Poppy came down the four flights. It took longer tonight.

And the door only opening a slow cautious slit.

"Mike—" Jamey saw the wild mat of dyed red hair in the murky light. Disappointment, yet intense pleasure; joy garroted by guilt. Mike.

"Hey, Jamey—" Mike opening the door all the way, Mike in old jeans and old green flower shirt from former times and that ancient tweed jacket, but Mike and Jamey in quick rough embrace.

"Goddammit, it's great to see you!" Jamey said.

"Great to see you, Jamey," Mike said. "That was funny in Portsmouth, huh?"

"Yeah," Jamey said.

"What're you doing in town?" Mike looked good, or at least better than he had in New Hampshire. His eyes were clearer.

"Oh, I—" Jamey hesitated. "I'll tell you about it. But I wanted to leave my guitar here. Isn't Poppy in?"

"No, not yet." Mike looked at his watch.

"I thought her last class was over at ten or so," Jamey said.

"Well, she ain't chosen to get back." Mike's smile, his voice, seemed unnatural. "I just had a little time, and I wanted to see her before I took off again. Been almost two weeks. Come on up."

They ascended, Mike ahead of him. On the third-floor landing he stopped: from behind a door came the cry of yet another newscaster reviewing Lyndon Johnson's announcement of the previous night that he would not seek reelection and that he had begun to deescalate the Vietnam war. They listened for a moment.

"Some news, eh, baby?" Mike declared.

"Sure was." Jamey shook his head. "I sure as hell never expected old Six Gun to get forced out like that."

Mike said, when they started up again, "When you think of all you silly people screaming, protesting, marching all these years, making goddam idiots of yourselves. And now maybe something's going to happen."

"Yeah," Jamey said, "and you were sitting on your ass the whole time."

On the top floor Mike said, "You still haven't told me what you're doing in town."

Jamey told him then where he'd been tonight and what had happened. But somehow the joy, the surge, was gone.

"Goddammit, that's great, that's great!" Mike put his arms around him. "Jamey, that's really— What's the matter? You don't have to look like that."

"I don't know." Jamey hesitated. "I thought it's what I wanted but I'm not all that sure now. I mean, I don't know what the hell the whole point is. At least what you do—at least that really adds up."

"Listen, baby"—Mike looked at him, the blue eyes intense behind the wire-rimmed glasses—"don't start that with me. What I do a lot of others can also do. What you do is something most people can't. And you've got to keep doing it!" He unlocked the door. "Hell, I can't hang around." He glanced again at his watch. "I'm late. Tell Poppy I'll get back in a couple of hours."

"Where do you have to go, Mike?"

"Brooklyn. I'm late and the goddam subways can drag at this hour."

"Take the Harley, why don't you?" Jamey said. "I mean, you might as well."

"Hey, that's an idea—" But the brightness went out in Mike's eyes; he still stood there by the open door, peering at Jamey, looking back into Poppy's apartment, then turning to look at Jamey again.

Jamey saw, at that same instant, what had darkened Mike's thoughts. Yet he couldn't say anything. He couldn't withdraw the offer; that would make his spontaneous gesture seem calculated and obvious. He said, "Look, if you don't want to use it—"

Mike's gaze still on him. Then: "Hell no—I want to use it."

An interval between them.

"There are some things I better show you," Jamey said.

"Right."

Mike fixed the lock so that Jamey could return. Then they started down the long narrow high-banistered stairway.

Jamey slowed; he stopped midway between the fourth and third floors. "Mike—"

"What?" Mike turning back to glance up at him.

"Look—" Jamey tried not to sweat it. "I mean, I can stow my stuff someplace else, I don't have to use Poppy's pad."

"Why shouldn't you?" Mike said.

"Well, I don't know. If—I mean, if you—"

"What the hell are you trying to say?" Mike faced him, one foot on the stair tread where Jamey stood.

And Jamey, looking at him, had to chicken out. "Forget it."

After a moment Mike accepted this, turned and started down the stairs, Jamey following, and deciding he should never have opened his mouth, not after seeing the way Mike looked, not after that. Yet feeling the way he did about him, confronting him tonight, making that offer of the Harley—it all misfired.

"Listen, Jamey—" Mike's sudden voice, Mike stopping now. Almost down to the second floor. "I don't like to talk about this any more than you do. I know what you started to say before—"

"I—"

"Let me finish it, huh?" Mike kept working the fingers of his right hand. "I mean, let's at least put it where it belongs—in case you're worried that you're playing it like a shit. Maybe you are. Or were. I know how it is, I know it's nothing you went out of your way to do. But that doesn't matter, not now. It's not the same with me and Poppy. I mean, with Poppy. I'm more or less —well, not more or less, but definitely persona non grata around here now."

"Look, Mike, you—"

208

"Let me finish, huh?" But he turned again and moved slowly down the stairs to the newel post, grasping it, his russet head down. When Jamey reached him he stirred, spoke, cleared his throat and spoke again. "I just can't hang around much anymore. Too much heat. Aside from that, it has to be like that. I can't let Poppy in for anything more. In a way I was almost glad you showed up."

But Jamey couldn't reach it: he kept thinking Mike was still talking about the threat of getting the fuzz onto Poppy. "Mike, for Christ sakes, don't put all this on yourself, unless you're only trying to cut me up even more. This has never been my idea of a good deal for anyone. I've wanted to tell you this, talk about it, a thousand times, but I kept chickening out—"

"Let me tell you something. Nobody makes it with Poppy without Poppy wanting it." Mike floundered, took off his wire-rimmed glasses, blinked, put the glasses on again. "Maybe what I ought to tell you is Poppy just doesn't necessarily like standing on the same corner all the time. My trouble is I stood there too long. I wish I hadn't." Then in a burst: "I wish to God I hadn't seen her last time—"

"What do you mean, Mike?"

He loosened his shirt collar. "I'm late. You want to show me that stuff?"

Outside Jamey moved the Harley, wheeling it to a place beneath the street light. He gave Mike the keys; he told him the way the oversize racing brakes responded and when Mike got on he readjusted the foot pegs. Mike listened to it all, though he was still as distracted as Jamey. "OK," Jamey said at length. "Just remember this is a beast you don't want to scramble with in city traffic."

Mike nodded, fitting the scuffed white helmet over his red hair. "I ought to get back by one or so."

Mike was no longer looking at him though. Jamey stepped back from the curb. He felt tight, pinched, that expansive, buoyant sensation drained out of him; that good groove he'd been in after his audition no more, gone, bombed out.

He heard the Harley snorting off, looked up. Just as Mike was curving south into Seventh Avenue, Poppy came around the corner.

Jamey started toward her at once and then he stopped when he saw that she was not alone.

Not that it mattered, her being with someone—obviously another student, some guy from The New School—for just seeing her again after all these weeks in New Hampshire was enough to turn him on.

"Poppy—" he called. Poppy in that splash of corner street light —Poppy, that miniskirted masterpiece of elusive flesh, her two feet never on the ground. Her hair was longer, ribboned up, almost sedately, that hair of palest chestnut framing the pale pinkish pallor of that face elusive to memory, the bronze sparkle of the wide eyes, Poppy nearing him now, diminutive, plastic, saintless in the cityscape. . . .

Going to her, meeting Greg Waters, who attended The New School's Information Processing Center, one of those industrious cats with good features and an athletic boyhood, taller than Jamey, fair, a kind of pragmatic visionary, talking now, his attention on Poppy, saying he hoped the sudden prospect of peace would ease him out of the draft. So different. "The idea of leaving people like Poppy and taking off in some Army bus just doesn't figure. Right?"

Right.

"Jamey, when did you get in? I mean, was it supposed to be this late?" Poppy said.

The audition.

"Yes. How did it go? How was it? I mean, was it terrible or what?"

Greg Waters shifted textbooks and notebooks to his other hand.

"It was terrible," Jamey said, "but it worked out. I think."

"Listen, Greg—" Poppy turned to the computer buff. "I'm sorry about this. I haven't seen Jamey in like almost a month."

"In other words—"

"Yes. But—"

"Saturday still stands?" Greg Waters said.

"Oh—oh sure, Greg."

Handshaking.

"Saturday. Right?" Greg Waters trying to nail it down, not particularly seeming to like it, but deciphering Poppy, knowing it was necessary.

Poppy nodded.

They went up to her new pad, a one-room apartment that had belonged to a friend of Florida's who, instead of showing up at the Whitehall Street induction center, split for Canada. For Poppy this was a posh place. It had a telephone. The floor was painted chrome yellow, drip-sprayed in a Jackson Pollack maze of shiny black. A large Chinese chest smelling of sandalwood and a big brass bedstead painted black with a coverlet of black goatskin; two peeling wicker chairs and a wall shelf of books. An improvised kitchenette and a commodious bathroom, painted all black, a rough and mottled surface beneath which were the evidences of all the previous civilizations occupying the building during the past six decades.

As soon as they were in the apartment Jamey let burst the news of the day's events, a whole reenactment of the recording-studio scene and of the Raven people and how one of them cut short "The Lyndon Tree" in the greedy, premature flush of peace in Vietnam. Poppy listened, eyes wide, not moving, standing splay-legged, still holding her books, throwing them to the bed then and crying out in great pleasure, kissing him, edging out of her shoes, moving around the yellow-black floor, going back and kissing him again.

Jamey said he had to take a shower. Right away. He was sweat-soaked.

"What did Mike say when you saw him?" Poppy said then.

"He said he'd probably be back by one or so. I'll clear out when he gets here. I'm still sticky. That audition really stoked me up."

"But isn't it fantastic!" Poppy declared. "Do you know what you're going to record?"

"I'm supposed to discuss it tomorrow." He hoisted his black turtleneck over his head, took off his ankle-high shoes and his socks. He went into the black cavern of the bathroom. "This guy, Greg—have you known him long?"

"Yes, well, you know, like a few weeks."

"Seems like a bright guy."

"He is."

Jamey stepped out of his pants and shorts; he stood by the partially open door. "Maybe you shouldn't have tied him down for Saturday."

"Why not?"

"I mean, I'm back now, I'll be around and there won't be any more of that shuttling back and forth to school."

"That was such a drag, wasn't it? Take your shower. Do you want some tea, baby?" Poppy asked.

Yes. He closed the bathroom door. He opened it again. "I have to see my parents tomorrow night. They think I'm still at school."

"Will you be able to live in town or—"

"I'm going to have to face my old man before I do anything. This is going to cut him up and he's going to expect me to get right into the business." Jamey tried not to let the images form.

"Are you? Why don't you take your shower, baby?" Poppy began to undress. "What a drag, your having to go through that whole scene."

"I wish to hell it was all over. Anyway," Jamey said, "I'll be in by Friday—Saturday latest. You can tell what's-his-name, can't you?"

"Jamey—look, I sent him home tonight. He wanted to come up for a while. I'll have to see him Saturday."

"Hey, come *on*, Poppy!" He grinned over at her, closed the door again, stepped into the gritty porcelain tub and turned on the shower, grateful for it, letting the cool needles pierce his skin, soothing him, washing down into the feverish pores of anxiety this day had brought.

Now nothing but night was coming into the room as Jamey, a towel of Poppy's around his middle, padded across the dim light of the room, across the yellow, black-splashed floor. Poppy, barefooted and wearing only her sleeveless T-shirt, poured the moo tea into cups and set them on the floor by the bedstead.

She was all a-smile in that misty, oblique way, going to him and her arms around him then, in the circle of her love, and the bath towel fell to the floor in the hunger of his longing and his love. He removed her shirt so that at last they could meet and he kept her there. Once she murmured something about the tea and he said yes, still holding her and touching her, rediscovering the joy of her breasts, yes and the fine satin plane of her belly and the sassy thrust of her buttocks, yes, oh Poppy, yes.

"Oooh," came the familiar yet always unrememberable sigh. She arched against him, her hand playful on him, tender, holding it gently at first, yielding slowly to the swelling in her hand.

And Jamey only said, only wanted to say, how he loved her and wanted her and wanted her to be part of everything that was happening to him. . . .

"Oh, Jamey—" Poppy's muffled response against his mouth, and then soon lowering herself and so delicately, as in a rite of devotion, caressing it, lavishing him with that devotion and tenderness and that abandon that could only be Poppy . . .

Soon he was cradling her to him on the floor, cradling her above him, and he was not even remotely conscious of the rigid black-splattered yellow hardwood floor that was their bed.

To the bedstead afterward to drink the now cold moo tea, to rest on the black goatskin coverlet. The tea was very good and when they finished she put the cups back on the floor, and he drew her back to him, her body so childlike and curved and fleshed with an infinity of age: oh Jesus, Poppy, how I love you, he would say over again. . . .

Then: "I don't know where we ever—"

"Ever what?" Her voice warm and close and tickling in his ear.

"I mean, why didn't we try to do something about—about ourselves, why did we waste all that time? I know part of it was me, I mean, because of Mike, but—"

"We didn't waste it," Poppy began.

"Yes we did. Or I did."

Poppy sat up then, her small narrow feet tucked under her, her breasts pale, almost luminous in the dimness, so absolutely eternal.

"I was thinking—" Jamey clasped his hands beneath his head, stretched out his body full length against the goatskin. "I've got to find some kind of pad around here. I'll be getting money, I imagine—at least I think I will. From Raven Records. Maybe you can look around for me, and on Saturday when I—"

"Why Saturday, Jamey? That's no good for me—"

"I thought—well, you don't really have to see this guy."

"I said I would," Poppy said.

"I mean, it doesn't have to be this Saturday; you can always change it," Jamey said. "Why don't you just tell him how it is."

"How it is?" The pellucid brown eyes seemed to take on a different cast, an opacity, as if she were suddenly apprehensive or frightened. "How it is? Look, Jamey—I mean, like I've just been through all this with Mike—"

"We're not talking about Mike."

"Darling"—Poppy hesitated—"if this is going to put you up-tight all the time—"

"All I'm saying— Listen, Poppy—" But he reached out and drew her against him. "Listen, Poppy, I don't know about anything except that I want you with me. I always assumed you wanted that too."

"Oh, I do—I do, Jamey, if—"

"If what?"

"What I mean is, I want it too, as long as—I don't see what's wrong with the relationship we have—"

"I want a better one. You're talking in circles, Poppy."

"I am?" She frowned; she reached to the table for her cigarettes and lit one. "Well, you know—"

"No, I don't." Abruptly he rose. He switched on the overhead light and went back to the black-painted bed. Disconcerted, he said, "I don't know what you're trying to say, Poppy, I really don't."

She inhaled the smoke, she shook her head. "Oh, Jamey, do we have to get into all this? Look, let's go out, go someplace—"

"I don't want to go anyplace."

"Do you have to be like that?"

"Like what?"

"Like you're suddenly pissed off. Oh, Jamey, is this going to be a whole new hangup—I mean, what's wrong with what we have?"

He said, "Am I going to see you Saturday?"

"Oh, Jamey, please—" Leaning over, her arms suddenly, almost desperately, around him, her voice in a tremble. "Please, Jamey, I love you, I don't want to lose it, I don't. But can't we let it alone, at least for now."

"Christ, Poppy, if you—" He stopped; for when he'd drawn back from her he saw for the first time the places on either side of her neck, the one on the right the biggest, a crimson welt. "Poppy —what is that? What happened to you?"

"What? Oh." She touched the bruise just below her right ear. She stirred, moved to the edge of the bed. "I guess it's pretty bad, but it's much better than it was. I mean, you should have seen it just afterward—"

"When?" He kept staring at her.

"When Mike was here—last week." She stubbed out the butt.

"Poppy—" He moved beside her to the edge of the bed; he put his arm around her, around that hollow of the curve of her slender waist. "What the hell happened? Mike did it?"

"Oh, it was a real bummer, that whole night." Poppy was sitting there, bending forward now, her hair hanging down, shielding her face. "Look, why don't we go someplace, Jamey?"

"All right," he said. "You don't have to talk about it."

"Well, it's a drag, Jamey." She stood up and turned off the ceiling light. "I don't think there's any grass left—" She came back from the kitchen. "One's all there is."

Poppy lit the joint and after a long deep inhalation gave it to him. They sat there smoking on the side of the bed. No words now, only the smoke between them. He remembered then the way Mike had looked before, what he'd said: *I wish to God I hadn't seen her last time—*

"I mean"—suddenly Poppy's voice—"oh, poor Mike. I just don't dig it anymore. He knocks himself out, rushing all over the entire Eastern seaboard, he kills himself, you know how he is, he can take anything. But when he gets back here and I'm gone or out with someone, like sometimes I see Greg or someone from The New School, Mike falls apart— I mean, he's knocked out, exhausted, and he goes right back on the meth. I didn't know he stashed right here." Poppy looked down at the joint in her fingers; she dragged in and exhaled and it sounded like an endless sigh. Then she said, "Last week I was with this person who's in my Indian Metaphysics class, I mean, we were just sitting around here having some tea and rice, and suddenly there is Mike. He seemed all right, I mean, you could see how beat he was, but he was all right. Not more than an hour later I could see he was on it, and then he started tearing the place apart, smashed both windows and then he grabbed me—you know how strong he is—

began choking me, I mean, he was strangling me, honestly, my eyes were coming out of my head and I screamed or tried to, I didn't have a chance, I knew he was killing me and I— Then something happened, I don't know, I think what it was was he suddenly saw us—himself—in that mirror and he dropped me and ran tearing out of here." Poppy looked away, handed the joint to him. "He wrote me three letters this week, and he called me yesterday. I think he's never going to get near speed again. I know that's true now. I'm not scared of him anymore. He's had it." Then: "I guess I have too. Oh, poor Mike. How can a guy like that— I mean, Mike is not an ordinary person, he doesn't get himself in that kind of hangup, how could he—?"

Jamey shook his head. "I don't know. I just don't know. I just can't accept it. To me he's somebody else, maybe I see him as somebody else, I guess I always have." After an interval, Jamey looked at her. "But maybe I'm beginning to dig how it can be. Even with someone like Mike."

"What do you mean?"

He crushed out the roach in the ashtray by the bed. "Maybe we ought to get out for a while, Poppy. I could pick up some grass at Florida's."

"He's not around anymore. He got busted," Poppy told him.

"He did?"

"About three weeks ago. A female narko."

He and Poppy silent again. Then Jamey said, "Look, about what we were talking about."

"I'll get dressed."

"Poppy." He reached for her arm. "Poppy, do you love me?"

"Oh, Jamey—I love you. But I mean, does it have to be just the way you want it? I mean, there are two of us." She looked at him, the eyes soft again but again agitated by alarm or uncertainty. "I don't think it will work your way, I don't see how it will, and why should we risk anything when we've got so much going now—"

The telephone on the Chinese chest rang; it rang five times before Poppy got up to answer. "Yes—Mike?" Her voice rose and at once she glanced over at Jamey.

But Jamey was still out of it, still back in the swamp she'd left him in.

"What? Yes, he is," Poppy was saying now. "You're where? Oh, Mike, you're not! You're not hurt or—" After that she turned to Jamey again: "Mike got in some kind of accident with your motorcycle and the cops picked him up. No identification and the motorcycle isn't his."

Jamey hurried across the yellow-and-black floor to the chest. He took the telephone from Poppy. "Mike?"

"Listen, Jamey, this is not very good. I—"

"Where are you?"

"At the Avenue A station. You know. Ninety-ninth Precinct. And I don't like this, baby. What's worse is that this was a lousy, a goddam puny, little accident, not any damage at all to your bike or to this guy's stupid Chevy, but this patrol car is on top of us right away and of course the fuzz want to see my license or my draft card. The whole thing is stupid but I'm worried because it can get into a bad deal. Jamey, could you get down here?"

"Certainly," Jamey said.

"I mean now."

"Sure."

"Show these idiot boys your papers and tell them you gave me permission to use the Harley and all. I think they think I stole it. Listen, Jamey, do you have any money or a check— No, I don't think they take checks. I mean, in case I need anything." Yet Mike sounded fairly cool.

"I have some money, and I think I have a check," Jamey said. "But you're right, a check is nowhere. I'll get right over, Mike."

"All right. Thanks a hell of a lot. Thanks, Jamey. Listen, don't worry Poppy about this."

Poppy was dressed when he hung up. He hurried into his clothes. He suggested she stay there but she refused. They walked very fast, not speaking. It was almost 1 A.M. when they reached Avenue A, the Ninety-ninth Precinct.

Aquamarine walls, iron rail, desk officer behind the pulpit-desk: the muster room.

Yes. Mr. Michael Stone Sturdevant was here. Upstairs at the moment. Meanwhile some information necessary. Just for the record.

Jamey stood there, Poppy beside him, talking to the man above them at the desk. Jamey produced his registration; he vouched for Mike having had permission to use the motorcycle.

The officer examined the document and also asked to see Jamey's license. He jotted notes. Yes. Mere routine. And Michael Stone ought to be coming down from upstairs very soon. Chairs over there if you'd care to wait.

Nervously Poppy lit a cigarette; she stepped outside and stood alone on the sidewalk for a while. And for a while as Jamey waited the room was soundless except for the ominous music of teletype.

From a door at the rear sudden motion: hurrying out was a young girl in tight denim pants and leather jacket, a chubby kid, freckled, with long hair, her eyes blurred, tears silvering her cheek; as soon as she passed through the entrance and turned into the street she began running, leaving behind the echo of a sob.

Jamey waited; he looked outside. Poppy came back in. She sought his face in her agitation. She said, "I think tomorrow I'm going back to my meditation." Then: "I thought they said he was coming right down." Her reproachful glance fell upon the desk officer.

To the rail Jamey stepped once more to talk to the man. No, the man said, nothing wrong he knew of. "Don't know what's holding him up."

They found out a few minutes later when the lieutenant came downstairs, a compactly constructed figure, his uniform somewhat rumpled. A man of cherubic countenance, he had a rather preoccupied, gray-eyed gaze. He moved to the desk and handed the officer some papers. The officer then passed him a green memorandum. He studied it, nodded. He turned to Jamey and Poppy.

"I'm sorry." The lieutenant was dividing his attention between them, but favoring Poppy. "Your friend isn't going to be able to leave right away."

"He's not? How long will it be?" Jamey said.

"It might be some time."

"I thought this was supposed to be only routine; I mean, I cleared everything with the desk," Jamey said.

"We'll wait," Poppy said. "I'm not leaving. I don't believe anybody around here."

The lieutenant moistened his lips. "Miss, I suggest you check with us later. I'm afraid it'll be a while."

"Like when?" Jamey asked.

"Hard to say. There are a few things that have turned up," the officer said—a show of sympathy, the air of a veteran funeral director.

"I don't see why he—" Jamey's voice rose. "I mean, we were told that this—"

"Yes, I understand," the lieutenant said. "But we'll have to hold your friend. It might be overnight. I suggest you contact us tomorrow."

"Overnight?" Poppy cried. Dismayed, she looked at Jamey, then back to the officer. "Oh, no!" Her voice cracked in sudden alarm.

The tone of doom. Jamey knew it, felt it, just as Popppy had. Jamey said, "Can I ask what's going on? I mean, what about a lawyer? If you're keeping him, doesn't he have the right to—"

"Of course, but it wouldn't be much help until we know more and we won't know more—that is, about the nature of the charge—until later."

"But we were told he—" Jamey started again.

"This may be out of our hands," the lieutenant interrupted.

"Look," Jamey said, "all he did was use my motorcycle. Nothing happened to the other car, no one was hurt. I don't know why you people are trying to blow this up into a—"

"I'm sorry," the lieutenant said. "Ten minutes ago I would have agreed with you." A pause, a sigh of resignation or impatience. "But it develops that the FBI may have an interest in this case."

"FBI?" Jamey's voice, like Poppy's face now, was explicit with apprehension.

"What I'm trying to make clear"—the lieutenant's fingers, in a kind of absentminded sensuality, stroking the black leather of his gun holster—"is that your friend will have to be detained. I'm sorry."

Jamey pushed back the hair from his forehead. "Is there anything he needs, anything we can do for him?"

"Could we see him now?" Poppy asked.

"I suggest you call back later."

"When? How soon?" Jamey said.

The lieutenant shrugged.

When Jamey inquired about the Harley, the officer said it would have to be held there another twenty-four hours.

Outside, they moved north along the avenue, not saying anything. Desolately they walked. Poppy kept her hands in the slits of her open pea jacket. After a block of total silence, she murmured, "Oh, the bastards, the bastards, the bastards, the shits!"

Jamey put his arm around her. He didn't want to talk. Or even think. He said, "I'll call the CLU."

An old woman, sleepless, and with a sleepless girl in her teens, sitting by the open window of a tenement, the girl's radio a-blast —The Doors, Jim Morrison's voice dark above a shudder of guitar runs: *The killer awoke before dawn, he put his boots on/ He took a face from the ancient gallery/ Then he walked on down the hall* . . .

"Oh, the bastards!" Poppy cried. "And now the FBI. That's the end. Oh, poor Mike. The bastards!" Her voice was giving way.

"Listen, Poppy—" Jamey tightened his hold on her; the small figure pressed tight against him now. "Let's wait and see." But suddenly something clotted his voice, a knot, and when he swallowed it seared his throat. Why did he have to give Mike the Harley? Why did he let him take it? After all of Mike's risks, all those ruses, all these months—now this. And on campus last November, and Jamey getting him free from the Feds—and now this, this stupid innocent little accident or nonaccident. Now this.

They were passing Tompkins Square Park, some kids dragging around and not looking the way they had when Jamey first came down here; now they looked pinched, flaccid; some wore satin sweatshirts with the word YIPPIE, but somehow the scene seemed nowhere.

Walking on now and now neither of them looking at the life in the park, as if neither of them had ever been there, as if Jamey had never stood in that band shell, his guitar warming against his chilled gut and facing those Saturday-night mobs of last spring; as if he had never seen or met that girl who was Poppy, that former zealot of Haight-Ashbury, disenchanted and seeking; as if he and Laura Barnes had never wandered and scurried around looking for the lost child whose mother was stoned; as if all of it belonged to a bad trip instead of a good one; neither of them now looking into the park or wanting to because now neither of them wanted to look anywhere . . .

Turning into Saint Mark's Place, passing The Electric Circus, and all the sidewalk nomads and all the straight people in turtle-necks and gewgaws, dressing now, or trying to, like the same people they once snickeringly put down. This street, not the same street he'd been on last spring, standing atop that VW bus play-ing, singing, helping to celebrate the planting of a tree . . .

Now Mike being locked up. Alone.

Jamey stopped. "Maybe we better not get this far away." He looked at his watch. Maybe they ought to start back and be closer to the station.

Poppy said yes. She took him to a place on First Avenue, The Great East Indian Deli and Tea Temple. "They have a phone there," Poppy said.

Soon then into the tunnel-like establishment, past the counter of delicatessen to the rear, a recording going, strings of the sitar, and the casual admixture of incense and pastrami; random Salva-tion Army furniture and a flicker of candles.

They found a bench in the murky, smoky room. Poppy lit a cigarette at once; when the sallow waitress appeared she ordered a cup of Temple Tea; Jamey ordered beer.

Another couple sat on the bench across from them, close, no room for anyone to put his elbows on the stub of table between them. The couple, not cool enough to stop gaping around, looked like two walk-ons in an uptown mini opera, he all Nehru, she all Nordic and bra-less: they were having Carob brownies and tea.

After Jamey started on his beer, he said, "Do you think maybe we ought to get in touch with Mike's parents?" Not realizing until now that he had no idea who or what or where they were; that neither Mike nor Poppy had even thought of mentioning them. "Do you know where they are?"

Poppy was slow to come back. Then she said, "I'm not sure about Mike's father. He remarried and I think he's living like in Seattle or someplace up north. And his mother is in Palo Alto, still hung up on roses and ladies' auxiliary. Forget it, Jamey." Then: "Once after they were divorced—it was funny—we went to see her and she looked pathetic and I felt sorry for her. You know?

And stupidly I tried to lay the *I Ching* on her, but—oh, let's forget it. Maybe we ought to call the station, Jamey."

"I don't know if it's long enough. But to hell with it." Jamey put down his beer. "I'll try it now." He made his way through the mob. The wall telephone was in the passageway near the one toilet. He dropped in the coin and dialed Operator and asked for the number. He got the precinct. He talked with the lieutenant. It was a short conversation. When he hung up he stood leaning against the wall, reluctant to go back. Going back then slowly to the table. Nehru and chick had split.

"Jamey—" Poppy looked up at him, squinting. "What did—"

"Look, let's get out of here," he said.

"Jamey, what did they say?" Poppy asked as soon as they'd gained the sidewalk. When Jamey did not answer her at once, she said, "Oh, the bastards!"

Jamey said, "The whole goddam scene is bad news, Poppy. The FBI identified him and that was it."

"What about a lawyer, what about—"

"I got into that but the lieutenant says this is not a civil case," Jamey reported. "I mean, Mike has no civilian rights, he belongs to the military." Jamey spoke faster now, wanting to get through it, the whole goddam black scene. He wished he wasn't part of it. He tried to talk briskly, as if that might make Mike's fate sound or seem less grim than it was. If that was possible. He said, "What they did was call the Army at Fort Hamilton and they sent a squad or a goddam regiment of MP's to pick up Mike. He will be flown back to California for court-martial there—"

"Oh, no!" Poppy cried.

Again he put his arm tight around her.

"Is—there isn't anything anyone can do?" Poppy said.

"Nothing, Poppy. They're going to nail him."

"Yes," Poppy said. "I know it. I guess I've always known it."

"I guess I have too," Jamey said. Then: "But a guy like that, like Mike!"

"Oh, the bastards, the shits!" Poppy cried again.

Moving along, he and Poppy, along the avenue and then again turning into Saint Mark's Place, moving past all the people on the sidewalk, some of the white kids wearing black armbands: SOUL BROTHER (I mean, just in case if the summer gets too hot, ya see, we're with you, in your bag, man), Jamey looking for any sight or sound but this didn't work for long, and he and Poppy moved on, apart, isolated, disconnected, and people must have thought they were zonked.

All the way westward to Sixth Avenue, waiting now for the light. The way it hit him now was that deep-lodged regret of the past, of what other things he might have done for Mike, of what he should have done. The way you feel at the sudden death of someone close to you—the rueful awareness of all your deceptions and half-efforts and errors . . .

For now Mike was like someone who has died.

And all the clichés spring out of their dusty corners: Did Mike go in vain? They shall not die in vain. But it was true, Mike helped—just as Jamey hoped he himself could help—to get into a lot of things that could maybe show the dark underside of America, and help the light get to where it belonged. . . .

But, oh shit, who cared now?

Mike getting it. Always the wrong ones who got it.

Just another existential happening?

Since last November two gone: losing Roy Billings' friendship or trust; and now losing Mike's great presence and the special aura of his energies and hopes.

Leaving what?

Him and Poppy.

At least there was that, and that had to be of the best. It had to, didn't it?

That night and for almost two weeks after, Jamey stayed with her. Yet how he felt, the particular pain of his feelings for Mike, did not kill what he (or she) felt when they were in bed: they each knew it, admitted it and still it could not change the kind of love they held for Mike.

Poppy received only one letter from Mike. From California. From the Army base where he was awaiting court-martial. Mike tried to come on cheerful: the legal counsel assigned to defend him was a plump blond captain, optimistic by nature, though this did not mean he was optimistic about Mike's fate. The poop was that he'd get a year. It would be worth it; at least it would be better than joining in the slaughter or being slaughtered. If peace came, which would not be easy, there was a chance the mothers might quietly let him out to help slice the military budget. *Meanwhile, Poppy,* he wrote, *I think the only real thing on the plus side of my life is knowing there is 3,000 miles between us and that there is nothing I can do to make it closer. So this might keep me sane or fairly sane. I tell myself—I've got a lot of time to tell myself a lot of things—I tell myself this can't go on forever and who knows, one day when the whole goddam nightmare is over, Poppy might come back to where she started from and maybe I'll be around and maybe a lot will have changed. Except for one thing. And you know what that is, baby. P.S. Tell Jamey hello. Don't give it all to him. Save some for when it gets foggy out here.*

When Jamey finally showed up in old Nittygritty City, he found several letters waiting for him: a long one from Mike; a short one from the draft board stating he had been reclassified 1-A and that if he wanted to challenge this, he would have to appear before the board and present his case; a card from Laura —spring recess in Baltimore, visiting at Lincoln Karr's.

A long letter from Lyle Stinnett: big protests forming against the University administration. Roy Billings had been elected chairman of the Black Student Council, Roy finally coming on strong.

He read the letters hastily: his parents were entertaining. He stood in the hallway by the telephone table, by the wall-papered ladies and gentlemen cavorting in Colonial America. The party in the living room was in that post-dinner drinking phase, food and booze blending to form the mix for social anesthesia. He could hear, at the piano, not the conventional, artistic touch of his mother, but the untutored agility of his father playing one of the gold oldies, "Between the Devil and the Deep Blue Sea."

Fred Mieland dominating the room, his bourbon glass a dark amber prism on the piano, his cigarette smoldering in the ashtray on the piano bench; Fred Mieland commanding the scene, all bright face, must set the pace. Friendly Fred with that winning smile, the jacket of his single-breasted tan suit open, his gut plumping out over the narrow leather belt. . . .

"Jamey—Jamey!" His mother was hurrying out from the kitchen carrying a small silver tray dark with chocolate mints; she almost dropped the tray before putting it down on the step of the stairway. His mother being or pretending to be very gay in that lime-green dress, her gray-blond hair in a kind of shapeless puff. Seeing him, her pale face bloomed with color and her lackluster eyes came to life with love and surprise—and then maybe with worry. "Jamey, what are— Darling, you're home, you didn't let us know, and here we are with all these—"

He kissed her, conscious of how slow her weight was returning, the figure still too thin, near brittle; her throat so much older than her years: a rueful knife of love cut through him. "Look, Mom— I didn't know you were entertaining a mob. We'll talk later. How're you feeling? I don't think you should have rushed into a party this soon."

"Oh, I love it. And look at Fred! It always does him so much good," his mother said. "It's all business tonight."

"I'll go upstairs; I've got a lot to do, Mom. After everyone leaves, we—"

"Be goddammed! That's not my son! By Christ—Jamey!" came Fred Mieland's cries of welcome; he was bounding away from the piano, the long figure striding across the room and out into the hallway: much rough man-to-man-hug-to-hug, his breath carrying the pungent scent of Bourbon County, Kentucky, his neck and ruddy face still smelling of the barber's witch hazel, the brown thin hair almost grayless, the ginger moustache all trimmed. A dapper cat. "Love a surprise, goddammit! Come on in, son. Got a glass with your name on it."

"Right now, Dad, I'd rather not; I mean, not right now."

"Have you had any dinner?" his mother asked.

"Yes."

"You look thin," his mother said.

"Never hear you saying that to me," his father said to his mother. Then to Jamey: "What's the secret, son? No booze and all women, heh?" Fred Mieland thumped his middle and straightened his shoulders. Then: "To what do we owe this pleasure?"

"Your father," Mrs. Mieland said, "is feeling no pain."

"Don't you believe it," Fred Mieland said. "I could go out right this minute and tell you almost to an inch the square footage of any plot just by looking at it from my car, passing by and listening to the radio and watching traffic at the same time. Come in here, son, want you to say hello to all these broken-down swingers."

"Dad, I—"

"Are you disobeying your father?" Fred Mieland spoke grandly and tugged Jamey forward. Jamey stuffed the letters into the back pocket of his Wranglers; he pulled down his turtleneck sweater and tried hastily to push back the hair hanging across his forehead. "Say, everybody, look what just walked in! None other than the other half of Mieland and Son, come next June."

A flanking movement, three couples moving in on him, the men switching their highball glasses so that they could shake his hand.

"Jamey," his father was saying, "meet Marty and Gert Simpson." Marty was in asphalt roofing.

"Howjado," Marty Simpson said.

"And this is Al and Cora Helstead." Al Helstead was in tiles and carpeting.

"Nize zurprize, keed." Al oozed out his imitation of Sid Silvers' comedy accent.

"You remember Lloyd and Bess Gray—they used to go down to the beach with us when you were just about as high as that guitar of yours. Well, they've moved back to town. Lloyd here is swindling the building trade with his new aluminum siding."

Handshaking. "Howarya, Jamey? You've grown a little, huh? Not burning any more draft cards lately, I trust." Laughlaugh.

"Hi, Jamey." It was Louise Yates and at first Jamey almost didn't recognize her. His father's secretary had never been part of the family social life. This was something new and he wondered how his father could take it this far. But there she was, Louise, all jazzed up, thin and a little too bowlegged in that pink mini, her complexion improved, and wearing a wig: gone was the mousy mop of yore; here was something long, the tone of sulphur, the feel of pillows.

"Hi, Louise." Yet Jamey was relieved to see her, a familiar face, even though her presence bugged him.

"How's Mr. Oaker, our hero? We hold him in fear, oh yes—" Louise, a nondrinker, was holding a glass of sherry and it jiggled as she half-sang his high school ode to the lecherous English teacher.

226

"Let's let old Oaker rest in peace, Louise," he said.

"Say, Jamey," said one of the men, "Whatarya gonna do with all that loot you're saving on haircuts?"

"Pipe down, baldy," Fred Mieland said. "What can we get you, son? No bourbon, eh?"

"Well, no thanks."

"Beer?"

He nodded.

"Louise, would you get that boy some beer, please?" his father said. Then: "Louise is assistant hostess tonight. I asked her over. Didn't want your mother to do too much. Just look beautiful."

His mother's smile was wan—a frail tribute to her husband's kindness? Or tact?

He saw Louise come back with the can of beer and the glass for him. He couldn't adjust. In the office it was different. But here where his mother was . . .

He glanced out to the hall, to the stairway leading upstairs to his room, a shrine preserved. He turned back to his parents and the guests. Standing there. A comic statue.

The homecoming of Fuckleberry Finn.

He downed some of the beer. Oh Christ, how he wished that what would happen later was already over with; he wished he'd telephoned last night and broken the news. Now it was all ahead of him, a whole drag of a bag he'd still have to get into.

"How about this, huh?" Fred Mieland had his arm around him and was steering him to one of the two brocade couches flanking the never-used fireplace. "Sit down, son, and tell me the worst." Looking up at Gert Simpson on the opposite couch. "Gert, when a boy comes home to visit his folks like this, you can always be sure something's wrong."

Laughlaugh.

"Louise, you wanna be a doll and wet this for me?" His father handed the secretary his empty glass.

Mrs. Mieland came over and sat down on the other side of Jamey.

Jamey turned to her. "Look, Mom, I don't want to bust this up—"

"Since when would you bust anything up?" She reached for his hand. "This is the high point of the evening."

"Correct!" Fred Mieland said. Then, addressing Al Helstead, the tile and carpeting man: "Wanna hear something, Al? This boy —OK, lemme sound like a proud papa—this boy has been hitting a straight A average right down the line practically."

"Let's not exaggerate, Dad." He sank deeper into the brocade, feeling alien to the fabric or to the night. "My grades fell apart this year—"

"Fred, you're embarrassing him," Mrs. Mieland said.

Louise Yates, her long wig undulating, handed Fred Mieland another bourbon and then went over and put an LP on the deluxe color-TV-radio-tape-recorder-stereo. Now the cushy, coozie sounds of the Weston Mantovani Riddle hundred-piece orchestra in "I'll Remember April In a Garden I Surrender Dear I'm Comin' Virginia."

Feet tapping, heads swaying, lids lowered. Al Helstead, in maroon blazer with bright brass heraldic buttons, got up and asked Bess Gray to dance; Bess Gray rising, discreetly tugging the periwinkle-blue shift out from under her ass and leaning her chin into Al Helstead and working around the free feels in perfect rhythm.

"Fred," Mrs. Mieland said, "I don't think we ought to force this on Jamey. Maybe he wants to go upstairs—"

"As a matter of fact, I do," he said at once. "I mean, I want to get cleaned up."

"Why? Going somewhere?" Fred Mieland said. "You got a date. Poppy?"

"No." No. No Poppy now.

"You just came home to see us? That's all?" His father had more of his drink. "Or was there something on your mind?"

"Fred, leave him alone," Mrs. Mieland said.

"O.K." His father nodded, glanced around at the party, but something was under him. Jamey could tell. Then: "You usually call us before you come home."

"I didn't have time. Ever since that audition happened I—"

"Audition?" Fred Mieland said.

"Oh—you had that audition, Jamey?" His mother leaned forward.

"Yes."

But he waited, watching his father's face, for the storm. He saw him turn and look idly up to the wall that featured some of his prize eighteenth-century American guns. Then his father turned back to him. "Had that audition? Well, how was it?"

"I think it went all right."

Jamey waited. Fred Mieland would let it fly now.

But his father said, "Well, how about that! Good going! That's damn good, going in cold like that. Really went all right, huh?"

"They're going to sign me up."

"What?" His mother's smile was spontaneous, her voice took on sudden vigor. "Jamey, is this the company you told me about—Raven Records?"

"Yes."

Fred Mieland put down his bourbon, lit a fresh cigarette. He stood up, went to the giant console and toned down the volume of music, and then he announced the news for the party to hear. Was it that he had to flaunt pride to his business friends? Was it that he believed Jamey's progress would add more glaze to the surface of his own figure? Or was it merely the old Mieland impulse to shine no matter how dark it was? "Who knows?" he was saying ever more expansively, as though he believed it. "Maybe next year I will retire and just concentrate on my gun collection, do some fishing and live on my son's income!"

Jokes and congratulations all around.

"When did all this happen, Jamey?" his mother said when this great party started grooving again. "Did you say today?"

"No. It was—well, it happened about two weeks ago," Jamey said.

"Oh."

"Two weeks ago?" His father sat down again. "You didn't even let us know. How much school did you miss?"

Jamey swallowed. "Listen, Dad, I can't talk about it now. After people have left, we—"

"Oh, Jamey, Jamey—" His mother's hands fluttered in an arabesque of dismay: she was already wired in to him.

"Look, I said I can't talk about it now. Not here—" He was up from the brocaded couch and moving out of the living room.

"Hey, Jamey—hey, keed, what about zomezing on that geetarr?" The voice of killer comic Al Helstead calling after him.

But nothing deterred Fred Mieland, Fred following Jamey

right into the hallway and almost pushing him through the open door into the "den"—chocolate sofa and chocolate tilt-back Heart-Saver Stretchout Lounger, chocolate wall-to-wall carpeting (a recent "gift" from Al Helstead's company), strawberry drapes and cushions, a rubber-wheeled thirty-inch-screen color-TV unit; spanning the bottom row of bookshelves, a complete set of the *World Book Encyclopedia;* on the shelves above, the mysteries and chillers, the Neros and Queenies and Bondies, all the old-time corn-pone hard-covers—the Irving Stones, Anya Setons, Taylor Caldwells; the countless "informative and instructive" books Americans like to grown on, books telling us how it is Inside Argentina, Inside New Zealand, Inside Wall Street, Inside Mozart, Inside Paul Getty; the coffee table piled with all those magazines of all those zip-coded one-word names that turn on readers to the quick and easy—*Build, Life, Guns, Hobby, Home, Marriage, Garden, Dash, Joy, Piano, Auto, Travel, You.*

"Now wait a minute"—his father's voice booming into the back of his neck—"what is this? Don't try running out on me like that, I want to know what's going on. What's wrong? I know something's wrong. Are you in trouble?" A harshly, suddenly sober Fred Mieland, his face pinched, showed none of that capacity for the warm smile everybody loved and talked about.

"Dad—" Jamey still tried to get out of the corner. "I don't want to foul up your party. We can discuss it later."

"Now. Not later. You're in trouble. I know it. Walking in here tonight, no warning, no nothing. I should have known it. Now, what happened? Is it something with that record company? Is that what it's about? You're going into this music business and you don't want to tell me. Is that it?" His father waited. "Or is it something else? You've got some girl in trouble? This Poppy. Is that it?"

"No."

"What is it then? You weren't kicked out of school," his father said. "God knows you did enough crazy goddam things to get yourself kicked out, but I know it isn't that, it couldn't be—"

Jamey had had to hoard his cool. Now, gathering breath. "I left."

"You left?" Fred Mieland knowing it cannot be true.

"I quit, Dad."

"Quit?" But Fred Mieland hesitated now, almost a smile, he stood still and hushed—as if, all this time of spewing out his questions or suspicions, he had been hoping to ward off or escape the real avalanche of unwanted news.

"Yes," Jamey said; at last it was out, said, uttered, released. Yes: and seeing that rage of crimson rise into his father's face, that look he had dreaded all these months.

From outer space, the living room, came the soothing sounds from another planet, another time: Erroll Garner piano patterns, "You'd Be So Nice to Come Home To."

"Why?" Fred Mieland stirred, shifted his stance.

"What?"

"Why?" His father's gaze still bullet-straight on Jamey.

"Well, I— It's complicated." As soon as he said it Jamey knew he was in deeper.

"Why?"

"I—"

"Let me get this right. I heard you say you quit. I heard correct. Or didn't I?" Fred Mieland said.

"I just— Look, Dad, I just can't discuss it now; I mean, it involves a lot of things."

But as he faced his father he grew tight, too tight, the feeling of never being able to articulate, never getting through. He wanted to bolt from the room, the house—even though he knew he could not blame his father for blasting him; it was just that he had this way of cutting him off, leaving him stranded, hung up, building more hostility. . . .

"Why? Why, son?" Now his father's voice was rising in a new and sardonic torrent of incrimination and self-pity. "Why? Was it because you couldn't wait to get into the business? Was it because you knew I'd built that extra space for an office for you? Was it because I was proud of you and the grades you were making in college? Was it because you decided it would be too 'corny' or 'square' to come home with a diploma and be a partner to your father?"

"Will you please—"

"Was it because you just want to be a bum, screw around all night with all these kind of Poppy kids you seem to know? Is that closer to it, huh?"

Yes, that's it, Jamey wanted to say, wanting to say anything that would hurt or crush him.

"Jamey—" His mother in the room now. Then: "Fred, you stop this. Go back in there with those people. They're your friends. You invited them. I want to talk to Jamey."

Fred Mieland did not move. "I already talked to him. And would you like to know what he did, your son, your precious baby boy, after almost four years? He's quit college—quit, would you believe it? He's a goddam dropout!"

"No—" His mother looked at him, the gray eyes so wide, one hand immediately touching the cloud of her hair. "Jamey, you didn't leave, you didn't really quit—"

"Look, Mom, will you please take it easy. I wanted to tell you about it, but tonight it—"

"Oh, Jamey—" A mist already rising in her eyes.

"Mom, I—" But Jamey was mute before her now shimmering gaze.

"Come on, Louise, you lead me to those ice cubes. Dilutes the booze and the booze dilates the blood vessels, my doctor tells me." Passing by the hall into the kitchen was Louise Yates, followed by Marty Simpson.

"Fred, will you please go back out there." Mrs. Mieland was trying to regain her composure.

"Tell him, tell your precious son," Fred Mieland, rigid and fever-eyed, said. "Tell him what I spent to build his office."

"Fred, not now. And anyway you know you rented it to that insurance man; you couldn't resist renting or selling anything. So please—"

"I want you to tell him what it cost us to build it!" Fred Mieland insisted in his implacable way. "And while you're at it, tell him about how many of those goddam anonymous phone calls we've been getting every time he does something too cute somewhere or what he's doing in this McCarthy campaign. And tell him about that letter I got from the Minutemen, that goddam threatening letter!" Bitterly to Jamey then: "Your mother was *afraid* to tell you about all this, she was *afraid* it would disturb your schoolwork!"

"Fred, please—"

"Did you hear what I've been saying?" his father said.

Jamey nodded. He wished his mother weren't here; he wished he weren't burned down. More anonymous calls, and now the Minutemen: so that his rising rage at his father was locked, blocked; and he was held where he was, held down, his resolve to clear out in the morning, to lay it out for his father once and for all—all this fell away as he stood there, nailed there by the spike of his sudden remorse.

8 : THE CITY

His mom *and dad mean a lot to Jamey and he consults them on almost everything he does. Well, teeners, you can see from this that Jamey—his first album,* Jamey's Time/ Raven Records, *is just released—is quite a surprise. It's true, he is a little mysterious in some ways, but in other ways he's just like the boy down the block. . . .*

Reading this, Muriel Hewes sits at her desk in the office at the rear of the improvised nightclub: though she has not yet met Jamey, even she must smile at this piece of copy which has been left here for him by the girl from Raven Records.

On duty tonight in the recently opened uptown cabaret, Muriel shares the work with half a dozen other women (ages thirty-five to fifty) who are running the place. Purpose: to raise money for college scholarships among the hard-core poor. All entertainers volunteer their talents. The superstars and the still unknowns like Jamey. The waitresses and bartenders—mostly students, but some debs and secretaries—also donate their services.

It's really marvelous the way it's going. This place is divinely swinging, getting so many good people from the arts to do their thing for something besides money; really marvelous the way they cooperate and help Muriel and her co-workers get this place off to such a swinging start, really divine, a really divine gas. . . .

Only ten o'clock on this night touching June. Entertainment doesn't begin until after 11 P.M., but already Muriel's body, her nerve system, begins to tingle with anticipation, with that elevation of her pulse that such nights give her, working with all these people, some of them virtually kids not older than Janis Ian or Leslie Gore. Or Jamey.

Admittedly she might never have known of him this soon, but she happened to hear his record quite accidentally last Monday; she heard it at the apartment of a friend, a TV-radio network official who was not interested in the music but who was always bringing home the new rock records for the insatiable attention of his son. Muriel asked him to play it twice, that's how excited she was about it, not that she said much at the time, you have to be careful, an adult—and Muriel is, after all, thirty-seven, a widow of four years, a mere size eight, but still thirty-seven—and you don't go around saying how much you dig this music.

Anyway, she did telephone Raven Records and talk to Carol Lachman about trying to get Jamey to do his songs here.

And she got him. He's due, past due, and Carol Lachman is supposed to meet him here in the office and—

"Hi, Mrs. Hewes." Carol Lachman has returned. "I suppose there's no sign of Jamey—"

Muriel looks up. "Oh— No, he hasn't come in yet." She returns the two-page typescript. "I was glancing through this, which I shouldn't have been doing, but I couldn't resist peeking."

"Oh, it doesn't matter. Just more *drek* for the July issue of *Pop-teen*." Carol Lachman, like many other PR people, looks harassed; a pale and dark-eyed woman, probably a year or two younger than Muriel. "I don't know what's happened to him. He is late sometimes. He works for his father out on Long Island and sometimes he gets involved out there." She looks at her watch.

"When I talked to him today he said he was coming in earlier. His girl friend lives downtown and I suppose that's it."

"Oh?" Muriel says. Then: "I had no idea he works at anything except his—"

"It's one of those family situations." Carol Lachman lights a cigarette and holds the match while Muriel takes one from her gold case. "Always makes it rough for me, setting up dates for him, the way he has to live two lives. Practically."

"I see."

"But when I told him about this place he immediately said yes. That won't be a problem." Carol Lachman then taps the two-page manuscript in her hand. "But this will."

Muriel says, "I'm mad for his record, I really am, as I told you Tuesday."

"All of us are," Carol Lachman says. "Almost no one in the trade has heard it yet. Except one DJ, and he didn't think it would make his playlist."

It is almost eleven o'clock when Jamey opens the door and comes into the office: oh, he's different from the way he looks in the picture on the album. His first glance at Muriel is uncertain, perhaps suspicious. Muriel tries to disarm him with a smile: her teeth are beautiful—all right, let's admit it.

Carol Lachman introduces him. He still seems angry or disturbed. That girl downtown?

But Muriel immediately tells him how she feels about his record. "I think it's fantastic," she concludes. Does she sound too enthusiastic, silly, phony?

Jamey stands there, lanky in the corduroy suit; the collar of the flower shirt is open, his blond hair a shaggy aureole. He holds the guitar case. He wears the big sunglasses with the white rims. When he takes them off now, he frowns at Muriel, his dark-blue glance still suspicious. She liked his recording? What song did she like best?

"Well—" Muriel is not prepared for this one. Her job here is to set Jamey up so that he can perform tonight: it is always a good audience, posh, and happy to pay the admission, which is called a contribution—minimum ten dollars, going up from there with no limit. But she must answer his question. It seems urgent. He is waiting to hear it. She lights another cigarette.

"Well—let me think. I'm embarrassed. I'd hate to say the wrong thing. Oh hell, the one I—well, actually, the two I liked best are 'The Lyndon Tree'—I used to live in Texas—and 'The White Cat.' I know they're different as can be, but I—oh, I liked them all, they are all marvelous." Defensively then: "I'm not an easy person to please."

Jamey is interested in what she has to say. The dark look is fading. More than anything else surprise marks his eyes: what does an old babe like you know? A test question then: what rock artists does she like?

Now Muriel is really embarrassed. He is interviewing her. Why? What does it matter? Her whitest smile then, and another drag on her cigarette before she answers: The Rolling Stones? Janis Joplin? Tom Rush? Dylan? She admits she still can't go all out for him. "I guess I'm much too ancient," she says.

He does not contradict her. But his smile shows for the first time.

"Look, Mrs. Hewes—"

"Please call me Muriel."

"Muriel—" He leans his guitar against the desk. "I'm all for what's going on here. What do you want me to do?"

Carol Lachman speaks up. "We were talking about it earlier, Jamey. It doesn't matter. It's up to you."

Jamey says, "Clem Vogel said he was coming."

"Yes. He's over covering The Gingerbread Bicycle. But he ought to be here by now." Carol Lachman advances and hands him the typescript. "Jamey—I brought this along. You said you wanted to read everything first and I told the magazine I'd give it to you. But don't take it seriously or literally; it's just something you have to let run if you want a—"

"What magazine is this, Carol?" Jamey asks.

"*Popteen.*"

Muriel Hewes notices the way he frowns as he begins to read. Oh, she would like to help him, do what she can for him: this boy looks so tough and so vulnerable. Or is this only what Muriel wants to see? Is this only another rationale for her compulsive need to somehow be part of anything or everything that the kids are doing? Like a redemption of her whole past?

Jamey looks up, for now another man has appeared. The girl

from Raven Records introduces her to Clem Vogel: a young man, in his mid-twenties somewhere, all nervous energy, the way he looks around, moves; wearing that ivory Mao suit, sideburns down to his jaw, long hands and long nose. He carries the early edition of *The New York Times:* POLICE AND STUDENTS BATTLE AT COLUMBIA UNIVERSITY, REVOLTS AT OTHER EASTERN COLLEGES.

Muriel does meet all kinds these days and nights—not only artists, but PR people, agents, managers, music publishers, record executives, as well as all kinds of politicians and men from government agencies who are now taking an interest in this new type of cabaret. Oh, isn't it a marvelous change from those years with her husband, living all that time with Malcolm in Arizona; and oh, what a divine change from that nightmare period when Malcolm was campaigning for Barry Goldwater, and Muriel being hostess at God knows how many dinners and breakfasts for the Goldwater people. . . .

"I bring you nothing but glad tidings, Pedro!" says Clem Vogel to Jamey. "We're generating a lot of heat from at least two of our distributors." He turns to Muriel: "Mrs. Hewes, I hope you appreciate what we are giving you."

"I do," Muriel says, and looks over at Jamey.

"I doubt if anyone could keep him away," Carol Lachman adds, and makes Jamey uneasy or embarrassed.

Muriel rises, opens the door and peers out into the club. "We're filling up."

"What're you going to start with, Jamey?" asks Clem Vogel. "'Lyndon Tree'?" He folds *The Times* and puts it on the chair by the door.

Jamey fingers the typescript. "No, I thought something else."

"From the album naturally," Clem Vogel says.

"Well, no."

"It's up to you, Pedro. But in case you've forgotten, we put in over thirty hours of recording time on that album."

"I was thinking of trying something new," Jamey says. Then: "You sound like Zak and Syd."

"Up your very royal, lover," affectionately answers the young man in the pale Mao suit. "What do you mean, new? What's happened to you today? You look out of it."

"I am—I mean, I was," Jamey says. "I had to wait about two

hours for that hassle with my draft board. And I wrote this new thing, the whole thing almost in one sitting."

Clem Vogel shakes his head. "Two hours? What took you so long? Man, you like to goof, don't you?"

Jamey grins. He picks up *The Times* and says something about all hell breaking loose at the school he went to, and he talks to Clem Vogel about a student there by the name of Roy Billings.

Muriel Hewes suggests it's time to leave. She consults her schedule again, and tells Jamey he is penciled in between Jefferson Airplane and Paul Newman.

A movement toward the office door. But Jamey is not part of it and Muriel sees that he has been reading the typescript.

Carol Lachman waits now. Clem Vogel lights a cigarette. And Muriel Hewes returns to her desk and goes through the motions of rearranging her papers, though reserving a covert view of Jamey.

Jamey was reading it: . . . *that's right, we're saying it now, all you faithful Popteeners will dig him, 'cause he's outasight. You'll recognize his golden look and the golden sounds he makes. No matter if he is singing of love or war, you'll know he is singing to you and when he sings "The White Cat" you'll know it's only you. What is Jamey like? What kind of girl does he prefer? His hobbies? His private life? One thing is for sure: he'll turn you on. His hair—yes, it's thick, long and like a summer sun! Eyes that nice dark blue, and a crooked grin too. Cool it, girls—he's kind of a loner, likes to get on his Harley motorcycle and ride through the night. Of course he's not always alone. He prefers girls who are natural. Be yourself is what Jamey says. He wears turtlenecks and tight denims and those big sunglasses. His favorite foods are shish kebab and apple pie, and he likes cosy houses with crackling fires—when he has enough time to enjoy them. In a word he's the kind of man you'd like your folks to meet (though if Daddy is too stuffy, he'll freak out!). But you'll find Jamey is groovy to talk to. He loves to talk to people. Private life? Sorry, girls. He's spoke for, as they say in the hills. At least he's taken for now anyway. We understand by the Moby Grapevine that his spare time is spent with a groovy California chick who is a student in New York. But he's never too busy to say "Hey, you" to all the new friends he's making and is bound to make in the coming year with his first album. All right, Popteeners, start flipping. . . .*

That was as far as Jamey could make it. "For Christ sakes, Carol!"

"Look, Jamey—"

"That's one thing I made clear, Carol." He moved around to Muriel Hewes's desk and dropped the crumpled typescript into the metal wastebasket. "You know how I feel—"

"I can't kill it, Jamey." Carol Lachman's melancholy eyes responded with a kind of desperate luster. "This dame who runs *Popteen*—it's her life, she *believes* all this, she actually sees it that way. She controls the taste of a million kids. I mean, after all, Jamey, you're just beginning and you can't go around at this point and—"

"I'm sorry," Jamey said. "But that kind of teenybopper corn— Maybe it doesn't matter and probably no one cares and I know other people do it all the time, but—"

Clem Vogel came over and put his arm around him. "Let's go out and see who can turn art into money. Listen, Pedro, lover, this crap for *Popteen*, I agree, is not for you. But the facts of life are still around and that readership buys records." Clem opens the office door. "Come on. You're in no mood to make decisions tonight."

True. Jamey stood there not leaving. His mood was indeed not of the greatest—not after working at Mieland Homes, Inc., a long drag of a long morning, and not after that long session he put in before members of his draft board arguing his case, presenting new statements from his doctor and a new set of X rays; and not after waiting at the pad on Sixteenth Street until ten tonight for Poppy to meet him and Poppy never getting there, not even calling him. . . .

All true. He turned. "It's out, Clem."

Clem Vogel consulted Carol. "He says it's out. Any chance you can get them to scrape all that corn off the cob and deliver something more acceptable?"

"I don't know." Carol looked at him and sighed. "I'll try."

Clem turned to him. "Pedro, lover, on the concert Saturday

at Colston College—you're going to have to be a lot more cooperative."

"I know."

"The campus concert is where it's at, and you're lucky to get this booking before most kids even know you."

Now, as the others started out of the office, Muriel Hewes showed him the side door that would take him later into the back room of the club and out onto the dais. He moved along with her, conscious of feeling less tight. Was all this *Popteen* hassle with Carol nothing more than his way of diverting his nervousness? For to be here, though it was not crucial, *was* crucial just the same, because he knew he admired most of the others who performed here and he knew he wanted to please them, win their vote, as well as rouse the audience who contributed as much as they could to get this needed program off the ground. He was beginning to realize that this was what he wanted to get into; it fired him up, this union between his work and what was going on around him. . . .

The "cabaret" was more like a meeting hall, very plain, with high ceiling and the plainest tables and chairs—though you could see everywhere the unplainest-looking people sitting here: jewels of the women refracted in the murky swirls of smoke made a light show in themselves; men in black tie, some in Edwardian ruffled shirts, others in Nehrus and Maos—the straight and the nonstraight all growing in the same garden.

Muriel Hewes led them to a table near the dais, which spanned diagonally across the right corner of the club. He sat down next to her. A volunteer waitress came over—she was about nineteen, with very long hair and that familiar look, that spirit that kept her turned on like all the other people he'd been with in New Hampshire or in the march on the Pentagon or the rallies on campus: Christ, she looked like she was plugged into God's circuit.

And Poppy—where was Poppy tonight?

Everyone ordered beer except Muriel, who asked for a vodka and Schweppes. She smelled very good, this middle-aged mini-skirted lady with the schoolkid's figure and coming on too strong as a folk/rock aficionado. *Mrs. Hewes woos the Muse. But who woos Mrs. Hewes?* But a dame who seemed to know or care a

241

lot about what mattered. She smelled good; that skin of hers, bronzed—as if she had a private franchise on the sun—slender arms and the full lips frosted pale, emerald earrings and that emerald ring sparkling its green nimbus. What was it Carol Lachman had said? She was a widow with much bread. Obviously. One of those chicks who take great care of themselves; her hair, he noticed, was carefully blended into a dark titian shade, curved and cut to reach just to her narrow shoulders.

Jefferson Airplane assembling on the dais now and soon they took off, and Muriel turned to him and said he would be on next and she couldn't wait to hear him. But then a guy came to the table and said another rock group, Love, would follow Airplane because they had to make a connection at Kennedy for San Francisco. Muriel introduced the man to Jamey. He was Roger Greenthal, one of the new young rock critics, who gave three nights a week, as a kind of MC, to the club. A cool cat but warm about Jamey's album.

The beer now, and after the Airplane, watching Love come on and set up, a group he had not yet heard, and listening to them now, to that way they had merging acoustic and electric guitars, the balance against the vocalizing.

When the set finished, Jamey felt Muriel's fingers on his wrist and she said good luck. He took a last fast slug of the beer; he welcomed the look, the nod from Clem Vogel, and rose and went back to the office for his guitar, not strapping it on yet, wanting to wait until he got out there, a way of action he found helpful under stress.

But hearing now the voice out there of Roger Greenthal generously talking about him: "—and his name is Jamey and we think he's worth listening to. His first album has just been released and I find it remarkable for its variety and the virtuoso use of his voice and the texture of his interior rhyming. What's interesting about Jamey, I think, is that among the new folk/rock composer-singers, his scansion is less free and more hard-edge, his viewpoint and style is more urban than rural, more city than country and certainly more Eastern than Western." Then: "I think tonight is Jamey's first time uptown since he started last year in the East Village. And next Saturday he will play his first concert at Colston College."

So that hearing all this Jamey froze, his fingers like icicles, his heartbeat harsh in his chest. The curtain of the stage parting then and Roger Greenthal's young and leonine head jutting forth and asking him if he was ready.

Jamey nodded and moved on out to the dais strapping on the guitar, keeping his head down, looking up finally, nudging his dark glasses up, facing into the sudden cone of light, and Roger Greenthal sauntering over and asking him what he was going to do. Yes, Jamey said he'd do some songs from his album, though first he would sing something else, something newer, inspired by the way the politicos were going to solve the problems of the ghetto by recruiting the funds and know-how of Big Business.

And so he began chording into the new song born that day in the anteroom of his draft board: "Poverty's Gonna Pay Big This Year."

Gotta get rid of the slums
Gotta get rid of the bums
Before those cats try to burn us
Gotta start to save the day
But we also gotta make it pay
Who can we turn to, to turn us
on?

Free enterprise, free enterprise,
That's who, yes, that's who
The smart money's gonna go into poverty
The corporations always invest
In the best
And that's poverty, yes, poverty.
So get in on the ground floor
Dig what the new approach is
Where the rat and the roach is
Oh yes, it's clear, man, very clear
Poverty's gonna pay big this year
Poverty's gonna pay big this year. . . .

When he finished the third chorus, someone, a single voice, booed—a lone cry, but everyone must have heard this cat: his whiskey tone like a ship's fog warning came as a sustained whole note against the 6/8 tempo of the applause, and then was lost; there was laughter too, and that told him where he was and how good it was to be there: oh, it was good to hear that kind of sound laid down for him, to feel it get under him, inside him, so that Jamey knew the way was wide open for the other songs and he did them, four from his album. . . .

If only Poppy could have been there.

When he finished there was a delay, for this was a casual cabaret: it was as if each night the talent grew out of an ad hoc roster. Greenthal, the evening's MC, was telling the audience Paul Newman would be there in a few minutes. Jamey went back to the office and left his guitar there. When he returned to the hall of the club, two "waitresses" stopped him, their faces a-flush. One of the girls spoke in such a rush he wasn't sure what she said; the younger one he understood: she said he was cool—the ultimate accolade.

As he started for Muriel Hewes's table someone called: "Jamey!"

He looked around. It was Mrs. Barnes. He saw she was with Cliff Robison and two couples. He wouldn't have thought Marion Barnes would come here. But obviously the place was now sufficiently in or chic. "Jamey"—she beckoned—"isn't this the funniest! Please have a drink with us."

Jamey said hello to her and Cliff.

"Sit down, Jamey." Cliff Robison hurried into the introductions. "We said we knew you and our stock zoomed." Cliff still appraising him. "Well, looks like a whole new ball game, doesn't it? Join us, Jamey."

"I really can't, Cliff."

"Come on," Cliff said. "Come on aboard. You're welcome in spite of those cracks about private enterprise."

Jamey remained standing. To Mrs. Barnes he said, "How's Laura?"

"Oh, simply wonderful." Marion Barnes trim and athletic, her hair still sheared to boyish shortness. "She'll be in town this weekend."

"She will?"

"With Link Karr. He came in for one of those interviews. With a business consultant firm. Did you know—no, I guess you couldn't—that they're going to live in New York? That is, after the wedding." Mrs. Barnes pausing, beatific. Then peering at him: "Oh, of course—you didn't know."

"No—no, I didn't." Jamey wondered why he should have been this startled.

"But look what's going on with you!" Mrs. Barnes said then. "Tell me"—her resilient hand dipping toward the dais—"when did all this happen? Just since you dropped out of school? And an album of your own already. Amazing. Isn't that the craziest!"

Yes, it was the craziest and he had to be going now. He shook hands with Marion Barnes and with Cliff and he said, "Say hello to Laura. Tell her congratulations."

Laura and Link. Well, why the hell not! But this soon?

Laura going the old safe and sound route? Making it with Lincoln Karr, town wedding, setting up another cocktail cage on the upper East Side, the round of weekly charity lunches, and Link hustling for the bread, ten to five every day except for those sessions at the Racquet and Tennis Club, to which some men of the New York branch of his Baltimore family belonged. And now Laura ending up like that?

(And—his guilt whispering—if it doesn't work out who would she or her mother blame? Oh Jamey, oh Jamey, I call your name!)

Back at Muriel Hewes's table. And she looked all turned on, the bronzed face so animated, her eyes bright as her emerald earrings, and she was grasping his hands in hers and saying he absolutely had to, absolutely *had* to promise to sing here once a week, and then saying could he and the others all come up to her "pad" for some late supper when the cabaret closed?

Why not? Jamey had missed dinner; he was very hungry; also he saw no point in bombing back to Sixteenth Street, where Poppy had let him hang. And it seemed only decent to accept the invitation of this mahogany-haired, middle-aged, chic, quasi-hip lady—a special fan of his, and probably the only one over thirty-five he'd ever have. Carol Lachman declined; she had to get back to her husband. Clem Vogel had to get back to his wife.

Now Clem Vogel leaned over. "Pedro, you had me falling right out of my tree! And I watched and listened very carefully." He looked warm, moist-browed, his Mao jacket hung open now. He then flipped back the small pages of his notebook, and then the producer consulted the pages with their big black scrawls, and then the critique began, for Jamey did not always do his songs the same way twice, and tonight there were some lapses and Clem Vogel proceeded to tick them off. "We don't want anything like this on that college concert."

One: too much vibrato in his voice at the last few bars of "The White Cat"; two: he used those cliché guitar riffs in the intro of "Everything to Live For"; three: and in "Madrastown," what about those sloppy chordal shadings?

It was much later, after Carol and Clem had left, almost closing time, when one of the waitresses who had stopped him earlier came by and said someone was at the bar asking to see him.

Who? Poppy? Or—

It was Poppy. Standing alone near the entrance. Not far from one end of the bar. Poppy, an uncertain smile hovering on that delicate oval of a face, the chestnut hair straight down hooding her cheeks. For an instant he lost all the anger he'd been hoarding, for an instant seeing her there, small and alone, all thighs and all covered above in that new high-necked white sweater (her mother had sent it to her along with the new buckskin shoulder bag). Ah, Poppy—she was nowhere and she was everywhere. . . .

"I couldn't make it until now, Jamey. I— Did I miss your—"

"Yes."

"I knew it. Oh, shit!" Poppy shook her head.

Resentment began flooding through him; his patience, his love lost in the inundation. "I don't know why in hell you bothered coming at all."

"Aw, come on, Jamey—if you're trying to shoot me down—"

"What the hell happened?" His question too belligerent.

"What?" She raised her voice. "Look, if you're going to—" Her words got lost in the blast from The Electric Egg, a new seven-man group with more amplification than genius.

"Come on." Furiously he gripped her thin arm and led her back through the club to the table and introduced her to Mrs. Hewes, and when the evening ended and they went outside to Second Avenue, Muriel flagged a taxi. As Jamey mounted the

Harley, Muriel, as if unable to resist the impulse, invited Poppy into the cab and asked if she could ride back with Jamey. "I've never been on a motorcycle in my entire life and I've always wanted to. Would it embarrass you if I hitched a ride? I'd love it if you'd let me."

Jamey looked over at Poppy: she shrugged, hostile, indifferent, and stepped into the taxi. Muriel gave the driver the address and climbed onto the back of the Harley, her minidress hitching up to her armpits but being turned on by the experience, and Jamey handed her his crash helmet so that her hair would not get totally ruined. Her arms around him and he could feel her tensing up, but holding on, and he made it a real scramble up Park Avenue to Seventy-eighth Street. In front of her building Muriel climbed off the bike as the doorman appeared. "This'll give him something to talk about for a while." Then: "Hello, Andrew. I've just discovered a way to beat the taxi problem."

"I see that, Mrs. Hewes," the elderly but unperturbed doorman said.

As now the cab with Poppy arrived. Muriel told Andrew to pay the driver and they all went in, up in the mirrored elevator to the eleventh floor to the nine-room duplex Muriel called her "pad."

This pad, when Jamey saw it, made him think. This brand of life. He paused to peer at the painting in the foyer, black on black. Jimmy Ernst.

"Well—" Muriel Hewes went to the record player, an austere but elegant teakwood cabinet, and put on some music, most of it not much older than day before yesterday. Muriel baby really kept up. This first disk, Richard Harris singing on the album of Jim Webb's work, *A Tramp Shining.* "Well," she was saying, and she glanced not without pride around the living room—which must have been at least twice the size of Poppy's apartment, and was packed with a thousand small possessions and mementos, like medals on a general's chest. "You two please make yourselves at home. I won't be long."

"Do you mind if I smoke, Mrs. Hewes?" Was that Poppy's voice? All that proper middle-class politeness sounded as authentic as it was rare or surprising.

"Of course not," Muriel said, and left.

And immediately Poppy was into her new shoulder bag and smoothing out a joint and lighting it, sitting back on the sweep of black velvet that was the divan, peering over at him.

He kept moving around as if wanting to lengthen the distance between them. He tried to keep his interest on the room. He decided it was too much, all the art and all the furniture and all the objects and gadgets and photographs and books and flowers —too much. He would never want to get loaded down like this, possessions wagging the dog of life. . . .

He could never groove on anything like this.

"Look, I don't know why you have to get all strung out." Poppy's feelings followed him, Poppy blowing grass and already cutting the floral miasma of the room. "I was coming uptown to see you but it was impossible."

"Forget it, Poppy." He turned and looked down through the expanse of glass wall to the fatcat facades in the Park Avenue night.

"I mean, I didn't know I'd get hung up, it couldn't be helped."

"With you"—he turned around—"it can never be helped."

"Well, it couldn't. They were all around The New School and I was just standing there after class talking with Greg Waters and they—"

"They?" Jamey walked right into it.

"I mean, it was this group trying to round up people to picket the George Wallace rally at the Garden. How could I—you know —refuse? I went with Greg and we picked up more people on Avenue A—"

"Umm." Then: "OK. Even so, you could have made it earlier—"

"Will you let me finish, Jamey?" Poppy said.

"There's not much point discussing it now," he answered. "I didn't ask you to discuss it."

"No, you just looked it." Poppy killed the roach in the elliptical ceramic ashtray. "I thought we weren't supposed to get in a fever every time someone is late or can't make it. I mean, it's right back to the whole bourgeois scene, isn't it? All I was trying to tell you, Jamey, is that I had to do this. Would you prefer me to cop out?"

"Certainly not," he admitted.

Poppy seemed stopped. Distractedly she fumbled with her bag. "My mail—from Mike and my father. I never even had time to open it." Then: "Well, we all piled into these cars and this VW bus, and outside the rally the idea was to put everybody on to what they were in for inside the place. But all these creepy types just went by holding onto their tickets and their silly little fucking flags; some of them hissed at us and we were—you know—definitely not making it. Then some guy in the group arrived with a lot of Day-Glo and what we did, about ten of us, we got up on top of the VW and went topless. One of the people painted the letters on us with the Day-Glo, and we stood up there in a line like a banner to gross Wallace out. I was the two O's in 'Poor Whites.' "

He squinted over at her. "Poppy, look, you don't have to get into a phony trip like that. You could never get away with it, not with all the cops around a place like the Garden."

"Who said we got away with it? Oh, we did for a while, like five minutes, before the bastards started after us—"

"Poppy, listen, since when are you trying to snow me?"

"Snow you?" In a sudden fume of indignation Poppy rose and went straight across the room to the window wall where he stood, and without a word crossed her arms and tugged her new white sweater up over her torso, up to her chin. He saw it then: the livid purple streaks forming two letter O's, each crudely painted around her breasts. . . .

But Jamey's anger still glazed his sight. Then without warning, this view of Poppy—all bunched-up sweater where her neck and chin were, the gaudy graffiti circling her bare breasts—suddenly this sight engulfed him and where his rage was there was an explosion of helpless laughter, and finally, as if he knew no other way to stop or gag himself, he leaned down and mouthed her decorated and impudent bosom, his tongue or his muffled laughter forgiving her for anything. . . .

It was the sound of Muriel Hewes's foot nudging open the door from the other room, coming as it did just in that quiet interval of the record between tracks, that signaled Jamey to pull down Poppy's sweater. If Muriel saw any of it, there was no way of knowing; she never cracked, her suntanned face putting out nothing but exhilaration as she carried this outsize tray to one of the glass coffee tables, the one in front of the black velvet divan where Poppy had been sitting, and there was all this food. When she looked around she seemed to sniff, she glanced down to the ashtray. The uncertainty on her face gave way to a slow smile. "Well"—she looked at Jamey—"I guess I have just about everything except—pot, don't I?"

"I have some," Poppy offered.

While from the record: "Hey, Jude."

Muriel said no thanks. "Or maybe I should. I never have." Yet when Poppy offered her a joint: "Oh, I think not." A short self-conscious laugh. "How square can one get, hmm?"

She sat down on the divan beside Poppy. Jamey pulled over a white side chair as Muriel heaped out a plateful of goodies for him: burnished turkey leg, a lime aspic, artichoke hearts, a beautiful golden apple. (The brand of life he condemned?)

Jamey bent to it as if all of his six-foot frame needed every grain and morsel to survive or as if his long day and the tension of this night had sucked out all his blood and marrow or as if his system craved nourishment to push him through tomorrow at his father's office. And tomorrow already here.

Eating, wolfing it now, as Muriel Hewes, with the exuberance of a teenybopper, turned herself on, legs crossed, brandy glass in hand, rapping away about her work with the "cabaret": she almost never got to bed before 3 A.M., unlike the nights of her married life, and how fantastic was the success of her work now and how much bread they were raising, how many poor kids would be getting a chance at college. Then: "I think one of the funniest sidelights to it is that so many of the people we depend on actually dropped out of school. Didn't you too? Didn't I hear that, Jamey?"

Jamey nodded; his plate clean now, reaching for the white napkin, pouring some more coffee from the small silver-ringed carafe. Muriel, the hostess, patching holes of silence left by him or Poppy.

Once as he reached for his coffee cup he sensed her eyes on him and he looked suddenly to pick up, intercept, the vibration, and then he turned his glance to Poppy.

Muriel rose and changed her seat, going to the big womblike

Swedish chair, as if she decided that sitting next to Poppy only deepened the shadow of age between them.

Another brandy after a few minutes: Muriel Hewes for the first time showing a certain sense of isolation . . .

(*Mrs. Hewes woos the Muse. But who woos Mrs. Hewes?* The stupid doggerel kept nagging at him. *Who ignites her fuse?*)

Putting the brandy glass down, Muriel Hewes excused herself and went out of the living room.

Immediately Poppy brought out the letters from Mike and her father. She scanned Mike's first, then began reading a section of it to Jamey. The cryptic style Mike had developed was necessary and both Poppy and Jamey knew how to decipher it:

. . . I am not exactly alone intellectually, which is maybe why this stockade is a bit overcrowded these days. The next stop in the life, times and peregrinations of Mike Sturdevant—unknown. And even if I knew, there is that little law here about "unauthorized contents" in letters. Your last one, Poppy, rated a lot of interest around here by those who checked it; they think your language is "colorful." Will check on regs about incoming packages. Meanwhile my health (physical) couldn't be better, as we get the kind of exercise here that makes it easier never to gain any weight. Nine months and six days to go. I hope. The state of the world has not improved nor has it deteriorated, which I thought would happen once I was removed from the scene. Keep writing. It's all that makes the days shorter for me. The news about Jamey is all he deserves and more. If he gets a big head and becomes obnoxious maybe you'll turn back to the baby who's saving it all up for you. . . .

Poppy opened the envelope from her father then. "Oh, it's just a quick note with this in it." She handed Jamey the large newspaper clipping. "You keep asking what he's really like—well, this is more or less what he's into now."

Jamey studied the photograph of her father at the head of a two-column report on the student strike at his college: a man of middle height with hair very shaggy for his age and gray sideburns down to the earlobes, a luxuriant moustache, resolute but delicate mouth; the eyes were much as Poppy had once told him, those of a "California Dreamer."

The caption beneath her father's picture said: "Professor Thomaston Edwards joins ranks of striking students."

"Certainly I'm with these kids," the report quoted him saying. "I believe in them. I think they're more honest, less selfish than my own generation. Of course they're impatient for action. Why is this? Well, I think Kingman Brewster, President of Yale, pretty much put his finger on it—in part he said: 'There are two understandable reasons for the impatience of the youngsters and the feeling on their part that action must take place now. One is the fear that the world will blow up if something is not done with immediacy and speed; and the second is that the more highly organized the society becomes, the more concentrated centers of power become, the harder it is for the individual to feel he makes a difference. One way he makes a difference is to be visible, and to be visible is to be impatient in your manner of protest—'"

Jamey returned the clipping from the San Francisco newspaper. "Your old man is quite a cat. You're a hell of a lot luckier than I realized."

"I am?" Poppy frowned.

When Muriel Hewes returned she tried for a while to stitch together enough words to extend the night or to keep it from bombing out. "Carol Lachman was saying something that surprised me, Jamey—"

"Umm?"

"About your working for your father."

"Yes." But let's stay out of that corner.

"Mrs. Hewes—" Poppy reached into her bag for another joint, got up and moved to the fireplace; she sat down on the floor in a lotus position. "I think maybe you're stepping on somebody's hot little foot."

"Why is she?" he had to say.

"I mean"—Poppy still addressed Muriel—"I mean, his father is like something else." She lit the joint.

"Is that bad? I gather it is." Muriel's gray eyes lively; tilting her head, the auburn hair in graceful swerve: but a discussion was under way and she was a happier hostess, this hippie manqué.

Poppy, he knew, was not going to drop it. "No, it isn't too bad; I mean, Jamey *likes* those bad trips sometimes."

"Look, Poppy"—he tried to reach her with his eyes—"you know how much choice I have."

Of course the warning didn't touch her, not Poppy: regardless of where or when, let it all hang out. "You told me if you got out of the draft you'd never go back." She was letting the joint smolder. "I mean, you decided it was something you'd refuse to do anymore. On principle. You said."

"I can't let them force me out," Jamey answered.

"You mean those mothers from the Birch Society and the Minutemen?" Poppy said. "But you already proved your point."

As far as Poppy was concerned he had made his defiance of the anonymous calls and the threatening letters, the warnings to his father to make Jamey shut up or get out. "I'm not quitting until the calls stop and the letters stop."

"I thought you said they had."

"Almost. But you can't give them an inch."

"Oh shit," Poppy murmured.

A pause.

Muriel Hewes leaned forward in her chair. "I think I'll change my mind, Poppy."

"What?" Poppy looked over at her.

"The pot. If you can spare some," Muriel Hewes said.

Jamey got Poppy's bag from the divan and took out the rest of the stash. He lit one for Muriel Hewes, and because it was her first time he didn't want to inhibit her, so he moved off across the vast living room. He passed the black iron spiral staircase that corkscrewed up to the second floor of her apartment. At the TV console he paused. He looked at his watch. He switched on the set. The late late news was already in progress:

"—the latest talks between the peace negotiators in Paris indicate the United States is still unwilling to commit itself to a total cessation of the bombing, but—"

"But," Jamey shouted back at the TV screen, "this week alone five hundred and sixty Americans died in Vietnam!"

"What? Jamey, did you say something?" Muriel Hewes's voice from across the room.

Now shots of the students at Columbia still fighting it out with police after the battle of yesterday, which went through until dawn. Other schools shown now, in Ohio and California, with students in violent dissent against the authorities . . .

Something galvanized his attention then: a familiar, blurred late-night view of Scott Memorial Quad, of the fountain—his alma mater, that erstwhile institution of midi-culture he used to call Mustang U. . . .

A flash and streak of lights, students in clusters and knots and others running or walking. A newscaster was saying now that they would transfer to the front of College Hall for interviews with two of the student leaders.

Jamey saw it then, that massive marble facade of Doric columns, that Parthenon without pediment behind which Chancellor Alvin Adams Ross had his offices, that red marshmallow of a rug in Rossboss' chamber where Jamey got the bad word. . . .

Out in front, lights and mikes were set up and a thousand students massed on the steps and lawn. . . .

Interviews came on, hasty, improvised—and who was that now? His buddy Lyle Stinnett, the long-legged fugitive from Virginia, stating for the cameras that SDS and other groups were pressing their demands against the administration, demanding more student control of the curriculum, demanding that agencies like the FBI and the CIA, with their hounding presence, wiretapping and other harassments, be barred from campus. Lyle answering the questions now: yes, they had occupied and were holding the rear wing of College Hall, and they would not leave until the University met their requests. Was it also true, a reporter was asking now, that they were inside to support the action of the Negro students who were occupying, holding, the central part of the building? Yes.

"I understand," the interviewer said, "that the Negro students have not asked for your support and that in fact they prefer you to leave. Is that true?"

Lyle said, "We stand for everything they stand for and we are giving them our support. I think it is a tactical necessity."

The camera panned to another part of the steps, and there being interviewed in torn white shirt was another buddy (former buddy?), Roy Billings, Roy very erect, half-circled by other members of the Black Student Council, and Roy saying in that precise, almost elegant way of his:

"No, we are definitely not coordinating our efforts with SDS or any other white campus groups. The black students are acting on their own. We have no plans to do anything except act on our own and we are not leaving this hall. We will hold it, police or no police, threats or no threats, until the administration accedes to every demand of every black student in this University—"

"And these demands, Mr. Billings—can you tell us what they are?"

Roy edged closer to the hand mike of the interviewer, his voice cool but with that underedge of derision: "Well, we've submitted our demands—small, petty items like wouldn't it be advisable to increase the number of scholarships for black people, and wouldn't it be advisable to put more black professors on the faculty, and then there are trivial demands some of us feel ought to be met, like courses in Afro-American history, black literature, and other courses that might hint something of the black man's place in our past. . . . What? What will we do if nothing happens? Well, you see, sir, if we are ignored this time we will simply tear this place apart. For openers. Yes, I am supposed to graduate, but you see it doesn't matter because as soon as I return to my home town I have already been selected for the honor of going into the armed services and fighting for my country. I'm not saying I will, necessarily, I am only saying I've been selected, like a lot of my friends here, because what we did here on campus and at the Pentagon last October impressed a lot of folks like General Hershey."

Cheers, cross-cries and shouts, and the camera swiveling away from Roy to cover the other black students . . .

Jamey turned off the set. He looked around, to see that Poppy had come over and was standing a little way behind him. And he saw Muriel crushing out the joint.

His attention returned to the TV screen, now blank and showing nothing but his own reflected image. He heard Poppy say something, and Muriel answering, and Poppy saying Lyle Stinnett was a law student and a friend of Jamey's and hers.

"That campus scene"—he turned to Poppy—"it looks like nothing but bad news." But saying it didn't help pull down the way his feelings had kept piling up during the newscast, the sense of regret, his not being there, his having left before the fight was any where near over. . . .

If he'd been back at school, if he'd been standing with the rest of them . . . though not standing with Roy.

But it was Roy's voice that stayed with him. Those echoes of how many other black students?

It was Roy who laid it all down. Jamey could never blame him. Even though he knew there would be more repression and more blood.

But the way Roy said it made it something Jamey felt all the way through. It was nothing new. Yet it was somehow newer and it hit him harder and it spurted his rage, his frustration, just the way the endless war did, and the way the shooting of Martin Luther King had this spring.

All the warnings, all the protests, the rallies, the hassles, the labor and love that so many tried to put into ways to stop it all— and nothing!

Yet now only wanting to get there. If he could be there tonight, on campus.

But he'd been there and he'd quit.

He turned to Poppy and he said they'd better split, he had to be in Nittygritty City first thing in the morning.

"You can go from here," Poppy answered. "I can get down-town."

Poppy, still pissed off, stranded, though he recognized what was in her eyes, wanting to be near, needing him because he *was* near, wanting all that loving that would light them both up, and it would be daylight before he got around to sleep.

And his father's office waiting for him sure as death, and that same hassle: Where were you, son? You look like you've been whoring around all night, what kind of time is this to show up? Either you work here or you live with that girl!

Jamey said, "I'll go back with you, Poppy."

"I mean—you know—you don't have to," Poppy said.

But he had to be with her.

Muriel Hewes was moving toward them, her miniskirt some-what rumpled, her legs and thighs so evenly suntanned, her cop-pery face suffused with a new radiance. She veered off and went to the record player, turning then and saying, "Would I be a bore, Poppy, if I asked for another?"

"I think—you know—we finished them," Poppy said.

"Oh— Doesn't matter." Muriel put on more music; this time, for the first time, it was Jamey's album.

Jamey said they had to go. He thought again of the office and he thought tomorrow afternoon he ought to call Lyle Stinnett.

"You're sure you won't have anything?" Muriel Hewes went to the glass coffee table, beatific on brandy-cum-pot and having such a fine time digging her experience. She must have been more stoned than she realized: she reached for the bottle of Courvoisier but clumsily let it slip from her grip, and it fell clashing against the edge of the table and then hit the white marble floor. The bottle splintered and almost at once the room was heavy with brandy fumes rising to merge with the smoke of grass. "Oh—" She seemed more shattered than the bottle; an unpoised hand touched her auburn hair. "I'm sorry."

When Jamey went over to pick up the fragments, she said insistently, "Oh no, please. The girl will be here in the morning."

As she accompanied them to the foyer Jamey could hear his voice coming from the record following him. He heard it this time like a stranger listening, for it seemed enhanced, richened (which it was, in all that manipulation of Clem Vogel, Clem not even waiting until after the recording, but doing much of it during the session, adding echo, mixing and blending as he went along).

He wondered if Lyle Stinnett or Roy Billings or anyone else on campus had heard the album yet. He had no way of knowing, and that telegram the other day from Able's Music Store probably showed Dave's personal enthusiasm more than it reflected an accurate opinion of the others in the college town.

But tomorrow, yes, he had to call Stinnett.

Out in her foyer now Muriel shook hands warmly with Poppy and then buzzed for the elevator.

As the stainless steel door slid open and Poppy stepped into the car, Muriel was telling him how much she appreciated his helping out tonight and not to forget next week, and she said "what a divine gas" her first motorcycle ride was, and her first smoke.

"Good night—" Impulsively Muriel Hewes kissed him then, and at once he felt the desperate thrust of her tongue.

As the elevator descended he noticed the way Poppy was looking at him. He said, "Well, I didn't ask for it. But she certainly gave it to me."

"You don't have to—you know—apologize," Poppy said, and hitched on her shoulder bag.

"I wasn't apologizing."

"I mean, if you turn this lady on, why not?" Poppy always asserting her manifesto of love (or living).

At the curb they mounted the H-D and he jammed down on the kick starter. It was very cool outside but moist. Rain soon. Roaring off now and Park Avenue at this late hour his private raceway.

At the apartment on Sixteenth Street, as they undressed, they talked about the cabaret and Muriel Hewes. He crossed the yellow-and-black spattered floor to the bathroom and got under the shower. Poppy was brushing her teeth when he finished. And he sat down on the edge of the john: pensive, agitated, he studied the dimpled hollows above her naked little rump. "I'm going to call Lyle Stinnett tomorrow," he said. "If I go up there, you'll come, won't you?"

"Depends when—I mean, if it's not a time when I have like a class or an exam." She began soaping the washcloth. "I have all that outside reading I haven't even looked at yet." She started cleaning off the Day-Glo paint. "But I'd like to go. Lyle is really a groove."

"Here"—he took the washcloth from her—"I'll get it off. Labor of love." When her breasts were free of the wheels of paint, she reached out and drew his head against her and he lingered there for a long taste of what he'd only begun at Mrs. Hewes's place.

So that they never made it back to the other room, and he sat down again on the john seat, Poppy straddling him—only ninety-nine and a half pounds of her but with that infinite weight of love and the purest dedication of that insatiable and velvet little diddlebox, that tender vise of thighs. . . .

"Ooooh, Jamey—"

It must have been close to 5 A.M. when they were ready for bed. Poppy had finished copying her notes for Indian Metaphysics. As she folded the black goatskin cover and drew back the gray unironed sheet, she said, "I could make it maybe day after tomorrow."

"What?" He got into the bed.

"I mean"—she was beside him then—"if you're going to get into that."

"Oh—well, yes, I'd like to. The problem is, I'm no longer a part of it. I'm going to call Lyle Stinnett tomorrow."

"Day after tomorrow—" Poppy paused. "I—I'm not sure; I can't remember if I said I'd go to that meeting or not."

"What meeting?" Sleep seemed so remote to him as to be almost irrelevant.

"You know—Mailer and a lot of people. It sounded interesting."

"Well, look, Poppy—"

"Oh, I'll forget it, I'd rather get into that campus thing with you." Idly her small hand tracked down along his belly. Abruptly then she sat up. "One thing I'm glad about."

"Hmm?"

"Like I'm glad you're beginning to make it now," Poppy said. "I used to be worried, I mean, right after Mike got caught. Oh, what did I do with those letters—" She started out of bed.

"Poppy—" He grasped her arm, pulling her back. "Wait a minute. What do you mean, you were worried about me? You never said anything about it."

"I mean, I was, well, worried about us. Everything was getting, I don't know, too tight, too much. Wasn't it?" she said.

"I like it that way," Jamey said.

She looked at him. It was not the first time she looked at him in this way: that cloud in her eyes dark as fear.

"I think," he said, "you have to have a kind of tension going if it's any real kind of love."

She pondered that and let it go. "No, I meant now that you're beginning to make it, it's better for us. Even if something happens like you're a tremendous great big all-out success or even if you turn into a shit, I—"

"Oh, I will, one of the biggest," Jamey said. Then: "Look, if we're going to talk about anything happening, what about you? What's going to happen to you?"

"When?"

"Oh, I don't know," he said. "Any time."

Poppy's tender smile: "How do I know? I feel like some tea. Do you?"

"No."

She padded across the Jackson Pollack floor and heated a pan of water. "I should have eaten some of that poison Muriel had. All Yin and no Yang." She fixed the Bancha tea.

"What do you really want to happen to you?" Jamey said when she was back in bed, holding the mug between her hands.

"How do I know?" She blew on the hot tea.

"I think maybe you like not knowing, don't you?" he said.

"Maybe," she said. "But I mean, I never want a blueprint or a fence. What we have going is just right." Then almost crucially: "Isn't it?"

He said, "I keep getting the same jazz at home. They're scared to death we're going to get married and here I am living with you and everyone back there keeps asking them if—"

"For godsakes, Jamey, you're not letting that bug you, are you?" Poppy said. "I thought—I assumed they knew just where it was. If they still don't, why don't you tell them. Even if they don't dig. At least you—"

"Christ!" He laughed. "I wonder what would happen if we did."

"Did what?"

"Get married."

Poppy stopped sipping her tea. She did not look at him. "My parents have that. Why should I try to top it?"

"I wasn't thinking about trying to top anything or anyone," he said.

"Well, I meant that's a whole special thing and I'm not into it, I'm really not." Poppy's voice thin, a hard melancholy. "And all those rules, I mean, all the unwritten ones, the ones you have to work at all the time. Who needs it, Jamey?"

"I don't know what we need," he said.

"I don't either." Poppy downed more of the tea and then put the mug down on the floor. "Except I think what we need is only to follow our—you know—arrows. If we follow our inner arrows that's all we need." She smoothed down her long hair now and was very quiet for a while.

"In other words," he said then, "we just head out to sea and the more fog the better."

"I guess." She murmured: it was there again, that indefinable ache beneath her voice.

"What?"

She swung around. A fierce rush of tenderness: "I love you."

"I love you."

Silence.

Then she said, "Why? Why really? Why?"

"I don't know," Jamey answered with absolute honesty, "unless it's that sometimes it's like this. Like now. Of the best."

Poppy's hand moving over his.

"Or because," he said, "this is the only good thing in a super-shit world."

As it happened he never called Lyle Stinnett—how could he when Lyle was holed up with the other students in the south wing of College Hall? But as it happened it was Lyle who telephoned him. At the office on this Wednesday afternoon.

"Where are you calling from, Lyle? Man, it is so great to hear that phony Old Dominion accent of yours!" Jamey leaned forward at the Simu-wood Steel Execudesk his father had installed for him this spring. "Where are you now?"

"Where am I?" The familiar cadences of Virginia rolled softly into Nittygritty City. "At this moment I am occupying the august chambers of the Assistant Dean of Men. Guess what I found in his private john? The current issue of *Playboy* as well as one of those dirty-old-man paperback novels." Lyle paused. "Jamey—I hesitate to put the buddy-buddy hand on you, but we need some help around here. I know you're going big these days—you're one of the most loved and revered dropouts this institution has ever let loose, in case you didn't know—"

"Fuck off, Lyle," he said. "I was going to call you the other day, then I realized I couldn't get you. I wanted to come up."

"You did?" Lyle said. "Well, let me tell you, we can use you, daddy, and how we could use you! Your album is all over the place."

"It is? Already?"

"Sure is. I can see why you put this place behind you." Then

Lyle said, "Listen, Jamey, any chance of your getting up here—say, by tomorrow? Is that pushing it? I mean, it's getting a little rough here now."

"Tomorrow?" Jamey hesitated: suddenly time was pinching him again. That's how it had been lately. His life, aside from his duties at his father's, was not as much his own as in the past.

Yesterday in New York he had had to make a hurried (overdue) trip to West Fifty-second Street to Local 802 to become a member of the union; he had had to pose for more pictures up at Raven Records; once again he had had to sign a dozen press kits, which the company then sent out by special messenger—this kit was twenty by fourteen and covered in black velvet and it contained his album, a poster-size photo and other items of hype.

Two days ago, through Clem Vogel, he had acquired—you had no choice—a manager, one kinky-haired, funky-eyed, ironhearted Irishman, Nat McGovern, who had a switchblade mind and who would also act as his attorney, and who was already trying to arrange more campus concerts after the one scheduled this Saturday night at Colston College.

Between times, all spare seconds since the early dawn he'd cut out from Poppy's bed, all his power was going into his new project: a long talking song or poem about Negro history: three nights in his room at home he worked on it, working in a storm, intermittently running downstairs for more TV—the whole phantasmagoria of Robert Kennedy's assassination and funeral and the faces of all the weeping Negroes, and LBJ soothingly telling the nation now now don't y'all take this so personally, we're not two hundred million sick people, just one sick person did this . . . *Oh, how long was everyone going to keep riding this plush supershit special taking them straight to Civil War II?*

Somehow Jamey worked through it and completed the song and taped it. But his obligation to the record company never eased off, every day or every night some stint to perform.

For example: since his name at Raven was already smudged by his having refused not one but two teenybopper magazines, he couldn't say no to a legitimate interview with a newspaper syndicate. As for the kids, naturally he liked them, but he didn't want to make it with them on this corn-pone level. Syd Held and Zak Silberman were coming on salty, and Clem Vogel urged him to cool it. Hence he then agreed to give another half-day to Carol Lachman and her Fame Machine.

But the one thing he wanted and needed most was time for his own work, and he couldn't seem to buy it or steal it. . . .

"If you could get up here tomorrow," Lyle Stinnett was saying, "that would be—"

Tomorrow. Thursday. Oh Christ. That session he had promised the Raven people he would go to: that bigbigbig interview with the bigbigbig DJ for what the trade regarded as one of the big-bigbig sendoffs on bigbigbig FM radio. Even Jamey would admit it was something that could only do him goodgoodgood. . . .

"There's only one thing, Lyle. I mean—well, never mind—"

"What is it? I figured it was probably too last-minute to get you but—"

"No—never mind, forget it. I think I can make it all right." Jamey went on before you could say Syd Held or Zak Silberman: "No, it's OK, Lyle. I had some kind of a thing with a DJ but I think I can put it off." Then: "Tell me something—are you people getting anyplace? According to the TV stuff I've seen—"

"I think we're holding our own," Lyle said.

"What about Rossboss?"

"Well, that part is getting rough," Lyle answered. "He's threatening to call in the police if we don't clear out by Thursday midnight. I want to use everything we have to hold out. It's been good going so far but a lot of guys are getting a little fatigued, to say the very least."

"What about Roy?"

"That's the main thing I called you for, Jamey. We're getting nowhere with him, and if you could help put across to him and the Black Student Council that they can't play this alone—I mean, together we can make it, I think. But separately—well, you know I feel the same way you do about that."

"Roy won't do business with me, Lyle."

"He might. At least he'll listen to you."

"I doubt it," Jamey said. "I found out the hard way."

"Now listen to me, Jamey: Roy is mighty predisposed toward you, despite what he says."

Jamey said, "This call couldn't be monitored, could it? I mean, they wouldn't do an impolite, naughty thing like that to us, would they?"

Lyle laughed. "Oh, never, never." Then: "You and I already have dossiers thicker than our college records. They'll use them when or if the time comes, so we might as well care less."

"What about Commencement?" Jamey asked.

"I'll tell you the sad tale when you get here. We're in Hall B, South Wing," Lyle said. "You sure you can really come up tomorrow? Something tells me you're in a squeeze and—"

"No." Jamey said it more firmly this time. "I'll be there. I'll take the train, the four-o-five."

"What about that two-wheeled monster?"

"In the shop."

Then Lyle said, "How's the light of my life, you bastard?"

"She's great, Lyle."

"You bringing her up?"

"I was. But now it depends on her schedule at The New School."

"I'd not advise it," Lyle said. "Well, listen, Jamey, I surely do appreciate your doing this. I realize you've got all these problems now, but that's the price of *la vie* glamorous."

"Fuck off."

"Up yours," Lyle replied.

Like olden golden times.

Down the steep steps of the train. His left hand gripped the handles of guitar case and bag. Even before he touched the wooden platform of the station, he heard the bursts: new sounds in his life, these young voices reaching him in shrill trajectories, shattering the late afternoon of June like a hundred dissonant horns:

"Jamey!"

"He's here!"   "There he is!"

"Jamey!"   "Welcome back, Jamey!"

"Hey, Jamey!"

"Sign this!"

"Please would you sign this!"

"Jamey!"

"I have your album!"

"Sign this!"

"JameyJameyJameyJameyJameyJameyJameyJameyJamey!"

Moving counter and crabwise through the cacophony of the new sounds in his life, yet feeling a tug of pure childlike pleasure at this recognition by strangers, while at the same time wanting to fly or sink out of sight beyond the reach and cries of the local boppies and campus kids:

To one of the battered 1959 Chevy taxis with its old Detroit Spaceage tail wings, and going straight to College Hall— Was that it? Yes, but with that mob across the wide tier of steps, in front of and behind the barricades, a tangle of wood horses, garbage cans, orange crates? Was this it, this Indiana-limestone flat-roofed Parthenon, was this the sacred temple in which Rossboss used to lay down the law and sacrament? (Excrement?)

He saw right away that getting into the building was not going to be easy. At the top of the steps you could see the students inside and the ones who were guarding the doors and windows outside, while all around there were these ragged groups of counterdemonstrators—ultraconservative, indignant students who got their balls off hurling threats and insults and hurling garbage and junk from some malodorous arsenal: the target now was Jamey.

"Hey—don't go in there!"

"Stay out of there!"

"This is campus, not Red Square!"

"Mao-lover!" yelled another as Jamey mounted the steps.

He kept going.

Thunk: an egg splattered against his left shoulder.

Louder somewhere above: "We Want a Revolution!" came the singing from the *Marat/Sade* play.

"Hey, Jamey—Jamey!" someone called from a friendly island.

"Stay out of there!"

"You want anarchy or education?"

He kept going up.

Plorrpp: a plastic bag of red paint came hurtling from the counterdemonstrators. Jamey was slow, but lifting his right arm, which held the guitar case, he shielded his face and caught it on his elbow, the bag exploding on his corduroy sleeve bright as a crimson flower.

He kept going, holding his suitcase and his guitar, shoulder splotched egg yellow, elbow gummy red: but gaining the threshold and hearing behind him the voices of righteous coeds shouting with ladylike delicacy at the campus right-wingers:

"Ball-less bastards!"

"Jerk-offs!"

"Sister fuckers!"

Jamey got through and into the great rotunda: Negro students everywhere, some standing, some stretched out on the floor, some singing, some in tight circles rapping passionately. But it was almost as difficult getting through here as it was getting up the steps outside, feeling now like a stranger in a foreign country without passport, though once or twice he thought he heard someone call his name.

To reach the south wing you crossed an enclosed bridge and suddenly you were in white territory, right in front of the lecture hall. This once familiar room of tidy one-arm chairs was now another scene: guys everywhere, sitting, standing, squatting, sprawled on sleeping bags; a debris of beer cans, coffee cartons, Coke bottles. . . .

Faint as it was as he passed, Jamey smelled the heavy sweet aroma in the staid lecture hall; it was obvious a handful of people were smoking.

Tomorrow's headline: MARIJUANA, DRUG-USING NEW LEFTISTS INFILTRATE STUDENT BODY IN CAMPUS REVOLT.

Someone's portable player, an album spinning beauty: The Beach Boys into "Wild Honey."

Down the corridor right of the bridge, to another familiar landmark, the door of the Assistant Dean of Men, except now there was a new sign: ASSISTANT OLD PHART OF MEN.

Inside the office it was Instant Reunion, leaders there from the different factions, all friends, and suddenly he had never quit school, scrambled off campus on the Harley that couldn't get him far enough away. He put down his suitcase and guitar. All friends here now, all spectrums from SDS to Lyle Stinnett and the CCA: yes, Lyle here, and Bob Lothar, editor of the campus paper, and Gary Einsberg, the premed, and Susan Sayres and Dwight and Claire Dougherty and Andy Ryan with Paula Heston, all around him now, all love and all talking at once; rushing at him with the shape of the scene: listen, almost five hundred people holed up in this wing alone, and the Negro contingent in the main building, and tonight was it, tonight they would either make it or bomb out. . . .

And now Lyle Stinnett stepping back from the others—Lyle, his thin hair limp, his jaw with the brown stubble of four days' growth, eyeing him, Lyle ambling and rambling around the office, coming to a stop before him, Lyle tall as a wall. "Well, I declare, look what just came in! It is my boy, my very own long lost son—why, you sonofabitch, you got messed up a bit, didn't you!"

Susan Sayres with a wad of Kleenex now trying to rub the egg and paint stains from him. Pointless, but part of the welcome. Yet Susan working away, the long chestnut hair undulating like a flag in gentle wind . . .

Settling down, and Lyle, sitting on the edge of the old phart's desk, getting into the basics: "The point is, Jamey, in my opinion they can break us easier this way because we're already in two parts. If we're solidly together, blacks and whites, it's going to make us a lot more impregnable, it'll take a lot more police to root us out of here."

"I know," Jamey said. "But I also know Roy."

"You said you'd at least try it," Bob Lothar urged him. "When Lyle called you, you said you'd at least try it."

"If you could get him for just this one night," Gary Einsberg said.

"If it doesn't work, then what?" Jamey had to keep it on the negative side, knowing the odds.

"Then we're no worse off than we are now," Lyle said. "Anyway, we've got a mob of people here and they've been here for days."

Finally Jamey said, "I better go see Roy now."

And out of the office, past the student-jammed lecture hall and across the bridge into the main building. He found Roy Billings with several other Negro students in the corridor outside the Chancellor's suite of offices.

But Jamey immediately felt that reserve or reluctance seize him as he saw Roy, or maybe it was that guilt alone had risen between him and his friend or just some vague embarrassment knowing Roy would know that he was merely another white emissary, mouthpiece for all those students who liked symbols, who understood symbols more than the hard-gut reality of where the truth was at. . . .

So that as he neared Roy, as he saw Roy looking up, Jamey tried to move more briskly, smile more, swallow down the hostile distance between them.

Saying hello to him and finding it was all as he feared, not of the best, nowhere near it: Roy's eyes, black stones, cold and unyielding; none of that easy, automatic front-talk, none of that funnysunny cheer the whiteboy puts out in a crisis, none of that whiteboy Hemingwayshit front-talk above the churn of bowels, none of that now, not with this blackboy from the wrong side of the Cleveland tracks.

"What're you doing back here, Jamey?" Roy taking off his black-rimmed glasses. "I hear you're a big rock star and—" He stopped, peering now at Jamey's corduroy jacket, at the shoulder and sleeve.

"I wanted to talk to you, Roy."

"Sure." Wearily Roy rubbed his now bearded face, and led the way into the sacrosanct chamber of Chancellor Alvin Adams Ross, to the flag-flanked desk where Jamey had once stood before a ladybird flapped down on campus; here he and Roy now stood in this unlikely (now likely?) context.

From beyond the noble windows in the gold of the June afternoon you could still hear the mobs of students outside on the steps and the sidewalks, the cross fire of voices between the groups, never ending, equations canceled out. . . .

"You're one of the last people I expected here," Roy said; there was that wariness which seemed to make his eyeballs bulge.

"Yes, well—" Jamey groped stupidly for a way to get through the intro and verse. "I heard about what was going on—saw you on TV, Roy—and I was coming up and then Stinnett called and asked if I— I mean, since you and I were always—you know—he asked me if I wouldn't try to talk to you about making this one solid-front fight. He feels—"

"I know what he feels, Jamey. I know what they all feel they're Westchester activists, Connecticut living-room liberals. And oh my, I am bleeding."

"Roy, what I don't want to see is the cops come blasting in

here and putting this thing down. If it's a solid-front fight I think they'll go easier and there'll be a lot less heads bashed in."

"Look, Jamey, now that you are getting to be a rock star why don't you stick to that, hmm? You see, I don't think you quite understand how it is."

"You don't think I understand?" Jamey shook his head. In dismay he looked around Ross's office, he looked over at the chair where he had sat last fall staring down at his knees. He looked back at Roy. "What I understand is you're holding out for a straight black front and nothing else, and I think there are times when that's stupid, Roy."

"You do?" Roy, cool and unruffled, reached for his glasses.

"Yes." Jamey was well beyond the first frontier of his discomfort. "It's stupid because you can lose this fight and stupid because what it shows is that you people are really much more interested in your own show—making this a black stand is more important than forcing the University to make the changes this strike is all about."

"You've got to be dreaming, friend." Roy paused, put on his glasses and read over a sheet of notes on Rossboss' desk. Then, coolly, he put away the glasses again. "Since when can't we do both? And since when does one have to be separated from the other?"

"Goddammit, Roy." Jamey loosened his shirt collar. "They're going to cut you up and you're not going to accomplish anything. You're being racist, it's a racist fight, not a student fight against the University!"

"One and the same, Jamey boy, one and the same. That's what you people have got to finally comprehend, isn't it?" Roy answered, though less cool now, somehow even ugly, and Jamey once more found it hard to look back to those early undergraduate years when Roy was just across the hall, Roy showing him pictures of his mother and father and his two sisters in Cleveland in front of that six-story rotting, sagging firebox; he and Roy sitting in Niko's late nights after Roy finished work at that bowling alley; Roy coming into his room to listen to new albums or tapes, and digging Aretha, Dylan or Smokey Robinson; Roy coming in to ask Jamey if he'd help him with that sosh quiz. . . .

"Roy, what I'm trying to tell you—"

"What I'm trying to tell you," Roy broke in, "is we don't want to win a fight just to win a fight. We've got to win it on black terms with black people!"

"But for Christ sakes," Jamey said less patiently, "you'll never make it either way. If they put this thing down, you lose as students, you lose as blacks!"

"Those losing days are over, Jamey. You better go back to Old Virginie and break the bad news to Stinnett. Just tell him—since he never believed it all the times I've told him—just tell him that the helping days are over too; we don't solicit help. That's been the trouble—too many of us have been asking for help too long and too many of us have depended on that help too long. Why do you refuse to see it like that?"

"I never refused and you know it. Goddammit, Roy, you know me better than that; why do you keep putting me down to where the redneck lives?" Jamey stormed. "I am someplace else and where I am is, I can't see you killing everything you want. All you're going to bring is more guns and more repression. Martin Luther King, and now Bobby Kennedy—and that's only the beginning. It's all they're waiting for, can't you see that? All they want is a real threat, a black revolution, and when that happens you are turning over the whole scene to riot control, law and order, and what that means is more blood!"

"It'll be white blood!" Roy's voice left no edge for doubt.

And Jamey stared at him for an instant. "I think you're wrong, Roy, you're wrong. They're just waiting for you, they're just waiting for that one chance to sing law and order, bring in the tanks and gas. Christ, I wouldn't keep fighting you on this if I didn't know sure as hell what's going to happen. Your only real strength, the thing that's really going to bug them, is a common front with the whites; it's what I've always told you—it's either coexistence or no existence!"

"That is shit, my friend."

"Roy," Jamey heard himself say, "sometimes you sound like you're more interested in Roy Billings than in your own people!"

"Why, you arrogant little—" Roy choking it off but reaching out in a sudden jab and shoving Jamey back—not just an ordinary push, but a vicious one that sent him staggering against the Chancellor's massive desk.

Even so Jamey should never have let go of his cool or his

understanding. Just a shove, impulsive. Except that Jamey didn't feel like that; that one jabbing push had all the hate that had sent the egg and paint exploding against him. . . .

And he was wild with resentment that Roy Billings should be so deliberately blind as to lump him with the enemy—Jamey of all people!

So wild or hurt (or blind) that he was already springing forward, lunging at Roy, jutting his arm straight out, thudding into his chest, shoving Roy back, aside, and going on across the office to the door.

Almost out.

A sudden harsh hand, palm or fist sharp and stinging against his shoulder, sending him into a spin, in a half-turn, and then each of them at the same time struck out for the other. . . .

Jamey jabbing, fisting right for the other's mouth—but the full thrust blocked and his hand crashed into Roy's and their arms locked in rigid hostility. . . .

Not until that instant when he was so close to Roy's face that he could see the tiny filament of hair sprouting from the mole near his temple, not until then did Jamey break his hold and spring back appalled, aware not only of what he had done but of how Roy would see it. . . .

"For Christ sakes, Roy—" Breathless, body trembling, his neck and armpits glazed with sweat.

"I—" Roy shook his head, working his long fingers, the glisten of pearls on his sepia cheeks.

"Listen, Roy—I don't know what the hell happened—" But in his mortification he could only shake his head, there was nothing he could say; even Roy seemed muted. And Jamey not knowing what else to do. Except to get out.

Going back, retracing his steps, past the halls, through the rotunda, where Negro students still stood ground against the high glass doors, and going across the bridge into the south wing: his body still trembling.

Carrying defeat.

And shock and shame.

Back in the office of the Assistant Old Phart of Men, and seeing the disappointment cloud over the faces of Lyle and the others who had somehow expected him to be the miracle cat, and all of them sitting around in this gloom of a room, trying to hit on other strategies, and getting nowhere. Susan Sayres and Sue Burke went out the back way and came back with a box of sandwiches and coffee. Laura Barnes conspicuously absent.

The dusk closing down the golden day, and then at ten o'clock through the open windows came the voice of one of Rossboss' aides, the voice through a bullhorn croaking in the sweet summer eve (like a pistol, echo of another gunshot, the one from the faroff City of the Angels, this sweet summer eve in the United States of Nowhere):

"—and there are just two hours left," came the bullhorn's strident warning from the sidewalk below. "The Chancellor has asked me to remind you that unless all students are out of the building no later than midnight, the police will be called in. Further resistance will meet with suspension or other disciplinary measures. The Negro students in the main building have also been informed of this. Two police units have been assigned. The administration is opposed to this, but it has been left no alternative. Chancellor Ross urges once again that all students be cooperative and avoid further conflict with the University. He assures all groups that the University will possibly consider the proposals and demands that have been made—"

Reasonable?

About as reasonable, Jamey thought now, as he and Roy wanting to bloody each other up.

Half an hour later some dissension among the students developed: some were talking about walking out in exchange for assured amnesty for all concerned. Lyle Stinnett, Bob Lothar and other leaders decided to call another meeting, and everyone left to meet in the lecture hall on this side of the bridge.

Jamey did not move. He wanted to stay here alone. It was as if he needed to talk with himself, to be alone in the aftermath of what happened between him and Roy:

To tell himself again that yes, Roy had started it, provoked it. But also telling himself there were all those centuries that made Roy do it, and Jamey had no such true reason. . . .

"Hey, come on, Jamey. We're going to need you!" Lyle Stinnett was by the office door.

"I've got your guitar." Gary Einsberg was holding it.

"Jamey—" Susan Sayres said.

He nodded.

He remembered he was going to telephone Poppy tonight. Poppy.

"Hey, Jamey—" Bob Lothar calling from the corridor.

He stirred.

Resisting. Why? It's why he'd come back here, wasn't it?

He'd come for all this.

For all of it (except the discovery that he might not be that exceptional person of goodwill he'd never questioned before, or that he might not be that exceptional person incapable of prejudice or violence).

If Poppy were with him now.

From her he would get what comfort there might be. Poppy was the music to soothe the savage breast. . . .

Yes.

She would say: "Maybe it's good this happened to you, maybe it shows how even people like us have to be like on guard. You have to learn how to withdraw from yourself to find your true self. If you'd only get into meditation, Jamey . . ."

Ah, Poppy, where are you now?

The mob in the lecture hall wasn't ready to get locked up in cohesive action. You could see that right away. He sat down in front, and up on the platform where Lyle and the others, all of them in huddling conference, and finally Lyle stepped to the mike and said they would like a show of hands on who wanted to hold out and resist whatever it was the police were readying for them tonight, but first a show of hands of those who wanted to cut out for a promise of amnesty and future talks with the administration.

Most people opted to stay. Some jumped up and shouted back, asking the floor to consider before it was too late the tactic that would be most realistic. Others objected to this way of putting it. But Lyle made the majority vote stick. Still there was indecision and resistance, and all those students up and down like pistons, all the shaggy-haired and the barbered, and the smooth-cheeked and the bearded, the plaid shirts and jeans and Wranglers, the seersuckers and madras and T-shirts—but Lyle finally hushing the hall:

Saying now—adding this in a rush like an ambulance speeding to a disaster—saying that in case some people didn't know it, Jamey, who used to be very much part of this campus scene, was back, was here, now, and they were going to ask him to come up, for if they were going to have to sit tight until midnight, wasn't this a better way to do it—"a concert for all you pot-head Communist activists who're going to get suspended for opposing the Old Phart Philosophers of College Hall."

And Lyle beckoned to him and he made his way to the platform in a barrage of applause and Bob Lothar came over and gave him his guitar.

By now he could see this, knowing why Lyle wanted him around tonight, and knowing that he would not have wanted it any other way.

The hall was hot. He took off his corduroy jacket. He strapped on the guitar, the leather strap a bleached gray across his black-and-white flowered shirt. He tuned the meerschaum gun.

He gave the concert, he gave the repertoire he would use Saturday night at his first official concert, the one at Colston College—from "Lyndon Tree" and "Everything to Live For" to the poverty song and "The White Cat."

Nothing he'd done ever went down like this. A captive audience, yes, but the kids were really all plugged in and he had to do "The White Cat" twice.

The hall had become hotter: more people had crowded in. From where?

And at the wide double-door entrance facing the bridge he saw now that many of the Negro students from the main building had come over, though they remained outside the hall.

He waited or hesitated, wanting to try his new one now. He saw the electric clock on the balcony balustrade: five minutes after twelve. No police. Unless . . .

He turned back and looked over at Lyle and the others, and they nodded.

Why not? If there was still time. Why not do it? All those nights working on it to finish it. So Jamey went into it, "When the Cymbals Are Still," with its long verse or prologue and its rambling uneven refrain, and keeping his guitar beneath, unobtrusive, blues-talking over it:

Opened my history book yesterday
Went through it all the way
Lookin' for those names in history's hall
Black people in history's hall
But I couldn't make this American scene
'Cause in history's hall
Seems like there must've been almost no blacks at all.

Now sure enough in that history book
Saw the same old faces
Read the same old sagas
Read all the eulogies
The epics
The eclogues
Ah, man, heroes all
And the professor
He said it too
And the TV spieler too.

So when I said how come all these cats
Are all a paler shade than pale
No one answered
And then someone said listen
Don't get salty
Don't say there are no blacks on the long roll of history:
What about Satchmo, Jackie, Sugar, Cassius, Harry and Sidney?
Well sure

But when the cymbals are still
And the drums have all died
And the blues have been cried
Is that all?

No.
But no one ever told me
I had to find out for myself:

'Bout the black kings in ancient Ghana
In the year seven hundred
And how in Africa
There used to be whole soul
Centers of black culture?

And in sixteen hundred
I never knew
There was a Negro-Arab University
In Timbuktu.

    No one ever told me
    I had to find out for myself:

'Bout all the swapping back there when
They traded rum for black men
And brought them
To America
Like on the Mayflower?
No, Jack—this cargo was black
And you wonder how they could put
All that stench in the hold
All chained together hand and foot
While Raphael painted, Luther preached
Corneille wrote, Milton sang
And the dark captives stretched their hands to God.
Hallelujah.

    But when the cymbals are still
    And the drums have all died
    And the blues have been cried
    Is that all?

No.
Beneath the blood on history's wall
Between the books and pages
Rage more black folks than you can recall.
Like there was a cat
Named Pedro Alonzo Nino
A Negro too, of the Christopher Columbus crew
And what about the black men who
Shared the mighty sight
Of the Pacific
With Balboa? Right.
And the black men with Cortez
Pizarro and de Soto?

    Not that the books or profs ever told me
    I had to find out for myself:

'Bout the Revolutionary War
I was never taught
How five thousand Negroes fought
Hopin' for peace evermore
And what about Peter Salem and Salem Poor?
Who? I never heard of them until
George Washington spoke their names
For bravery
At Bunker Hill.

Ever hear of Crispus Attucks?
Not sure?
Well, he was a black man too
A runaway slave
But he led a charge
And lost his life
In the Boston Massacre
On that eve of blood
Dying in darkness
As in darkness he is forgotten
Forgotten is Jean Baptiste de Sable
The first settler of Chicago town
Accordin' to fact and even fable
A brave man, a trader
And the son of a Negro slave.

But when the cymbals are still
And the drums have all died
And the blues have been cried
Is that all?

No:

Or didn't you know about Phillis Wheatley
Who used to be a slave
But who wrote
Poetry,
Lyrical lines people would quote
And that George Washington would quote
This wisp of woman
Delicate face
Born in Africa
In some unknown place.

And what about a man
Like Benjamin Banneker
An astronomer
And famed mathematician
Thomas Jefferson digging this black
For his remarkable almanac

Not that anyone ever told me
I had to find out for myself:

'Bout the first Negro newspaper
Freedom's Journal it was called
Though lost in history's storm
This journal put out
By Samuel Cornish and John Russwurm
And do you remember
Sojourner Truth
The freed slave who ran with the abolitionists?
Or Frederick Douglass?
No?
How come?
Too long ago?
Maybe.
Or too black?
Could be.

But when the cymbals are still
And the drums have all died
And the blues have been cried
Is that all?

No:

Oh yes
I know about Booker T. Washington
And George Washington Carver
But no one ever told me
About a man called Du Bois
This black cat who got a Ph.D.
Degree from Harvard
His mission: to see lynchings end
To get voting for his friends

And that was far back
Nineteen ten
Yes, they've been tryin' for a long tryin' time
To get what is right and fair
But no one hearing them
Until war is in the air
Like World War One,
Almost half a million black
In that one
Or World War Number Two
They let a black man die
Just like you.
Sure, sure, make your sad fugue
But why don't you blow the bugle
For the others
Like James Weldon Johnson
Countee Cullen
Langston Hughes
Richard Wright
Marion Anderson
The Duke
Ellison
And Baldwin

But when the cymbals are still
And the drums have all died
And the blues have been cried
Is that all?

No:

What about Oscar De Priest
Or Arthur Mitchell
First black men elected to Congress?
Then far far from home
In the long winterland
Went Ralph Bunche overseas
To widen whitey's eyes
To win the Nobel Prize
For peace
Well, sure I knew that
Though I'm not sure if I knew

Gwendolyn Brooks
Won the prize of Pulitzer
For poetry
Though her books
Aren't in my public library

And there's a doctor
Ever hear the name
Daniel Hale Williams?
Who is he?
Could it be the same
Who performed the first open-heart surgery
In this country?

Not that anyone ever told me
I had to find out for myself:

'Bout how many black boys
Slug their feet in the Vietnam heat
Dying in Asian anonymity
For that ever-lovin' white community
But when the roll is writ
Why are the ones who're black
The ones they seem to omit?
Yet now and then
Someone—by what grace—rises
To word and deed
To lead his people
Toward a dream
You all know who I mean
So loved and needed
But what happened to that dream
On that shattered eve of April
On that winged balcony
In Memphis, Tennessee?

And when the cymbals are still
And the drums have all died
And the blues have been cried
Is that all?

No.
Not anymore, not anymore

No No No
No No No
Not anymore

No!

The hall rocked this time with the thunder of their response; it broke over Jamey's head, it ricocheted in pulsing sound waves, touching him in that way he had come to know, sparking that special flash or surge inside him—it was different from the boost of vanity or professional pride other kinds of entertainers experience. This was that endorsement from his peers, that total communication and involvement between what they felt and what he was doing. . . .

When that happened he hoarded his gift and his guitar. The trouble was it sometimes seemed so temporal, momentary, and just when you thought you were turning people on or that what was going on between you would help shake up what Lyle Stinnett called the "World of the Old Phart Philosophers in High and Low Places"—just when you thought this was really under way, you saw that nothing seemed to change or that nothing but bad news seemed to be happening and you ended up flat on the ass of your discouragement and self-doubt.

But this time, this instant there seemed to be more. Beyond the faces of all the students his attention was again drawn to the Negroes crowded around the open doors, some of them even applauding. That's when he saw, against the jamb of the right door, the figure of Roy Billings.

Roy there.

Immediately then he hurried off the platform, down the steps and up the side aisle. He would pass Roy, though telling himself that he was really on his way to the office to put in that call to Poppy. Holding his guitar close to his side, he made his way to the rear, nearing Roy now, slowing.

It was maybe half a second, no more, as he hesitated, lured, hopeful, by the way Roy was looking at him. . . .

No more than that half-second when he veered just a fraction rightward toward him, seeing Roy stir, a movement of his hand as if he was going to come over or stop him and say something . . .

But it never happened, for in that flashing interval Roy turned away and joined the other Negroes, who were now recrossing the bridge into the main building.

Whatever it was Roy might have wanted to say to him, Jamey never found out.

And he never made it back to the office, never got to call Poppy that night. Swinging around now, he saw the sudden chaos in the lecture hall, heard the shouts. He looked all around and then he saw the door close to him, the closet where maintenance equipment and fuse boxes were; he pulled open the door and shoved in his guitar, turned and started back into the hall.

"What is it?" he asked one student who was charging up the aisle.

"Don't know. Smell it!"

What was happening was something no one had foreseen, and what happened was not the way it had been during the antiwar battle with police last October.

This time—no one ever discovered if it had been accidental or if it had been calculated strategy—the police did not circle the scene, they did not deploy their squads of geniuses to all quarters, but sent them instead only into the main building to rout out the Negro students, cutting off the others. But almost simultaneously, the lecture hall became the target for another group of counterdemonstrators outside, but a very concerted action.

Below outside, in the crescents of street lights you could see the torches and the signs: TOWN VETERANS OF VIETNAM and NATIONAL WAR VETERANS OF AMERICA. They had moved into this strike and were now hurling through the two high clerestory windows these stink bombs, proficiently made and with a powerful stench that seemed almost lethal, at least to Jamey.

Almost exactly like that summer five years ago when he was sixteen, working for his father, working with the crew bulldozing an orchard which had been sprayed with DDT—the same reaction this time, though it didn't hit him at once, but now it came: the stinging in his throat and chest, the tearing in his eyes.

Obviously the purpose was to force all the people in the lecture hall out the fire exits and into the open. The strike would be broken, making the building free for police and authorities to take over. Instead, everyone turned and started rushing out the back away from the fumes, going right across the bridge into the main building. To find themselves head-on with nightstick-wielding, helmeted police. Jamey—harder hit than most of the others—followed or tried to, but fell behind, struggling for breath, blinking the sting of tears from his eyes, turning then, groping, choking, coughing, pushing open the rear fire door and making it down the concrete steps into the campus, gasping for the fresh air.

It made the DDT seizure mild. Alone, he moved around to the area beneath the steel-framed bridge. It was damp here and he lay on the grass, face down, stupidly inhaling the night dew as if it would yield more oxygen for his need.

It didn't. For a while he lay there, paralyzed, stupid, enraged.

He kept pushing his hair back and wiping his eyes, but this irritated them more. When he called out to two students hurrying past, the sound that issued from his throat came in pain, thin, scratchy, alien, comic as Tarzan talk. . . .

Finally getting around to the front of College Hall, he walked right into the beginning of the end: TV lights and cameras and newsmen and radio people; police bullhorns croaking, urging all students in the area to leave, return to dorms; police carrying other students to vans; spurts of police running down the students who were still firing paving bricks, bottles, light bulbs. . . .

But it was already clear the strike had been broken, the odds going to the riot-trained blue boys.

While—as if this were some jazzy American sports spectacle—hasty interviews going on with the police captain, the Dean of Men and Lyle Stinnett (held by two plainclothesmen), and Reverend Tillou now asserting "all this could be traced to the Vietnam war and that unless it was stopped it would destroy the University."

The sports event needed only a razor-blade sponsor to spur sales to an accompaniment of lacerated skulls and contusions of the face and neck.

A senior faculty member admitting into a mike: "We have no more credibility with the students and the administration doesn't talk to us."

Someone saw Jamey. A mike was thrust at him, a bright light burning into his blurring eyesight. He turned away. No interview.

He remembered something else then. Colston College. The first of his campus concerts. But he knew that he would never be able to raise much more than a hoarse whisper or frog's groggle in time for the concert: it would have to be called off. And no one to take his place (except maybe an electronic sound robot or Robert Moog at the controls of his entire sound-synthesizing equipment).

By the next day the count showed: forty-three students hospitalized, 139 arrested; thirty windows broken; two fires in two rooms of an adjacent building; seven policemen injured. Lyle Stinnett, Roy Billings, Lothar, Einsberg were charged with inciting riot and criminal trespass, and arraigned in court before noon.

And of course the University issued their suspensions.

Within twelve hours Jamey's father had the dubious pleasure of seeing his son's face in several newspapers, along with many quoted segments of "When the Cymbals Are Still," and the TV coverage was thorough. To his father at the office came another letter from the Minutemen: *We have our crossed gunsights on you.* And there were three harsh and anonymous telephone calls. Within two days the pattern was made clear: Hometown National—Your Friendly Bank—turned down three mortgage applicants wanting to buy Mieland Homes.

Jamey received a very complimentary telegram from Laura Barnes, who had read all about "Cymbals" in the campus paper.

He received, also, a telegram from Muriel Hewes.

He received a touching telegram from Mrs. Martin Luther King, Jr.

He received a telegram from The Great Society Gross-Outs.

He received a telegram of particular (and surprising) enthusiasm from old Dr. Murdoch, his "Old Phart" professor in Sociological Theory III.

(A week later he received a letter from Mike, now removed from the stockade and continuing his year's sentence at a federal penitentiary.)

But slowly, under pressure from all quarters, the Chancellor began to bend, and the University took under serious consideration most of the proposals and demands which had set off the student strike.

At first the Messrs Syd Held and Zak Silberman, of Raven Records, and Jamey's manager, Nat McGovern, were very pleased: all this exposure for their new boy.

Until Jamey, in pain and under medication, telephoned Poppy and told her what had happened to him and asked her to get in touch with Clem Vogel and Nat McGovern to tell them that the concert at Colston College would of course be out.

Nobody at Raven, nor anyone in the office of crusty Nat McGovern, could groove on this announcement.

And when Jamey got back to New York three days later, after stopping off at Nittygritty City for that final bummer with his father, he went with Poppy to Rockefeller Center to the office of his manager and attorney. McGovern gave him a magnificent nonwelcome.

Nat McGovern: heavy-lidded eyes of ruthless vision, clear as a jeweler's lens; Nat fat but natty in his slate suit, black silk tie and hundred-dollar black London-built shoes; Nat cutting off outside calls and speaking from his cold clean desk behind which, on the sterile white wall, not his diploma from Columbia or Harvard (he liked to repeat the ancient epigram: "The three dullest things in the world are home cooking, home fucking and the Harvard Law School)—nor did the wall hold the other usual certifications attorneys feature, but rather the unsterile photographs of some of his superpeople, all in folk/rock, all under thirty, all as crusty or egomaniacal as Nat, but all of them like babes of compliance in his managerial nursery.

Nat glancing at Poppy and then bringing his frigid gaze back to Jamey: "—and it isn't only up to you whether you want to win or not. It's up to me. Because everybody who is on Nat McGovern's team plays to win, otherwise they can leave and go back to the bush leagues. It's one of my conceits, Jamey, that the people on McGovern's team all have the win factor in their blood. I took you on because I recognize what you have to offer. If you want to kill it, that means a parting of the ways. By kill—a case in point: you are now dead at Colston. They had to refund all moneys of their advance sale. Case in point: a wire from the executive secretary of the Association of College and University Managers. They are asking for more protection built into their contracts with you. Case in point: the campus dollar is now the biggest dollar spent on the live arts in the United States, forty million dollars a year just on pop concerts. Case in point: all brokers and campus managers have dead-level trust in Nat McGovern's people and in Nat McGovern's word. What you've done, Jamey, can never happen again. The word is *never!*"

"Look, Nat, I—" Jamey began, but even a few desperate syllables seared his still sensitive larynx.

"Spare yourself," Nat urged, and without warning focused his glacial gaze on Poppy. "Poppy darling, if you are turning off, that is a mistake. It is a serious mistake if you think this boy must not be tucked tightly into the money bag. It is understood that in private matters he is all yours, Poppy. But in his work and commitments he belongs exclusively to McGovern. Case in point: you said earlier Jamey didn't break this date at Colston deliberately and that all he was doing was following his own—I quote—arrow."

"Nat"—Jamey tried again—"don't lay it on Poppy. What I did I'd do again, even though—"

"If a man refuses to learn from his errors"—Nat McGovern maintained his Olympian authority—"it suggests some cell in the blood, some element in the win factor is absent." A pause, a cogent lifting of those heavy lids, facing Poppy. "Unless it's something else. Unless perhaps he is involved with some person who might not *want* him to win."

"Listen, Nat—" Jamey forced more power out of his voice.

But now Poppy, who had seemed lost in the giant-backed leather chair, sprang up and stood between him and the attorney —almost funny, her narrow shoulders working, tilting her head from side to side as if to peep out from the long bronze hair, her thighs beneath the microskirt so white against McGovern's somber desk, Poppy in a wrath, far from the serene scriptures of Tibet, Poppy a petite Portia, her small hand raised, index finger jabbing out, Poppy saying: "Don't you try to put me down that way! I don't even want to look at you anymore! I mean, you're nothing but another walking hangup of Western Man and like don't you tell me you understand Jamey, because you're too strung out on that fucking blood factor and I feel—I feel like what am I doing in here!"

That was as far as she got, all other words locked inside her:

she seemed lost again, inert, but just as swiftly she turned and went from the office, almost running out.

Jamey was on his feet.

"Jamey—" Nat, unperturbed, raised a restraining palm, French cuffs studded with onyx links, a flag of restraint. "Jamey, this is too bad. She fails to dig me. She fails to see what McGovern is really about: after all, why did I sign up a boy like you? There are dozens of very talented kids popping in here every hour of the day. But why did I choose you? Merely to bulge your money bag? Or because I happen to believe in what motivates you. This is what's important to me! When I'm alone. Money and the win factor—these are merely ways of assuring you intellectual independence and bodily nourishment when you reach the doddering old age of forty. Now you can forget I ever said this."

Jamey looked at him.

If Nat's oblique (but accurate?) shot at Poppy had wounded her, it was also true that it was Poppy's outcry that had made this otherwise oak-hearted indomitable man lower his guard.

The message reached Jamey. He accepted it. Somehow it even touched him. And when he left the office, he began, though he wasn't conscious of it, to turn into another path of the rock garden.

9 : THE CITY

"HI, HELLO on you! Well, what d'ya know? This is The Billyman Coe Show—WYTX-AM—and tonight I'm gonna hip you to the newest sound going down. The name of the game is Jamey! So hang in there, tigers, while we plug in some of the Top Ten as well as the others making the toppa the charts. Hey now, let's groove this, Number Nine this week. Yeah, it's outasight, it's Now!"

OK, laugh, let that handful of highbrow FM DJ's laugh, or blast him. Sure he lays down all the clichés. Why not? Yes, he feels real bad, cries all the way to the bank every week, cries every time he opens that fat portfolio of securities, poor Billyman Coe.

He doesn't look thirty-nine; looks more like thirty: jiving almond eyes in a pink chunky face; his He-Vi hairpiece has been replaced by the more luxuriant He-Vi wig with sideburns slashing down the side of his face like black scimitars. Swaggering brocade coat and gold medallion hanging from a gold chain; his pants bell-flared. Tomorrow night the costume will be different —he has eighteen ensembles—and Saturday night at his Record Hop he will wear the gold lamé, which, like the others, are tailored to enhance his matchstick frame. He has a wife, a son of twelve and a girl friend of nineteen, though he is letting her go in favor of someone more mature—the new receptionist, who is twenty.

Billyman Coe talks fast, talks loud; he sits across the table from the engineer, a ledge between them and all the cartridges scheduled on tonight's playlist are already stacked. Vertically—minibooks on a shallow shelf, each tape running no more than three minutes, but Billyman gets some of them shaved to two minutes and forty-nine seconds: you add up the seconds shaved off, and you can slip in at least one or two taped commercials extra in your nighttime slot. . . .

Acne and blemished skin are slipped in by the engineer now, and then Billyman comes on: "That's right, Billyman ain't just hypin' you—I promised you Jamey and Jamey you're gonna have, and now Number Six on the Coe Tally-O, dig it, it's fab because this is where it's at."

Number Six is pressed into play. He glances over to Jamey, who is sitting in that glass-walled room waiting to come on for the interview, which is dropped into the last segment of the show—Jamey there now surrounded by all those chicks and friends. These guys seem to always have a gang around them. A regular entourage. Like a magnet sucking up carpet tacks.

Jamey sits there behind the glass, all that thick yellow hair slanting across his brow. That face of his is a scowler: look, baby, if you don't like it, take off. Billyman Coe is favoring you with your record on the daily playlist and it's only Number Thirty-eight on the charts. Billyman is playing it again tonight. For free. Certain labels, certain people, would have to slip plenty of bread into his side pocket for the kind of plug Jamey's "The White Cat" is getting these nights. As for those other cuts on the album, all those protest songs—forget it, baby. Not that Billyman Coe rejects all of them. He appreciates some of that stuff. Once in a while (once a month) he'll press in a Dylan or Country Joe for his listeners. Hell, once in a while, no skin off his.

This show is paced and it's Billyman Coe who paces it, even though under the recent system the weekly playlist is set by a committee under the program director. But as long as the show goes, Billyman pretty much gets his way, as long as mail and phone-ins and sponsors don't drop off. If that happens, forget it. He is out. He's been out before. Wouldn't be the first time. A DJ is a bird of passage, friends. Billyman started at twenty-two in Buffalo but he was slugged out of that slot for balling the wife of the vice-president of the station. Then Billyman got himself a new slot in AM radio in Dayton, Ohio. From there to Miami, from there to Bridgeport, from there to Cleveland, from there to Chicago and finally this hot slot in New York . . .

Beer, more beer frothing in the commercial now, as the engineer sends home the next cartridge.

After beer: "And don't forget, tigers"—Billyman jumps in fast and frantic between tapes—"next Saturday, the Billyman Coe Record Hop at the Rainbow Ballroom with the grooviest groups around and the light show that turns you on—so make it fast for those tickets at your neighborhood music store. Admission three dollars." Billyman can push this with real heart. He gets 20 percent of the gate, which goes into the kitty, along with his salary of $40,000 per annum, plus his share in that indie label (the stock is in his sister-in-law's name). "All right, you groovers, here it comes, it's here, Number Seven! Hang right in there, tigers, The Billyman Coe Show is coming on with Jamey! That's right. Cool it, girls, I've got him all boxed in glass. Well now, all right, here it is, Number Seven, and it's gonna sock it to ya!"

The engineer presses in the cartridge.

During the play one of the staff steps over and hands him memos. Ah, he's really hyping this up tonight, all these telephone calls coming in. When Number Seven is over, he comes on: "Hey, hello on you! Seems they're jamming that switchboard with calls, all those questions about Jamey. What's Jamey wearing? Does he look like on his album cover? Well, just hang in there, tigers, we'll get to you and your questions, and here we go now with Billyman Coe, yes, here it is, grooving up there fast, your fav, Number Five!"

More acne and pimples, more beer, more Record Hop, more

giveaways, more hair shampoo and curl straighteners and more pimples and more beer.

But exactly at ten-forty-six, for the last segment he moves into the interview with Jamey; Jamey is across from him now in those tight white Wranglers and white denim work jacket, black cotton shirt, button-down collar open, big black sunglasses, white-rimmed.

"Hello on you again. And what d'ya know? It's The Billyman Coe Show. And here he is, that groovy young man with a guitar and the sunflower hair, the folk/rock writer and singer who is where it's at, the young man who has a lot to say and it's getting all over the place, like his groovy new hit single 'The White Cat.' Well, hello on you, Jamey."

"Hello," Jamey answers.

"Jamey, I don't know how we're gonna get in enough time, so many calls—they've been callin' in all evening. First, Jamey, what in your opinion has made 'The White Cat' the hot contender for Top Chart placement? Is this the type song you prefer? Some folks insist you're really heavy with the political and social scene. Do you agree? Is it true you lost several college concert bookings because of that strike last June at your alma mater? Do you pre-fer American cars or that foreign iron? Another question fans are breathing on my neck: is there any special chick who's got the inside track in your life? That's just a sample of what's coming, so hang in there, tigers, we'll be back right after we hip you to the face cream that will change your life—did I say love? But listen—"

The engineer buries the cartridge and the acne pitch spins.

Billyman Coe swivels around to smile over at Jamey's gang of followers and friends behind the glass-walled gallery and then he confronts his guest: but Jamey's scowl is like the day before yesterday when there was that storm and the sky went black. Forget it!

Yet Jamey mastered the smile once the interview began; it was something you learned to do, something Nat McGovern stressed: either go all out or don't go at all.

So that now on this somnolent, sultry September night, in the sound box of the studio, he answered the questions he'd answered many times before, though this session with Billyman Coe and his store-bought hair was really a supershit special. . . .

"Well now," the DJ was saying, "I see over there you've got a whole army of friends in the visitors' booth. Now here's something people listening in want the real info on—don't get mad on me, Jamey, but among all those chicks up there, is there one gal who is a little more than just a friend?"

Jamey gave the punch-card replies meant to safeguard privacy, but glancing over now to that "army of friends"—yes, and Poppy watching him, her smile not elusive yet somehow oblique or partly withdrawn, and then turning away to say something to a new friend of theirs: Roger Shens, a native of Barbados, part-time bongo player and Ph.D. candidate in philosophy at New York University, Roger with that shiner welting up to distort the beauty of his bearded cinnamon face. (The other night at that pub, some Alabama cat's way of objecting to how Roger had his arm around Poppy.)

Jamey could see Muriel Hewes nearby, and he saw someone waving: Karen McGovern, Nat's stepdaughter by his third marriage, Karen built for bed and a walking chapter out of any shrink's laboratory record. Poppy said of her the other night: "She thinks she invented fucking and like no one else can get the inspiration." Poppy sounding off because of the way Karen had of somehow turning up everywhere, somehow always trying to mix with the pack on Jamey's tail.

Seated over there beside her was Florida, recently released from a stretch for possession and selling, Florida, who had now attached himself to Jamey, being his self-appointed bodyguard, and Jamey keeping him on, helping out during his probation, trying to steer him out of the drug scene. . . .

As for all those boppybirds up there—

"Tell our listeners something else, Jamey." Billyman Coe leaned far forward. "Your family. I'm sure they mean a great deal to you. Do you get any time away from your busy life to see them? They must be mighty proud of you, all the groovy things happening to you and like that. Now don't tell us there's a—here it comes—generation gap between you?"

Jamey cringed behind his smile. He spoke mainly about his mother, who was the musical influence of his kid days.

Father? Oh no, no gap, no crap, not anymore, not as of this past summer, not since Jamey began to realize what was happening to him, and seeing that Fred Mieland would not want to admit it, so that he had to push him into that final corner, the two of them alone in the office, the five-o'clock bourbon bottle on the desk, and Jamey into the treatment Mieland Homes was getting from your friendly Hometown National Bank, and finally saying what the unseen enemies hoped he would say: "Look, Dad, I tried to stick with you even though I know I can't put in much time anymore, but I wanted to stick it out to show them they couldn't work us over that way."

"Sure, and I feel the same," Fred Mieland saying, and reaching for the bourbon again. "We both agree."

"I know what it's costing you," Jamey said. "I know it's costing more than money. And it's going to get worse. I thought we could kill it, but—"

"There are other banks"—somehow Fred Mieland's protest sounded thin—"more banks than buyers. I've got a good thing riding now with County Loan and Trust."

"That's not going to stop the calls in the middle of the night and that's not going to stop them from getting more serious," Jamey said. "When I saw Frank Beldon at the bank yesterday, the way he acted—I mean, the way he tried not to act—"

His father frowned as if suppressing a jab of pain. "Well," he said, "whoever's behind it, once they know we really mean business—"

"Dad, the only answer is my getting out. For good. Then at least they won't have any claim on you anymore."

"I want my son here, goddammit!" his father declared. "I'm not giving in to the bastards." But Fred Mieland's voice lost force.

Jamey tried not to look at him: but seeing that his father was holding out more to keep his son with him than to defy his anonymous enemy.

Jamey saw the slow disintegration of all his father had created. He also saw that at last he himself could be freed from Nittygritty City. "What I'm trying to say is that I'm definitely getting out."

"You're doing nothing of the kind!" Fred Mieland pounded his veined parched hand on the desk and the bourbon glass jiggled. "Goddammit, they're not going to push us—"

"I'm leaving," Jamey said again. Then: "Actually, at this point I think they'd rather see me stay here so they can keep harassing you. This way we give them no more ammunition."

"Won't have it, I told you. I don't care how much you have to be away, your name is still on this door!" his father blustered.

"Dad, please don't try to snow yourself."

"You listen to me—"

"Dad, it's out." This time Jamey spoke so quietly, so distinctly, so slowly, it gave his father no further pretext to resist.

"You—you really insist on this?" Fred Mieland said, but even before Jamey could repeat it, he saw that his father had already shed ten years, his bourbon-blushed face already softening, rejuvenated by this act of begging Jamey not to quit, when of course it was the only answer, yet now relieved that he didn't have to show defeat or weakness in his son's eyes. Another game. Like the game he played with Louise Yates, playing it in every way except the way it really was.

So that Jamey could leave his father's office with its long familiar, long drag-down Kountrylodge. Knottypine walls and its Kountrykraft furniture and payoff furnishings; he could leave, letting his father have the satisfaction of thinking Jamey was the one who was copping out. . . .

"Now let me lay this on you, Jamey—" Billyman Coe's best margarine manner. "Since 'White Cat' has turned out to be a real breakaway, I mean, it's really outasight, what's the rock horoscope show for the future?"

When the interview was over and Jamey was posed with Billyman Coe, and while he was autographing the album cover, the tape of "The White Cat" was going:

The White Cat
Is a nowhere place
Where the smoke curls up like ebony lace . . .

At last getting out of the studio—but Christ, how did he acquire this mob of people?—as he moved into the corridor, Muriel Hewes, miniskirted, her auburn hair longer now and wearing a long string of green beads (from Bergdorf's) and a silver peace symbol (from Tiffany's), Muriel touching his arm. "You know, I feel like a fifteenth wheel, Jamey. Do I look it? God, I must look ancient with all these—" nodding toward the others.

Jamey stayed close beside her. He could crank out a lot of affection for her. She had become for him a kind of shield. But the others moved along all around him, mostly girls: Carol Lachman's younger sister, two Brooklyn high school seniors, at least seven boppybirds from out of noplace, squealing and squirming, plus a blond journalism major from Sarah Lawrence, plus a promo man from Raven, plus Poppy and Roger Shens, plus the ubiquitous Karen McGovern. With Florida leading the way, his jaundiced eyes a-gleam, his rubbery frame bending into the scene.

Florida holding open the elevator door, deciding which among the faithful could cram in, leaving the others to wait for the next one.

In the elevator Karen McGovern pressed herself against him— Karen, big eyes and big breasts (and working all four like unsecret weapons), whispering, "Jamey, what about later? Is it OK? I'm going down to meet these people at The Electric Circus and I could meet you there—" her breath warm, a mist of beer and pot and minty chewing gum, this wildest of boppybirds, age nineteen, who'd been bribed with goodies by the mates of her mother's many marriages; Karen, who had bombed out of three schools and who was now working in Nat's office because he felt she needed a steady exposure to work and challenge; when he discovered her pinwheel mind had stopped at Jamey, he asked him to kill this thing quick. Jamey tried. But Karen wasn't buying.

Nor was Poppy, who now resisted anything connected with Nat McGovern's office. Though never saying so, never even mentioning Karen's name except that one time. It was the same with his new and demanding life, but lately you could see that it was cutting her up.

Even now, packed into the elevator, he could sense her resentment, reaching him like a bitter scent. Yet in a way it pleased him to get under her like that, because Poppy was the only one he wanted to get under.

In the black marble lobby, before he could go to her she was next to him. "See you tomorrow?"

"Tomorrow? Poppy, I've got that concert at Syracuse." Then:

"Aren't you going to wait for me? Only an hour." He was en route with Muriel Hewes to the cabaret on Second Avenue, his fifth appearance there. Money for college scholarships piling up in the cabaret's coffers.

"Well"—Poppy's wide eyes sparked with something more than bad news—"well, I'll see you when you get back. Maybe we can like talk without all the locusts—"

"Listen, Poppy, I'll be down at the apartment soon as I finish at—"

"I won't be there, Jamey." The faintest alarm rang beneath her voice. "I mean, you've got your essence and if you want to—you know—destroy it, well— Anyway, I have this date." Poppy was on her way, quick as a zephyr: he saw her leaving, Roger Shens, the guy from Barbados, pushing the revolving door for her, moving with her out on the sidewalk, and Jamey could tell that tonight bongo drums or philosophic discussion would be merely the overture. . . .

Poppy's walk so dainty but with that subtle strut, having served him notice and having at last betrayed a defiance or alarm that would be acted out not on Sixteenth Street but at Roger's place: it had been coming for months.

And he would not or could not do anything to stop her. Not the way she left him feeling now.

He looked around for Muriel. But Karen McGovern was already reaching for his hand. He withdrew it, cutting his smile. He hurried toward the side doors, the others—Carol Lachman's sister, the two high school seniors, the long-legged journalism major, the seven fluttering boppybirds from Who-Knows-Where-Westchester, the promo man, and (always) Florida—in the vanguard.

"All right, give the man some air, please!" Florida warned the new swarm of girls waiting just outside.

But of course one of them got through to clutch Jamey's denim sleeve, rapping plaintively: "Oh, Jamey, would you, oh would you please sign this: to Linda—Linda Folsom." As Jamey signed her autograph book, she chirped on: "My father, he's a salesman for—you know—beads, novelties, and he said he heard you sing one night down on Saint Mark's Place before anyone ever heard of you—"

By now you couldn't stop the others, at least twenty of them clutching at him: these chicks who didn't dig what he was all about but who had to plug in, identify with yet another pop icon.

"All right, let him live, let him live, willya, girls, please!" Florida finally clearing a swath for him.

As soon as he saw Muriel he went to her and together they hurried toward Sixth Avenue to his car, a rented Corvette (Nat McGovern insisted for tax purposes that Jamey rent everything—apartment, car, audio and recording equipment).

But in the Corvette was Karen, skirt blithely up to but a fingertip touch from her quivering box, there was Karen McGovern in the bucket, and she was grinning: All right, I tried it and it's not working.

He had to dump her, but because she took it the way she did, he could not resist smiling and he heard himself say yes he'd see her later at The Electric Circus.

And knowing Poppy and Roger Shens would be beyond the overture by that time.

He waited as Muriel got in. He turned to peer down each end of the crosstown street. He removed his sunshades. No sign of Poppy—gone, swift as a wind from nowhere . . . Why, Poppy, why why why?

He went around to the driver's side. Was this like a strike, Poppy's newest action? Always being around and then suddenly in a gossamer moment vanishing. This was new, recent. And letting the ache in his chest pulse up and letting the ache in his groin grow until sometimes it hurt unbearably if he walked too fast or absently shifted in the saddle of the Harley . . .

(And all this pussy palpitating around him all the time; he was unable to turn anywhere without all this pussy pressing for his nearness, his time.)

He drove to the cabaret with Muriel Hewes. Florida and most of the girls plus a handful of new boppybirds were hanging out in front, but Florida now springing forward, taking his guitar, easing the way for him and Muriel. And then parking the car for him and coming back, sitting down with him at the bar, while Muriel went to the office to put in some work time with one of the other charity ladies.

It was past 1 A.M. when he finished and put his guitar back in its case. Time to split for The Electric Circus. On impulse, on need, on hope he telephoned Poppy's pad. But no answer. He had a beer with Florida. Karen McGovern loomed richly on the screen of his libido: he saw her looming in the midst of that mixed-media circus of surreal madness (a fragment from Hesse's novel *Steppenwolf?*).

But he decided not to make it, and he asked Florida to go downtown and give Karen the word: if she was going to get more messed up, it wouldn't be because of him, at least Nat couldn't put that on him.

This time when he went back with Muriel to her apartment, he didn't leave after an hour or two. This time he went up the iron spiral of stairs to the second floor of the duplex, Muriel just ahead of him, waiting then, reaching out for him, arms up around him and under him, her brandy-tipped tongue flicking and fanglike in his mouth.

No more talk now, not like it had been downstairs in the living room, with Muriel for the first time letting him know (since he had never asked her) more about what she was made of: those "fantastic" years with her husband in Arizona in that sprawling air-conditioned estate and giving all those breakfasts, luncheons, dinners and all those terrace barbecues, all to push Barry Goldwater for President in 1964; but no, her husband, Malcolm, had not been as square as she was making him now, a terrific man except—yes, that giant exception, his blindness, his compulsion to revive the "world of past values and virtues" that had made "America supreme." Yes, but this same husband quixotically announcing a trip to Europe, no notice whatever, and then all those trips, halfway around the world, and buying her "fantastic" jewels in Paris and clothes in Rome; being on the loose, he was a separate person outside his other self. Until they returned to Arizona and his getting into that chairmanship of Arizona Overland Chemical and Natural Gas, and getting into the doom of the Goldwater campaign, again neglecting Muriel and all else to work and speak and push all his energies around the clock until two clean-cut, drunk, blonde All-American girls in cheerleader skirts and Goldwater straw hats found him dead in the corridor of the convention hotel in San Francisco.

Muriel returning to New York like someone rising out of a

miasma of blinding sunlight and her ears still a-buzz with the maddening drone of air-conditioners and lunatic oratory . . .

But now Muriel nude.

(Lewd? Herself? Dior? Exude . . .)

Her lime-green panties a puddle of lace on the white carpeting by the white bed.

Yes, Jamey digging her more precisely now, seeing how it could be that all she might want was to blast away (rock) the sounds of that dead life, and why it was he who was finding himself in the bed of this thirty-seven-year-old flower child . . .

Yes, Muriel still hung up on sex, despite a widowhood that was anything but lily white . . .

You could see and feel it: Muriel Hewes was malnourished and wild with the banquet of this night, and that effluvium of need spiking her eyes and hands and loins, and being all over him now.

With Jamey in his present state in no condition to prolong that feast, yet out of pity and affection and esteem wanting to make it a super night for her and even for himself.

Somehow prolonging it as if it were a point of honor: all of him bringing it to all of her and she bringing it back to him, the titian hair flung back off the pillows onto the sheet, her pale pedicured feet alive as her fingers, and Jamey slowly—as slowly as he could make it—slowly edging her body to the side of the bed until finally, half standing, his knees braced against the bed, his hands under her and lifting her just enough to make it for that slow depth of locking, her fingernails denting deeply into his flesh, her legs in a rigid coil around him. Drawing back from her now and then getting her locked into it, he kept it like that, thrusting from the soles of his feet and up through his knees and thighs, until her brandy breath carried from here to Tucson her ceaseless cries: ohgod ohgod ohgod ohgod ohgod ohgod ohgod ohgod ohgodohgodohgod . . . !

Afterward, their nakedness with that dull shine, the afterglow of orgasm. Muriel seemed very quiet, and leaning away from him toward the bed table and taking a cigarette from the gold case; it was as if she was letting him know she would not impose any talk, any demand, or maybe it was that she hoped her undemanding cool would encourage him to make it again and on other nights. . . .

But Jamey was already beyond that, lying there now and wondering why it had been great with Muriel, even though it really wasn't, and there wasn't that long flash like when he was loving Poppy.

This still bugged him; it often did: what made the difference? The basic nature and form of a woman, the basic sensation of balling a woman—what was there that left you feeling dulled or lost most times, while with Poppy there was this surge that came over him and did not leave?

He turned slightly and glanced at Muriel, lying on her side now lighting a cigarette, the remarkably young curve of her back and buttocks—yet when he was making it with her, he lost that vision of her. . . .

Was that it? Losing it all while you are making it? Muriel did things to the eye, she had something, some configuration of her breasts or contour of her thighs, the sloping hollow of her belly— he had imagined it, caressed her everywhere, but then as the fever rose and being in her, somehow you forget what there was that turned you on, whatever mystery or topography of the flesh, you forget it, you get lost in all the basic feels and smells and in the end you were nowhere. . . .

With Karen McGovern would it be the same? He knew, he was almost sure it would, he knew she didn't have it, that for all that supersex grabbing him, he would get lost and again spill it all inside her and not even know anymore what it was that had set her apart from anyone else. . . .

When you balled a girl like that you always forgot the special lure or beauty that had kept you so turned on. . . .

But with Poppy it was never like that. Why?

He tried to put it together: the special excitements of her body or her look, all that kept his eye and mind on that wavelength. Nothing got lost when they made love: she had, he saw now, that way, some mysterious way or gift of always keeping the total image of her body in his consciousness, that look of hers, even sending out the colors bending through her mind. . . .

So that with her there was that rare happening, being inside her while never losing the sight and essence of her.

How, why, did Poppy have it?

Or is this something that happens only when there's love?

Muriel was stubbing out her cigarette. He reached across her and turned on the table radio, dialing into another DJ, and there wasn't all that cornpone talk and little schlock-rock, The Beatles spinning out and The Kinks coming in.

Was that Muriel's voice now, yes, beneath The Kinks, Muriel singing the rest of the lyrics.

It made him grin inside.

In the half-light now he was able to lose for a few minutes the vision of Poppy and the vision of the bearded cinnamon face of Roger Shens. . . .

But only for that burst of time, and then it was back on him.

Muriel turned around, her body lightly grazing his, and he turned to meet it, needing to turn his back on all other visions. . . .

Muriel murmuring with that kind of wry put-down of herself, "I suppose you could say this is one way of narrowing the generation gap."

"It must be one of the best." Jamey pressed her against him, but this time somehow he couldn't make it the same way, too many things were getting between them, and he did not want to think of what was happening with him and with Poppy. . . .

Even though it was part of Poppy's way, even though he always accepted it, for it implied honesty and none of that supershit deception—even so, he knew it was different with Poppy now and he knew it was getting to be different with him.

It was at Yale, in Woolsey Hall, that Poppy without warning reappeared. And when he saw her there backstage as he arrived, it was, outside of his work, the first real surge in over two weeks—Poppy materializing out of the fog of war that had risen between them. Poppy here tonight suddenly. The return of Ruby Tuesday. Looking at her and nothing but that rush of his love reaching out for her.

After two weeks . . . two centuries. He'd been at Cornell, Colgate, Syracuse, Dartmouth, Middlebury, Bennington and three colleges that hadn't even been in existence when he'd been born.

A new Jamey? A paragon? Punctual and cooperative? No

choice, not after the way he'd had to bomb out on Colston last June. But this fall, one auditorium or hall after another. And gyms . . . Those basketball backboards had become part of the landscape of his concert life: making the circuit, moving ahead or after Jefferson Airplane or Simon and Garfunkel or Donovan or Tim Buckley or Arlo Guthrie or The Cream. . . .

And still surprised at the gap between what students felt and what was really going down. Syd Held and Zak Silberman like most people had forgotten something called the Vietnam war, people soothed by the synthetic perfume coming out of the Paris "peace talks." But the students he appreared before and talked to were more uptight than ever about the breakdown between them and the government. . . .

It kept coming back to him, that feeling he'd had so often, of living or working in a wilderness. All he and his friends and all the others had pushed for, all the sweat against the war, all the hope in McCarthy or Kennedy, all of it adding up to zero: the old phart politicos still the ones who were making it. . . .

He kept trying to ward off the shadow of Fuckleberry Finn, only shaking it during some of the concerts: that's when he felt that bond with them, getting into those songs.

Then it was of the best.

Though it ended there. All else was turning into a prolonged bummer:

Of the worst.

Not enough time to work on new projects. Not enough time or freedom to get into the rallies and benefits he wanted most to be part of . . .

Not enough time to . . .

Plus having to change his format. No more being alone with acoustical guitar. All that was changing beginning tonight. Raven Records as well as Nat McGovern had forced him into the new corner: now Jamcy would appear at major concerts backed by this four-man group—flute, organ, drums, strings. The old nights were gone. He was part of a production now, a presentation, slick, slock, schlock—not that bad, not really, but it meant carrying more of a load, and this kept cutting him up. . . .

Forgetting all of that, all of it now, seeing Poppy here, yes, there with Florida, others standing around, one of the concert staff and a guy from the *Yale Record*.

Poppy seeing him now and going to him at once like a mist veiling out the harsh edges of reality—ah, Poppy, that diminutive work of art, her eyes wide and deep on him, a Poppy without the familiar strip of skirt a-flutter above her thighs. Now Poppy, as if deliberately wanting to be beyond the New Haven context, was wearing those floppy wide-legged pajamas of Indian silk and that floppy wide felt hat the color of the flower for which she was named (it wasn't until this past spring that he'd found out her father during part of World War II had been stationed in France and had never forgotten the sight in April of wild near-scarlet poppies in the green fields of Normandy).

Poppy enveloped in all this swirl of silk looked like a child playing grown-up, except these clothes weren't mother's, nor did the impudent sculpture beneath them belong to Ma. Yet despite the panoply of her newest veneer, there was that inner glow of her person, as visible to him as the sight of distant fireworks across the dusk of a summer lake. . . .

Ignoring everyone, he kissed her and then, leaving everyone there in the wings, hurried her into the dressing room, and in the white sunburst of lights kissing her again, feeling the coolness and the slimness of her arms around his neck.

"I-love-you-I-love-you." Her mouth moving against his neck.

"I love you, I love." His voice muffled into her hair. The floppy wide hat fell to the floor.

And not moving, staying together, entwined, and not saying very much except those mouthings and murmurings, the language of lovers—yet he knew from the way they held each other that each was afraid to break away, as if they could only hold their new truce by holding each other.

But time was against him. "Christ—" He had to let her go. "I've got to get out there, Poppy, and run through the music with that group. Did you see them?"

"Yes, and I saw all those amplifiers and I thought like I must have the wrong place," Poppy said. "I asked Florida about it. How is he?"

"So far he's great."

"I mean, it's funny, the way he's—you know—getting to sound

more and more like you." Poppy had found her image in the bright glass. She bent down to pick up her hat.

He was slow to draw his eyes from her. "You look really cool. Dig you in that, Poppy, you look like a kid." Not until he'd said it did it occur to him that he'd identified something about her he had never noticed before.

Her smile was on him, though she said, "But Florida's not into anything, is he?"

"Not that I know of, not yet," Jamey said. "I mean, it's kind of lousy sometimes. He'll be around once in a while when I break out some grass. I don't know. I guess that prison wall really still closes him in. I doubt if it will last, but I'm not anxious to be the one he gets into it with. Mostly what he's doing when he's not working is making it with all the pussy around now."

Poppy smiled. "He gets all the leftovers, hmm?"

"Well, you know what I mean," Jamey said. Uneasily he glanced toward the door. He could hear the musicians. "Poppy, listen, what made you come?"

"I wanted to be with you," was all Poppy said. But saying it in that way of hers that made you put away any other questions. Then: "You look different."

"How?" he said.

"I don't know." Poppy peered at him. "I mean, it's nothing I can— Well—you know—it's like you've got a lot more in your head."

"Well, I have," he said, but he recognized that inadvertent flick of disapproval on her face.

"Listen, I'll be right back." He turned. "I have to see Florida and get out there—"

"Look"—she touched the brim of the floppy hat—"if it's about Karen—"

"What?" He stopped at the door.

"I mean, it doesn't matter if she's at that motel," Poppy said. "I went there before and I saw that silly fucking bourgeois Jaguar of hers parked in front of your door like it was a big yellow penis —which I guess is what she'd like it to be. I'm not trying to put her down. I mean, I'm not trying to—you know—begrudge any-one's pleasure. Only it's—"

"I was going to tell Florida to go out to the motel and—"

"No, don't, please. Let her rest in peace," Poppy said. "I mean, can't we go like someplace else?"

"Why, yes, sure—"

"Give her a night off." Poppy's cool seemed real, too much so. "Unless you—"

"No, we'll go someplace else. I mean—well, look, Poppy, she's been kind of following me all over—"

"Lots of people follow you around," Poppy said. "Oh, did you ever make it with that nice lady?"

"Who? You mean Muriel?"

"Yes."

"Well, yes—that once, that night you had to see Roger." Jamey hadn't wanted to say it but the scene was already falling apart. If he'd gone out to work with that group—

"Well," Poppy was saying, "at least everybody's following their arrows. That's something."

"You sure as hell followed yours." He sank into it.

"Being uptight like that isn't the answer, Jamey."

"What is? Meditating my way out of it?"

"I mean, I don't go around saying Roger or any other person is following me all the time and I'm all helpless and nothing I can do except dive into his pants the minute I check into some hotel a hundred miles from New York or—"

Jamey stared at her: Poppy with that sometime gift of divination choosing at random a parallel of what had happened between him and Karen.

"Hey, I'm mad on you!" Karen McGovern had imitated Billyman Coe on that afternoon two weeks ago, Karen at Syracuse University, parked in the yellow Jag outside his motel three blocks from the campus; he had just come out, still talking with the guy who was interviewing him for the *Daily Orange*. He waved to her and kept going, the kind of put-down that would have sent any other girl on her way. But Karen was still there when he came back at five-thirty, Karen moving with him into the motor lodge, upstairs to the hall with the giant ice-cube machine, Karen sticking right with him like a shadow, and into his quarters, passing Florida, alert by the open door of the adjacent room.

Florida stepped in just as Karen was closing the door. "You need me, Jamey?"

"Florida"—Karen frowned—"what's the big deal? Can't you get lost *once* in a while?" She pushed the door against him.

"Hey, listen—" Florida shoved his foot forward.

"Forget it for now, it's all right, Florida. Thanks." Jamey ended it. To have the hassle continue would have made too much of it.

Yet when they were alone Karen seemed suddenly inhibited, that aggression or hostility gone: she floundered there amid the Scandinavian units of bleached wood furniture; she combed her long hazel hair and she put mascara on the lashes of her dark-green eyes.

She watched him as he went over to the desk to open the letter from Richmond, Virginia, from Lyle Stinnett, in answer to his: Lyle writing now that his second draft deferment was running out and that he was hooked, ordered to report in a month. And telling him that in Cleveland Roy Billings "never got the OK from the Army medics. I think they wanted absolutely no part of him. Since then he's working with the Black Urban Authority and apparently getting a lot of action. As for good old Chancellor Ross, assume you read of his forthcoming resignation."

Karen lit a cigarette. She kept alternating her gaze between him and the window. When Jamey started reading the letter again, the part about Roy Billings, she said, "All right, I get it. I'll leave as soon as I have this cigarette."

When he glanced over at her, the look on her face made him regret having shot her down so many times. "It's all right, Karen."

"Oh, what the hell, Jamey. I had it coming. Won't be the first time I—"

"What?" he asked as she let her words hang there.

"To hell with it," she said.

"What were you trying to say?"

"Oh, just one of those dull creepy things like, this won't be the first time in my life people don't beg me to stay," Karen said.

Jamey wasn't sure what to say then. Except: "Well, it's just that I'm in a kind of rush, Karen."

"When are you going to be back in New York?"

"In a week," he said.

"Jesus, how I hate that place," she said vehemently.

"You mean Nat."

"Nat and a lot of other creeps including my mother and— Jesus, that place gets me down," Karen said.

"Maybe you ought to go back to Chicago, finish school—"

"Chicago? That's where my father lives!"

"Oh."

"He'd start running the minute I got there!" She looked away when she said it. Her tone was bitter yet there was that swift breath of softness: it was the only time now or after that she ever let down her guard. Then: "Can I ask you something?"

"Sure."

"You really like him—Nat, I mean?"

"What? Well—yes, I do."

"You do?" She moved to where he was standing by the desk. "That must make you a fan club of one." She kissed him then. "I wish I could be."

"Be what?"

"Your fan club of one." Karen waited, an almost wistful air in the backwash of what she'd said, though this did not last, and in an abrupt or desperate movement she thrust her hard aggressive breasts against him.

He should have made his move then.

"Why couldn't I stay here?" Karen's hand was on his chest.

He didn't answer immediately. And her hand stirred and then she was tugging at his zipper and slipping her hand in, her ravenous fingers finding him.

He resisted it.

For at least three and a half seconds.

Sometimes chicks like Karen who were badly hung up and who seemed like such hostile hotpants aggressors turned out to be nowhere when the moment of truth came. But from the way Karen made it, the way she reached it was like a brutal freak-out. This bed in the motel in Syracuse, like the others to follow it on his tour, must have always had her name on it. . . .

But it would not work tonight in New Haven. He would have to send Florida out to give her the bad word. He could see Karen in that pile of quasi-Colonial motor lodge off the Wilbur Cross highway, Karen really burned down—yes, he could see her, a

witch in a twitch all night, refusing to leave and using Florida to
spit her invective on. . . .

No, he couldn't do that, that would be begging her for trouble.
He knew her now. He wanted no part of anything like she could
hand out, and his sending Florida there would be begging for it.
He would have to go there himself and break it; it didn't matter
how, but he knew she would never accept it unless it came from
him, not from Florida, whom she held low as a pimp. . . .

Somehow Jamey would break it.

"Look," Poppy was saying, "I didn't come here to get into this,
Jamey. I mean, I know you have to work and—"

"Hey, Jamey—" The drawl of Florida beyond the door. "It's
seven-thirty and everybody's waiting for you."

"Right there," Jamey answered. He turned to Poppy. "Listen,
baby, all I know is you're here and that's all I want to know.
Come on out with me. You can watch it from the wings when—"

But no, Poppy said she wanted to see it from the audience.

"I'll have them get you a seat," he said.

"Jamey—" She went to him. "Can we, I mean, can you like
shake all those characters afterwards? For once?"

"Watch me!" Leaving now, with the new truce and the worst
of it already over between them: Poppy, who could vanish but
who could return and lay it out cold so they could start clean and
fresh. Or almost.

At eight-fifteen the auditorium of Woolsey Hall, from where he
stood in the wings, looked near capacity: the Yalies and townies
in a mix of sarapes, admiral coats, Co-op T-shirts, army-navy-
store jeans and work shirts, miniskirts and long multihued stockings and the inevitable J. Press tweeds—the hall itself a stalwart
reminder of past times, the mighty organ pipes rising, a phalanx
of brass at the back of the stage, the twin colonnade of columns
flanking the hall, the baroque cupola over the balcony. . . .

While now Jamey's backing, the four young musicians in their
vermilion capes and ruffled shirts and wild plaid pants, waiting
out there for Jamey to come on, the amber spots shafting down
on him from either side of the proscenium.

On signal he stepped out into the blaze, wearing what he usually wore—the white jeans and white denim work jacket and

black button-down shirt, the black glasses white-rimmed. And as he walked out he was strapping on his guitar. He still had enough suntan so that he could ignore makeup. He moved to the center to stand in front of the group and the banks of electronic equipment, and standing there now, and while making his final tune-up, telling the audience something about his first song, "The Lyndon Tree."

The concert would go tonight. Poppy out there. That marginal jab that would turn him on. (When he'd given that first campus concert at New York State in Long Island and his parents were there, he'd felt inhibited somehow and never really got plugged in until near the end.)

So that tonight he was sure the Yale appearance would be of the best.

It was. He was knocked out. And hoarse.

What he didn't know until he'd finished the concert was that Nat McGovern had come up from New York and his resilient girth had been somewhere in the darkness of Woolsey Hall, Nat not making his presence known until Jamey was through, the curtain down.

Then Nat moved in: with his black dispatch case of notes, letters, telegrams, the newest contracts, data on his next recording session for Raven.

Poppy saw him too and gave Jamey that look and moved away to wait, calmly, coolly, waiting in shadow for Jamey to split.

Instead, as it turned out, Nat McGovern made the gesture of going to her and inviting her to join him and Jamey at Casey's for food and drink. Of course there would be business, but—

"Thanks, but I won't be able to make it," Poppy said.

Jamey urged: "Poppy, come on, it won't take all that much time and—"

"I really can't make it," Poppy said.

Florida's spindly frame eased into the scene, Florida with his pale nicotine complexion, in his denim outfit—a kind of adaptation in blue of what Jamey wore—Florida, his sandy mop merging into long sideburns, Florida saying, "Jamey, that cat from the *Record* is still waiting and there's a photographer from the *Register*—"

"McGovern will be at Casey's," Nat said, though not leaving, pausing as if to ponder—Nat in his black silk suit, black shoes and black tie, deciding then, and his plump hand on Jamey's arm, steering him into a far corner at the rear. "There's something I have to discuss. In case we're not alone later." Nat with that kind of chill and funky gaze upon him now. "Am I misinformed or not, Jamey? Is Karen here in town with you? I promised her mother I'd check. I know she was at Syracuse and at—"

It was bound to come like that and Jamey should have been ready. "What about it, Nat?" he said. "I mean, I stopped trying to keep up with Karen."

"She keeping up with you?"

"Look, Nat—Poppy's here tonight. I haven't seen her in almost three weeks."

"If Karen doesn't show up in New York tomorrow morning, someone will be out to get her. Where is she?" Nat waited, friendly and calm, even seeming indifferent as he tugged at his impeccable white cuffs.

"I don't know where she is." Jamey tried it that way.

Nat McGovern shifted his ponderous stance. "Let's level, kiddo. I have a serious, a very serious, responsibility with her. It's part of my marriage. Marriage seldom interferes with anything I do. But this is a serious matter. My wife is terrified Karen's going to end up in real trouble. Something else. Has she ever mentioned a boy by the name of Dirkwood, Emmett Dirkwood?"

"No."

"This is a boy who she's been seeing. Until you. And her mother feels he's the answer."

"I hope he is, whoever he is." Jamey glanced at his watch.

The gesture was ignored. Nat said, "Emmett is a straight kid, and also very bright. Top fifth of his class. He's in law at Columbia. A brain. But Karen is like some exotic foreign country to this boy and he wants to live there. And that's what my wife wants to see happen. He's the answer if Karen's going to have any kind of stable future and not end up in a clinic for kooks. This is private business, Jamey. I assumed you were otherwise occupied." A long look over to where Poppy was standing now, near the master switchboard. "I assumed that or I would have made you privy to all this to begin with."

"I'm sorry, Nat. I mean, if she's going with this cat, she kept it a secret. I'm glad you told me."

"In that case I count on you for action. Where is she now? I have to live with her mother."

"I'm not sure," Jamey said.

"You are lying. Please don't try to be gallant with McGovern."

"I don't know where she is," Jamey said.

Nat was not amused. "See you at Casey's soon as you're through with these people here."

"Nat— Look, Nat, I have this date with Poppy. I didn't know she was coming up and I—"

"I came up here tonight also. The only free time I had. Tomorrow night I have to fly to L.A." A final tug at the white cuffs. "Casey's. In an hour. Or less. I know you'll be there."

Jamey looked around the dim cavern of the backstage area: more people seemed to have come. More boppybirds too. From where? He looked over at Poppy. He palmed back his damp hair.

Karen McGovern still waiting. In a twitch. In that motor lodge by the Wilbur Cross highway.

It was after midnight when he got through the interview and the photos and all the rest of the supershit rituals.

And Poppy waiting here, so patient now, all love, swathed in that Indian silk and looking childlike and almost comically demure in the floppy wide-brimmed hat. Going to her now, he said, "Look, I'm sorry, Poppy—"

"It's all right."

"I've got to see Nat McGovern. No way out of it, Poppy. So you've got to come along this time. Then we'll—"

"I told you before, I really would rather not, Jamey. I'll wait. Somewhere. Where do you want to make it?"

"I'll have Florida take care of it." He was still only marking time, filling in until he could get away from Nat and get Karen the hell out of New Haven and environs. But he couldn't spare Florida for that now. He needed him to make the arrangements for later, for Poppy.

So that, pinched for time when he reached the restaurant, he decided to telephone Karen at his motel. "Karen, I—"

"Where are you, Jamey? I was just thinking I'd better come in. Do you want me to pick you up?"

"I'm with Nat at this restaurant."

"Nat? Oh, Jesus, what's *he* doing here?"

"It's business." Jamey tried to tell her how it was. "Here's the thing, Karen. I— Nat's here and, look, why don't we forget tonight? You ought to return to New York. Nat is in a real sweat about it. So is your mother."

"Those two creeps can get lost!" Karen turned the words like a knife.

"I mean, look, Karen, they are putting it all on me, I'm not used to anything like this. It really cuts me up. You go back to New York and I'll call you tomorrow."

"Tomorrow you're going to be at the University of Connecticut."

"Oh, that's right."

"You prick."

"Karen, will you try to get this straight? Tonight's out. I'll call you from—"

"You of all people! Why does everybody have to be a prick!"

Jamey sighed; he pushed open the door of the telephone booth as if to lure in some air, to cool his forehead, to bank down the rising fires of all his discontents. But all he could feel now was the unwanted heat of his life beating down on him like the blaze of spotlights. He could see Karen now, her long dark hair already taking on that electric luster of combat, the angry emerald eyes sparking in the empty motel room, that look on her he'd seen several times when someone or something wasn't going the way she wanted it to go, that pulsing of her nerves showing at her temple. Now he heard her low voice dropping half a note and taking on that abrasive edge: "Either you come out here or—" A sudden pause. "Jamey darling, are you with someone else? Like Poppy? Who is it? What's happening?"

"What's happening is Nat and your mother," he said.

"Why do you have to keep mentioning those creeps!"

Jamey said, "Why didn't you ever mention this guy—Kirkwood—"

"Dirkwood," she corrected him. "What's that got to do with anything?"

"Look, Karen, I'm late as hell now. Nat's here waiting for—"

"You must be at Casey's. I'll come over."

"Karen, I told him I hadn't seen you, I said I had no idea where you were—"

"That turd won't believe it. I might as well come over and tell him and anyone else around who's bugging you to get lost—I mean lost!"

"Karen"—he pulled the door shut—"listen. I—I'll get right out there as soon as I'm through with Nat."

"You will?"

"Yes."

"That's my honeybaby. How soon?"

"About—oh, I don't know—around one or so."

"I'm waiting, honeybaby. God, I can't wait," Karen said.

But she would have to wait. For by the time he finished the long drag of a conference with Nat McGovern, he felt choked with impatience; he also felt fury at himself. And he decided to let Karen hang out there. He wouldn't see her. He'd let her cool her stupid, sad, beautiful ass and by tomorrow Nat could take over, or her mother.

He was not going to be flattened by her or anyone else, not now, just when Poppy was back.

Late that night he drove to The Inn, just southeast of New Haven, where Florida had taken Poppy, and he stayed there with her until after noon the next day. He had about three hours left before starting for the U. Conn. campus in Storrs.

At two o'clock he telephoned the motel where he and Karen had been staying. There was no answer in his room. He felt free to go there then. When he drove over with Poppy he made a slow and careful pass around the horseshoe-shaped building and the parking grounds. No sign of the yellow Jaguar.

Near the rear of the sprawling motel he parked. He left Poppy in the car and went in for the rest of his gear. He was not surprised to see the condition of the room: pillows, sheets, clothes, portable radio, everything had been broken, torn, twisted by the tornado of Karen's helpless, stupid temper.

When he left he carried out his suitcase and his battered second guitar. He had just passed beneath the concrete canopy at the rear car entrance and was starting for the parking area when it happened:

He heard or sensed someone somewhere behind him. Instinctively he turned or started to. Just enough to recognize Karen, partially hidden behind the concrete post of canopy, Karen's arm jutting out, the revolver in the sunlight.

The sound of the shot was almost lost in the backfire blasts of some truck passing beyond on the highway.

Jamey did not fall at once. There was that stunned instant, the sting or burn of the bullet in his back near the right shoulder, just that stunned blurring instant or two and the black nausea in his throat and the dizzying tilt of vision before he fell.

10 : THE COUNTRY

THE NURSE, Elda Reens, is a tart-tongued and sour-eyed woman who, until this Jamey got on her shift, was known among her colleagues, particularly the younger ones, as "Reens, that crud."

However, these days it's a new Elda, suddenly high on the popularity poll in the Albith Annex of Grace New Haven Hospital. And the new Elda is making the most of what has come her way: after all, it's the first real chance she's had since she's been here to get her foot in the door of the "club."

On the way to the cafeteria now she passes a young nurse's aide rolling the library cart along. "He's leaving tomorrow. Is that true?"

"If Dr. Wayde says it's OK," Elda answers.

The girl sighs. "The nice ones never stay long, do they?" She pushes the culture cart forward on its rounds.

In the cafeteria it is so light—all those windows with the October sun, all those bright Formica tables and chairs. Elda picks up a cup of coffee with cream and two sugars, and goes to one of the empty tables, just as she usually has done in the past: except today, you can bet your last bedpan, today the table won't be empty for long. She will soon have company.

Sure enough. Two other nurses have caught sight of her and here they come, coffee cups in hand.

"What's new, Elda?" the youngest one asks.

"Well, now he wants this map." Elda taps it against the table. "I had one of the orderlies get it at the gas station."

"I wonder what for. I wonder where he's going." The other one is greedy for information.

Elda Reens tries to look impassive.

"Who else has been to see him?" asks the first nurse. "Did you ever find out who that woman was? You know, the one brought him the Sony TV for a present?"

"Oh, certainly. It's a Mrs. Hewes."

"The one with the dark-red hair."

"Yes. Mrs. Hewes." With authority, Elda can release this small item for them to taste and chew. "She's a very personal friend of his. That much I happen to know. And rich. Likes 'em young." She has no way of knowing what Mrs. Hewes's tastes are. But it doesn't matter: almost everybody who came in there was some kind of case. And the clothes they wore! You take this girl friend of his, Poppy whatever-her-name-is. Talk about your weirdos—well, this kid takes the cake. Like the day they brought him into Emergency, and this Poppy in those silk pajamas and that big hat looking like God knows what. And that one called Florida, talk about your nuts! And that lawyer McGovern and that young fellow from the record company with the sideburns down to here and wearing that jacket from China or India somewhere. The only decent people so far have been his mother and father. Really nice. You wonder what they must think, a thing like this happening to their son, their only son. . . .

"You know, I wanted to get him to sign that second album of his," the younger nurse is saying. "I went all over New Haven looking for it. Sold out everywhere. And all those singles of his—not one left."

"Naturally," Elda concedes wisely: a scandal like that is bound to boom his records. Personally, she heard his album once and she can't see it for dust. Isn't there enough misery in the world without someone like this Jamey Mieland having to write songs about it? When Elda was a young nurse, at least you could sing the melody and it was pretty and the words you remembered, the nice easy way they rhymed. But this Jamey—what all the fuss is about she'll never know.

She finishes her cup of coffee.

"Oh, don't rush, Elda. You never finished yesterday about what happened after you walked in on him like that—"

Elda shakes her head. Who would think nurses, of all people, would fall apart like a couple of moronic teen-agers just because someone like this Jamey is a patient here. "Well, it was nothing much," she begins. "What I mean is, he was just necking. Like. With this Poppy. He was still partially immobile but that didn't stop either of them. When I walked in she just got off the side of the chair, sort of pulled at her skirt—what there was of it—and smiled and asked me if it was Tuesday or Wednesday."

They nibble at this for a while. Then one of the nurses says, "Everybody is saying she's the reason the other one shot him."

"No." Here Elda can let them have the true inside. "No." She masticates each word, for this is authentic and she doesn't care if they repeat it. "As I understand, it's more complicated than that. This Karen McGovern turns out to be a psycho."

"Anyone give me odds she'll get away with it?" Noah Berman, an intern, stands by the table. Absently he jiggles the stethoscope that hangs out from his side pocket.

"Not me—I wouldn't." Elda readjusts her cap, clips in the bobby pin again.

"In this country people get away with anything," the intern comments righteously.

"Some people do." Elda favors him with that sour gaze. He's a fine one to talk. Even if it isn't true, and it isn't, somebody said when he's on night duty he does it with that new young nurse right on one of the examining tables in Gyn.

"Well, she's out on bail," the intern is saying, "and they're going to tuck her into some country-club-type sanatorium. My, my."

Elda rises to leave.

"Elda, I'll be glad to take that map up for you, if you're busy." The youngest nurse smiles at her own transparent guile.

"Another time, dear," Elda says.

"That map—why is it so important?" the other nurse asks.

"I have my own theories," Elda answers: this will carry her higher on the poll during this last day.

"Like what? Come on, Elda!" the nurse urges.

"It's none of my business. And it's too soon to say anything. A little too soon." Elda moves off quickly now to keep intact her current mystique.

She takes the elevator to the fourth floor and goes straight to Jamey's room, which has that awful view of those big concrete test tubes of the new Knights of Columbus building. She opens the door, and there is Mr. Luck himself. Half an inch is the difference between his being alive or being dead, less than half an inch, according to Dr. Wayde, the surgeon who removed the bullet (it had gone through muscles, scapula, posterior chest wall, pleural cavity, lodging in the anterior chest wall and caught in a rib bone). A fraction of an inch more and this Jamey Mieland would have been cooling off in a drawer in the morgue.

But now there he is, sitting in the armchair. The sutures were removed yesterday morning.

And this Poppy whatever-her-name-is is in the other chair and she is reading a book and moving her lips from time to time.

"Here's that map you wanted." Elda hands it to him.

He thanks her. Poppy looks up from the book.

Well, Elda feels, with so little time left before he leaves, she ought to stay around as long as possible. She dawdles. Puts fresh water in the carafe by his bed, rearranges the flowers in the vases, moves about amid all the clutter—that tiny TV, the radio, the guitars, the piles of books and newspapers, the tape recorder. Talk about some people having just about everything!

She dawdles. But she does not hear a choice word from Jamey. Or this girl of his.

He is opening the map though, and then closing it. And now he keeps looking at this girl.

There is nothing else for Elda Reens to do. Too bad. She'll have to clear out. She has other patients on the floor. Not that you'd know it. So it's clearing-out time and she still hasn't even picked up a clue about the map, she still hasn't been able to catch a hint about where Jamey is going. Too bad.

He opened the map. He found the place. He studied it for a long time. Still he didn't say anything, waiting for the excitement —or was it apprehension?—in his chest to subside. His gaze swung to Poppy, who was reading. He still hadn't told her. He wanted to make sure. He was sure now. Maybe it took a bullet or near-death to shock him into it, but somehow he had to make the break: get out.

Get out from under the orchestrations suffocating the lyrics of his second album; get out from under the way they were butchering the singles cut from his LP's.

Get out, get away from the flip-flapping boppybirds, away from the super-selling supershit of the Billyman Coes; away from the strangling mob; away from the super psychophants; away from the Syds and Zaks and Nats; away from the killers of his time . . .

Maybe away from himself—the self that was beginning to like what was happening to him.

"Poppy." He gripped the map.

She looked up from her book.

He told her then that he was going to get out. Tomorrow. He told her what he'd been thinking about in the darkness of these nights in the hospital room.

He kept watching her face, seeing how the shadow of disbelief or surprise was giving way to a clearer light.

Abruptly now she rose and the book dropped from her lap. She came to him. "Jamey, you're— Are you really going to do this?"

He nodded.

"I mean, you really are?"

He nodded again.

"It's—it's such a big—"

"I know," he said. "And I can't wait!"

Still Poppy hesitated. She still couldn't seem to catch hold of the reality of it. He told her more. He told her how he had been feeling, the way the whole scene kept strangling him and how his creative time was being robbed by the mobs around him.

Now it was Poppy who nodded. Then she said, "What about Florida?"

"I thought of that too," Jamey said. "I think I can get him a job as road manager for The Gingerbread Bicycle."

"I see," Poppy said. Slowly there grew in the bronze eyes that final shine of love or reassurance, and then she was on the arm of his chair and her arms were around his neck. "I was sure I'd lost you for good—I mean, I never thought there'd be any way you could like walk out—"

"I didn't either."

Exuberantly she was kissing him. As if in celebration. Then: "When we get back to New York this time, it'll be—we'll be like two different persons."

"We're not going back to New York," Jamey said.

"Not right away? When?"

He opened the map. He altered his position to favor his other side. "What I thought"—he pointed to one section—"I thought we could rent a place, maybe buy one. I don't know. This part around here, it's very beautiful and it's remote. I can get back to work, get into everything I've been unable to do. It's nice and quiet. When you're there you're really out of it."

"Oh."

"What's the matter?"

"Nothing." She walked away from him. "I just assumed we'd be in New York."

"What's the difference?"

"Well, in New York you're not, well, boxed in."

In sudden desolation he looked at her. "Poppy, you don't want to go."

"Oh, I didn't say that. It's just that, well, you know—" She seemed to flounder and then in a burst, clutching at the words, she said, "And what about Nat McGovern?"

"What do you mean, Poppy?"

"He won't let you just walk out like this," she said.

He peered at her in astonishment. "Since when are you worried about Nat McGovern?"

She blinked. "Well—maybe I *am* worried about him." Hastily she added, "He won't let you just walk out. And that's something you ought to think about."

"Poppy"—he stared at her—"you've got to be kidding. Since when are you suddenly all common sense and worries?"

"Well"—Poppy answered him almost defiantly—"I don't see how you can just pretend Nat doesn't exist." She began to walk around the room with its pale-green walls. "He'll never let you go. You're money—you're his money boy. I know him. I know he's not going to let you walk out."

"Wait a minute, Poppy. What is this? You sound like two other people."

"Well, it's true. You've got all those commitments, those dates. And contracts. And what about that nightclub Nat was discussing?"

"For Christ sakes, Poppy, that's what it's all about! That's why I'm getting out! And you know it! What are you covering for? Two minutes ago you were all over me with joy and happiness!"

She blinked again. "All I'm saying, Jamey"—she faltered—"all I'm saying is, you shouldn't go rushing off into the woods somewhere until you make sure Nat isn't going to stop you or sue you or something like that."

"OK, Poppy." Dismally he looked at her. "Come off it. Let's not lay this on Nat." He paused. "One last thing I ought to tell you is that right now Nat's too involved with Karen. Lawyers. Psychiatrists. He's trying to get her out of this. And everything I've said in this case will help get her out of it. He has to be on my side. He can't antagonize me now. He's got to let me go. So let's not get hung up on that. If you don't want to come with me, say so. But don't keep getting into somebody else's bag just because you don't know how to tell me you aren't having any."

No answer.

She seemed to be squinting. "Well, I, at first—you know—didn't think of what it really meant." Then abruptly: "And there's something else. What about The New School? I mean, I just started the new term and I couldn't walk out if—"

"Poppy—" muting his temper. "What're you trying to build here? You float out of Berkeley for the Haight and you float out of there for the East Village and then you float into The New School last winter. Since when does getting into another scene make you nervous like this? What're you trying to say?"

No answer.

"Poppy, did you hear me!" Jamey said, noticing only then that she was biting her lip, and then he saw that her eyes were blurring with tears. "Poppy—"

She turned away and moved to the window. Her narrow shoulders kept shaking.

"Poppy—" He went to her. He grasped her, brought her around to face him. "What is it?"

No answer at first.

"You just don't want to go? Is that it? You don't want to make it this way?" Jamey said.

"No—" She cleared her throat. "I mean, yes, I do. I do, Jamey. It's just—" She hesitated. "It's just that, how do we know if we go out someplace in the woods somewhere—it might just box us in. It might turn out to be like a terrible drag, like we're vegetating. And I keep worrying maybe you'll begin to miss what you used to have."

Slowly he said, "You're sure that's all that's worrying you?"

She nodded slowly. She reached out and touched his hand.

"Listen, Poppy, listen, baby, that's why I'm doing this. I want to do it before I really start missing anything." Then he said, "I saw how it was going, I found myself resenting it a little less and liking it a little more. It's very easy to like. The trouble is, no matter how you cut it, you end up in show business. And that's what I don't want, that's not for me. When that happens something goes out of you."

Poppy began, tentatively, to show that slow half-smile, yielding now, slowly, but yielding, or settling for whatever answer she had been looking for.

And Jamey moved in on it, his arm around her now, guiding her back to the armchair. He had to lock it up now. He opened the map as soon as he was seated. All his new hope was in his voice.

"It's right in this section. I was driving right through there— wait until you see it, Poppy. This section around Bridgewater and Roxbury. You'll fall right out of your tree!"

"When were you there?"

"I was coming down Route Seven from that concert at Bennington. On the way to Yale. I took Sixty-seven across." He felt very warm. He undid the top buttons of his white pajamas.

"You and Karen—"

"I was alone. She went back to Syracuse to get her car."

Poppy frowned, peering at the patch of bandage on his chest. "Oh, why couldn't she have stayed up there!" she cried.

He did not say anything. How many times had he seen that pistol of hers, the snub-nosed, palm-sized .22 in the open glove compartment of the Jag, so casually protruding amid papers, maps, cosmetics, flashlight. . . .

Now he folded the map into a smaller square. "I think what we ought to do is just drive up there, see some real estate people and see if there are any good houses in this Bridgewater section or—"

He looked up. A nurse's aide had come in with mail. Poppy went to the door and took the letters. The girl kept staring over Poppy's shoulder, trying to mask the interest she was showing in Jamey. When she left, and she moved like a turtle, Poppy handed him the letters. He glanced through them. He stopped. "This one is from Roy—"

"Roy?"

"You know. Roy Billings."

"Oh yes."

Jamey was opening it. "He never writes. This is history. The last time he wrote was summer before last, I think." Jamey began to read the letter immediately. But the telephone rang. He asked Poppy to take it. (No more Florida bounding across the room at the first ring. Florida would be missed; Florida sleeping it off today in the Central Plaza Hotel, where Poppy also had a room. Florida's eyes were getting that yellow glaze; he seemed strung out: idleness was poison for him. Yes, he'd get him that job; if not with The Bicycle, maybe with The Gross-Outs, who were gigging around the East.)

Poppy held the telephone. She said to him, "It's a Mrs. Karr—"

"Karr? Oh, Laura—" He wanted to speak to her. Poppy brought over the telephone, trailing the long cord. "Laura!"

"How are you, Jamey?"

"Well, great. Or almost. Thanks for your wire. Are you in New York?"

"I'm in New Haven. Is it possible to stop by?"

"You mean you came up here to see me?" Jamey said.

"Yes. Can I come for a few minutes?"

"Where are you now?"

"At the Co-op."

When he hung up he said Laura would be over in about ten minutes.

"That's very nice of her, coming up here like that," Poppy said. Then: "What does Roy Billings say?"

Jamey picked up the letter again. That cool black ballpoint script of Roy's, neat, precise. Like the way he spoke. The letter came from the Hough Street headquarters of the Black Urban Authority in Cleveland. Jamey said, "I had to get damn near killed to get a word out of Roy. I don't know why I love that sonofabitch."

He read the letter aloud:

Dear J: I am glad you are doing all right. Or so I have read. As I keep saying, in this country the guns get into the hands of the madmen, the bullets into the bodies of the sane ones.

I heard your new single, "When the Cymbals Are Still." Someone here at the Authority had it going the other day. Very fancy stuff. I suppose I liked it better the way you sang or talked it with just a guitar that night in College Hall just before the bust. But hearing it now with all that musical background, it was more like a big lush patriotic marching song. Since when am I a critic? I'm sure my opinion won't hurt the record's sales. Or am I only trying to revenge myself for the way you once blasted that history paper I wrote during sophomore year?

Jamey looked up. "Christ, I wish I could say he was wrong. I begged Raven not to dub in all that shit. I begged them."

He resumed reading the letter:

On the 15th of next month at the Oberlin College auditorium they are having one of those so-called Angry Arts festivals. They want to raise more money for our ghetto rehabilitation project. I was asked to speak. But I refused. We can use the money and we'll accept it. However, I do not believe in going there and holding my black hand out to that audience. Best intentions notwithstanding. I suggested to them that perhaps you could take my place—if you're free, which I doubt. They jumped at the idea. If you are interested you might let me know. Having antagonized you with my unsolicited comments about one of your records, I don't necessarily expect you to fall all over yourself to answer this.

Meanwhile take care of yourself. And watch the company you keep. I do. Roy.

He put down the letter.

"Ooooh!" Poppy said. "Is that man pissed off on certain people!"

Grimly Jamey nodded. "He's trying to get under me again. But at least he's writing, at least maybe we're not as far apart as I thought we were. One thing about Roy. He's into something big, and he's putting all of himself into it. Which is more than I've done. At least lately."

Softly the door had opened again. Nurse Reens. She said Mrs. Karr was outside.

When the nurse, in slow motion, finally left, Jamey murmured, "Eleanor Rigby."

"'Keeps her face in a jar by the door.'" Poppy added more of The Beatles' composition.

And then Laura Barnes Karr was in the hospital room and there was a rush of talk and then Poppy floated out, going to the solarium. She had to get her ticket for tonight's recital of Indian dancers, and she had to write letters to her father and to Mike.

As soon as they were alone there was that weight in the air, that sense that this was a mistake, that it had to bomb out; he and Laura now trying to dial in on a wavelength that would work; or maybe all it was was that there seemed to be something about her he could not dig, not yet anyway.

She talked but did not stand still, she moved around the room like a woman distractedly examining an apartment up for rent but who has no intention of taking it.

Not until he asked her to sit down on the other chair was there the beginning of repose. Time had been between them for so long that it was not easy to get into anything.

Jamey stirred in the armchair. "When Poppy said it was a Mrs. Karr, I had to stop and think for a second."

"I realized that, but—" A kind of shrug.

He said, "You look great, Laura."

Meaning it, even though there was a change and he wasn't sure about how it worked: the coed had become a young matron; that indifferent slimness seemed to have given way to something else. Gone were the sweaters, the loafers, the shoulder bag, the tight denim pants; her long amber hair no longer streamed down but was cut to just above the shoulders; she wore one of those little suits you always saw advertised by Bonwit Teller or Bergdorf in the first section of *The New York Times*, a fawn-colored, short-skirted, double-breasted worsted, chic and safe. Her black stumpy shoes matched her alligator bag.

Suddenly he was truly glad she was here. "Christ, Laura, it's really great of you to come all this way. How's Link?"

"Working hard. Eight to five. Practically. He hasn't even had time for tennis—" Pausing now as if too conscious of the way he had been looking at her. "Actually, I didn't come only to see you. There was a luncheon meeting I wanted to go to—hence, this uniform."

"Oh."

"One of those regional affairs. You know." She seemed relieved to dive into this. "Reports on the antipoverty program in the East. And the Arts Council. I'm involved in some of it. As a matter of fact"—stopping abruptly, but going on then—"as a matter of fact, the same day I, uh, read about you in the papers, that was the day I was going to get in touch with you. They were having this kind of street fair on One-hundred-thirty-eighth Street—lots of rock and roll and all that, and I thought even though it would be mostly black people, I thought it would be marvelous to get you, but—"

"I was kind of hard to get that day." Jamey tried to make it easier for her.

It helped. She said, "Mother, my dear mother, told me she saw you at that cabaret last spring and that's what gave me the idea." A small laugh. "You want to hear something funny? My mother. The way she drops your name into conversations now. You wouldn't believe it." Mimicking Mrs. Barnes then: "'And here's the funniest—this boy Jamey, he was always up here chasing after Laura, and we used to worry about what would ever become of him—isn't that the craziest?'"

Dutifully Jamey laughed.

But somehow after that they fell into a hollow of silence.

So that Jamey reached back into last year and they talked about school and the rumors of who was going to replace Ross-boss as Chancellor and what some of the people were doing, like Stinnett, Einsberg and Susan Sayres.

"Did you read about Roy Billings?" Laura said then. "I mean, the way he's involved in the black movement around Cleveland?"

Jamey said yes and he told her of the letter he had received this afternoon.

And then another gap of silence. This one seemed deeper and was longer. Jamey buttoned the collar of his pajamas. Laura glanced at her watch. He said, "When—when did you start in on this stuff uptown?"

"Oh, I—well, actually, I know you're going to laugh: it started when I was one of those Sunday volunteers helping to paint, sweep and clean up the neighborhood—"

This time he really had to laugh: Laura still the loyal straight optimistic liberal trying to paint away four hundred years of the white man's sins, sweep out the debris of the white man's long brutal indifference. Yes, Laura still there.

"I knew that would get you," Laura said. A smile cracked the young matron's earnest, Pre-Raphaelite features. Like times of yore.

"No—" But he laughed again; sometimes when he laughed he could feel it where the stitches in the wound had been.

"Well," she said, "I have to do something, don't I?"

"Oh, sure."

"I mean, you didn't think I could just stick up in that apartment or just go to those auctions at Parke-Bernet? Not with Link away so much."

"But you're happy. Right?"

"Right."

Then he said, "Did Link know you were coming to see me?"

"Oh, certainly. Actually he wanted to come too. But he had a meeting—oh, this is really godawful, Jamey—he had to join the Young Republicans Club—I mean, he didn't have to, but he did it. Sort of to keep his boss happy. He almost had to do it. More or less." Uncomfortably Laura waited and when Jamey said nothing, she suddenly looked around. "Oh, I forgot." She rose and went back for the package she'd put on the bureau when she'd come in. She presented him with a bag of grapes. "I passed this marvelous fruit store. I know how you like them. Or did."

Still did. He drew out a small cluster of the pale-green seedless grapes. As soon as their sweet tartness touched his tongue he was right back in that borrowed apartment near Tompkins Square Park that Sunday morning he and Laura were in bed with *The Times* and he'd tried to press a grape into her navel. . . .

He found himself watching her now. She stirred and said, "Have I changed that much?"

"What? Oh. No—no, I was just thinking of something."

"Oh." Laura shifted the alligator bag on her lap.

"That Sunday," he said. He recalled the time.

At once she said, "That's not why I brought them."

"What?"

"I mean, that's not why I brought the grapes. I brought them because there was this marvelous fruit store and—"

"Oh, I know that, Laura," he had to say.

In the stillness you could hear voices in the adjacent room. And somewhere dimly a radio.

"But you"—Laura said then—"I was sure you were thinking I've changed. Have I? I mean, that much?"

"Haven't I?" he answered.

"Oh—well, not to me, not really. After all, that's how I remember you. In a way."

He nodded. Those times in the hospital in Mesa, Alabama. "That's right. We're right back to that."

Again she stirred as he watched her. "I'm pregnant." It came bluntly. "I know it doesn't show."

"Pregnant?" he said. Then, "Hey, that's really great, Laura! The only thing that shows is that you look very healthy."

"Yes." She smiled brightly. He wondered if her voice seemed joyless.

"How long has this been going on?" Jamey said.

"Three months. Actually—well, at the time we thought it was a good idea to start early—" Laura stopped, looked away, then, hastily correcting herself: "I mean, we still do, of course."

Jamey nodded and smiled and tried to show her he hadn't

noticed. Not knowing how to get out of this corner, he finally turned to that old game of theirs: "Well, Mrs. Karr"—his voice gruff, avuncular—"now that you're going to be a mother, a parent, would you say you've come full circle? From anarchy to responsible citizenship? And what about your child? How will you bring it up? Like your mother brought you up, I hope."

"Right." Laura took it up. "Yes, it's all well and good to rebel a little but when you get a family of your own you know what life is really all about. Right?"

"Right," Jamey answered. "And I'm glad to know you'll appreciate what it is to be a parent, and I know you're going to bring that child up right. Right?"

"Right." But Laura's tone seemed strained as her smile.

"Ha-ha. Yesterday's rebel is tomorrow's responsible citizen," Jamey said. "Nothing wrong with these kids a good haircut and some real pride in their country won't cure. Right?"

At least this helped, however little, to ease the air again. He passed her the bag of grapes and then had some more himself. Not until then did she say, "I—I suppose you've had to cancel a lot of things."

"Yes," he said.

"Isn't that a damn shame," she said.

"I don't know. Is it?" Jamey said.

"What do you mean, Jamey?"

"Just that it looks as though I'm going to cancel a hell of a lot more."

"Oh. Why? What's happened? I mean, I thought you were all ready to leave the hospital."

"I am. I'm also ready to leave a few other things," he said. "I'm going to take off some time, Laura. I'm going out to the country for a while."

"Jamey, why? Just when you're—"

"Mainly because I don't like what's happening to me," Jamey said. "And even if I did, the whole scene is getting futile. I mean, you get up on some stage and knock yourself out and everybody cheers and you think Christ, we're really making it. What you forget is that your audience is young, sure, but all the others—the ones who move the machinery, who get the real action in Washington—this mob is geriatric! I've had it. Listen, Laura, I wouldn't even be surprised"—he heard himself release the thought that had just been born—"if I ended up bucking for my degree and becoming a goddam teacher!"

"Jamey— God, you really are, well, discouraged, aren't you? Was that me? Did I bring all this on? I couldn't have."

"Of course not."

"I mean, I get so damn discouraged myself. Sometimes," Laura said then. "Oh, I'm not saying it's all the time."

He nodded. "Let's forget what I said."

"God, it's wonderful. Talking to you, I mean. I haven't had a—" Again it went unfinished, because the nurse peeked in and announced that Dr. Wayde was on his way.

Laura rose and opened her handbag. "Listen, Jamey—we want you in for dinner. Let me give you the number." She scribbled on the back of an envelope and gave it to him. "If you should get into town, will you call? Actually, I'm there most mornings—"

"I'm going to be away quite a while," he said.

"Yes. But—"

"If I get in I'll call you, Laura," he said. He moved to the door with her. "And look—I hope everything works out—"

She was nodding and changing her bag from one hand to the other and then she was backing out of the room with her smile, and you knew the smile would not live as far as the elevator. And she was gone.

In less than a week he and Poppy were into it, that autumnal treasury of Connecticut colors. A whole new scene. What he craved now. What Poppy already seemed to take to herself. The house, between Bridgewater and Roxbury, was set far back from the road, forming a green enclave of privacy.

It was a white clapboard Colonial house built in 1780, the property of a writer who had suddenly split for Europe because, according to the realty man, he got disgusted with the way the American way was going. "Can't understand it," the agent had said. "Here he lives in the greatest country in the world and he doesn't like it."

Jamey had let it pass: wasn't he renting this secluded house for many of the same reasons for which the owner had left it?

And now after living there for almost two weeks together night and day in a new pattern of closeness, he was sure he had made the right move for the present. Like the bullet wound in his chest, his woes and discontents were healing as he remained remote from the supershit over-turned-on life he'd been living.

Living like this was something else. Though the Eastern autumn was a phenomenon he had grown up with, for Poppy it was an ecstatic experience, and of course she had returned with zeal into yoga. The thing that was newest for both of them was the enveloping quiet, the air of rustic domesticity. He and Poppy had fallen into a kind of rhythm: he would go into the small studio behind the house and work, or try to, on new material during the late mornings; they would have a light lunch and go walking to the granite quarry nearby or through the woods and Poppy would stop from time to time to root up sassafras to make tea with; in mid-afternoon he would try to work again and then later in the house they would have tea and music, and most times they would smoke.

On this day, a rainy one, the work did not go much better than it had been going; he still couldn't get plugged in. At half-past one he returned to the house.

"I'm getting nowhere, Poppy," he said as soon as he came into the long tavernesque living room with the old pine paneling, the cavernous stone fireplace, the walls hung with the collection of Early American primitive portraits. He leaned against the side of the fireplace and palmed the rain off his hair.

"You keep saying that," Poppy said. "But all it is is that you're still unwinding, and maybe it's too soon to get into anything." Poppy barefooted, in washed-out jeans and sweater, her long hair hanging in two plaits tied with narrow green ribbons.

"Maybe. I hope you're right." But he had to smile as he looked across the room to one of the portraits, an Early American child whom Poppy had curtained off with a new poster (Roger Shens had given it to her) of a newly discovered guru, the Maharishi Karisha Yogi, who had set up shop in London and was gaining a great following among the young of Britain and the U.S.A.

"What's the matter?" Poppy said.

"Oh. Nothing. I was just wondering what the guy who owns this place would think if he came in here now, trying to dig that London yogi."

Poppy glanced at the bearded guru. "I'll get the tea. It's ready." When she brought the cups of Bancha tea in from the kitchen, she put them on the Queen Anne coffee table. She took the cushions off the couch and placed them on the floor in front of the hearth. "Oh, that damn fire fizzled out on me again. I was sure I had it going this time."

Jamey got more paper and kindling and restacked the logs. The fire caught. When he turned around he saw that Poppy had been watching him the whole time. "I don't know why I still can't do it right." She tugged at her sweater. "My mother and father, they used to build fires on trips—like we'd be camping overnight in the Redwoods and they could start a fire in a rainstorm." Poppy laughed about it. But ever since they'd come to the country the shadow of her paragon parents fell deeper across Poppy's landscape. She picked up the teacups and brought them over and put them on the floor. "That antique table is really a drag, isn't it? Too high for us to use. What we need is a low one."

He nodded and sat down on a cushion in front of the hearth. Poppy said, "Are we smoking?"

"I am." Jamey waited while she brought the stash: he stared at the fire. How long would it be before he could get locked into serious work? What the hell was happening?

Poppy lit a joint and handed it to him and he drew deep on it and passed it back to her. He drank the tea, and for a while he forgot about the work. He and Poppy sitting on cushions before the fire and hearing the music of rain playing on the windows and clapboards. But then they were talking about his hangup, and Poppy said with that soft, rather remote smile, " 'The superior man does not permit his thoughts to go beyond his situation.' "

"I'm very unsuperior right now," Jamey said. "What is that from?"

"The I Ching," Poppy said. She looked at him and then rose and got a book from the table. She sat down on the floor again and started reading to him, picking up from where she had left off yesterday afternoon; it was a Sanskrit work translated by Sachindra Majumdar. Once into this, reading softly, her long-lashed eyes lowered, she could often reach him, soothe him, and always he liked just watching her.

She put the book down after a while and poured some more tea: ah, he was far away from all of it now, far from the fatcat jungles of bummerville. . . .

"Who the hell is that, Poppy?" His bland euphoria was jarred; he turned. In the driveway, a magnificent mass of green-and-white iron, the 1965 Dodge hardtop jolted to a power-brake halt.

"Oh—" Poppy leaned forward, peered out into the rain. "Oh, I think that is—yes, it's Mrs. Stells."

"Mrs. Stells?"

"The cleaning woman." She came once a week.

"Is this her day?" Jamey asked.

"I don't think so. I've forgotten," Poppy said.

"Christ."

Poppy said, "What I'll do, I'll have her do the upstairs. I thought she wasn't coming until tomorrow." She opened the front door to admit the woman, a widow who had never left Litchfield County in fifty years and glad of it, a stalwart figure with leather skin and sagging bosom; she had a brisk manner and paranoid eyes, like the warden of a women's prison.

Mrs. Stells carried her own equipment: dust cloths and pink rubber knee pads. Immediately she sniffed the unidentifiable odor in the fine old room. She kept moving. When she came out from the kitchen she said, "Where do you want me to start today, Mrs. Mieland?"

"I thought the upstairs, if you don't mind," Poppy said.

"Ayeah."

"And my name is not Mrs. Mieland," Poppy reminded her quietly, her smile very bland.

"Oh?" The woman's rugged features remained unperturbed.

"My name is Edwards. Poppy Edwards," Poppy informed her.

"Okeydoke," the lady warden said, and glanced coolly over at Jamey, or down at the floor cushion where he sat. Then she went back for the vacuum cleaner and mounted the steep stairs to the second-floor bedrooms. Though she was gone her presence remained: the drone and moan of the vacuum cleaner.

Jamey rose and crossed to the back of the room to his tape recorder and put on a spool he'd made of a Ravi Shankar concert.

But of course the afternoon was killed. He said, addressing the ceiling, "How long does she stay?"

"Last week she was here, I don't know, like half a day. I'll make some more tea." When Poppy returned from the kitchen she said, "We're almost out; there was just enough left for now." She paused. "While Mrs. Stells is here I might as well shop. We're out of everything. Maybe I'll drive to that new health-food store—you know, on Route Seven—we don't have any more macrobiotic flour and soy oil. I love it when I've been out and come back and—you know—smell the smoke from the chimney."

"That's really one of the great things here," he said.

The next noon Poppy was serenely preoccupied baking whole-grain bread. She had come back from the health-food store the day before with thirty dollars' worth of organic items. And now on this afternoon when Jamey walked into the kitchen from another round of work, he found Poppy still at it, Poppy barefoot and in an old fawn-colored miniskirt and a University of California T-shirt, earnestly at it like a little Pilgrim chick. She stopped what she was doing and removed a towel from the two loaves of freshly baked bread.

Jamey inhaled the savory air. He took a knife from the drawer and cut off the heel of one of the loaves and munched it slowly. "Of the best, baby," he said. "Maybe this'll pick me up."

"Why? What's the matter?" Poppy said.

He didn't answer.

Poppy said, "Is it the work? What's wrong?"

"A lot. But—" Jamey said. "Look, why don't we go outside."

"Like what, Jamey?"

"Let's get some of that sun," he said. "It's great out there."

"Was it yesterday? That call from Nat?"

He hesitated. "Partly."

"About Karen?"

"No—though we talked about that too," he said. "And Clem Vogel called also. While you were out shopping. He's trying to build up more pressure now." Clem Vogel had also put him down: *Listen, Pedro, all this griping of yours about success. You're not a success. Not until you know how to cope with it, ride with it, make it work for you, not against you. That's what it means. Don't rap about success until you know how to cope with it.* Then Jamey said, "It's the way they're escalating the pressure on me. Christ, I don't want to talk about it."

"It's a question of ignoring them, Jamey," she said. "You just have to remember your mind is made up and that you're beyond all of it now."

Outside they went. It was one of those matchless idylls only October can create. They walked down the slope of lawn to the pond and they sat there by the fine white birch, and then they went back up, moving beneath the russet canopies of maples. Behind the white house they lay down on the grass, close to a clump of forsythia, the leafless branches like green whips.

It was fine and warm, and soon he took off his shirt, and Poppy slid out of her skirt. The feel of sun was too good, so that they got rid of all their clothes and just stretched back supine on the grass. They lay there like that, glistening with the first film of sweat, dappled by the forsythia branches, the blades of grass soothing and tickling; they kept their eyes closed and he could hear that quivering trill of birds all around them.

Ah, this was of the best, a pantheistic groove!

Poppy beside him and getting the same vibrations, so that they turned facing each other, letting their bodies touch and become adhesive in the moist gold of the afternoon sun.

Once Poppy said, "This is nice."

He said, "Make you think of anything?"

"That night at school, you mean the place by the river?"

"No, not Platt's Landing," Jamey said. "Before that. That night in Newport during the festival—"

"Yes—" Poppy's fingers trailing along the back of his thigh.

No hotel rooms in Newport summer before last. They used their sleeping bags and slept on Newport Beach with unprivate and good communion with the hundreds of other temporary nighttime residents of the shore. Until police scattered everyone at 7 A.M. Then he and Poppy scrambling back on the Harley.

Poppy stirred now and he drew her over him, Poppy slippery, beautiful, a lissome mermaid between him and the sun, ah yes, this was how it could be, wrapped, entwined, like a part of nature.

Supersensitive is how it made you feel. Innocent, erotic conspiracy of nature, a ladybug weightless and orange on his ankle, the sibilant riff of a bee whirring around his ear, a breeze ruffling, the zephyr coolly feathering between his thighs . . .

"Oh, don't move, don't move. Stay like this." Poppy murmuring.
All day he would stay like this. Yes, all day.

But too soon he heard it.

That sound. From where? What was it?

Who?

The sun daze of Poppy's voice: Was that someone in the driveway?

Christ.

Yes, oh Christ, a car, truck, a hell of a sound, unwelcome as war, yes, that action in the driveway, and now Poppy was scooping up her clothes, scampering away into the back of the house, like music fading.

Other sounds nearing. Into his jeans.

As a man came charging, warty face down, charging, gripping a hose line, moving in to within a yard of where Jamey now stood: the oilman grunting in the sun to replenish the tank buried like a secret lode in the earth.

"Hot, huh!" The oilman bent down, keeping the nozzle embedded in the iron orifice (the only completed coupling of the day).

It was sunless the rest of the week, and one morning, very early, Jamey woke up and couldn't get back to sleep. He lay there beside Poppy a long time. As soon as she opened her eyes, he said, "I've been thinking—I think I'll go over to New Haven today."

"Oh? You decided?"

"Yes." He would see about making the transfer, finishing there for his A.B. and going on for his Master's so that he could get into teaching.

"Maybe you ought to wait," Poppy was saying.

"Why?"

"Well, you know, maybe it's just that you're still hung up and discouraged." The tip of Poppy's foot stroking his calf.

"No, it isn't only that," Jamey said. "But what if I want to teach someday, and I'm sure I will."

"You're really looking ahead, aren't you?" Poppy said.

"I guess so."

"Why don't you wait and see how you feel about it later?" Poppy said.

336

"Like when?"

"Oh, I don't know, Jamey. Just later." She kissed him. And then her warm and drowsy nakedness was no longer beside him.

He arose then. He would shave, dress, go to New Haven. Today. He paused in the hallway, watching Poppy.

Poppy into her yoga, in the other bedroom, on the bare planked floor, in the lotus position, into her first mantra, relaxing, sounding the om, inhaling deeply through her nose (the nose is for breathing; the mouth for kissing and eating, she would say), and then the very long exhalation before continuing with the hatha-yoga, emptying her mind of the clog of the world.

He liked to watch her. She did not tire easily now, her energy and control had become fantastic, so supple; and beautiful to watch her in all these sculptural arabesques. And always the periods of pure meditation. Her face serene, not beatific, but registering the total void she had made of her mind and body. Sometimes she didn't even know he was near. (Once she had said, quoting Bhagavad-Gita: "The yogi whose mind is controlled and concentrated on the Self is likened to a lamp which is without a flicker in a windless place.")

That day he went to Yale; he went to the office of the Registrar and picked up the catalogues and other information he wanted. He stopped by at the Co-op to buy some records, but the moment he got to the lower level of the store the scene turned sour, a lot of people watching him and some boppybirds moving in, so that he cleared out in a hurry, buying nothing.

He was on his way back, passing through Roxbury, when he saw the sign on the green: outdoor auction at the Episcopal Church in Bridgewater. On impulse he drove over. He stood at the back of the row of folding chairs on the lawn of the parish house; the auction was already under way. He stood there a long while; nobody noticed him. On impulse he bought a table. It wasn't until he bid it in at forty-two dollars that people looked around and then he could hear his name, and since none of the people there was young he knew it was in connection with the shooting, not his work.

But he got the table. An antique it was not. It was secondhand and low and lacquered black, exactly what Poppy had been wanting. He wedged it into the trunk of the Corvette and he had to keep the lid up all the way back to the house.

"Poppy!" he called out as soon as he was in the living room. He saw that the cleaning woman, Mrs. Stells, had been here again: all the cushions had been taken off the floor and returned to the couch and armchair. "Poppy—where the hell are you?"

"You've been gone practically all day, I couldn't—" Poppy in from the kitchen, but staring at the little table he was holding. "Where did you—where did that come from?"

He told her about the auction.

"Oh, it's lovely, perfect, perfect, just what we need." She came over, examined it and then set it down in front of the hearth; then she got all the cushions and put them back on the floor in a crescent around the table.

Her eyes sparked with small lights—surprise, contentment, all lovingness. He noticed then that the poster of the London yogi had been moved to the fireplace wall to cover yet another Early American primitive painting. He told her about the trip to New Haven and about the church auction: "Closest I've been to a God box in a long time."

Poppy said, "Aren't we maybe loading up on too much?"

"What difference does it make? You've been saying ever since we got here we ought to have a low table; it's something you wanted."

"Yes. But it's just that"—her eyes losing that light like sudden dusk darkening the day—"it's just that, well, it's funny how you can get hung up on a lot of little domestic things, isn't it? I mean, I suppose it was pretty stupid of us—"

"Listen, Poppy, when I walked in here with this thing, you flipped, didn't you? I mean—"

"Oh, yes, yes I did, and I'm still glad you got it. But—oh, you know what I mean," Poppy answered.

"No, I don't," he said.

"Jamey, it's just that, well, if things keep piling up on us, it can get to be like too much, can't it?"

"I'm not hot to acquire a lot of possessions, if that's what you mean," Jamey said.

"Yes, but look, look how it's getting with us—"

"With you?" Jamey said.

338

"Oh, Jamey—" She stirred uneasily; for a moment her eyes showed a glint of fear, an animal cornered. But this passed and she got up and said why didn't they smoke for a while and why didn't he put on a record.

The grass and the music moved bending, clouding, around them, and it was good; but later that night and the next morning, Poppy still seemed quiet and pensive.

In the kitchen she fixed her tea and made the pot of coffee for Jamey, and they decided to have breakfast on the terrace at the north side of the house, but it was too cold: a raw mist of prewinter glazed the fields, wildflowers, the bark of trees, and they went back inside again to the slope-ceilinged alcove off the kitchen and sat down around the mulberry-red hutch table. Poppy lit a cigarette and stared out the window to the bird feeder hanging from the fruit tree.

Jamey said, "I was thinking. Maybe I'll drive in to Nittygritty City. And get back tonight. Do you want to make it?"

"Oh—I don't know." Poppy kept looking outside. "But why don't you if you want."

"I should see my father. I've been putting it off—"

"Yes."

"I'd like to get it over with, and I was thinking I'd stop in town and pick up some books and records I left at my place. We can use them here," Jamey said.

"You miss it?" Poppy said.

"Hell no, it's just something I ought to do," he said. There were still loose ends from his days in the office and his father still kept after him to come in and clean up his affairs. Since his official departure his father's company was no longer harangued. The hounds of hell muzzled.

Poppy looked down at her cigarette. "It's none of my business, but if you're planning to see anyone, you don't have to use your father as a—"

"Come on, Poppy."

"Well, she has been writing to you a lot and it—"

"Muriel?"

"No. Laura."

"Oh—well, I might have a fast dinner with Muriel. It's one of the few places I can go and eat in peace, without a mob moving in," Jamey said. Then: "How come you're suddenly getting onto Laura?"

Poppy shrugged. Poppy in jeans, turtleneck, her hair in a ponytail, that gaze still pensive. "I guess it was that you were talking about her last night. About her marriage." Poppy began to speak more rapidly, even brightly. "It must be—I guess it must be the worst to be pregnant and know your marriage isn't making it."

Jamey nodded, though he was puzzled. "I don't know if it's really that way, I only thought that's how it seemed."

"Yes."

"But—" Jamey paused. "Look, what is all this, Poppy?"

"All what?"

"On Laura," he said.

Poppy twisted out her cigarette in the ashtray. She said, "I think I'm a few days late."

"You are? Are you sure?"

"I think so. I lost my calendar."

"How could you be? If you—"

"I forgot to take my pill. Twice, I think. I didn't say anything about it because, well, you know."

"Oh."

She got up and fixed another cup of tea. When she came back to the table she said, "If I'm caught, I'll have to find someone for an abortion."

"Listen, Poppy, let's wait and see."

She didn't reply.

He drank more coffee. As the silence grew in the long morning. Then Jamey heard himself tentatively say, "We could always get married."

"What made you think of that?" Poppy said.

"Well, if you're pregnant—I mean, if you are," Jamey said.

Poppy frowned. She rose. "I can't think of a worse way to get into something like that." Distractedly she moved to the stove and lifted the teakettle and placed it on another burner, though she did not turn on the gas. She came back to the table. "There are one or two people I can talk to in town who I think could—you know—help me out; I mean, they'd know where you can go. I think I'll—"

"Listen, Poppy, I'll—"

"Oh, isn't this the drag of all time!" she cried.

Two days after that, a chill and hazy afternoon beneath a pewter sky, they were going to take a walk down to the quarry. Jamey was in the driveway, waiting for her to finish dressing. He had not even tried to work on any of his new compositions. Two days nowhere.

Poppy came out of the house now, in her wheat-colored jeans, leather sandals, T-shirt and the Australian bush jacket. She did not say much until they started downhill on the rutted dirt road. But her face was sunny. "Well," she said then, "that was a lot about nothing."

He looked at her. "When did it happen?"

"Just now. When I was getting dressed to go out," Poppy said.

They moved on. As they neared the steep part of the road he slid his arm around her, and then they turned left and started up the path to the quarry. Jamey said, "At least now we won't have to go through the whole bit."

"That would have been something," Poppy said. "I can just see us."

"Yes," Jamey said. "So can I."

Laughter touching them for the first time in two days, a fine free feeling, the way it had been when they'd first come up here.

"As a matter of fact," he said then, "it isn't all that stupid. I mean, if you don't *have* to do it, it's not such a horrendous idea."

"Umm," Poppy said.

They reached the quarry, the great crags and plateaus and caverns of pristine white stone and slate-hued stone and stone streaked with dark veins. They sat down on a ledge, their legs hanging down over the edge: below, a vast granite bowl still holding the autumn's rain water. Jamey said, "I wonder what would happen—I mean, how it would be. If we did." He paused. "It's possible we might even like it."

"Oh?"

"Well, it's possible."

Poppy's hand was unexpectedly on his. "We might," she said.

"But you doubt it," he said.

"Well—" she said.

341

"Well, what it is, it's the idea." Jamey said. "Or maybe the idea of seeing if we could beat it—I mean, without the hangups of everybody else, all those old pharts hung up and doing everything all wrong. You and I, Poppy, I think maybe we could beat it."

"Do you really think we could? I mean, if we ever did anything stupid like that?" Poppy said.

"I don't see why not," Jamey said.

Poppy was looking at him. "We must be like idiotic."

Jamey said, "How the hell did I get into this?" Then: "Oh well, it's nice to think of anyway. At least it was. Or is."

And it was. The novelty of the unexpected image flashing up, the whole scene suddenly taking on a shine, an exhilaration that rocked him. He started to say more, but Poppy had abruptly withdrawn her hand.

"Let's go back." Her voice faint. She was on her feet.

Nothing more was said until they started down the path from the quarry. Then Jamey said, "You copped out of that one, didn't you, baby?"

"What's the matter with you?" Poppy spoke to the hard clay road where you could see embedded the dull plum glints of garnets.

"Nothing's the matter with me." But he resented feeling hurt, he never expected to feel cut up like this. "I mean, you made it sound like the end."

"It probably would have been." She buttoned her bush jacket and accelerated her pace, her small sandaled feet dainty and dusty on the road.

"How do you know? What makes you so goddam sure, Poppy?" Jamey said.

"Well, I—I just know we don't want to get into that. At least not now," Poppy answered.

"Why not?" Jamey suddenly felt himself taking all of it too personally—how else could you take it?—resenting, resisting her coolness, her fear, her alarm. He wanted to get through to something inside her and he wasn't sure how. "Why the hell not? What you're doing right now, Poppy, is just turning off. As if you don't know who I am, as if I'm some cat you met a week ago!"

"I can't talk to you," Poppy said. "All I was trying to say, Jamey, was that for now it's—"

"I know what it is with you—" But he held back.

"What?"

They turned right into the other road, passing the white house and the house in the woods with the Peugeot in the driveway.

"Maybe"—Jamey felt his way more softly—"maybe you want to keep going the way you always have, maybe life is something you don't want to get too deep into."

Poppy's head was very erect. "Is that what you think?" Her eyes squinted straight ahead. At nothing.

"What I was thinking," Jamey said, "was how great your parents are and why you sometimes say maybe they're too great. Maybe what it is, Poppy, is they've got you snowed."

"I never said anything like that!" Poppy's defiance crackled like the fall leaves beneath their feet. "What's that got to do with us!"

"You're scared," Jamey said too harshly. "Maybe you're scared you can't ever top anything they do. Including the kind of marriage they have. I mean, they gave you all this mobility, all you ever wanted, they gave you a childhood right out of the books—"

"Right out of the books? Since when?" Poppy stopped, her body rigid. "I didn't ask you for your opinion!"

"I think maybe you want them backing you up all the time, that's part of it," Jamey went on. "As if you're afraid to face anything. Love or marriage, the whole deal. Anything. You're scared to death of any kind of real commitment. You can't give up that childhood!"

"Oh, Jamey—fuck off!" Poppy spurted forward, trying to hurry beyond him or his voice.

He caught up with her. "Listen, Poppy"—he grasped her arm—"all I'm saying is, maybe what you had was so good you're afraid to let go of it, you still want it all, all that protection. It's like playing kid all the time, it's like the only way you can beat the game is by holding on to the way you've been going, from whim to whim, idea to idea, scene to scene, or man to—"

"Oh—" Poppy cried out, and twisted her arm free and started running up the road.

Again he overtook her: only this time her face was averted and when he touched it it was wet, hot, her cheeks searing with tears.

They walked back toward the house and he didn't know what to say because he had already said too much. Regret burned through him. And he couldn't take back what he'd said or change it.

"I guess the mail's come," he said; it was something to say. He stopped at the mailbox on the road, but Poppy kept going on down the driveway and into the house.

He reached inside the metal box. There were several letters. He noticed as he shut the box that a VW with motor running was parked nearby: there were four kids in it, two boys, two girls, and they were gawking at him.

He moved down the slope of gravel. He hurried; he didn't even look at the mail. He found Poppy sitting on the small brick hearth of the kitchen fireplace; she was wrapped in silence. He said something about the mail again. He glanced at the envelopes: a letter for Poppy from Mike, another from Roger Shens, another from her father. Forwarded from Nat McGovern's office there were several letters for him. But he put them down on the counter. As soon as he handed Poppy her mail she rose, and before he could even talk to her she was out of the room.

Distractedly he sat down where Poppy had been and after a while he glanced through his letters: a request for him to appear at an antiwar rally; a request to be part of a benefit to raise money for another Negro ghetto rehabilitation program; three requests from former McCarthy and Kennedy groups.

Poppy remained upstairs. He waited a long time. But no action. He cleared out of the house. He took the Corvette and had it gassed and oiled for the trip to his father's and to New York tomorrow morning.

That night was not good. He couldn't kick down the wall he had raised between them. Yet the instant they were in bed, in the darkness, Poppy turned, her movement almost convulsive, and flung her arms around him; she never spoke, holding him as though she was scared he'd leave, holding him in a way that seemed beyond loving, for she never let go all night, all night her arms around him.

In the morning she was up before he was, and dimly he could hear her in the other bedroom, into her yoga.

It was sure as hell not a day to leave. He tried again to get her to drive in with him. But no. She said she wanted to stay in the country. Her voice, like her eyes, seemed flat, without luster.

But if yesterday had been a bummer all the way, it was like an overture to today.

Driving in that morning, he turned on the radio, listening for anything that would blast out the other sounds inside him. (He heard on WDAI his recording of "When the Cymbals Are Still"; he heard on WNEK "The Lyndon Tree"; he heard on WMTA "The White Cat.") Dialing into Ray Stevens singing: *Mr. Businessman: . . . Tuesday evening with your harlot/ And on Wednesday it's your charlatan analyst . . . You've got air-conditioned sinuses/ And dark disturbing doubt about religion . . . And while your secretary's tempting you/ Your morals are exempting you/ From guilt and shame . . .*

Soon into the noon news: all bad. A newscaster cranking out more tripletalk from Trixon, and more of the same from Old Six Shooter in Austin, Texas . . .

"Another outbreak of trouble in Cleveland's East Side—" The voice ticked it off: the trouble began as a small incident in a tavern in the Hough sector, looting followed, then fire-bombing and finally shooting between police and people in the neighborhood. . . . "Nine persons were shot to death." The newscaster's voice cool with statistics. "Of the nine dead, six were civilians said to be associated with black nationalist groups. The youngest, Roy Billings, twenty-three, was a leader in the Black Urban Authority. He was found partially burned in a frame house that had been tear-gassed and had caught fire from the shells. Billings was also shot twice in the head. Automobiles and buildings were scarred with bullet holes and according to police—"

There was no place to pull over to the side of the parkway. Jamey held the wheel tight, he fought to counter the sense of faintness, he felt the hard throb in his chest. He kept driving, he kept stupidly twisting the dial trying to tune in other newscasts. . . .

345

Stupidly he kept dialing: there could be a mistake.

He got it again.

No mistake.

It had happened.

But to Roy.

To Roy, who was never out for private power, never out to make it just for himself.

Roy, who had started out with nothing from nowhere and who was someone they needed . . .

By the time he reached "America's Garden of Living," Nitty-gritty City, he had heard the news again, and he stopped and bought a *New York Times*. It was all there, all of it confirmed. True.

As soon as he got to his house, as soon as he had talked with his mother, before he left for his father's office, he put in the call to Cleveland. It took a long time to get a free line to Roy's home.

It was past two o'clock when he spoke with Mr. Billings, Roy's father. Though he knew Jamey, he was too stunned to say much or respond to what Jamey tried to say.

Except that when Jamey said he wanted to come to Cleveland, Mr. Billings said no.

Jamey called later and asked for Roy's older sister. A stranger, a neighbor, answered and said the family was not there.

Then he called Connecticut twice. He wanted to talk to Poppy. She must have been outside or out walking, for there was no answer. He called Gary Einsberg. He was out. He called Laura. She was in. Yes, she had heard the news too. And for a long time they talked about Roy. She said would he like to come by, but he said he had to get back to Connecticut.

To Poppy.

To what else?

For all the way driving back he kept asking himself if he had been right, holing in like this in the country, turning off, trying to think, trying to work. . . .

Removing himself from where it counted, copping out at a time when he should have stayed with it . . .

(Like Mike. Like Roy.)

Wrong or right. Get back to the city.

346

That was the first thing he'd tell Poppy tonight: he had to get back into it. Hiding out was a luxury he no longer wanted.

Maybe it meant having to reverse his stand. OK. He would admit his failure in the country, the explosion of an idyll. . . .

"Poppy!"

Soundless. Two lamps were on.

"Poppy!" He shouted it: but immediately he knew or sensed the void; no one was here. A house can tell you that immediately; there is that deadness that comes into the fibers of the walls, into even the dust on a windowsill or tabletop, as if all life has ceased. "Poppy!"

He kept looking for her, first in the kitchen, then in the library. Upstairs then to the bedrooms. Trying the small studio out at the back of the house.

In the living room again, standing there weighted, inert, looking stupidly all around. Wherever she was, she must have left after dusk: the lamps were still on. Yet there was this dead feeling, like the house itself.

She was gone. Not just out for a while, but gone.

It wasn't until he went back into the library that he saw something she'd left—Poppy could never go anywhere any time without leaving a trace. On the open slant-top desk where the telephone was he saw the envelope of the letter Mike had written from the federal penitentiary. On the back of it she'd scribbled in that high looping style: "BOAC." A telephone number. A flight number.

Tonight? When? Where to?

Now it was a quarter to eight.

He stared at the scribbled notes. He swallowed the stone of his resistance to what he knew was true.

Not even a message for him—unless it was upstairs and he had missed it before.

Up the steep steps again. Nothing there. The closet gaped: her clothes gone. He saw that her books were gone too. He gazed around everywhere. The bed. Unruffled, dead, a wasteland where less than twenty-four hours ago her slim sweet nakedness had been close, and the way she'd held on to him as if fearful of his leaving . . .

He heard it then. The telephone. And he started down the

347

stairs, leaping down the steps, almost slipping on the bottom tread, hurrying to the library. It had to be she.

It was.

"Poppy—for Christ sakes, where are you?"

Her voice small, from a far planet: "At the airport. Kennedy—"

"Where are you going—for Christ sakes, Poppy, where are—"

"London."

"How did you—"

Her father. Of course. Who else? She'd called him in California and he'd wired more money to her in care of the airline.

"Poppy—what is it? Why? What're you—"

She was going to study with Karisha Yogi. "It's something I've got to do, Jamey."

"How long is this for? Where are you going to stay?"

"I don't know yet."

"What is it, Poppy?" His hand damp on the phone. "Is it because of yesterday or—"

"No," she broke in. "I don't know. It doesn't matter."

"Poppy, baby, listen, kill the trip, can't you cancel it? I'll come in, I'll get there—I mean, you can't take off like this!"

"Jamey"—her voice was wavering—"I knew if I didn't do it today I'd never do it. And I—you know—I have to do it."

"Why?"

An extended silence. "What else can I do?" she said.

"Love me, stay here, is what you can do!"

"Oh, Jamey," she cried. "Jamey—" she began, and stopped. Above her a jet pierced the sky. "I have to go now, I think people are boarding the plane."

"Listen, Poppy, you can't leave now! There's so goddammed much I—" He tripped across the words. "I'm going back to New York. Back into it. You've got to be with me. I've got a thousand things—goddammit! You can't do this, Poppy!"

"Jamey—Jamey—"

There was nothing after that.

He hung up. He moved into the living room that Poppy had robbed of life, Poppy following another arrow into another gossamer path. . . .

Except this time he wasn't part of it.

If it was blues anyone wanted, he could deliver them: right here. Without playing a chord or uttering a sound. It was in him and all around him in this eighteenth-century box. (This Poppy-less house, now even more out of context with his life—funny even, if you wanted to dig it in terms of McLuhan or Buckminster Fuller. And he didn't.)

Thinking like this, in random tandem thoughts, anything that would get him through the long night, Jamey not knowing what in hell to do, finally just moving around the living room like some stupid sleepwalker.

Then he would stop, put on some records or try to play his guitar, but of course nothing worked and everything always fell back to Poppy.

Like now, looking at that low lacquered table, looking at it in dismay, a black weed threatening the rosy garden of her child-hood.

Sometime in the middle of the night he fell asleep on the couch. When he awoke it wasn't even seven o'clock. But at least he woke up ready to act. That morning he reserved the last seat on a TWA flight leaving for London that night. His passport was bent, mildewed by neglect, unused since that two-week student junket to Greece in 1965. But tonight he'd dust it off: tomorrow morning he would be in London, tomorrow he would go straight to the ashram of Karisha Yogi. . . .

Had to. What else could he do?

Coffee, more coffee in the kitchen. The cabinets gravid with Poppy's macrobiotic foods and grains. He finished the coffee, walked around the kitchen, stopped by the window; and he went all through it again.

Look, he told himself, while you were putting Poppy down all the time, what about yourself? Telling Poppy how she was al-ways floating, drifting from one thing to another all her life. What about Jamey Mieland quitting his father's office, quitting school, quitting Raven, quitting the country?

What next?

Forget it. Pack.

What was he hanging around for? That magical call from Poppy, Poppy calling him to say what?

Packed now, ready to close the house, the six-month lease a loss. Let it all hang out.

In the entry hall he set his guitar back in its case. Not until that moment did he remember. Not until then: Cleveland.

"Christ!"

He looked up, addressed his image in the wall mirror: Christ, he must have been zonked right out of his stupid mind!

Forgetting Cleveland. Like blacking out.

But during the past twenty-four hours he couldn't have remembered his own name.

Cleveland: day after tomorrow. Fifteenth of November. To that festival at Oberlin College, Roy turning it down but setting it up for Jamey. And nothing short of death or a broken right hand should have kept him away. And Roy's funeral tomorrow, the fourteenth. He'd get to Cleveland a day ahead. To the funeral. Uninvited.

Christ.

And here he was like some clown in heat ready to zoom off for London. He'd kill it, cancel the reservation soon as he got into town. It could wait until then. What he had to do now was leave here. Split. Lock the door, follow the realtor's instruction, put the key in the woodbin beside the house.

In the driveway he lowered the top of the Corvette to the November sky: sunless, a dim damson day.

On the road now. Again. Through the village of Bridgewater, past its serene center, the two white churches and Gowan's store and the post office, the flag flying. Fly Old Glory to inglorious times. . . .

O Poppy.

Curving fast now through the green glen and into the next county and soon gaining the parkway.

Radio blasting now: Cleveland still all over the wavelengths. And Roy cut down. Roy. *In this country the guns get into the hands of the madmen, the bullets into the . . .*

Dial it out!

And here he was rushing forward. Once again. While it seemed most people were rushing the other way:

But can you hear the bells or are they muffled by the gray

flannel mantle of mediocrity? As now all the geriatric cats come to an arteriosclerotic halt to look backward.

And here he was rushing forward. As if this was the beginning instead of the end.

Radio blasting still.

Dialing it out. Very cold, colder. Wind storming through his hair. He edged up the turtleneck sweater tighter to his chin.

Cleveland: he'd start for there tomorrow. Yes.

Listen: near Triborough Bridge, the radio, his voice:

The White Cat
Is a nowhere place
Where the smoke curls up like ebony lace
And . . .

O Poppy.

Straight onward. Yes. Passing the intersection telling you: TO LONG ISLAND. TO AIRPORTS.

No airport. Not anymore.

Tomorrow he'd be in Cleveland.

Yes.

After that, after he got back, he'd face the rest of it: yes, into the whole Raven bag again, the Zaks, the Syds, the Clems, the Nats, the boppybirds, the . . .

Yes. And back again into all the supershit.

But that couldn't matter now. Not anymore. Suddenly it was no longer relevant, was it?

That modest sign now: New York City.

Yes.

O Poppy.